SKY BREAKER

ADDIE THORLEY

PAGE STREET
PUBLISHING CO.

PAGE STREET
PUBLISHING CO.

Copyright © 2021 Addie Thorley

First published in 2021 by
Page Street Publishing Co.
27 Congress Street, Suite 105
Salem, MA 01970
www.pagestreetpublishing.com

Distributed by Macmillan, sales in Canada by The Canadian Manda Group.

25 24 23 22 21   1 2 3 4 5

ISBN-13: 978-1-64567-130-5
ISBN-10: 1-64567-130-5

Library of Congress Control Number: 2020944742

Cover and book design by Kylie Alexander for Page Street Publishing Co.
Author photo by Jordan Wallace

Printed and bound in the United States

FOR LOR AND COURT, THE WORLD'S BEST SISTERS

I'M GLAD WE DIDN'T KILL EACH OTHER AS KIDS, BECAUSE I DON'T KNOW WHAT I'D DO WITHOUT YOU NOW.

"For love is like a tree; it grows of itself; it sends its roots deep into our being, and often continues to grow green over a heart in ruins."

—VICTOR HUGO, *The Hunchback of Notre Dame*

CHAPTER ONE

ENEBISH

Darkness rises around me like a shield—girding me with armor, enfolding me in steel, deflecting the whispers that climb the cavern walls like goblin spiders.

It's easy to tell when people are talking about you: They huddle into groups and throw hasty glances over their shoulders. They murmur in hushed tones and jump when you enter the room, their smiles too wide, their faces too bright.

I want to tell the shepherds not to bother. I'm hidden in every inky shadow, pressed into every murky corner of these caves. Which means I hear every skeptical and disapproving word they utter.

Sand scuffs beneath my knees as I crawl along a narrow ledge jutting over the mouth of our cavern like a swollen lip. Nearly a thousand homeless shepherds are camped below, their tents and animals spread throughout the system of limestone caves hidden beneath the sand dunes of Verdenet.

I heard countless rumors of the caves when I was young. Traders claimed they were an ideal place to take refuge from snow squalls and hide from caravan raiders. *If* you could find them. According to Southern legend, such a staggering number perished in search, the dunes are composed of disintegrated bones rather than sand—that's what makes the desert look so white. But we accomplished that part of our journey without much trouble—the *only* part that hasn't been riddled with it—thanks to the darkness. The tendrils took me by the hand and led me eagerly toward the eternally blackened tunnels and shafts.

Though, I don't think anyone in our company would call the caves ideal. They are frigid and gloomy, with wet floors and walls covered in luminescent moss that, while beautiful, is deadly to the touch. And don't even get me started on the goblin spiders and fire geckos and the banshee vipers that scream like a dying child when they lunge from their crevasses to bite your ankles.

It's the last place nomads accustomed to the boundless grasslands and open sky of Ashkar would choose to live. The last place *I* would choose to live. But when you're being hunted by the Imperial Army for liberating a notorious criminal, and then you've been *betrayed* by said criminal after they allied with your greatest enemy, you have to make concessions. Hide somewhere no one would suspect. Somewhere no one else can find.

Temujin taught me that.

"Enebish!" My name ricochets through the tunnels so loudly, a cloud of bats take flight. I bolt upright, underestimating the height of the serrated ceiling and the sharpness of the rocky floor. The back of my head bashes against a stalactite and my bad leg drags across a protrusion of rock.

I close my eyes, curse behind clamped lips, and pull the cocoon of darkness tighter around me, wishing it could block out voices as well as light.

"Enebish!" they yell again. It has to be at least five shepherds, all shouting at once. My entire body shudders. The complaints and demands are never ending. And the most ironic part is, the shepherds doubt and disparage me with one breath, then cry for my help with the next. I am the problem and the solution. Their scapegoat and their savior.

Which is to be expected, I remind myself. A good leader lives and dies by their successes and failures. They are confident and unflappable—no matter how grim the battle—until the war is won.

You wanted this chance.

Now all I want is for more than two minutes to pass without being criticized or summoned. I want to *actually* disappear for a few hours to bathe in the geothermal pools hidden at the backs of these caverns, where the rocks are yellow and the water is electric green and surprisingly warm. Hopefully hot enough to scald away my exhaustion and anxiety and doubt.

I try not to consider what that says about me—that I want to be alone again, so soon after two years of solitude at Ikh Zuree. That I'm ready to surrender my title as leader just two weeks after guiding the shepherds from the desolate grazing lands outside of Sagaan.

When Serik's voice joins the shouting, I sigh and release my hold on the darkness. If he's entered the fray, it means one of two things: it truly is an emergency—or he's so tired of the shepherds' squabbling, he's going to strangle someone, which will *create* an emergency.

I pick my way down from the ledge and amble toward the shouting. I should probably hurry, but my feet drag through the puddles. And, for once, it has nothing to do with my old injuries. The first dozen or so times the shepherds summoned me like this, I raced from my bedroll with my heart in my throat, my mind spinning with every horrible scenario:

The tents were on fire.

Shoniin scouts had found the caves.

The children had brushed against the deadly moss.

But no.

Cezari had tied his goats too close to Yimran's camp and they'd eaten large holes through their blankets during the night. Now Yimran's family would freeze to death and they were demanding recompense from Cezari. But Cezari couldn't give them his blankets or *his* family would freeze to death.

"We have a Sun Stoker. No one will freeze to death," I assured them with patient platitudes and gracious smiles. After which, I had the immense pleasure of spending the entire day patching the slobbery blankets. Yimran's family insisted they shouldn't have to do it. And Cezari didn't have time, since his goats were clearly starving. He had to take them aboveground to find whatever meager weeds were growing through the sand.

By the time I finished mending the blankets, my fingers were as gnarled as an old woman's and my skin was covered in pinpricks of blood. I was too young and wiggly to learn how to sew when I was a child in Verdenet. And Ghoa was more concerned with teaching me how to draw blood, rather than stanch it.

When I presented the blankets to Yimran, do you think he or a single member of his household thanked me for my efforts? Of course not. They snatched the pile of blankets, careful not to let our fingers brush, lest I infect them with my scars or wickedness or whatever it is they're afraid of, and hurried away. They even cast wary glances over their shoulders, as if I might throw the sewing needles into their backs like knives. *After* I helped them.

The next time, the shouts had been so frenzied, I thought surely there was news from the scouts. Or someone had fallen down a shaft and died.

The latter wasn't too far from the truth.

Emeric had been moving his bedroll in the dead of night so he could sleep right in front of Serik's heat, instead of waiting for his turn in the rotation. That night, he accidentally stepped on a dog's tail, and when the creature yelped, the jig was up.

The group wanted to cast him down a shaft. Or banish him to the punishing desert. Someone even suggested I bring the stars down on him, which earned them a glare as hot as a bolt of starfire.

"I don't just throw stars at people," I growled.

The shepherds looked down and away. At their feet or at the rocks. Because they saw it with their own eyes: how I'd tried to kill Ghoa. How I'd ravaged the Sky Palace with starfire during Temujin's rescue.

I take full responsibility for what happened in the Grand Courtyard. The night and starfire are *my* obligation. But I *do* blame Ghoa for framing me for a massacre. For manipulating me and deceiving me to the point that I felt compelled to use my power against her. I nearly let her turn me into the monster I'd spent years running from. A monster these people will never forget.

The shepherds part as I limp through the main cavern toward the commotion, but it doesn't make me feel important or revered, as it did when I was a member of the Kalima warriors. Instead of bowing with respect and veneration, the shepherds recoil and raise their hands to cover their faces, as if I might slash them with my beastly claws. Or bring the night crashing down on them for sport. No matter that I haven't so much as raised my voice since we left Sagaan.

I am not responsible for Nariin! I want to fill every tunnel and crevasse with the truth. *Why bother calling for my help only to scramble away when I answer?*

I didn't expect the shepherds to warm to me immediately.

But I did expect them to give me a chance. Ghoa and the Sky King had left them to freeze and starve to death on the winter grazing lands. And the unified Zemyans and Shoniin will invade Sagaan any day—if they haven't already. These weak, flailing shepherds would have been the first to perish. Or be taken prisoner.

I make my way around a cluster of stalagmites that form a sort of partition between the caverns, and slip into the smaller room, where we've been storing food and supplies.

Serik stands in the center of the space with his arms outstretched, holding back two shouting men who have large riotous groups gathered behind them.

"You're trying to kill my family!" the older of the men, Iree, roars.

"Only because *you're* determined to kill *us*! You broke the code first!" Bultum, a round-cheeked and generally good-natured shepherd, screams back.

"I'm going to kill you *both* if you don't stop hollering!" Serik bellows loudest of all. Flames leap from his palms, and it wasn't on purpose if his surprised yelp is any indication. It does, however, effectively force both sides to lurch back.

If there's one person who's discovered they dislike leading even more than I do, it's Serik.

"We should let the shepherds tear each other apart," he'd muttered only two nights into our journey across the grasslands, during which time we had to deal with a broken wagon wheel, arguments over camping spots, unfair grazing rotations, and places where people could build fires. "Survival of the fittest and all that."

I'd rolled my eyes at Serik's overblown suggestion. "They'll settle soon enough. They're just frightened and anxious and out of their depth. Think of all they've been through. We must be patient."

Little did I know the shepherds *wouldn't* settle. Their panic and paranoia would only grow. It wasn't long before Serik's dark thoughts began circling my own mind.

"I'm glad to see you're de-escalating the situation." I flash Serik a teasing smile as I approach the standoff. We learned quickly that you can either laugh or cry at these exasperating disputes, and I try to do the former for the sake of both of our sanities.

"You try reasoning with them!" Serik flings his arms above his head, and another burst of heat rushes from his hands. His control over his Kalima power is still tenuous at best, and his aggravated gasp makes me smile even wider. Which makes him even madder, but I can't help it. He's kind of adorable when he's frustrated: his freckled cheeks get all ruddy and he pulls at his hair, which has grown nearly to his ears now.

"We only want what's rightfully ours!" Bultum's small but terrifying wife, Emani, yells from behind him.

"Our portion of grain doesn't belong to you," Iree spits back, and several others in his company agree. "If your family squandered your portion, you can't dip back into the grain and take ours."

"What are you talking about? We've had nothing for days—can't you see that?" Bultum gestures to his family, who do, indeed, look rather emaciated. But no more than anyone else. Between the snow-covered grasslands and the punishing sand, Ashkar is not a bountiful or forgiving place in the winter. We're all slowly starving.

I join Serik in the center of the fray, which causes both sides to retreat even farther. "What's going on? Who's stealing from whom? And why? We portioned rations just this week."

It was an excruciating process. We had to convince all of the shepherds to place their provisions into a common collection, which was then redistributed evenly to ensure everyone had food. The ones with plenty were obviously incensed and the ones with empty oil casks and grain sacks reached greedily for the piles.

"Exactly!" Iree jumps in. "We were all given portions, but they're dipping into ours." He points at the half-filled burlap sack in Bultum's hands.

"Because we had no portion after you stole ours!"

"How dare you accuse us of thievery!" a young man behind Iree shouts.

I wait for them to stop yelling, trying to keep calm, since Serik is rubbing his temples like he might explode. "What do you mean you had no portion?" I ask Bultum.

"I mean exactly that! When I came to collect our rations, there was nothing to collect. Iree has never liked me because my sheep produce finer wool, so I knew he was to blame and I made restitutions where necessary."

Iree's eyes look as if they're going to pop from his skull. "Your wool is no finer than ours!"

"I'm certain your portion is here." I rush to the stacks to conduct a thorough search. "Maybe it just fell behind the rocks or was misplaced in a different pile?" But there's nothing in any of the potholes, nothing tucked behind the outcroppings.

"You want us to perish so there will be more for you!" Emani cries, melting onto the shoulder of an old woman next to her.

"You want *us* to perish!" Iree's family shoots back.

"You're bickering over nothing!" Serik's boot knocks the bag of grain from Bultum's hands. Everyone falls silent as wheat scatters across the wet cave floor. "These meager rations won't keep us alive for much longer anyway."

"Serik!" He's right, of course. But I want to kick his head as hard as he kicked the grain for admitting it out loud. For giving the shepherds even more reason to fear and doubt.

"Thankfully, we won't need the rations much longer," I say quickly, making my voice cheerful. "We'll find King Minoak soon. Then we'll rise against the imperial governor and retake Verdenet. Once we're in Lutaar City, there will be plenty of food. It's only a matter of days."

Serik cuts me a weary look. Temujin is the one who informed me of the Sky King's attempt to assassinate King Minoak. Temujin is also the one who claimed Minoak survived and escaped. And Temujin has proven less than trustworthy.

"You said it would be a matter of days when we arrived last week," Iree groans.

"Precisely," I say with more conviction than I feel. "We've only been searching for a week. That's hardly any time."

I look to Serik for support, and even though I can tell he'd rather continue spewing his depressing realism, his hazel eyes meet mine and he nods. "These things take time. We must continue to have faith."

"Time is the last thing we have," Bultum says, snatching up the now empty grain sack. "We won't survive much longer."

"You and Iree can split our portion to counteract the shortage," I offer, because I clearly have to give them *something*.

Serik gapes with horror, but it's too late—I'm already handing over the bag of wheat.

"And we'll assign Azamat to guard the cavern," I say. He's old and far from honorable—he stole my staff as soon as I entered the winter grazing lands back when I first left Ikh Zuree—but he has no family, no loyalty, and, most important, he's so stubborn, he cannot be bought.

This seems to appease Iree, Bultum, and their families. Though, they don't thank me. That would require acknowledging I did something right.

"Do you know how hungry I am?" Serik mutters as the groups trundle their separate ways.

"Did you have a better solution?"

"Oh, I can think of a few. . . . If you let me knock out their teeth, they won't be able to eat. Problem solved. *Or* we could let nature take its course and allow the shepherds to starve. Then the survivors can eat the weaker people who perish first."

"Serik!" I swat him hard.

"I know, I know. Patience, resilience, no cannibalism. Blah, blah, blah."

"There's nothing 'blah, blah, blah' about it. You've always wanted to be a warrior. Well, here we are. In the heat of battle." I gesture across the cramped cavern, so overrun with bleating animals and bickering shepherds, it's impossible to hear yourself think.

Serik appraises the group with narrowed eyes. "I guess I imagined being a Kalima warrior would involve more adoration and swordplay and less . . . thankless drudgery."

He massages his blistered palms. Barely an hour passes when he isn't required to warm the chilly air or heat the bathing water or clear a path through the drifts of snow and sand so the shepherds can leave the caves in search of roughage for their animals. Half the time he doesn't even manage to accomplish these tasks. His power is too new, too volatile. He stands there, ears red and face grim, as the shepherds shake their heads in disappointment—as if he *should* be able to flawlessly control the sky after mere weeks with a Kalima power.

Surprisingly, Serik never snaps at them. And he never stops trying. But every day his smile grows a little duller, his eyes a little less sharp and squinty. And sometimes when he's asleep at night, I feel his power flare and sputter. He shivers and whimpers in his bedroll.

It's too much strain for a warrior so new to their power. Too much strain for *any* Kalima warrior.

After tracking down Azamat and getting him situated at

his post, Serik pulls me around a corner, out of sight of the shepherds. The glowing algae paints strange green patterns across his face that make him look even more exhausted.

I lace my fingers through his and squeeze. "Just a little longer. I promise. The scouts will return anytime, and I'm certain they'll have found King Minoak."

"But what if they haven't?" he asks without looking at me. "I'm not doubting you," he adds gently. "I hope you're right—that Minoak lives and wants to lead us—but perhaps we should start making a contingency plan, just in case he's—"

"Don't say it." I cut Serik off before he says the word that will ruin everything.

King Minoak isn't *dead*.

He can't be dead.

I refuse to even consider it. And we can't make a "contingency plan," because we have no other option. Without the aid of Verdenet, we will never be able to liberate and recruit the other Protected Territories, which means we'll stand zero chance against Ashkar and Zemya.

I try to pry my hand free, but now Serik tightens his grip. "En, you know it's not in my nature to be tentative or levelheaded, but we can't will a king into existence. Just as we can't allow these people to starve to death. Or freeze if my power runs out." He flexes the fingers of his free hand and frowns. "Some of the shepherds have been counseling and—"

"They've been *what*?" My shrill voice echoes all around us. "Why didn't you tell me immediately? If they're plotting behind my back—"

"No one is plotting behind your back."

"Do you think I can't hear, Serik? They're always grumbling and whispering and criticizing me. You don't have to lie to protect me."

"What are you talking about? No one is doing any of

those things."

I pry my hand free, fold my arms, and scowl.

"Yes, they complain," he finally admits. "But not specifically about you. People are allowed to have conversations and opinions. If you outlaw that, our rebellion will start to feel an awful lot like the Imperial Army. And just because Ghoa and Temujin betrayed you doesn't mean everyone else is going to do the same. . . . Try to have some faith," he tacks on quietly.

It takes everything in me not to roll my eyes. Assuming my allies won't turn against me is as foolish as assuming the snow squalls won't ravage the grasslands this winter when they have every year before. And since when does Serik spout lines about faith?

When I don't respond, Serik takes me firmly by the shoulders, as if tightening the reins of a skittish horse. "Some of the shepherds are discussing entering Verdenet," he says.

"If we do that, we'll be subject to the imperial governor! We won't be able to venture beyond the walls of Lutaar City and continue our search for King Minoak. Even if we miraculously find him within the capital, we'll no longer have the element of surprise to retake Verdenet."

"But they'll have shelter and food, which is the most immediate concern. They've been through so much already. And they think we may be able to raise a resistance once we're inside the city."

I squirm. "It will never happen. The people of Verdenet would have done so already if they could."

"Maybe not if they're lacking leadership. I think—"

"You agree with them!" I fling my arms, forcing Serik to release me.

He sighs. "I never said that, En. I just think it might be good to have another plan. Options are never a bad thing."

"We don't *have* options. If we enter Verdenet, we'll be

trapped. Imprisoned. Which means we'll be sitting ducks when Kartok and the Zemyans attack. They'll conquer Verdenet and all of the Unified Empire, and our efforts and suffering will have been for nothing. We'll be subject to an even more merciless ruler than the Sky King. Why am I the only one who sees this?"

Before Serik can respond, a chorus of shouts ricochets down the tunnel, coming from the direction of the main cavern.

I drag my hand through my unraveling braid and the little muscle beneath my right eye jumps. "If they're fighting over rations again, I swear to the skies I'm going to . . ."

"The scouts have returned!" The message echoes off the rocks and into my ears and I practically collapse with relief.

Thank the Lady and Father.

I rush back toward the cavern, my bad leg dragging painfully behind me. I've been straining it too much lately, bustling across these uneven floors and scaling the slippery walls. I need to be more careful. The only thing that could worsen this situation is if I'm unable to lurk and listen for deceit.

Serik hurries after me. As soon as his stride matches mine, he slips an arm under my shoulders. I don't stop him or complain. He's only trying to help. And I'll get there faster and preserve my strength with aid. But I don't let him support all of my weight. I refuse to put myself in a position where I could be dropped.

Not that I think Serik would drop me.

But I didn't think Temujin and the Shoniin or Ghoa would drop me either.

We burst into the main cavern and hurry to where a horde of shepherds gathers around the three scouts who have been scouring the desert for Sawtooth Mesa. It's where the kings of Verdenet have always gone for their Awakening—when priest-esses of the First Gods chisel the royal tattoo onto their legs. It's a sacred ritual: The future king lies faceup on the tabletop of sandstone, completely bare and vulnerable before the Lady of the Sky for three days. The weather She chooses to send is representative of that future king's reign. After the ceremony, kings often return to the mesa to pray and meditate. But the Ashkarians wouldn't know this because they don't worship the First Gods and they showed no interest in learning our traditions. And the temple is located in the center of the mesa, cut into the earth like ant tunnels, making it completely invisible from below the butte.

When Minoak wasn't camped near the Lady's Lake, where infants are presented to the Goddess for naming, or hidden in the Father's Arms—a small oasis blossoming in the middle of the desert—Sawtooth Mesa came to mind next. It's the perfect hiding spot for a hunted king, as only his people would know of it.

"What news?" I call as we hobble closer.

King Minoak isn't with the scouts. That's the first thing I notice. But that doesn't necessarily mean anything. He's a king; he wouldn't risk following strangers without proof of identity and guarantees of our intentions.

The second thing I notice is how the scouts flinch at the sound of my voice. How they refuse to meet my eyes.

"Well?" I demand. "Did you find him?"

"We didn't even find the mesa," Lalyne, the most experienced tracker among the shepherds, says.

"*Nothing?*" My last shred of hope rushes away with my breath. "But I gave you detailed directions. . . ."

"To a place you've never been!" calls a shepherd from behind me.

I shoot the man an irritated glance and step closer to the scouts. "Did you cross the dry river basin? Are you sure you counted the dunes accurately, from straight beneath the guiding star?"

They stare at me without a spark of frustration or conviction. And now that I'm looking closely, their faces hardly look sunburned. Their boots aren't encrusted with a week's worth of snow and sand.

Did you even try? That's what I want to ask. But I tighten my fists, smothering the starfire flaring in my hands. I must be a calm, confident leader. "This obviously isn't what we hoped for, but we'll organize another expedition—"

The cavern explodes with complaints.

"We'll never find this hidden mesa, because it doesn't exist!"

"And neither does your missing king! He's obviously dead."

"Otherwise, he'd be raising a rebellion and retaking Verdenet himself!"

"No. He wouldn't," I answer resolutely. "He knows better than to charge into a fortified city unprepared. He's waiting for the opportune moment. And reinforcements." I gesture to the gathered group, and the burst of derisive laughter almost knocks me off my feet. I feel like a cat, dangling from a wobbly branch by a single claw.

"You can't honestly think *we're* reinforcements. Look at us!" an elderly woman calls.

"We are just the beginning," I say. "Enough to get Minoak through the gates of Lutaar City. All of the Verdenese inside will rise with us once they see their king is alive."

"And what if he isn't?" Iree shouts. "I say we enter now!" His family loudly agrees, no matter that they're more prepared than anyone to wait a few additional days, thanks to the rations I sacrificed.

"We can't just stroll into Lutaar City!" I don't mean to get emotional, but my voice rakes and rattles like a Bone Reader's poker.

Serik catches my elbow and tugs me a few steps away from the group. "Breathe, En. I know you think finding King Minoak is the only way. And it's a noble plan, it is. But sometimes the necessary pieces just don't come together. It doesn't mean you've failed. It just means we have to keep an open mind."

My eyes are hot and itchy and my voice scrapes against my tingling throat. "You're giving up on me too?"

"I haven't given up on you. Don't be absurd. It just might be a good idea to listen to the majority in this case and find a way to defend against the Zemyans from *inside* Lutaar City, where we'll have food and shelter."

I break free from Serik's hold, twisting my bad arm in the process. Pain explodes along the thick purple scars above my elbow. The algae's florescent colors spin as I stumble into the winding tunnels, half blind and gasping. Serik calls after me. I can feel the shepherds' judgmental eyes on my back. And I can't stand any of it for another skies-forsaken second.

Throwing a cloak of blackness over myself, I wind farther and farther. Deeper and darker. Into the protective arms of the night, where no one else can reach me.

CHAPTER TWO

ENEBISH

The tunnel ends in an inky blue-black cavern that's never seen a speck of light. I flop down onto a stone slab that juts over a spring filled with little translucent racer fish, and close my eyes. Serik and the shepherds may be ready to give up and enter Lutaar City, but we *can't*. The shepherds won't cooperate unless they need us, and they won't need us in there. Not until Kartok and Temujin arrive. But then it will be too late. We'll be trapped. Enslaved. Obliterated by the starfire Kartok siphoned from me in his false Eternal Blue.

"How do I make them understand?" I tilt my head back and look up at the Lady of the Sky. I can't actually see Her down here, buried beneath a league of limestone and sand, but it feels right to lift my face in reverence. I stare at the craggy ceiling, where yellow goblin spiders dangle from silver-spun webs. As I pray, I swirl the tendrils of night like a painter, brushing them gently over the gloom until the spiders and mold and stalactites are covered with glimmering wet darkness. Then I spatter it with an array of gemstone stars. Last, I sculpt

Orbai and send her slashing through the blackness.

My breath catches as she soars above me. My hand trembles as I trace her shadowed wings. "Where are you?" I whisper, even though I know: she either perished in the burning *xanav* or lives eternally bound to Kartok through his Loridium healing magic. But my question is also for the Lady of the Sky, who led me to the shepherds and showed me the way to these caves, but then failed to guide me to King Minoak, the most important piece of this puzzle. "Come back. Help me. *Please!*"

My sobs fill the cavern—shrill, agonized wails that cover the sound of Serik's footsteps. I don't realize he's behind me until he says my name.

"What are you doing here?" I nearly tumble into the pool as I whip around. "How did you find me?"

"I was worried about you." Serik ducks into the cavern. A tiny ball of yellow light flickers in his palm, no bigger than a globeflower. I could loosen my hold on the blackness so he doesn't have to expend his fledgling power, but I don't. "As for finding you, I stumbled along, always choosing the darkest tunnel, until I ended up here." Serik's smile is so proud and adorable, I *almost* let myself smile back. He's much better at summoning heat than light out of necessity, so the tiny matchstick flame hovering above his hand is a big accomplishment. "Seriously, En, are you all right? You were screaming like you were being tortured."

I am being tortured.

"I'm fine." I turn back to the pool, watching the strange fish. It's unsettling, how you can see straight through their scales and bones to their rapidly beating hearts. I feel like my skin is just as thin. Like my sputtering heart is on display, despite my efforts to shield myself.

Serik sighs and shuffles closer. "Please don't shut me out. And don't shut the shepherds out either. We need to stick together or everything will devolve into chaos."

I raise a skeptical brow as if to say, *Hasn't it already?*

"*More* chaos," Serik amends.

After a quiet minute I say, "*We* need to stick together. You and me. If the shepherds see you doubting my plans, I have zero chance of earning their respect or leading an uprising against Kartok and Temujin and the Imperial Army. Don't you see how they look at me? How they whisper and shy away? And did you see the scouts? They're not even trying to find Sawtooth Mesa. No one is taking this seriously, because they want me to fail."

I rip up the gnarled shoots growing through the rocks and toss the oily leaves into the pond. The little fish swarm to the surface, snapping at one another as if these are the last scraps of food on earth. The water clouds with red, and it feels so fitting. So telling. I'm being eaten alive by my own.

"Don't be ridiculous," Serik says. "No one wants you to fail. They wouldn't have followed us into the desert if they didn't think this was their best chance at survival. Sabotaging you would only hurt themselves."

My hair tangles across my face as I shake my head. "You don't understand, because they adore you. They need your heat. But they treat me like a faulty cannon liable to explode at any second."

"I know it's difficult after everything you've been through, but if you want someone to trust *you*, it might be helpful if you try to trust *them*. Something as simple as a compromise, or even just acknowledging their concerns, could go a long way."

I laugh. I'm not about to trust anyone else. Not after Temujin. And Ghoa. And Kartok. And the Sky King. The list just keeps growing.

Serik scoots closer. The otherworldly heat of his body is even more pronounced in this remote cavern. It prickles across my skin like sunshine. "If you can't trust them, trust me." His warm fingers glide across my cheek and curl around my ear. I scrunch my eyes shut and let my forehead plunk against his chin. The parchment and pine ink scent of the monastery is fading from his cloak and robes. Now he smells of wild: of sun and sand and smoldering wood. It suits him even more.

"We can't give up," I whisper. "Minoak is close. I can feel it."

"We have to give them something, En."

"Fine," I relent. "We'll send the scouts one more time. If they don't find King Minoak in five days, we can enter Lutaar City."

Every word slashes my mouth like a knife. It's the last promise I want to make. But I know it's what Serik wants to hear, and the gesture goes a long way. His eyes squish into crescents and his lips quirk into a crooked smile. He presses a light kiss to my forehead, then takes my hand. Leading me back to the shepherds, who won't be nearly as grateful.

"You and her are welcome to stay here and twiddle your thumbs as long as you want!" Iree booms when Serik announces our plan. "I'm leaving at first light."

Cheers of agreement fill the entire system of caves. The roar can probably be heard from Nashab Marketplace in the heart of Lutaar City.

"Do you think it's wise to march into an occupied city in broad daylight?" I shout over them. "It would be far more prudent to enter under the cover of darkness so the imperial warriors can't track your every move. And you need me to do that."

The shepherds wave me off. I know I should keep my lips stitched tight and let Serik reason with them—he'll get far better results—but their cold dismissal, after everything I've done for them, makes my temper bubble over like a lidded pot. I snatch a handful of the black tendrils flapping around my face and drench the cavern in darkness.

Screams ping from wall to wall, and I momentarily revel in their terror. In their helplessness. If they insist on treating me like a monster, I might as well give them something to fear.

My conscience flares at the thought, and I immediately loosen my grip on the night. This is how Ghoa would think. This is how she would react: with harsh threats and vicious punishment.

Serik blinks over at me, his brows crumpled and his lips pursed, conveying exactly what he's thinking: *What are you doing? Stop driving an even larger wedge between yourself and the group.*

I toss my hands in frustration and shoot him an equally pointed look: *Then do something. Make them agree. You're the one who suggested we compromise.*

Serik closes his eyes and rubs his temples. His voice is hollow and ragged when he speaks, "If you don't agree to support this final scouting mission, I won't provide heat."

The shepherds recoil, looking at Serik the way they've always looked at me.

"It's only five more days," he says feebly.

"Less if you locate King Minoak quickly," I cut in, turning to the scouts. "Replenish your rations and prepare to leave immediately."

Lalyne sets her jaw and regards me for a long, uncomfortable minute, her lined face hard and her eyes even harder. I stare back. Grudgingly, she nods and the other two scouts snatch up their satchels and clomp toward the supply cavern.

When Azamat sees us, he rises from his stool and lets us pass with an official wave of his staff. The rations are divided by variety: grain in the far corner, dried meat in the other, and cheese made from goat's milk along the far wall. "You may each take a parcel of cheese and two strips of meat from the sacks labeled for the coming week," I say.

The scouts rummage through the supplies and end up clustered around the meat. "There isn't a bag marked with those dates," Lalyne says loudly. Loud enough for any shepherd who might have followed us to hear.

"What do you mean there isn't a bag?" I hurry to the ever-dwindling pile. "I took inventory again just a few hours ago and everything was in order." I paw through the sacks again, only to discover Lalyne is right. An entire sack of meat is missing.

"Azamat!" I whirl around. "Did a family pick up their allotment early?"

"No one's entered the chamber since you left," he says with a lift of his chin.

"Are you certain? You never left to fetch water? Or accidentally fell asleep?"

Or accepted a bribe?

Or joined the plot to sabotage me?

"I don't fall asleep on watch," he says with a sniff.

I try to keep my voice level. Calm. "Then did *you* take the bag of dried meat?"

Azamat's knobby fingers tighten on the staff and his leather-worn face pinches. His shout rumbles through the cavern. "Why assign me to guard the food if you believe I'm the one who's stealing it?"

I wince. It shouldn't be possible for such a thunderous voice to come from such an old, wiry man.

"Enebish didn't mean to accuse you." Serik elbows past me, but it's too late. The cacophony of complaints that only just died down resumes with twice the fervor.

"More food's gone missing!"

"We won't last another day!"

The hysteria builds like the pitter-patter of rain, until the shouts are a downpour. The cave is so flooded, I can barely keep my head above water.

"I'm sure the bag has simply been mislabeled. Or misplaced," I call out. "I'll take stock again. Then *I* will guard the rations."

Azamat protests loudly, as does everyone within earshot, but I grab his staff—which is actually *my* staff—and use it to press him out of the cavern like a stubborn sheep. Mercifully, the staff takes a large swathe of the clamoring crowd with him.

Once a space is cleared, I position myself in the cavern's opening, arms and legs extended so my hands and feet are flush with rock on both sides, like a human wall. The shepherds mutter and glower as they disperse, murmuring that I'm the least trustworthy of everyone, but we all know the real reason they don't want me to guard the rations: they *want* the food to disappear. Just like they want the scouts to return empty-handed. Any reason to abandon my plans. They're willing to throw away our only chance at freedom for a smelly tavern and a hunk of bread in Lutaar City.

Serik trudges away last. His steps are slow and he scrubs his hand over his exhausted face. I know I'm not making things easy for him—he'll spend all night apologizing and giving out extra warmth to appease the shepherds—but we must all make sacrifices.

I certainly am.

And at least they appreciate his efforts.

The hours creep by slower than the pale green snails climbing the cavern walls. No one wanders by to chat with me, as they did with Azamat. But I don't want visitors. I don't want to be distracted—purposely or inadvertently. And I have the darkness. The only companion I need.

The tendrils curl around my wrists and twine through my fingers. They coil up my legs and wind around my torso, wrapping me in a velvety embrace. I breathe out and in. Relaxing, re-centering.

It's impossible to gauge the passage of time without ever seeing the sky, but at least a night and day pass without trouble. By the time the shepherds settle into their tents the following evening, however, my eyes burn and my lids droop as if weighted with stones. My body is so heavy, I slide lower and lower down the wall. Maybe I was harder on Azamat than I should have been. The seductive lull of sleep is almost as irresistible as the night.

I rest my eyes for a second. Just a moment. No one would dare steal the rations while I'm sitting right here. . . .

I don't know if a minute passes, or if it's several hours, but from deep within my cocoon of slumber, I feel the slightest nudge. I groan and wave my hand, shooing the pesky mouse or fire gecko. But then the feeling comes again, and this time I realize it's not a nudge so much as a pull.

A yank.

The threads of night, resting slack in my palms, slide away, burning like rope as they go.

What in the skies?

My eyes fly open and I lurch upright, scanning the ration cavern. It's barely ten paces across. An intruder would be a mere hand's breadth away from me.

My muscles tense, prepared to pounce on whoever has the audacity to steal from the entire group. But I force myself to wait as I scan the darkness.

At first I see nothing, but as I gather up a handful of night and tug it back, like the blankets Ghoa hoarded when we shared a bedroll as children, an outline shimmers into focus.

I don't recognize the thief right away; they're on the small side, with skinny legs poking out from beneath a tattered hem and a hood pulled over their hair.

My palms prickle with starfire as I watch them sift through the sacks, snatching a bit of this and a handful of that. Taking whatever they'd like, no matter that the rest of us are starving too.

How can you be so selfish?

And even more curious, how can they *see*?

I sit there, coiled like a banshee viper in the cavern opening, waiting for the opportune moment to strike.

When the thief finishes raiding what little food we have, they heft the sack over their shoulder and creep closer. Closer. I snap my eyes shut as they glance down at me—just a careless guard, overtaken by sleep. But as they hop over my legs, I reach out and grab their ankle.

"Gotcha!"

A deafening scream fills the cavern as the thief falls. The sack of stolen rations hits the ground, and I howl with indignation as our precious food rolls through grimy puddles.

"How dare you!" I roar, leaping onto the thief's squirming body. My old injuries are a dull buzz compared to my rage. I grab for their arms and try to pin them to the ground. For a second they're so still, I think I've managed it. Then the ribbons of darkness heave and I tumble backward—into a whirl of pitch black, as if they pulled a rug out from beneath me.

I'm so stunned, I lose my grip entirely, and both the thief and the night wiggle free.

The intruder retrieves the mostly empty food sack and they're already several paces ahead by the time I clamber to my feet. Which is a problem, since I am not a fast runner.

"Stop!" I bellow, sprinting as fast as I can despite the jolting pain. Panicked thoughts whirl around my brain: the Zemyans are here, using my siphoned power. Except why would they bother stealing our food? So there must be another Night Spinner among the shepherds. Except I would have known. I would have felt them sooner. We would have been playing tug-of-war with the threads of darkness all this time.

I fly into the main cavern, where sleepy-eyed shepherds spill from their tents, gaping with horror. All of them yelling at me when they should be yelling at the thief.

"They're stealing our food!" I point at the hooded figure, who's already halfway across the cavern, but every eye remains on me.

I try to rip the cloak of darkness off the thief, but they're too far away and their grip is too strong. My hands are too shaky.

"If you're not going to help, at least get out of my way!" I shout as I plow through the throng, throwing elbows and ramming shoulders.

I'm nearly to the tunnel the thief slipped down when someone dodges in front of me. "Stop this, En!" Serik looks as mortified as the rest of the group. "There's no one here. You're frightening everyone."

"Just because you can't see them, doesn't mean no one's here!"

Serik places his hands on my shoulders and holds me tight. "I know you're desperate, but do you really think this is the best way—"

"This is the *only* way. Move!"

Still, Serik doesn't let go. Leaving me no choice. Not only is the thief stealing our food, they're somehow wielding the darkness. They can't get away.

I fling the night over myself like a cloak and drive my knee into Serik's stomach.

"I'm sorry," I cry as he crumples. Then I dodge through the crowd much more efficiently and charge into the tunnel.

Too late.

There isn't even a fleeting glimpse of the thief. Only dozens of tunnels branching off in a hundred different directions. Growling with frustration, I slam my good hand into the wall. That's when I feel it: the push and pull of the darkness. Every time I tighten my grip, the thief pulls back. Connecting us like a tether.

I dart ahead again, following the pull right, then left, then right again. Where in the skies are they going? I'll never find my way back. A second later, cold air slaps me across the face and the ceiling explodes with stars. My feet sink into the still warm sand, slowing my progress even further.

Why would they leave the caves?

Panic seizes my lungs as a third possibility enters my mind. If the thief isn't Zemyan or one of our own, they must be from the outside. And if that's the case, stolen food is the least of our worries. They could reveal our location to the imperial governor in Verdenet. Or sell us out to the Zemyans.

I beg my feet to move faster, but the sand is deep and my bad leg throbs. The thief races up the nearest dune, widening the gap between us. Until the tug of darkness is so faint, I can no longer feel it.

Crashing to my knees, I tilt my face heavenward and cry out to the Lady and Father, screaming at the distant, glinting stars. And that's when I remember that darkness isn't the only weapon at my disposal.

Don't!

My mind dredges up images of the burning Sky Palace, but I don't have a choice. I have to think of the safety of the group.

The thief is a Night Spinner.

I have always been the only one—other than my mentor Tuva, who died when I was thirteen. Where has this person been hiding? Why haven't they been recruited by the Kalima? Is this a challenge of some sort?

There's only one way to find out.

With a desperate shriek, I reach for a dagger of starfire and hurl it at the smear of shadow stealing over the dunes.

CHAPTER THREE

GHΘA

THE SPICE TRADERS LOOK LIKE THEY'RE GOING TO WET themselves.

A pathetic man and woman hunch behind their rickety cart, faces pale as sand, hands trembling. Skiffs of yellow turmeric and rusty paprika escape the burlap sacks and float on the breeze. I grin as I inhale the pungent air.

Frightened witnesses are cooperative witnesses.

"Have you passed any caravans along this route?" I demand, gazing down from Tabana's towering height.

They eye my warhorse—her sleek black coat draped in imperial blue and gold. Then their gazes continue upward, to the saber gleaming through the folds of my cloak, the glint of my lamellar armor in the harsh winter sun, and settle at last on the tinkling strands of my ponytail, singed white with frost.

"W-we've seen no one, C-Commander," the man babbles, dipping into a pathetic bow. "Not a soul."

"You're halfway between Verdenet and Sagaan on one of the most heavily trafficked roads in the Unified Empire," I say

29

quietly. Dangerously.

"Most people choose not to travel this late in the year," the woman says.

"Which is how I know you couldn't have missed them." I slash my arm, and frost ravages the spice bags. "Surely you've seen wagon tracks or footprints in the snow? Or heard the braying of sheep? Voices, even, that seem to come from nowhere?"

Just because they haven't *seen* my traitorous sister and her ragtag group of rebels doesn't mean they aren't here. I *know* Enebish would have run to Verdenet. I know it as surely as the heady burn of ice overtaking my fists. Yet somehow she and Temujin and his Shoniin, and every skies-forsaken shepherd on the grazing lands, has vanished without leaving a single footprint or wheel mark in the snow. I feel like I'm tracking shadows, chasing phantoms.

Which isn't far from the truth.

I nudge Tabana forward and the traders scream as her platter-sized hooves nearly sever their toes. "Do you know the punishment for obstructing imperial justice?" I ask, twirling my fingers idly in the air.

The woman screams as intricate patterns of frost climb the wheels of their cart. I nudge a few fractals onto their cloaks, let them nip at their cheeks. The man drops to his knees, babbling incoherently.

"Tell me what you know!" I shout.

Before he can confess, a screech fills the air. My eyes snap up to the sky, and invisible fingers seize my lungs. For one breathless moment I'm convinced it's *her* eagle, diving at me with blood-soaked wings, daggers of ice still protruding from her chest. But as the raptor streaks closer, I see it's too small, too spotted, and too *alive* to be Orbai.

The imperial falcon glides overhead, releases a scroll of

parchment, and climbs back into the low-hanging clouds before I've unrolled the missive. The frosty strands of my ponytail harden further, scraping the back of my neck like a blade.

Whoever wrote this letter hasn't given me an opportunity to reply.

I unfurl the parchment.

Return to Sagaan at once.

The note isn't signed, but the Sky King's hand is unmistakable. A flurry of annoyance billows through me as I stare at the ornate loops.

"Find them. By any means necessary," he'd ordered me from the bowels of the treasury, where I led him to safety during Temujin's thwarted execution. We sat in prickling silence for hours, listening to Enebish's starfire ravage the Sky Palace and the Grand Courtyard. Finally he spoke: "I'm giving you complete control. Full confidence. Prove I'm not a fool to continue putting my faith in you."

But how am I supposed to *prove* anything if he recalls me before I've had the opportunity to search? It's barely been a week.

A week should have been more than adequate. A competent commander would have found them in days. Hours.

I can't tell if the voice of censure is coming from myself or the Sky King, but it makes no difference. We are one and the same. His will is my own.

The spice traders scream, which is when I realize I've crushed the missive in my fist—though not before freezing it. Brittle shards of parchment escape my fingers and slash around us on the wintry breeze. The woman falls to the ground beside the man and they cover their heads, finally ready to cooperate. But orders are orders. Without a word to either of them, I bring Tabana around and dig my heels into her flanks.

We ride northward for five days, the snow-streaked grasslands blurring past, until the city of Sagaan rises up around me. A fortress of towering spires and impenetrable walls surrounding the glittering splendor of the royal complex. What *used* to be the royal complex, I correct myself as I gallop into the wreckage. The white façade of the Sky Palace is blacker than crumbling coal, the spires are ensconced in scaffolding, and the acrid tang of smoke still blankets the air.

The rebuilding will take months. Years. An opened wound, left to fester.

No matter how many times I see the devastation, I will never get used to it. And I will never forgive Enebish. Not only did she turn her back on me, but she turned her back on the Sky King. On our empire.

"Welcome home, Commander," Reza, my page, calls from the front of the blue stone treasury building.

I look past the boy, my eyes narrowing into slits. This smoldering wreckage is *not* my home. And where in the name of the Sky King is Varren? My second-in-command always greets me to relay messages and reports from the war front. Why am I stuck with this knobby-boned *child* who knows nothing? He isn't even supposed to address me—or leave the barn—and I'm about to remind him of this, but his eyes are so eager and adoring and he pulls his shoulders back in an effort to impress me. This small show of veneration defrosts my anger a fraction.

Until he opens his mouth again.

"Did you make any progress, Commander?" Reza asks hopefully.

My back goes rigid. I dismount and toss the frozen reins at his face.

I would *be making progress if they'd let me do my job instead of summoning me back to Sagaan.*

"What do you think?" I bark to avoid the question.

Reza beams and gives me the Kalima salute, even though

he's magic-barren, and hurries off to the stables with Tabana.

I march up the steps and slam through the heavy brass doors of the treasury. It's nearly as cavernous as the Sky Palace, comprised of two wings that intersect like a cross. Silver molding adorns every wall, and a glass dome crowns the center of the spiral staircase. When sunlight streams through the diamond-cut panes, the vivid blue walls glow like lightning bugs on the grasslands.

I used to think it was beautiful. Serene, even. I would sneak over here and sit in the stairwell when I needed a break from the endless bustle of the Sky Palace. It reminded me of slower, more carefree days, when Papá would bring me to his office and teach me to balance ledgers and manage the royal coffers. I always found the steady clink of coins and murmured transactions so comforting. Like a song, in its own way. But ever since the Sky King claimed the treasury as his temporary residence, those soothing sounds have been replaced by the clomp of boots, the rattle of weapons, and, ever more increasingly, the sound of his raging criticism.

"Varren!" I call, my own voice grinding with exasperation when he isn't waiting in the atrium beneath the glass dome either. And Cirina isn't ready with towels and a change of clothes. The thin coat of irritation varnishing my skin like sweat hardens into ice. How dare they summon me, then fail to prepare for my arrival!

"Varren!" I yell again as I storm toward the vault—our newly minted war room. It's the only place prying ears and treacherous arrows won't breech. When my second still hasn't appeared by the time I reach the hidden door, covered in oak paneling to match the rest of the hall, I vow to demote him.

I spin the lock.

Right, left, right.

"There had better be a damn good reason for disrupting

my search," I say as the door swings inward. "What could possibly be so important?"

My voice trails off and my boots freeze in the threshold. Arctic flurries whip around my wrists as my arms slap against my sides. There, seated at the long ebony table we dragged in from the assembly hall, is every Kalima warrior. Including Varren. And at the head of the table sits the Sky King.

"What's this?" I look from face to face, trying to keep my voice level, but it pitches higher with each word. "What are you doing here?" I point at Iska and Eshwar. "You're supposed to be patrolling the highway between Sagaan and Lingosk." I turn to Karwani and Vanesh, who stare at the table as if it's inlaid with gold. "And you're assigned to watch the fish market a day's ride from Chotgor." They all look down and away. My heart pounds so wildly, it echoes off the steel walls. Filling the tiny room.

I take a deep breath and let it out slowly. If everyone has been recalled, it must be for a good reason. "You've found them?" I ask hopefully.

Still no answer.

The ticking of the clock has never been so deafening.

I spit out a hysterical laugh. "What sort of conspiracy is this? It isn't any wonder we haven't captured the traitors. You're not even looking for them!"

The Sky King rises with maddening slowness. "Just because they're not following *your* orders doesn't mean we aren't hunting the traitors."

I try to make sense of his words. "Whose orders are they following if not mine? You gave me complete control. Full confidence. *Find them. By any means necessary.* . . . Is that not what you said?" I think back to his command, how he stared at me inside this very vault with such pride and conviction. What about all the routes and rotations I've mapped? All the missives I've written? All the detailed reports I've received?

Did they carry out any of it?

My hand instinctively goes to my saber. "I don't understand."

The Sky King casts me a look that's both pitying and condescending. "You've been erratic and unreliable, so we did what was necessary to keep you out of the way."

"Erratic and unreliable?" The words drill into my flesh like Zemyan arrows. My pulse throbs wildly in my throat. "What are you talking about? I'm neither of those things!"

"You put your feelings for that monstrous sister of yours above your duty and the well-being of Ashkar," the Sky King accuses.

"I *never*—"

"You helped her sneak out of Ikh Zuree to complete an unsanctioned mission." He raises a finger and counts off my crimes. "Then you lost track of her in Sagaan, allowing her to join forces with the Shoniin. When you finally recaptured her, you were unable to extract any useful information, and instead of killing her, you let her thwart Temujin's execution and escape. *Again.*"

With every word, the walls press closer. At least half of the Kalima exchange small, lurid grins. "I didn't *let* her get away!" I shout. "I ran to *you*, my lord. To protect you and guide you to safety. As any good warrior would."

"And by so doing, you ran *away* from *her*."

I blink at him, my eyelashes crusting with frost. "You can't possibly think I would defend Enebish after she tried to kill me!"

"Perhaps not consciously. But familial bonds run deep. Sometimes deeper, even, than love for one's country . . . and king."

"These accusations are absurd!" I cry. "Varren, tell him! You were with me every moment. You know I would never . . ."

Betray my king and country. I can't bring myself to utter the horrible words.

I lean across the table, staring desperately into my second's eyes. We've rarely left each other's sides since we were fifteen, when neither of us could best the other in the sparring ring. He was strong but I was fast, and no matter how many times we fought, it ended in a draw. Until, one day, it didn't. His eyes met mine and, with an unspoken nod of agreement, he let my fist crash against his temple.

I generally despise quitters, but this was different. Varren's surrender was a message. A vow. He would defer to me. He would put my needs above his own. And it solidified his place at my side. He's been as steady and immovable as the Ondor Mountains ever since. A quiet, towering presence. My rock.

"Varren, *please,*" I beg, hating the waver in my voice.

Our eyes lock, just as they did that day in the sparring ring, but instead of yielding, he straightens in his chair and his face twists into a scowl. It makes the dragon tattoo prowling down his cheek look like it's baring its teeth.

"A more competent commander would have spirited me to safety *and* captured the traitors," the Sky King continues. "There's no room for error during these tumultuous times. Certainly not if you wish to lead my most elite regiment."

A cannonball of outrage slams into my chest. Blowing me to bits as my mind fits together the pieces of their treachery. "You planned this from the beginning." I laugh bitterly as I point at each of them, coming to rest on the king. "I haven't had your *trust* or *confidence* since the attack, have I? That's why you allowed me to ride out on so many scouting missions—so you could sharpen the knife to stab in my back."

"We had no choice," the Sky King says, calm as ever. "We knew you wouldn't go quietly, and now is hardly the time for infighting. You can tell people you chose to step down, if you wish," he adds as if he's doing me some great favor.

Anger howls through me. My hair grows heavy with frost and my cheeks crackle like ice. I let out a guttural scream because I have given this country everything. *Everything!* I can't just tell people I *stepped down*. I refuse to be removed at all. Never, in the history of Ashkar, has a commander of the Kalima warriors relinquished their title for any reason other than death. I would be the only one. The embodiment of disgrace and failure. I wouldn't be able to show my face anywhere in the empire. Not even at my parents' estate.

Especially not there.

Memories rise before me—their smiling, tearstained faces on the day I was sworn in as Commander; their pride so tangible, I could reach out and clutch it to my armored chest.

I refuse to have that ripped away.

With a growl, I unsheathe my saber and hold it out in front of me. "If you wish to remove me, you'll have to kill me." Then I extend my left arm and push the frost and fury swirling in my core out through my fingertips, forming a glittering blade identical to the one in my right hand. I swing the twin sabers in front of me and stare my warriors down, daring them to attack.

More than half of the Kalima shoot to their feet, and that deliberate act of betrayal hurts so much, I nearly whimper in pain.

But I bite back my screams. Sever my emotions.

I don't need these traitors.

And I don't *want* them.

I stomp my boot into the floor and a thick coating of ice sweeps beneath the table and chairs, slicker than the Amereti in winter. I lower my head and bare my teeth, but before I can charge into the room, an earth-shattering rumble shakes the walls of the treasury. The steel vault groans. Books and quills clatter from the shelves and slide across the ice.

"Earthquake!" Cirina yells, ducking beneath the table for cover. But this doesn't feel like any earthquake I've experienced. The shudders come in waves. Almost like detonating cannons. Only harsher. Stronger.

"What in the name of the Sky King . . ." I turn and squint down the hall. A second later, the massive glass dome over the stairs splinters. The cowards behind me scream as shards of colored glass fall like rain—even though we're in no danger of being hit.

I remain silent. Still.

Listening. Watching.

It's almost as if we're under attack, but from whom? The Zemyans are advancing, but they couldn't have reached Sagaan this quickly. They only just captured Ivolga. And Temujin and his pitiful rebels don't have this kind of firepower. They're all magic-barren deserters.

Save for one.

Enebish's scarred face fills my mind: twisted with outrage during our argument in the spire salon. As if I did something unforgivable at Nariin rather than what was necessary to defend our country and fortify the Kalima. We needed a strong leader after Chinua's death. Someone seasoned and dependable. It would have been disastrous if I'd been removed. Plus, the merchants could have easily been Zemyans. I had to counteract the threat.

Another boom shakes the walls, and my muscles stiffen with ice—harden with certainty.

"Don't you have a scrap of honor?" I scream for my sister as I jog toward the shattered dome. "How can you turn your back on your family and country like this?"

How can you?

I don't know if she actually spoke, or if it's the ghost of

her voice spitting the accusation back at me, but Enebish's face fills my mind again, bristling with fury and snarling for revenge. She looks just as she did before she flung her starfire at my chest—like an executioner wielding her blade.

There's a moment of eerie quiet. Like the deep gasp of breath before a scream.

Then every shred of light is sucked out of the treasury.

CHAPTER FOUR

ENEBISH

The desert skyline flares with light. A second later, vicious heat sears past me as the starfire I summoned slams into the crest of the nearest dune. Sand sprays into the air, even higher than the explosion Serik created to destroy the Shoniin's encampment in the Eternal Blue. The debris blots out the stars and bitten moon. It strangles the cactus wrens as they fill the dusty sky.

I hold my breath and wait. The thief was well ahead of me. Almost out of range. But after five long seconds, the night rebounds with a *snap*. The stolen tendrils slingshot back to my hands and a shrill cry rends the night. An intense, visceral shudder works through me—the feeling of a thousand scorpions scuttling down my limbs.

If you're not Enebish the Destroyer, why do screams still follow you?

It takes me much longer than I'd like to reach the wreckage. Long enough that my impressive attack will have lost most of its impact, but I eventually catch up with the thief. They're dragging themselves through the sand on hands and knees. The ravaged ball of starfire smolders behind them, churning noxious white smoke into the air.

I don't bother shrouding myself in darkness. There's no point.

"I can't believe you thought you could steal from us without consequence," I say, my voice cold and hard. "Or beat me at my own game."

The thief glances back and squeals. They hoist themselves to their feet and try to run, but the starfire grazed their left calf, leaving a long strip of shiny red skin. Burned to the bone.

"Stay back!" they yell, reaching skyward.

I freeze, bracing for a return volley of starfire. But the pricks of light above us barely quiver. "You don't know how to call them, do you?" A twinge of laughter creeps into my voice.

The thief grumbles and surges forward, but thanks to their newly inflicted injuries, they're no longer faster than I am. We limp on and on and on through the desert. My thighs burn and sand collects in the corners of my lips, but with every excruciating step, I manage to close the distance. I'm so focused on catching them, I don't realize we've scaled a series of switchbacks and crossed a flat stretch of rock, until the thief drops into a square hole cut into the earth.

My heart stutters with disbelief as I peer over the edge—at the long colonnades and sandstone altar. At the ornate mosaic walls and hand-carved columns. A place our scouts swore they couldn't find. A place they claimed doesn't exist.

Sawtooth Mesa.

"Wait!" I cry, my mind scrambling.

The thief limps on.

I leap into the temple without considering the drop, and land in a painful crouch. Zaps of electricity climb my injured leg like wasps, but they're easy to ignore. My entire body is tingling. Buzzing with newfound energy. I take off after the thief's retreating shadow, more determined than ever to catch them.

They knew the way to the temple of the kings, which means they are Verdenese. And of high rank. They could know something about King Minoak.

The sandstone altar, on which every king of Verdenet has been tattooed, dominates the center of the space. The thief ducks under it and streaks into the colonnades beyond, which are made of intricately patterned orange and white tiles. When standing close, they depict small scenes of life in Verdenet. But when viewed as a whole, they turn into an impressive mural of the Lady and Father. Down the length of each wall, there are at least twenty doors that undoubtedly lead to twice as many halls. It could take weeks to find the thief once they disappear inside—*if* I ever do.

"Wait! I just want to talk to you!" I gasp.

Labored, breathy laughter trails from the thief. "You nearly took off my leg! I'm not interested in *talking* to you."

Their voice is higher than I anticipated. Softer too. It makes me pause for half a second before spitting, "If you don't stop, I'll obliterate the temple!" I thrust my hand skyward, praying they can't see how much my arm is trembling. I don't want to destroy this sacred place—not to mention throw away the only lead we've had in weeks—but they've seen too much. They're plainly up to something.

They halt, eyes popped wide in the darkness. "You wouldn't."

"Wouldn't I?"

Their heavy breath fills the quiet.

"Answer my questions, and I'll be merciful."

Still no response.

"This isn't an invitation; it's a demand!" I yell, tugging a bolt of starfire closer.

The thief remains silent, but behind us, a second voice calls, "Ziva, is that you?"

This voice is deeper and accompanied by the shuffle of much heavier feet. I whip around, looking for a second assailant, but to my surprise, the thief—Ziva—shouts, "Stay hidden!"

That only makes the pounding footsteps quicken. "Why? What's wrong?" The questions are cut off by a grating cough.

"Run!" Ziva screams. "As deep into the temple as you can! I'll find you when it's safe."

"You won't be finding anyone if you're dead," I cut in— loud enough for her accomplice to hear.

"Ziva!" the unseen voice cries again, closer. I widen my stance, spread my fingers, and stare down each bejeweled doorway as if a lion might leap out.

It turns out to be a fairly accurate prediction.

A dark shape emerges from a door to my right—large and broad with filthy sand-crusted furs draped over bare shoulders and bloodshot eyes peering through a tangle of hair. They even roar as they charge at me.

Tingles ignite my throat and my palm sizzles as I grip the starfire tighter.

Ziva tries to erect a protective wall of night around the man, but it doesn't affect my vision in the slightest. He, however, trips in the sudden dark and crashes into a pillar. As he crumples to the ground, moaning and clutching his side, Ziva throws herself in front of him. Though, it's a needless sacrifice.

The starfire is already slipping through my slackened fingers, drifting back up to the heavens as I squint at the mewling figure.

The man might be wearing the rags of a beggar, but he has long gray hair the color of storm clouds and thick-muscled legs that are covered in tattoos from knee to ankle, and the golden rings climbing the ridge of his left ear are almost too numerous to count, especially as he thrashes in pain.

But I do count. All the way to seventeen. A number only one man in my country is permitted to wear.

"King Minoak?" I gasp.

"Don't be ridiculous," the girl spits at me. She hovers in front of the king of Verdenet, scrawny arms outstretched. "We're homeless outcasts. I'm sorry I stole your food; we're just desperately hungry." From beneath her hood, I catch a glimpse of a round face, unmarked by a single wrinkle or line. Dark curls escape around her full cheeks. She can't be older than twelve. Maybe thirteen.

What is a *child* doing with King Minoak? I assumed if he survived, he would be with guards. Or warriors. Not a young girl.

Yet, it's clear she isn't just *any* girl.

Ignoring Ziva's request, I edge closer. "I—I never doubted you were alive," I stutter, suddenly tongue-tied and bumbling as I gaze down at my king. "And I knew you'd come here."

Irritation at the scouts' pathetic efforts rankle me. I found the missing king on my very first attempt. Proof that they've been trying to undermine and sabotage me.

Except they wouldn't have been able to see Minoak or the girl, I realize as the pane of blackness Ziva erected between us crumbles. They probably couldn't see the mesa at all. . . .

"How long have you been hiding here?" I ask. "And how long have you been able to do that little trick with the darkness?" I nod at Ziva's hands.

"We're just passing through. And I don't know what trick you're talking about," she retorts. She lifts King Minoak under the arms and tries to drag him back into the colonnade, but her burned leg gives out and they hit the ground hard.

The king clutches his side with a moan. Dark crimson stains

bloom through his filthy tunic—the kind of wound made by a dagger, not the result of a nasty fall or starvation. And judging by the amount and pattern of the blood, the dagger was at least the length of my hand, and the attack came from behind. Uncontested.

Which means Temujin's tales about the assassination attempt were true—for once.

"Now look what you've done," the girl barks at me. "That wound had nearly closed."

I ignore her accusatory scowl and rush to help. "He needs stitches and poultices to stave off infection." I reach for the corner of Minoak's tunic to inspect the wound closer, but the hiss that flies from Ziva's mouth is fiercer than the growl of a banded leopard.

"I just want to help," I assure her. "I've been searching for the king. I need to bring him back—"

"Of course you've been searching for him! Everyone has. All you empire dogs are desperate to finish the job after I killed the first assassin."

It takes a moment for Ziva's words to compute. When they do, my mouth slowly drops open and I appraise her in a new light. "*You* stopped the assassin?"

"Yes," she says quickly, before her voice breaks and fades away.

"Who *are* you?"

She draws her shoulders back and her honey-brown eyes burn into mine, as fierce as the desert sun. "I am Zivana Bonwatu Yimeni, Crown Princess of Verdenet, and I will end you if you lay a finger on my father."

I had almost forgotten the king had a daughter. She was so young when my village burned; they hadn't even performed her hastening ceremony yet. Now here she is, on the run, trying to nurse her father back to health when she's barely old enough not to need a nurse herself.

"I'm no empire dog, and I don't want to kill your father," I tell her again. "Quite the opposite. I am Verdenese. Minoak is my king. I want to see him restored to the throne." I gesture to myself—my tattooed calves, tanned skin, dark hair and eyes.

"I don't care what you look like. A loyal citizen of Verdenet would never throw a *star* at me, chase me through the desert, and threaten to bring the entire mesa down on us. You're clearly one of the Sky King's warriors."

"What makes that so clear?"

"Everyone with power is."

"Does that mean *you're* one of his warriors?" I raise a brow at her. "We seem to have a lot in common. . . ."

"I don't know what this is"—she holds up her hands—"but I do know I'm nothing like you. I would never help a greedy pig ravage my country."

"Neither would I. That's the entire reason I'm here. I want to free Verdenet and the other Protected Territories. I want to place King Minoak back on the throne. But I obviously needed to find him before I could accomplish any of this. All of those people hidden in the caves are of the same mind."

"I don't believe you."

"That's fine, but it's the truth, and if you come back with me—"

"We're not going *anywhere* with you."

"What other choice do you have?" I look gravely at the chalk-faced king. His hand clutching his side is entirely covered with blood and his lips murmur unintelligible words. He's thin beneath the rags and furs. As thin as the girl.

"I don't know, but I'll figure it out *without* your 'help,'" she says, dismissing me.

I scoot closer. "You've done an impressive job keeping your father hidden and alive, but he needs medical attention—you both do." I nod at her burned leg. "And food. It's okay to change course and accept help."

It isn't lost on me that this is the same speech Serik has been giving me since we left Sagaan. But the circumstances are completely different. The shepherds don't actually want to help. They want me to fail. They offer aid with one breath, then slander me with the next. While I, on the other hand, am willing to do anything, sacrifice anything, to save my king and my people.

King Minoak coughs again. Thick, wet droplets of blood speckle his lips. When the fit finally releases him, he loses consciousness, his head lolling onto Ziva's lap. While she screams and grips him by both cheeks, commanding him to wake up, I sidle even closer.

"Without you and King Minoak, we'll never be able to reclaim Verdenet. My group will perish in the caves or be forced to enter Lutaar City, where we'll be subject to the imperial governor. And without treatment, your father will die of these wounds, no matter how hard you've worked to protect him. We need each other."

"We don't need help." Ziva stubbornly shakes her head.

Burning skies! I'm tempted to mold the darkness into a giant hand and smack her across the face with it. Instead I huff out a breath and look to the Lady of the Sky. "You've set me with so many impossible tasks—and it's my honor to perform them—but I beg you to have mercy on me this once and soften the heart of this belligerent child."

Ziva gazes at me, head cocked to the side. I'm certain she's going to give me a tongue-lashing for calling her a child, but she says, "You worship the Lady and Father?"

"Of course I do. I don't know how many ways I must tell you: I am like you. I am with you."

She narrows her eyes even further. "Swear on your immortal

rest in the realm of the Eternal Blue that everything you've said is true."

I laugh at the irony of her request. At how I thought I had already reached the Eternal Blue.

"I don't see how any of this is funny," she snaps.

I bite my tongue and look down. "I'm not laughing at you. I've just been used and lied to so often, it's strange to have someone believe *I* am doing the double-crossing."

"Are you?"

"If I wanted to kill the king, I could easily do so now." I gesture to King Minoak's limp form. "But everything I've said is true. I know how it feels to think you can't trust anyone, to feel like the entire world is against you, but I swear on the memory of my parents, who perished ten years ago during the Zemyan raid of Sangatha, I'll do everything in my power to see your father reinstated."

Ziva glances down and trails a finger across her father's bearded, weatherworn face. "Fine. We'll return with you. But I won't hesitate to call the night at the first sign of trouble." She raises her hand, fingers outstretched, and I quirk my lips with amusement. She drops her hand and looks sheepishly at her feet. "I forgot that my threats mean nothing to you. You're much stronger."

She waits, as if she expects me to encourage her, but I nod and say, "I am."

While Ziva gathers her things, I unfasten my cloak and lay it on the cool stones beside King Minoak. He's still unconscious, and he weighs twice as much as a sand cat, but I manage to roll him onto the cloth. Then I remove the fur from his shoulders, press it to his wound, and bind it with strips of cloth I tear from the hem of his robe. It's crude and far from sanitary, but it should control the bleeding while we hike back to the caves.

When Ziva returns, she surveys my handiwork and gives a small nod.

"Did you get everything you need?" I gesture to the satchel slung over her arm, and she hastily pushes it behind her back. Out of my sight. As if I'm a skies-forsaken caravan raider. "Honestly? I was just trying to make conversation."

Ziva lifts a corner of the cloak and throws her weight forward. "Less talking, more pulling."

CHAPTER FIVE

ENEBISH

At the mouth of the cave, Ziva hesitates and glances back at her gray-faced father splayed across my cloak. "Are you certain—"

"We've been searching for him since we left Sagaan. They'll be overjoyed." I charge into the tunnel, forcing Ziva to follow, eager to present King Minoak to the shepherds. Here's proof I was right: the king of Verdenet lives. And I found him, just as I said I would, despite their impatience and skepticism and sabotage.

If this doesn't earn their respect *and* their trust, nothing will.

"We're saved!" I holler as we trudge through the tunnels. We're a long way from our cavern, but I can't help myself. I need to scream the good news. I'd rearrange the stars and write it across the sky if I could. This changes everything. This *fixes* everything. We can finally leave these caves without compromising our freedom.

The closer we get, the faster I walk. By the time we skid into the vastness of the cavern, I'm practically running, Ziva panting beside me. Her father is as still as ever on the cloak, but he's *here*. Living, breathing hope.

"King Minoak lives!" I shout, my booming voice rebounding off the limestone walls. I release the cloak and step aside so the group can see Minoak for themselves. "*Now* we can enter Lutaar City and proceed with our plans to liberate Verdenet."

The bustle of the cavern abruptly ceases. Women look up from their cook pots, spoons still in hand, and the youth hauling buckets of water and scraps of food to the animals pause mid-step. Even the most difficult, loudmouthed men, like Iree and Azamat, quit squabbling and turn.

I'm not sure if it's the early hour causing them to blink and gape—dragging King Minoak back across the dunes took the better part of the night. But they're staring like they can't see the massive Verdenese man lying at my feet. Or maybe they're unable to grasp the magnitude of what it means?

"How is *he* going to save us?" someone shouts.

Ziva shifts from foot to foot, her sandals creaking. "You said they'd be overjoyed." Her hands clutch the sides of her tattered dress, making her look far younger than she did in the colonnades of Sawtooth Mesa. Smaller too.

"Is he even alive?" the same voice yells. I'd wager it's Emani—Bultum's cantankerous wife always has something to say.

"Of course he's alive!" Ziva lunges in front of her father and clenches her fists. The darkness thickens. I reach out to steady the threads, but they squirm and twist with confusion, unaccustomed to heeding two masters.

Stepping protectively between Ziva and the shepherds, I grit my teeth into a smile and force a laugh. "What sort of welcome is this? We've found the Verdenese king! We should be celebrating! Our plan is in motion." I clap my hands and stretch my smile wider, willing the shepherds to let me have this small victory. But they continue to stand there, frozen and frowning.

It was foolish to envision a triumphant return, like the parade of warriors that marches through Sagaan after hard-won battles, but I expected more than *this*. The shepherds have never been so quiet. Not even when a battalion of imperial warriors marched past our caravan on the grasslands, and our lives literally depended on staying silent beneath my blanket of darkness.

It's because they don't want this. They never *wanted this. They never believed in you or your plan.*

"I can't win, can I?" My voice trembles like Ziva's. Except where hers was timid and frightened, mine is furious. "No matter what I do, it will never be enough."

There's a flash of movement near the back of the cavern. Serik spills from the adjoining tunnel, the trackers behind him. "Enebish! You're back, thank the skies." His entire body seems to unclench, and a look of pure relief washes over his freckled face—despite the fact that I kneed him in the stomach and bolted.

If anyone should be angry, it's him. But he's jostling through the throng of shepherds to reach me. Coming to my aid yet again.

My chest floods with the same emotion I felt when he appeared through the smoke in Kartok's burning *xanav*—a welcome ache that tantalizes my insides like warm vorkhi.

"Where did you go? And why is everyone standing around . . ." Serik trails off as he notices King Minoak splayed across the cloak. His hand leaps to cover his mouth. "Who's *that*? They look like a bloody carcass left to rot on the side of the road."

Ziva flinches. "You try tending a knife wound in the desert without herbs or bandages!"

Serik appraises the girl through narrowed eyes. "And who are you?"

"This is Ziva, the Night Spinning food thief I chased from the cavern," I say.

Serik sputters and his eyes constrict even further. "Why in

the skies would you bring her back? She stole from us! And we already have too many mouths to feed."

"Because *this* is her father—His Royal Majesty, King Minoak of Verdenet." I plead with my eyes. If Serik reacts well, the shepherds will follow suit. He's who they trust—he's who they look to.

But Serik is Serik, and he's never had to set any sort of example.

"*This* is King Minoak?" he says with disbelief. "How will he lead us anywhere?"

The shepherds resume wailing, and I glare at Serik, my warm fuzzy feelings drying up. "Thanks for that," I snap. He tries to apologize, but I've already turned back to the group: "I know King Minoak isn't his strongest at the moment"—the understatement of the century—"but we'll have him fixed up in no time."

"How *much* time?" several people demand. "And with what supplies?"

"Look at him! It will take months!"

"Months we don't have!"

"King Minoak is our only hope of freedom," I say, trying to stay calm as I explain for the hundredth time, but even I can hear the desperation creeping into my voice. "Please, just trust me—"

Their shouts pelt me, one after the next.

"I knew following a criminal was a bad idea."

"We should enter Verdenet."

"What good has trusting you done us?"

You're not a human icicle, frozen on the grazing lands! I want to scream. *And you won't be slaughtered when Temujin and the Zemyans conquer Sagaan.*

I could go on, but I grind my teeth together because telling them does no good. They see only what they want to see.

As the chaos builds, Ziva melts to her knees at her father's side and shields him from the assault, as if their words are arrows. I throw another desperate glance at Serik, but he tosses his hands and shakes his head. We're both so far out of our depth, we might as well be drowning in the Zemyan Sea.

You were a fool to think this would work, an insidious voice whispers in my ear. *A fool to think even desperate people would follow you.* A crushing weight presses down on me—heavier than the league of rock and sand above my head—and my ragged breath is so loud, I almost miss Ziva's shattered voice, rising from her huddled form.

"W-what if I asked you to trust *me?*" she yelps. Her words are so faltering and the shepherds are so loud, she has to repeat herself three times and climb onto a tall protrusion of rock before they hear. And it would have been better if they didn't.

"Why would we put our trust in a child?" an ancient shepherdess barks.

"And a thieving one at that!" someone else growls.

Ziva clutches her skinny arms around herself. She begins to shrink, but then she peers at her father and stands back up. She pushes her chin-length curls behind her ears, looking more like the fiery girl I chased to Sawtooth Mesa.

"I'm not a child!" she shouts at the ornery old woman. "I'm thirteen. And I know how strong my father is. He will retaliate against the empire, once he's able. I also know that running to Lutaar City is futile. The imperial governor feeds people one day, then executes them the next. It isn't a long-term solution."

"We don't have *long* to wait!" Azamat calls.

Ziva purses her lips. "When did I say anything about waiting?"

"Do we have another choice?" Serik asks.

"We go to Namaag," Ziva says, as if it's the simplest, most obvious solution in the world. And maybe it would be if it wasn't *exactly* what Temujin predicted King Minoak would do when we sat and speculated on this very subject in Kartok's false Eternal Blue. The Shoniin and Zemyans could already be lying in wait along the route.

I shake my head, but Ziva continues, her voice growing with conviction. "My aunt Yatindra is married to the vice chancellor. Relations between our countries are strong, and Ashkar's presence has always been minimal in the marshlands, so there's little threat of being caught. If you help me transport my father to safety, I'll convince the Namagaans to join us in our march against the imperial governor."

For the first time since we entered the caves, the shepherds aren't yelling. I can see them turning the plan over in their brains: Food. Shelter. Protection. Reinforcements. It's only a weeklong trek to Uzul, the Namagaan capital. One week, and their suffering could be over. It's a good plan—essentially the same as mine, only we'd be recruiting the Protected Territories in a different order. And the shepherds aren't outright saying no, which is a victory in itself. But when Ziva looks at me with a wide smile, I shake my head.

"It won't work."

"Why not?" She leaps down from the boulder and plants her hands on her hips.

"Because you could use us to transport you and your father to Namaag, then cast us out."

Ziva recoils, her dark eyes glassy with hurt. And beneath the hurt, a quiet, simmering rage. "Do you honestly think I would abandon the people of Verdenet? My father is the *king!* I am the crown princess. I'll return to fight for my country with or without this group."

"Don't take her cynicism personally, little princess." Azamat throws a venomous look my way. "That one thinks we're all traitors—accused me of stealing the food she set me to guard."

"I don't— I never . . ." My voice takes on a desperate edge. "We must also think of her family's ties to Namaag. Scores of assassins are hunting King Minoak. They'll surely be waiting along the caravan route."

"Enebish refuses to believe any of us are capable," Lalyne, the tracker, says to Ziva. "She accuses us of insurrection and incompetence, no matter that she set us with an impossible task. We never would've found you or your father—not while you were hidden beneath the cover of night."

"Which is *exactly* why we don't have to worry about assassins or Shoniin scouts spotting us as we travel to Namaag!" Serik jumps in. "Now we have *two* Night Spinners to conceal us."

"*What?*" I demand.

"We all know how exhausted you are, En. Ziva can help."

"You can't be serious!" I retort. "She doesn't know the first thing about Night Spinning."

Ziva jerks back as if I've slapped her. "I knew enough to steal food out from under your nose!"

"I didn't know how to wield my power either," Serik continues. "But you learn quickly when you're thrust into the fray. And you can teach her, En. Mentor her. She's already shown promise. She concealed King Minoak all this time."

The shepherds whisper and nod more eagerly, pulling away from me like the threads of darkness at dawn.

"Do you realize what you're suggesting?" I ask Serik in a low, dangerous whisper. I *can't* just mentor Ziva. Ghoa destroyed me. I want nothing to do with another relationship like that. And if I allow Ziva to help, I won't have complete control of the night. I won't be able to ensure everyone's safety when she inevitably makes a mistake. Or purposely sabotages us.

"Loosen your hold on the reins and stop being so suspicious," Serik says. "We can do this, but only if you trust us. We need to use every advantage at our disposal, and Ziva's offer is a good one."

Behind him, the shepherds nod. Ziva raises her chin, a

challenge in her eyes.

"What if my power flags?" I persist, even though I know it's pointless.

"What if *my* power flags?" Serik says solemnly. "Every day, I burn closer to the end of my wick, and when I reach it, we'll all freeze to death."

"But—"

"If you have a better plan, let's hear it!" someone shouts.

They know I don't. Without proper treatment, King Minoak will die. And we can't invade Lutaar City without him. We need the Namagaans to join our rebellion eventually anyway. I'd just hoped to recruit them later, when our numbers were more impressive.

"I have a bad feeling about this, Serik," I say, my heart buzzing in my chest like the wings of a dragonfly.

Serik's face softens. He twines his fingers through mine and tugs me closer, tucking my head beneath his stubbled chin. "I know it's hard," he whispers for my ears only, "but we're your allies. If you can't trust us, this rebellion is doomed before it's truly begun."

I clutch his hand tighter. I know Serik's right. I'm not being fair. I'm treating everyone as if they're going to betray me—as if they already have. But how can I be anything but wary when Ghoa framed me for a massacre and Temujin tricked me and Kartok siphoned my power and stored it in his urns?

"We can do this," Serik murmurs into my hair. "Have faith."

There it is again. That word. Coming from Serik.

He gives my shoulders a squeeze, then turns back to Ziva and the crowd of waiting shepherds. "Gather your belongings! We leave for Namaag at sundown."

CHAPTER SIX

GHӨA

EVERYONE FEARS THE DARKNESS TO SOME DEGREE. IT MAKES the walls feel closer. Sounds seem louder. Every whisper of breath is sinister and every prickle on your skin is menacing.

It renders even seasoned warriors like the Kalima useless.

Their shouts fill the vault behind me and spill down the long treasury hall, low and high, shrill and warbling, as they realize what the darkness means.

What Enebish has done.

She isn't acting in self-defense or rescuing the "weak."

She is *attacking* us.

"Do you know what you're *doing*?" I roar into the blackness. We'll never be able to stand against the advancing Zemyans if we're locked in battle with one another. Maybe that's the aim? Temujin has never been concerned with keeping Ashkar strong—always stealing our rations and cannons, luring our soldiers away and releasing prisoners. He probably wants Sagaan to fall. Wants to see the Sky King dethroned. Wants to end the Kalima.

And Enebish supports him.

Part of me wants to scream and flail like my comrades trapped in the blackened vault, but I refuse to give Enebish and Temujin that satisfaction. Plus I have an advantage the others do not: I'm accustomed to Enebish's darkness. As accustomed as a person can be without the ability to spin the night, that is.

Stretching out my arms, I feel my way across the glass-strewn atrium and back down the corridor, breaking into a run once my hand is flush against the wall.

When Enebish's power first presented, she stayed up all night fiddling with the ink-black threads, as she called them, drenching our entire room in impenetrable shadow. She never would have stopped practicing—she never would have even known the sun had risen—if I hadn't woken up screaming most mornings.

In time, I grew less terrified of the oppressive blackness. But I will never forget how my heart raced that first morning. How I felt like I was choking, suffocating. Falling down, down, down a never-ending well.

Just as my honorless, double-crossing warriors are now.

They continue to fight and thrash, desperate to escape the vault.

When we first chose the space for our war room, the close walls and jutting shelves seemed like a good thing. An extra layer of protection. But in the dark, the obstacles might as well be prison bars. Not even the Sun Stokers can counteract Enebish's darkness. They snap their fingers, but every spark is doused in an instant, leaving the most elite warriors in Ashkar to grapple helplessly for the door.

I feel my way to the threshold and lean against the frame, listening to their weakness. Picturing their desperation. I ran back to them on instinct—to rally them to defend our king and city—but now I'm tempted to leave them here. It would be so easy to slip down the hall and out the door. Let them try to escape and orchestrate a counterattack without me.

This is what happens when you "dismiss" your commander, I'd crow as I watched Enebish and Temujin overtake them.

Or even better, I could seal the door with ice and fill the air with frost. Trap them in here until they're too cold to move, too frozen to escape. A gift for the Shoniin.

I reach for the door, my lips carved into a grin, when my mother's warbling voice and my father's stricken face appear through the blackness. They're seated in the music room at our estate, as always, but instead of rushing to greet me, eager to hear of my victories, Mamá is sobbing over her embroidery and Papá is pacing the room, downing glass after glass of vorkhi.

"How did you, alone, escape?" he asks.

"Was there nothing you could have done to save them?" Mamá cries.

"We're so grateful you survived, but . . ."

But, but, but!

I could never face my family or the people of Ashkar without my warriors. No one will revere a commander who left her battalion to die—even if they deserved it—because the people will never know they conspired against me. No one will allow me to speak ill of the dead. Especially not if the Sky King is among them. In the eyes of Ashkar, *I* would be the traitor. The coward.

No better than Temujin.

I want to shout and rage at the injustice, but I let out a long breath, tighten my ponytail, and smooth my hands down my leathers. I will never forget their betrayal, and I will *never* forgive them, but if I must save my warriors to salvage my reputation and reclaim my position, so be it.

"Stop moving!" I shout.

They continue jostling and yelling, punching and scraping.

Crawling over one another like feral dogs as pops of light from the Sun Stokers flare in and out.

"Listen to me if you want to get out of here!"

Again they ignore me. Or maybe they can't hear me. Thankfully, I have ways to make them listen.

Placing my palms on either side of the door frame, I press my cold outward, sliding it across the floors and along the walls like the giant blocks of ice we cut from the Amereti each winter. That's how my Kalima power has always felt: like a crushing weight I must unload. Almost too heavy to move.

I can't see the blue and white fractals overtaking the walls, but I feel the power shoot through my fingertips. My body shivers with delight as the temperature plummets. Colder and colder until breath clouds my face and tickles my cheeks.

"The commander is attacking us!" my warriors shout.

"She's defected to the enemy!"

Of course that's what they'd think.

The loudest voice sounds like Bastian, and I make a mental note to annihilate him at our next training session.

Assuming there is a next training session.

"Unlike *you*, I haven't betrayed anyone," I retort. "I'm trying to help. But if you'd rather perish at the hands of Enebish and Temujin, by all means, keep fighting me."

To my astonishment, the jostling ceases. Probably out of habit or sheer desperation, but I'll take it. "Reach out in front of you. If you can feel the table or chairs or anything at all, shove them together in the middle of the room. Then step back as far as you can. Press yourselves against the walls."

I give them exactly one minute to complete this task before I center myself in the doorway, raise my hands, and send a blast of ice hurtling at the furniture. It streaks through the blackness like a long, white spear, visible for a fleeting instant, before it hits the pile with a *crack*. It sounds like the entire room is shattering, and my warriors gasp. The Sky King cries out. Though, it's completely unnecessary. My aim was true. I can feel my ice seeping into the wood, binding each piece together and freezing it to the vault floor.

"Eshwar, lightning!" I command. After a brief hesitation, Eshwar hurls a snapping bolt of electricity at my makeshift firepit. As soon as the furniture bursts to flame, I shout at the Sun Stokers, "Fuel the blaze!"

All five Sun Stokers dart forward, palms up, and direct their strength into the fire. The resulting wave of heat and light is so intense, I have to shield my face. Enebish's darkness dives at the wood and snatches at the leaping flames, but unlike the Sun Stokers' individual flares, this fire is too big, fueled by too much wood, to douse. And thanks to my base of ice, every obstacle in the room remains cemented to the floor. Which means, for a few blessed seconds, there is enough light and space to navigate to the door.

"Move!" I shout.

This time I don't have to repeat myself.

We spill into the hall, and the sudden wall of darkness feels like tumbling into a grave—one of the mass burial pits I've dug for fallen Zemyans. I always assumed they would repay the favor if I perished in battle. I never dreamed it would be my sister, along with defectors from our own army, who would put me in the ground.

Another wave of outrage washes over me.

How dare she? *How dare she!*

"Form a line behind me," I order, "hold on to the person in front of you, and do exactly as I say, when I say it." I wave my arms and stumble forward until my left hand finds the wall. Then I take a deep breath and close my eyes. I feel safer in the blackness of my own mind than trapped beneath Enebish's shroud. It also makes it easier to fall back through time, to my childhood, when I would skip down these corridors hand in hand with Papá.

From the vaults, Papá's office is seven doors down and up a flight of stairs. But going up will only trap us, so I guide the Kalima past two more doors and feel my way across the atrium to the perpendicular corridor, which will lead us to the rear entrance. Temujin will want to make a spectacle. He always does. Which means he'll charge through the grand entrance so all of Sagaan can see his accomplishment. How he surprised and trapped the Kalima warriors. While he puts on a production, we'll slip out the back. What we'll do once we're out in the open, completely exposed, is another question. But our odds will be better out there, where we have room to fight and unleash the power of the sky.

I increase my pace to a jog. The king's hands are like shackles around my wrist—sharp and bitter cold—but he doesn't question my actions or make threats. Neither do the Kalima.

They will never question me again.

I plow ahead, counting the distance to the exit. Twenty paces. Ten. I remove my hand from the wall and extend my arms to shove through the double doors, but the sound of a high-pitched whistle makes me slam to a halt. The Sky King and several others crash into my back, their complaints peppering me like shrapnel, but I hiss at them to be silent. The whistle grows louder. Nearer. My stomach lurches. It's a sound that preludes death. A sound I always equated with victory until Enebish turned on me at Temujin's execution.

"Get back!" I whip around and shove blindly at the Sky King. He falls into Varren, who stumbles into someone else, but if they complain, I don't hear it. The boom of exploding marble drowns out every other sound.

Debris pelts my face, and a wave of scorching heat throws us back down the hall. As if we're no heavier than tumbleweeds.

Which turns out to be a blessing, since the entire end of the corridor has been bitten off by a ball of starfire. It smolders red and gold as it rolls to a stop against the blackened wall. I stare at it. Bewildered. Then furious.

They attacked from the rear entrance.

Frustration snowballs inside me until my vision flares white. I was wrong. I don't know Temujin as well as I thought I did, despite the fact that he's been tormenting me like a vengeful ghost for months now, prodding invisible wounds he couldn't have known existed.

"Snow Conjurers!" I scream. The heat from the starfire feels even hotter than the blaze I started in the vault. Melting my icy core. Thankfully, the Snow Conjurers don't need additional instruction. Flakes of the heaviest, wettest snow fall from the ceiling of the treasury and smother the flames. I urge them to continue, and the snow builds into a wall of solid white that seals off the burning hall. It won't hold Temujin and Enebish for long, but hopefully long enough.

"Freeze the floor!" I call as I charge back the way we came, relying on the faint glow of the dying starfire to guide us. The rest of the Kalima follow, the Ice Heralds at the rear, painting the tiles with sparkling strokes of ice.

"We can't use the grand entrance," the Sky King says in a shrill voice that sounds nothing like the man I've served for half my life. He isn't wrong. Those doors will either be obliterated like the rear entrance or the traitors will be lying in wait in the courtyard, ready to ambush us. "We're trapped!"

He *is* wrong about that. There's another way—a way I imagined as a child, staring out the floor-to-ceiling windows of Papá's office while he finished his work.

"What are those tiny bridges?" I'd asked, my face pressed against the glass, enthralled with the lacy wings extending from his second-story room to the building adjacent. They looked like a highway for birds. Only birds didn't need a highway. They could fly.

"Those are called buttresses, my dear," Papá said. "They keep the building steady, help to hold it up. And they look rather nice, don't you think?"

If we can reach them, they will look better than nice.

"Why are you leading us *up*?" Iska mutters when I bang through the seventh door on the left and pound up the steps. "We'll be treed like snow leopards. We might as well surrender down here."

"If you want to surrender, stay. If you want to escape and return to fight another day, follow me," I say as I slam into Papá's office.

The familiar scents of pipe smoke and his bergamot cologne hit me, both comforting and paralyzing. He and Mamá retreated to the safety of our estate after the attack on the Sky Palace, but if he were here, he wouldn't doubt me for a second. Papá is proud and supportive to a fault—evidenced by the awards from every minor concert or competition I've ever participated in, plastered to the walls and dangling from the ceiling. The gauntlet of medals slap my cheeks, making the pressure even more overwhelming.

I stumble through the pitch black and crash into Papá's gigantic desk, toppling papers and making a mess of his carefully arranged quills. Once I've battered through the furniture, I lift my hands and ease forward until my palms meet the chilled windowpane. Then I spread my fingers and pump my bitter cold into the glass. I can feel it shudder and expand—like a bowstring drawn too tight.

With a loud *pop*, tinkling glass falls across my boots and down the outer wall of the treasury, where it smashes against the cobblestones. I don't know if it's because my hearing is heightened in the dark, but the sound is louder than a cannon firing.

If Enebish and Temujin didn't know where we were before, they do now.

"*Go.* Hurry!"

"Go *where*, Ghoa?" Varren asks. "You can't expect us to jump out a second-story window."

"Of course not. There are buttresses. Walk across to the adjacent building. Hopefully it hasn't been invaded."

"How?" someone shouts.

"We can't see!" another voice interjects.

"Scoot or crawl," I shoot back. "Do whatever you must. Just go. We cannot be captured. They'll kill every one of us, then Ashkar will have no hope of recovery."

"Do as she says!" the Sky King bellows behind me, and despite everything, my racing heart flutters with satisfaction. Vindication.

"We can try to provide some light," Weroneka, one of the Sun Stokers, says. She and the others feel their way to the window and raise orbs of light as Lizbet ventures out onto the buttress. She's the smallest and lightest of all of us and, as a Breeze Bringer, she can wield the drafts of wind to steady her balance. She's the natural choice to make the first crossing. I keep sight of her brown braid until she's halfway across. The Sun Stokers' orbs grow smaller and dimmer every second, shrinking from the size of melon fruit to potatoes, but Enebish's power is flagging too. Every time she snuffs the Sun Stokers' light, the oppressive darkness lightens a shade. Ink to midnight. Raven to charcoal. It's a battle of stamina, and she is out of practice.

Vanesh, another Breeze Bringer, mounts the buttress next. He shuffles out a few steps, then turns and extends his hand to the Sky King. Varren helps the king navigate the jagged window and steadies his balance until he catches hold of Vanesh. Then the two of them creep forward slowly. Painfully slowly.

"Faster!" I hiss. But the Sky King is too wobbly—encumbered and off balance in his heavy fox fur cloak and pointed slippers. "Lose the finery!" I order. Vanesh turns carefully, hands trembling as he fumbles with the buckle of the Sky King's cloak. Which is stuck. Of course. Vanesh is still tearing at the clasp when the darkness ripples. The sky flares orange, and my ears ring with a deadly hum.

"Turn back!" I shout.

Too late.

Several balls of starfire whiz past the window, demolishing the courtyard and east wing of the treasury. Varren leaps back into the room, but Vanesh and the Sky King are too far, nearly to the apex of the buttress, and moving slower than ever, thanks to the king's hysterics. He's shouting threats and gesticulating wildly instead of putting one foot in front of the other.

Time slows to a crawl. Another burning star careens from above. It crashes through the center of the buttress, and I see every growing splinter, watch every falling fragment, as the structure crumbles.

No.

The Sky King screams. Vanesh flails, grasping for a ledge that isn't there.

I throw myself forward, arms raking across the broken glass, as if I'll be able to catch them. They fall in slow, eerie somersaults, like the fluttering seeds of a globeflower. The Sky King thrashes while Vanesh tries to reduce their speed with frantic bursts of wind.

From across the divide, Lizbet adds her wind to the current, and I almost think Vanesh and the king will survive. But then another bolt of starfire slams into the battlements of the treasury. An enormous chunk of blue marble breaks away, like a glacier collapsing into the sea. It slams into Vanesh first, wheeling him around, then breaks across the Sky King's back.

His spine twists unnaturally. His face goes slack. Screams flay my throat open as I watch the Sky King of Ashkar, my lord and master, plunge into the darkness below.

I bury my face in my hands, oddly thankful for Enebish's blackness. So I don't have to see my king and comrade painted across the cobbles.

Behind me, the Kalima are silent. I can't even hear them breathing.

Our lungs have been crushed—like the Sky King's.

He can't be gone. There has never been a more powerful leader in the history of Ashkar. He is transcendent. A god on earth. And a god cannot be flattened like an insect on the cobblestones. They *can't*.

Sobs rattle from my swollen throat, and I howl into the quiet. How could Enebish do this? How could she *murder* our king?

"Don't disgrace them with your tears," Bastian snaps behind me. "This is your fault."

"My fault?" I whip around, my face so hard with frost that it crackles and pops.

"You shoved him out onto that narrow beam. You probably wanted him to fall. You probably told your monstrous sister to come."

"If anyone is at fault, it's you—all of you double-crossing traitors!" I fling my hand at the Kalima, frost shooting from my fingers and skimming over their heads. "If you'd been following my orders instead of conspiring behind my back, we would have caught Enebish and Temujin before they attacked. We wouldn't have been sitting ducks—"

"Quiet," Varren says.

"Don't you dare silence me!" I roar. "How could you betray me like this? After everything? You're supposed to be my second!"

Varren's tattooed arm winds around my face and his

meaty hand covers my mouth. When I try to scream, nothing comes out.

"Quiet," he says again in a gruff whisper.

That's when I hear it. The sound of voices in the courtyard—the rebels undoubtedly discovering their bloody prize. Only the voices sound too smooth and susurrating, the cadence too fluid and lilting, to be Ashkarian.

A new wave of panic dances down my spine.

"Zemyans," Cirina whispers.

Except that's impossible. They couldn't have marched to Sagaan already. And Enebish would never fight with them. They murdered her family and burned her village.

But then I never thought she would align with Temujin, either. Or attempt to kill me. I know nothing about what she would and wouldn't do. Her starfire is as undeniable as the foreign shouts filling the halls below.

My sweat freezes the moment it leaves my pores and rolls down my face like tiny gouging diamonds.

This changes everything.

Temujin and the rebels taking Sagaan is infuriating but rectifiable—once Enebish's darkness peters out. The Shoniin hardly have the numbers to hold Sagaan, let alone the empire. And the people weren't at risk of violence. The Unified Empire wasn't in danger of collapsing. But if the *Zemyans* are here—if the *Zemyans* are taking our capital—there's no end to the possible devastation. They'll raze our cities, imprison our people, and if they manage to capture a Kalima warrior—as they've been trying to do for decades—they'll kill us. Or worse: taint our power with their devil magic. Twist it into poison to use against us.

I stumble back, unable to catch my breath. This is all I'll be remembered for: the death of the Sky King. The fall of the empire. Not my impressive victories at the war front or my legendary march to the beaches of Karekemish. Not my unmatched leadership or the strength of my ice.

My ice.

I look down at my hands, barely visible in the oppressive dark. If I can forge a blade of ice, why not a buttress?

The thought makes my muscles quake. The ice will have to be ten times longer and ten times thicker than a saber to support the weight of a person, and I'll have to maintain it for several minutes, which could burn through my power.

But it's the only option.

Our only hope of escape.

If I can lead the Kalima to safety, we can regroup. Retake Sagaan. I'll be heralded as Ashkar's greatest warrior, despite all of the obstacles, and *people*, who stood in my way. I'll be their savior—the commander who refused to back down after unspeakable tragedy.

"Stand aside!" I cry, fighting my way back to the window. I grip the sill and hiss as the protrusions of glass sink into my palms. My fingers slip as my blood wets the stones, but I close my eyes and envision how the blue marble buttress fit against the wall. A perfect seal. Then I re-create the arch, but instead of an impossibly thin and intricate adornment, I fabricate a rudimentary slab that's twice as wide as the original. It's practically a highway. If my warriors can't make it across, they don't belong in the Kalima.

Behind me, the angry shouts fall away.

"King of the Skies," Varren whispers as they watch my creation take shape. The bright bursts of ice slashing through the black are strangely beautiful—like ghosts, dancing across the sky.

"Go," I croak out. My nose is bleeding. My hands are shaking. The effort of speaking is too much. A small fracture forms in the center of the arch. I have to grit my teeth to smooth it. "Now," I pant, sweating with effort. But still they hesitate.

Only when the hall door slams open and boots vault up the stairs do the Kalima move.

Bastian looks at the buttress, then at me, his gaze heavy with respect and perhaps a twinge of remorse. *Good.* He ambles onto the ice and the others follow. With every stomping boot, my energy flags. My vision swirls like blood in water.

Hold on. Just a little longer.

But what if I don't have longer? The cautionary tales we use to frighten new recruits aren't entirely false. I watched Enebish's mentor, Tuva, turn to dust during the Battle of a Hundred Nights, when we conquered Chotgor.

Varren and Weroneka mount the bridge last, just as the Zemyans crash into Papá's office. Ululating whoops and battle cries fill the room—sounds that have haunted my nightmares for the better part of ten years. I shake my head because I still don't understand how they marched to Sagaan so quickly. Or why Enebish is aiding them. I watched her rescue Temujin. I know she joined forces with the Shoniin. But the Zemyans are here, attacking us with her night power. Which can only mean one thing:

She's even more treasonous and deceitful than I realized.

When Varren and Weroneka are halfway across the bridge, I release the windowsill and try to pull myself onto the buttress. But my legs are shaky and my eyes are bleary. When I look down, there are two windows and two buttresses and I can't tell which is real. The Zemyans surge across the room, smashing Papá's desk and rending every ribbon and medal.

"Varren!" I shriek. "Help me!"

He turns, his eyes even wider than they were at the sight of the Zemyans—I *never* ask for help.

"*Please!*" I cry as I drag myself forward.

From the safety of the adjacent building, the other Kalima

warriors yell something I can't make out.

Weroneka looks back at them, but Varren keeps staring at me.

Crushing hands close around my shoulders and yank me back inside the treasury. I scream and kick and reach for my cold, but there's nothing left. I gave every drop of ice to the buttress. I grapple for my sword, but my arms are jelly and the Zemyans easily trap them against my sides. I stare at my battalion across the shadowy distance. Faces I have known for years. People I've risked my life for. They owe me this. Ashkarian warriors never leave a comrade behind. Especially not their commander.

The Kalima bark at Weroneka and Varren again, and each word jabs my stomach harder than the Zemyans' fists: "Melt. The. Bridge!"

Varren and Weroneka exchange a faltering glance. It's light enough now; they could wield the power of the sky without misfiring and hitting homes or bystanders. The entire Kalima could batter the Zemyans with wind and rain and lightning until I'm free.

But they don't.

With a grim nod at Weroneka and a fleeting look at me, Varren turns and sprints to safety. Weroneka follows, her smoldering hand melting the escape route *I* provided.

As the buttress falls, my heart falls with it.

No one looks back as the Zemyans wrestle me to the floor.

And no one lingers to hear my screams.

CHAPTER SEVEN

ENEBISH

I FORCE A SMILE AS THE LAST FEW SHEPHERDS DUCK OUT of the cave and into the net of darkness I hurriedly knit. My stitches are loose and clumsy, the blanket lopsided and unwieldy, allowing hooves and wagon wheels to occasionally flash into view. But it's the best I can do after our grueling journey from Sagaan and the weeks I've spent starving, bickering, and spying on the ungrateful and unreliable shepherds.

I'd thought my time concealing the caravan across the continent was behind me. We should be storming Lutaar City, reinstating King Minoak, then freeing the other Protected Territories to make a stand against the Zemyans and the Sky King. But here we are. Trekking to Namaag with a half-dead king and a group of "rebels" who are ready to abandon our cause after a few weeks of hardship.

I peer up into the undulating darkness, desperate to find the Lady's face in the ever-shifting shadows.

Can't you lighten my load, even a little?

"You should sit down," Ziva says. "You look like you're

going to collapse." She pushes away from the opposite cave wall and offers me a hand.

I ignore it and brace myself against the slippery rocks. "I'm fine. Just tired from chasing you across the desert last night." I spear her with an accusatory glare. "Unfortunately, I won't be sleeping tonight, either—or any night—since you convinced the shepherds we have to leave immediately, and it's safer to travel when my power is strongest." I flip my hand at the ambling group, my right eye already twitching at the straying sheep and uneven pace, and we're mere steps outside the cave.

It's going to be a long week.

"You could let me help." Ziva's voice is tentative but her eyes are hopeful.

"Don't you need to look after your father or something?" I nod to the litter in the middle of the group, balanced on the shoulders of our six strongest men.

"There's nothing I can do for him until we reach Namaag, and I'll follow your orders with exactness. I know I'm new to all of this." She waves a hand, sending the tendrils of darkness swirling, which makes it even more difficult to keep the net taut and steady over the group. "But I did manage to conceal myself and my father for almost two months."

I give my head a terse shake. "Concealing an entire caravan is far more difficult than concealing two people. You can't just toss the darkness at random. There must be order and discipline so that the tendrils lie flat and move seamlessly with a group this large."

"So teach me."

I laugh. I can't help it. "It isn't something I can teach in a minute or two. It takes years. A lifetime of training."

And I don't want to be a mentor.

My own mentor, Tuva, was so patient and encouraging. I remember her cooing-dove voice and graceful artist's hands, swirling through the darkness with the ease of a paintbrush. For the longest time, I thought she was too timid and fragile to be a good warrior—or a respectable mentor. Especially after my childhood with Ghoa. But now I see how strong and humble she had to be, entrusting me with her knowledge and assuming I would do right by it.

Tuva would have agreed to train Ziva without hesitation. But I'm not half the Night Spinner, or *person*, that Tuva was. The wreckage I made of the Grand Courtyard is proof of that. She *never* would have been so thoroughly deceived by Temujin and Kartok.

"No," I say in case Ziva mistook my silence for consideration.

"But you *clearly* need me. And Serik said—"

"Serik doesn't know the first thing about wielding the darkness, so he doesn't get to dictate who can and can't be trusted with it."

"Is this about trust or ability? Because before you said—"

"It's about both!" I snap.

"I trusted *you* enough to follow you back to these caves." Ziva's voice grows shriller by the second. "Don't I deserve the same courtesy?"

"You only came because you had no choice. And you *can* help by keeping up and keeping quiet." I point to the back of the caravan.

Ziva grumbles something I can't decipher and stomps ahead. I'm positive she's cursing me, but that's fine. Better than fine. My life will be much easier if she despises me enough to stop pestering me.

I seal the blanket of darkness behind us and take up the rear of the wagon train. Far ahead, at the front of the group, there's a flash of gold in the blackness. My breath automatically catches, even though I know it isn't Orbai—it's only Serik's goldwork cloak. But my heart can't stop hoping, and breaking, all over again. I'd give anything under the skies to have her here with me.

Gold sparkles again as Serik mounts a wagon and squints for me at the end of the procession. During the arduous trek to the caves, he was forced to trail the group and melt the snow to remove our tracks. He never once complained, even though I know he felt alone and unappreciated back here. Now it's my turn, since we don't have to worry about tracks in the sand, and it's easier to manage the net of darkness, where I can adjust for the shepherds' obnoxious wandering.

Secretly, I'd hoped Serik would decline to lead the march to Namaag so he could walk with me, but he didn't. He couldn't. The shepherds trust him and, more important, they listen to him. As they should—he works so hard to be a good leader. I just wish I could be up there with him instead of stuck back here eating dust with the seething princess.

Serik waves when he spots me, but when he sees Ziva walking ahead, his smile falters. Shame drags at my shoulders. I know what he's thinking: *This isn't you. Don't let Ghoa and Temujin turn you into a cynic. We need Minoak. Which means we need Ziva. Which means you need to play nice.*

You know you've hit rock bottom when Serik has become the voice of moral reason in your head.

I look away and turn my focus to the shadowy dunes. Where Temujin and his Shoniin are undoubtedly lying in wait.

For the first few leagues, I jump at every sound. My fingers grasp for the darkness with every flicker of movement on the horizon. But two days pass and the Shoniin never come. No one does; the roads are all but abandoned. I don't know if it's due to the terrible weather—the wind is still cold and punishing, pelting our cheeks with sand and whipping the animals into a frenzy—or because we only travel at night, but we encounter one solitary man leading a sorry-looking llama.

Where are they?

Perhaps I was wrong. Maybe Sagaan didn't fall as easily as planned, and the Shoniin and Zemyans can't spare warriors to patrol this road. Or maybe the siege ended so quickly, they've already conquered Namaag and we'll be greeted by Kartok and Temujin when we reach Uzul.

I try to picture the continent under Zemyan rule. Will they spare the young? The old? The ancient cities, with their stunning architecture and rich history? Or will they burn everything to the ground, like my village in Verdenet? Will they execute the Sky King? Ghoa?

The image of her head on a block fills my mind, her expression grim and defiant as a Zemyan blade hurtles toward her neck. I tell myself I don't care. She deserves even worse. But I can't stop from flinching as the steel slices through her flesh.

Another night of travel passes—which means another night of sweating and straining to conceal the meandering group. It also means another night of staring at Ziva's pathetic slumped shoulders. She walks several paces ahead of me but well behind the shepherds. She isn't tall enough or strong enough to help carry her father's litter, and the shepherds aren't the most trusting of people who aren't like them. More specifically, of people who are like me.

Every day, she tries to worm her way into the throng; and every day, the shepherds ram their shoulders together, creating a wall to keep Ziva out.

To keep *both* of us out.

Add to that Serik's increasingly frequent backward glances, and the irritating notes he's been passing to me through the masses, asking if Ziva and I are making progress, and I feel like I'm going to explode. Or collapse. Probably both.

Fine.

I grit my teeth and force my bad leg to move faster until

I catch up with Ziva, who's kicking dust at the shepherds' backs. I won't be her mentor, but I suppose I can try a little harder to be her friend.

"They're kind of unbearable, aren't they?" I say.

Ziva jumps and scowls at me. "What are you doing here?"

"Walking. And talking to you, if that's okay?"

Her frown deepens. "Why would you do that?"

"I'm sorry for how I've been acting. I'm just frazzled and exhausted . . . and hurt," I add in a small voice.

I haven't wanted to admit it, as if acknowledging how Temujin and Kartok and Ghoa destroyed me will somehow give them even more power. But it actually makes me feel slightly better. Stronger. Because that feeling—that vulnerability—is what separates me from them.

"Believe it or not, I know a thing or two about being hurt and betrayed," Ziva says after a long silence. "*Your* empire—our supposed protectors—tried to kill my father."

"I'm sorry," I say. And I mean it. "That's never what I fought for."

She nods and we're quiet again, gazing out at the midwinter desert. The shepherds see nothing beyond the tunnel of blackness, only the path ahead, where I want them to go. Like blinders on a horse. But Ziva can see everything: the dunes, tinged purple in the moonlight; the frost dusting the tiny cactus blossoms; and the fox slinking through the brush and pouncing on an unseen quarry.

"When did your power present?" I ask, trying to sound friendly.

"Why do you want to know?" Ziva eyes me like I'm trying to trick her. "When did *your* power present?"

"At the stroke of midnight, on my eleventh birthday."

She snorts. "Of course it did. You must have done something *quite* heroic."

I know she's mocking me, but I shrug and answer truthfully. "Not really. Zemyan raiders sacked my village, Sangatha, when I was eight, and set fire to our hut. My mother pushed me out the window to save me, but I fought my way back inside. I refused to leave them to die. But it was too late. The roof collapsed. I only survived because I was barely through the door and avoided the worst of it. I guess the Lady of the Sky appreciated my effort."

"Both of your parents perished?"

I nod. "Along with most of my village."

"I don't know if my mother is alive," Ziva admits, voice choked. "I couldn't save them both. There wasn't time. Papa was bleeding, and I didn't know if there were more assassins lying in wait. So I ran."

"I'm sure your mother's fine," I say, though I'm sure of no such thing.

"If being trapped in the palace with the imperial governor is *fine*," Ziva mutters darkly. "And that's the best-case scenario."

"But you were able to save your father. The king! Which is an incredible accomplishment. How did you manage it? Did you use your Night Spinning?"

"My Night Spinning came *after* we'd escaped. At first I thought the taunting shadows were a curse—punishment sent from the Lady and Father for killing a man."

"But it's the opposite. The power was a reward for your bravery."

"If you consider stabbing a man in the back an act of bravery." She says it so softly, I almost mistake it for the shifting sand.

"He wasn't an innocent man. He was an *assassin*."

Ziva furrows her brow and looks straight ahead. I want to press her, but I force myself to keep quiet, giving her space to fill the silence.

After almost ten minutes she blurts, "I—I didn't even mean

to kill him. It was the middle of the night. I should have been asleep, but I was thirsty and on my way to the kitchen for a glass of milk when I stumbled upon three dead guards in the hall. I wanted to scream, but I saw a shadow slip into Papa's chamber, so I grabbed one of the guard's blades and followed. I've had swordsmanship training since I was five, so I felt confident that I could at least frighten them. I figured they were a thief, picking around the royal apartments for gold and jewels. But then I saw them lean over Papa's bed and raise a knife.

"I don't remember the rest. I only know that I've never moved so fast in all my life, and I've never seen so much blood. It was everywhere. Gushing from Papa and the assassin, staining the bedclothes and the carpet and my nightgown. As the assassin hit the ground, I dragged Papa out of bed and into the hall with every intention of taking him to the healers, but the floor below was filled with stomping boots and shouting voices—all of them Ashkarian. So I dragged Papa down the servants' stairs and to the barn, where I found a cart. I managed to heft him onto it, and then I started running. I was too terrified to think about where we were going, or how strange it was that no one stopped us. Now I know it's because they couldn't see us. I called the darkness without even realizing it."

Silvery tears slide down her cheeks, and she paws at them furiously. I feel a sudden kinship with her—not quite tenderness, but understanding. "You've been through a lot."

"And that's just the start of it!" she says with a hysterical laugh. "Now these infuriating black ribbons won't leave me alone, but they won't cooperate either, and my head is always pounding and my throat is always scratchy. I feel like I'm losing my mind." She slices her hand through the air and the whorls of darkness scatter and dodge every which way, disrupting my tenuous hold. But I don't snap or complain as I guide the tendrils back into place.

"Kalima powers can be overwhelming at first, but rest assured that this is the Lady's will. Saving your father *awoke* your power, which means you passed your test."

"So why does it feel like I've failed?" She tucks her curls behind her ears and looks over at me, eyes glassy and yearning.

I don't say a word. I can't give her what she wants. I *can't* teach her to wield the darkness. And she shouldn't want me to. I'm a failure. The last person on the continent who should be giving lessons or advice.

"*Please—*" Ziva begs, but I cut her off.

"*Please* don't ask me to do something we both know will end disastrously."

"Do you honestly think I'm that hopeless and incompetent?"

No. I'm *the one who's hopeless and incompetent.*

But I lie and say, "Yes."

Because that will get her off my back.

And that's what mentors do: lie.

Ziva resumes ignoring and avoiding me, and my conscience resumes pricking. Only now it's a constant throb, rather than the sharp, fleeting twinge I felt when Serik's eyes caught mine from the front of the caravan. But I don't know what to say. I don't know what to *do*. I tried being nice, and it backfired. She doesn't want a friend. She wants a teacher. And I will never be that.

As the temperature warms and swathes of swampy wetland begin to intersperse the shrinking sand dunes, the mood of the group improves considerably. The shepherds start to laugh and sing. A few of them even acknowledge me, and not just to complain.

We reach the craggy cypress groves that cover most of

Namaag at sunrise on our final day of travel. Space is scarce—
we all have to squish onto the tangle of roots that act like a
causeway above the mud—but it's safer if we spend the more
dangerous daylight hours hidden in the shade of the trees.

I manage to find a little nook, tucked away from everyone
else, and spread out my bedroll. The knobby knees of the trees
are far from comfortable, but at least they're dry. And I'm too
tired to care. My hands won't stop shaking, my nose is dribbling
blood, and the blanket of darkness is beginning to fray and tear.

Thank the skies we'll reach Namaag tonight.

Cradling my head in my hands, I lie back and watch the
thick clumps of moss sway in the breeze, so green that they're
almost black against the backdrop of the sandy-white dunes.
We're straddling two different worlds: one foot in Verdenet,
the other in Namaag.

"The marshlands clearly suit you," Serik says, appearing
from out of nowhere.

I bolt upright. "What are you doing back here? Who's
managing the front of the caravan? You know how the
shepherds are—you can't leave them alone for a second. And
they need your heat!"

"Relax." Serik spreads his bedroll out beside mine. "The
marshes aren't nearly as cold, if you haven't noticed, and I left
Azamat in charge."

"Azamat!" I attempt to lurch to my feet, but Serik catches
my arm and laughs.

"Yes, Azamat. They'll be fine for a few minutes. Besides, it's
practically a straight shot from here to Uzul, and all of it on
raised root paths. They'd have to try to get lost."

"You give them too much credit," I grumble.

"Maybe because you never give them enough . . ." Serik's
voice is soft, far from accusatory, but it still itches like a
crusted scab.

"They haven't earned it."

"Haven't they? When you step back and look at how far they've come—how much they've endured—it's pretty remarkable."

"Spoken like a true 'hero of the people.'" I shake my head and tweak his freckled nose. "Did you come back here just to make me feel bad?"

"That, and it's cold sleeping alone." He shoots me a cheeky grin as he burrows into his blankets, pressing as close to me as possible without actually climbing into my bedroll.

"You're never cold. And what about Azamat? Sounds like you two are getting close. . . ."

Serik barks out a laugh. "Azamat is too bony to cuddle with—and have you smelled his breath?"

"It's impossible *not* to smell his breath." I chuckle. "I catch whiffs of it all the way back here."

Serik's arms snake around me, and I let myself melt into his warmth, press my face against his chest. "I've missed you, En," he murmurs into my hair.

"You've done an excellent job leading the caravan," I say.

He waves a dismissive hand, but his hazel eyes twinkle with satisfaction. "No one's gotten lost, and the shepherds haven't killed one another—and *I* haven't killed any of them—so I suppose it's a success. You've done well too, shielding us." He turns on his side so we're face-to-face. His freckles blend together—a swipe of gleaming bronze across his nose—and I want to trace my finger over the dots. "But I still worry it's too much, En. I see how your hands shake, how pale and hollow you look. How the darkness occasionally falters . . ." he adds, his voice gentle but his expression piercing. "Even the strongest warriors need help sometimes. And you have help. Right there."

He nods over my shoulder, to where Ziva's sitting on a low-hanging limb, trying for the thousandth time to fill her hands with darkness. When she inevitably fails, she tosses her hands up with a curse and nearly knocks herself into the murky water.

"Honestly?" I deadpan.

"I know you're not keen on training her," Serik says, "but I think it would be good for you both."

"How would that be good for me? Look at her! I'm already exhausted, and *that* will make it even worse."

"Perhaps initially, but it'll ease your burden in the long run."

I hope to the skies I'm not stuck with Ziva for the long run, but I know better than to say this out loud.

"And it would be good for the group," Serik continues. "The shepherds may be more inclined to trust you if they see you trusting *her*."

"It won't make a difference," I grumble. "They'll despise me no matter what."

"But they've never deliberately gone against your judgment. . . ." Serik is quiet for a minute, his finger tracing tiny circles up my arm. "Why do they have to *earn* your trust, En? You've always looked for the best in people and given your trust freely—until circumstances proved they were undeserving."

I push away from Serik, shaking my head in disbelief because he *knows* why. He was there! That naïve, idealistic version of myself died when Ghoa *and* Temujin *and* Kartok rammed their knives into my back.

I stagger to my feet, ready to remind him of this, but before I can let my verbal daggers fly, a familiar screech fills the air.

My heart slams to a halt and I look skyward—at the streak of golden feathers diving into the trees.

CHAPTER EIGHT

ENEBISH

"Orbai!"

Her name rips from the depths of my belly—as natural and instinctive as breathing.

Tears flood my eyes as I watch her weave gracefully through the trees. I've felt her absence like a missing limb. Like she tore out my heart and carried it away in her talons. But now it's back. *She's* back. And I'm whole.

I call her name again and run toward her, arm raised. So deliriously happy, I forget she could pose a threat—until she dives at King Minoak, resting quietly on his litter. Her talons rake across his chest, ripping off a wide strip of tunic—and skin—which she takes with her as she ascends back into the canopy.

For a second the only sound is Minoak's groan.

Then Ziva starts screaming and the shepherds follow suit. They run in a hundred different directions while I watch numbly, detached from my body, as my eagle soars to the edge of the thicket and lands on the shoulder of a figure dressed in Shoniin gray. Orbai places the bloody scrap in their outstretched hand, and they wave it overhead like a flag.

I can't breathe. I can do nothing but stare at my best friend, perched on the shoulder of one of *them*. I didn't expect to see her again until we killed Kartok and severed the Loridium bond. But of course he would send Orbai to taunt me.

To weaken me.

"Enebish!" Serik's so red in the face, he's probably shouted my name at least ten times. "Why in the skies is Orbai with them? Attacking us? *Do something!*"

I blow out a breath and glance up at the wispy shadows lurking beneath the canopy. Such little darkness remains. The few lingering threads are desperate to avoid the rising daylight, but I make a frantic grab for them. If the scout makes it back to Kartok and Temujin, the combined Zemyan and Shoniin armies will return to slaughter us.

It feels like I'm scraping the bottom of my well of power, but I manage to catch hold and slam the tendrils to the ground.

For a second nothing happens. The shock hits me like a punch to the stomach. I've gone too far—pushed my power too hard for too long. This is how it feels to be magic-barren. Then something tightens deep within me and the night billows outward, rolling over the sandy waterway between the marshlands and dunes. Swallowing the rosy-pink morning—and the scout.

"We have to stop them!" I take off running and trip immediately. My body is weak and woozy. The cypress roots entangle my bad leg.

Serik appears at my right, breathing heavily. At least a dozen other shepherds flank my left. Lalyne and Azamat and Iree and Bultum. All united for the first time since leaving the grazing lands.

"Throw your starfire at them!" Azamat shouts.

The scout's still in range, stumbling through the last of the flute reeds. If they reach the sand dunes, they'll run for leagues, unhindered by the marshland's rocks and trees. We'll never catch them. Not even with the darkness.

"Finish them!" Iree cries.

"Quickly!" Bultum agrees.

I choke on an agonized wail. They're right. I *should* bring the stars down on the scout. But I *can't* because Orbai flies directly over their head, trailing the scout how she used to trail me.

"What are you waiting for?" Lalyne demands.

They don't know what Orbai means to me. They won't understand. "We're still in the marshlands." I grasp for an excuse. "Do you think King Ihsan will join our cause if I lay fire to his kingdom?"

"Enebish." Serik whirls around, his face drained of color, his expression grief-stricken. "Orbai would understand—"

"No!" I sob. I can't kill my bird. I *can't*.

And Kartok knows it.

Help me. I fall to my knees, begging the Lady of the Sky to intervene.

"I'll do it." Ziva emerges from the back of the group, her hand already thrust heavenward.

A bout of nausea grips me. "You can't even fill your palms with darkness! There's no way you can—"

Ziva smashes her fist into the sand with an earsplitting scream. Above us, a blinding crimson star streaks across the golden morning, speeding toward the scout.

And Orbai.

My heart thrashes. The world blurs, as if trapped behind a pane of ice. I don't consciously choose to summon another star, but suddenly it's there, scorching my hand, and I throw it.

Not at the scout, but at Ziva's volatile strike.

"What are you doing?" The shepherds cry and cover their heads as the bolts of starfire collide.

The explosion is more violent than anything I've ever experienced. Even more devastating than when I laid fire to the Sky Palace. The sky bursts with light, a hundred times brighter than the sun. White fire and popping sparks shred through the blanket of blackness. A second later a boom shakes the earth, bringing everyone else to their knees. I half expect the ground to fall away completely. It feels like the world is splitting in two. Devouring itself.

As torrents of ash fall, the ground settles with a groan and the brightness fades. My vision returns just in time to watch the Shoniin scout reach the crest of the dune. They turn, wave their bloody memento from King Minoak, and vanish into the desert, Orbai screeching behind them.

I cough and droop back to the boggy ground. It feels like handfuls of wool have been shoved in my ears. Unfortunately, it's not enough to block out the shepherds' rage.

"You're completely out of control!" Lalyne rants.

"They'll come for us now." Iree tries, and fails, to gain his feet. "You've condemned our families to death!"

"Ziva's starfire was unstable," I say desperately. "It could have obliterated us. I had to counteract the threat. . . ."

My voice trails off as the words register: *I had to counteract the threat.*

It's exactly what Ghoa said to me at Nariin.

I press my cheek into the wet sand and take big, gasping breaths.

"Her starfire didn't look any more unstable than *yours*," Bultum says.

"I can't believe you'd rather sacrifice these innocent people than give me a chance," Ziva spits out, her voice razor-sharp.

"That isn't it. . . ." I drape my arm over my face, as if blocking out the horrors will change what happened. "It had nothing to do with you, Ziva, and everything to do with my eagle."

It's the truth. And the exact wrong thing to say.

Iree's eyes do that bulging thing again, coming even closer to bursting than they did over the stolen rations. Which seems like such a trivial squabble now. "The eagle?" He points at the empty morning sky. "You sacrificed us all for a *bird*?"

"No, that came out wrong." I cast Serik a pleading look, begging him to step in and defend me like he always has, but he continues staring off into the desert, his brow furrowed and jaw tight. As if he's angry. Or disappointed. But how can he be? He's the only one who knows what Orbai means to me. And it truly was the safest option. Ziva's dangerous and untrained.

"We should have known better than to follow Enebish the Destroyer!" The shepherds continue to hound me. "Add a thousand more lives to your death count!"

I should stay quiet—nothing I say will help—but I can't take their derision and mistrust and ingratitude for another skies-forsaken second. "*I* didn't want to come this way!" Angry words dart from my lips like a colony of agitated bees, stinging everything in sight. "I *knew* the Shoniin would be watching this road. And I warned you. But, once again, no one trusts my judgment."

"For good reason!" Ziva flings her hand at the sky, where ghostly strands of smoke still stain the blue.

I laugh bitterly and turn away, furious that they could be so obtuse, exhausted from constantly defending myself, and overwhelmed by the horrible possibility that there's a parcel of truth to their accusations. Despite my good intentions, my efforts always *do* seem to result in the loss of innocent lives. I am Enebish the Destroyer no matter what I do.

"I'm sorry," I murmur, my voice small and breaking. But no one answers. I don't know if it's because they didn't hear me or because they're *choosing* not to hear me. Either way, I give up and direct silent pleas to the Lady and Father instead. They're the only ones who might take pity on me now.

Forgive me. Strengthen me. Show me what to do.

A lightning bolt of clarity doesn't strike, and answers don't miraculously appear in my mind—as they do when I'm writing in my Book of Whisperings—but while I pray, I feel warm, steady arms wrapping around me. Giving me the tiniest nudge. Helping me up off the ground.

"We need to go," Serik finally says with a tired sigh. "We don't know where the Shoniin and Zemyans are camped, and we need to be within the walls of Uzul before they arrive."

"I'm not going anywhere with her." Emani, Bultum's terrifying wife, levels a finger at me.

"Please don't make this more difficult than it already is," Serik pleads. "It's easy to cry for blood when that blood won't stain your hands. We're all just doing our best. Including Enebish."

The shepherds mutter and scowl and complain loudly, but they let me follow them back to where the rest of the caravan waits—to hundreds of additional people who will be just as furious with me.

I decide now is not the time to mention the even bigger problem they all seem to be overlooking: King Ihsan will never welcome us into Namaag. Not if he knows the Shoniin and Zemyans are coming for us.

No one speaks to me, or even looks at me, for the rest of the day. Which isn't so different from before. I prefer it, in fact. It's quieter, easier, better. Or it would be, if I didn't have to watch the shepherds praise and coddle Ziva. As soon as we set off into the marshes, they sucked her up into the center of the caravan, petting her hair and offering her water, taking a sudden interest in her story, as if her wayward starfire saved them singlehandedly.

If they want to applaud someone for misplaced bolts of starfire and rash and dangerous decisions, it should be me. But she's the hero and I'm the monster, no matter that they'd all be dead if Ziva had been leading them from the start.

My waterlogged boots catch on a protruding root, and as I crash to the unforgiving path for what feels like the millionth time, an unexpected thought seizes me: Is this how Ghoa felt when the Sky King began addressing his missives to me? When the Kalima flocked to me, instead of her, for advice? When the crowds in Sagaan cheered loudest for my power?

Of course, I would never maim Ziva or frame her for a massacre, but chills overtake me, despite the much warmer air of the swamp. Where is Ghoa now? What's happening in Sagaan? I want to know, and at the same time, I don't. I'd be lying if I said there wasn't part of me that hopes she suffered a horrific death. But if she's dead, that means Kartok and Temujin succeeded in taking the capital. And the thought of their scheme proving victorious, and knowing *I* had a hand in it, makes me nearly as sick.

There is no good option. No positive outcome.

I try to distract myself with the scenery. I knew Namaag would be wet and thick with trees, but nothing could have prepared me for the otherworldly beauty of the marshes. Rivers tangle and twist through the forest, each a different color: from midnight blue and algae green to silty brown and sulfur yellow. The air sits heavy in my throat and tastes sickly sweet with rot.

It's the only Protected Territory I've never visited—King

Ihsan allied with the Ashkarians long before I was born, when the Sky King convinced them to build aqueducts to Sagaan to end the drought, and they've caused little trouble since. There's never been a reason to send the Kalima. We were busy engaging Zemya and acquiring the other territories.

A strange iridescent insect buzzes around my head, louder than the spice grinders in Nashab Marketplace, and the air fills with the calling of birds. Never in my life have I seen so many birds! Herons and egrets and ducks and ibis. Under other circumstances, I would adore them, but every snapping beak and rustling feather reminds me of Orbai—attacking King Minoak, choosing the scout, abandoning me when I needed her most.

Fury and heartbreak war for control of my heart, so all consuming, I don't realize the caravan has ground to a halt until I slam into the back of a wagon. I expect to receive a death glare from its owner, but they don't glance back. No one does. The entire caravan is entranced, gazing up at the city of Uzul just ahead.

It's built high up in the canopy, on platforms and bridges that connect one behemoth tree to the next. My jaw hits my shoes as I take it all in. If any king should be called the Sky King, it is undeniably Ihsan. His feet probably never touch the earth. The roofs of the houses are thatched with moss, and the walls are constructed to look like leaves, blending perfectly into the foliage. Copper pipes that look for all the world like branches run beneath everything, sucking water up from the marsh and feeding it into the treetop homes.

Everything is green—as green as Kartok's false Eternal Blue. Except for the flashes of yellow and orange and turquoise darting through the dense greenery. At first they register as birds, but as I squint harder, I realize they are *people* hustling down the thoroughfares.

We don't resume our march again for a long while. I presume Serik and the head of each shepherd family are discussing the tactics of our entrance—things that no longer involve me—so I nearly jump out of my skin and into the murky water when someone touches my elbow.

"Have you ever seen anything so incredible?" Serik's hazel eyes glitter and there's a new bounce to his step. Such a welcome change from the shadow-eyed wisp he's become over the past weeks. "We made it, En."

Barely, I want to say, but I refuse to take this moment from him. And he's right. Namaag is unbelievable. I smile and hook my arm through his. "We made it," I echo, "which raises the question, what are *you*, noble leader, doing back here with *me*?"

"Ziva thought it would be best if she approached the Namagaans first, alone, so I had a moment to spare."

Of course Ziva wants to go alone. Then she can make it look like it's only by her good grace and connections that we're allowed into the city.

"Stop that." Serik digs his elbow into my side. "I can hear every awful thought running through your head."

"Stop listening to my thoughts if you don't like them," I say with a wry smile.

Serik tugs me closer so his warm side presses flush against mine. "I understand why you're frustrated with her."

"*Frustrated?*" I choke on a cynical laugh. "She tried to kill Orbai and made me look like an erratic, unhinged traitor."

"She's far from innocent, but your response had just as much to do with the shepherds' reaction. You attacked Ziva's starfire instead of the scout. For good reason, though," he adds before I can get angry. "You had to. Sometimes we can't stop believing in our friends, even when they seem hopeless and lost. You never know when circumstances will change. Or when new truth will come to light."

He looks over at me with those earnest crescent-moon eyes, and I melt. Completely and utterly incapacitated by the closeness of his lips and the fluttering in my stomach.

"You're announcing your thoughts again," Serik whispers.

"Are you fonder of the message this time?" I ask.

"Much." His gaze drops to my mouth, but he reluctantly pulls away. "There's still one thing I don't understand—what was Orbai even doing with that scout?"

"Kartok healed her with Loridium, a type of Zemyan magic. It bound her to him," I mumble, hoping the words will hurt less if I only half say them.

"Is that why she didn't come with us when we left the *xanav*?"

I nod.

"And you didn't think it was important to tell me this?" Serik manages not to yell. Barely. "Skies, En. Temujin and Kartok know what she means to you. They know they can use her to manipulate you and endanger us."

"I'm sorry," I say softly.

Serik sighs. "I should get back, but I wanted to check on you and ask you to please help this to go smoothly. We need to convince the Namagaans this rebellion will work, which will never happen if they see us squabbling among ourselves. We need to present a united front, a capable—if not formidable—battalion."

If anyone else was giving this speech, I would roll my eyes and shove them off, but I nod and say, "I know."

"That means trusting me, and the group, to make the right decisions. And showing a willingness to trust our potential allies. And no more secrecy."

"Isn't that a little hypocritical?" I ask.

Serik's brow crinkles. "What are you talking about?"

The shepherds are still keeping their distance, but I lower

my voice and step closer anyway. "King Ihsan will never welcome us if he knows we're being pursued by the Shoniin and the Zemyans. He's notoriously stingy with aid. Namaag only supports neighboring nations if it doesn't pose a threat to their own land and people. Which is one of the reasons I didn't want to start our recruitment here. They're the only Protected Territory that hasn't been exploited by the Sky King because Ashkar is so dependent on their aqueducts, so they don't share nearly as much hostility toward the Unified Empire."

"We don't technically *know* that Temujin and Kartok are coming, so we don't need to tell them anything," Serik says, and now I'm the one pinning him with a dubious look.

"I suppose we also don't *know* that the sun will rise each morning, but it's such a forgone conclusion, we don't bother considering what would happen if it didn't."

"This definitely isn't sun-level certainty," Serik argues.

"What happens when Kartok and the Zemyans scale these gigantic trees to get to us? King Ihsan will feel used and blindsided. He won't come to our aid and he definitely won't join our rebellion."

"I disagree. Fighting with us is preferable to being conquered by the Zemyans . . . and it doesn't matter if it's dishonest. It's our only option. We just have to hope the scout is slow and the warriors Temujin and Kartok send are even slower. The grasslands are harsh this time of year, and they have no Sun Stoker."

I gnaw on my lower lip and look up at the treetop city. "There's so much that could go wrong. . . ."

Serik takes my shoulders and forces me to look at him. "This is exactly what I'm talking about, En. Things could just as easily go right. Try to see the positive. We'll never be able to convince the Namagaans to forge this alliance without your help, but we're doomed before we even enter Uzul if you lead with suspicion and allow the past haunt you. Let it go—for yourself. For all of these people depending on us"—he motions to the shepherds—"and for your captive people in Verdenet."

I stare into his eyes, so warm and soft and hopeful, despite everything. "Fine. Find me a shovel," I say with a reluctant nod.

Serik's face twists with confusion. "A *shovel*? Why do you need a shovel?"

"Because I'm finally ready to bury the past."

CHAPTER NINE

GHΘA

THE ZEMYANS LAUGH AND CONGRATULATE EACH OTHER AS they shove me into the back of a covered wagon. It reeks of sweat and vomit, and I cringe as my face smashes into the boards and slides through something wet and gritty.

Get up! Fight! Stop being pathetic.

But my mind can't convince my body to move. Not even as the Zemyans spit into my hair and slam the door. I don't see the point. I'm not the peerless commander I thought I was. My warriors *left* me. After I saved them. And if I move, I will have to accept that this is *real*. That all of this is truly happening.

The Sky King is dead.

The Zemyans have taken Sagaan.

I still don't understand how it's possible. They were advancing, yes, but they would have had to sprout wings and fly to reach the capital so quickly.

Unless *someone* in Ashkar helped them. Snuck them in.

I see Enebish's starfire demolishing the buttress and crushing the Sky King for the millionth time, and her name explodes from my throat like a cannonball. "Hypocrite!" I bellow. "How *dare* you condemn me for what happened at Nariin, then go and do something even worse! You'll be responsible for ten times as many deaths!"

No matter how deeply I breathe, I can't seem to fill my lungs. No matter how tightly I clutch my forehead, I can't slow the blood pounding my temples like fists. Enebish is the closest thing I've ever had to a sister. The one person I was certain I could never lose. She owes me everything. I have always been her everything.

And this is how she repays me.

You shouldn't be surprised. You shouldn't allow it to hurt you.

It *doesn't* hurt me.

But as the wagon lurches forward, I see her dark eyes peering up at me through the smoke of her burning village in Verdenet. I feel her tremble in front of me on the saddle as we ride back to Sagaan. I hear her breathing even out with sleep, her thin body sinking into mine as if I'm the most comfortable bedroll she's ever slept in.

"Enebish!" I scream her name again. I know she's nearby. "At least have the courage to look me in the eye as you drive your knife into my back! How can you fight alongside the people who murdered your parents? How can you help them destroy the empire that gave you refuge? Do you realize what this means for Verdenet?"

She doesn't answer, because she's a coward. But that doesn't mean she can't hear me. I take a deep breath and continue shouting. I have enough accusations to fill the entire journey to Zemya. But after less than five minutes, the wagon creaks and a pale face fills the small, barred window on the door.

"Hold your tongue, or I'll hold it for you," a gruff voice

threatens. I can only see the upper half of the man's face. His eyes are the color of a glacier, framed by thick blond eyebrows, and pale patchy stubble covers his sallow cheeks. It's hideous and unnatural, as if all the color was leached from his body as punishment for his wicked magic—just as the legends claim.

"If you want to silence me, come in here and do it!" I spit.

He chuckles and the sound sends gooseflesh racing up my arms. "They told me you were fiery. I'm delighted to see you're living up to expectations. It will make our time together so much more interesting. As for your tongue . . . why would I come in there when I can quiet you from here?"

His bone-white hands slip through the bars, grasping for me. I scramble back, well beyond his reach, but his arms *grow*, stretching across the compartment like the taffy Mamá used to make each year on the Sky King's birthday. I press myself against the farthest wall, but the Zemyan easily catches me. His knobby fingers squirm between my lips and grab my tongue.

I scream and claw at my mouth. The pain is staggering, blinding. It feels like the farriers' tongs are wrenching my tongue. I have to make it stop. But my fingers find nothing to grab. There's no hand inside my mouth, even though I can *feel* it there.

It's all an illusion. His vile Zemyan magic.

I curse for a full minute, wishing it was in fact his hand. At least then I could bite him. When I finally run out of breath and fall silent, the pain abates. But the instant I open my mouth to resume yelling, the wrenching fingers return with a vengeance.

"You'll quickly learn it'll be much more pleasant if you cooperate," the Zemyan says.

"Filthy, depraved sorcerer!" I yell, even though I know it will cost me. I need him to know I *won't* cooperate. I will *never* cooperate.

I grip the iron bars and summon my ice, commanding them

to bend, to shatter. Willing the entire wagon to explode. But of course it doesn't. My palms don't even feel cool against the metal. I emptied every reserve I had to save my traitorous warriors. It could take days, weeks, for my power to regenerate. *If* it ever does.

I sink back to the floor and seethe as the wagon lurches onward, league after league. Day after day. My captors don't bother feeding me. Each night when we make camp, firelight flickers through the bars and the smell of roasting meat fills the air, but the Zemyans don't fling even a splinter of bone my way. Instead they feed the excess to their dogs—small, mangy mongrels that gulp and snap loudly.

I make a vow, then and there. When I escape, I will roast those mutts on a spit and eat them for spite, savoring every sinewy morsel. Then I'll whittle their bones into arrows and put them into the hearts of their masters.

The longer we travel, the warmer it grows. Wetness floods the air, blowing down my neck like a hot breath. The smells of salt and sand somehow overpower the putrid stench of the wagon.

The last time I breathed these foreign scents, *I* was the one leading the charge. Riding down from the Usinsk Pass on Tabana, the Kalima streaming behind me like a never-ending cloak as we stormed Karekemish. Not only did we breach the Zemyan capital, we advanced all the way to Empress Danashti's seaside palace before we were finally driven back by their magic. The empress's best sorcerers made it look as if the entire city were sinking into the sea, and we thought we would drown if we didn't retreat.

I had never seen the sea before, and it felt dangerous in a way I couldn't describe. Bigger than I would ever be. I had been so certain that nothing in the world could be more endless than the grasslands, until I saw those waves, rippling into eternity. A million shades of blue, each one deeper and darker.

The closer we get to Karekemish, the more impossible it becomes to sleep. The air is heavy and thick and revolting, and I sweat all night, my Kalima power still too depleted to summon cooling drafts. Though, I wouldn't be able to sleep in the heart of a blizzard with the way my thoughts are racing. My panic escalates every day as I think of Sagaan. Of the Zemyans, sinking their claws deeper into my country, now that there's nothing and no one to hold them back.

We have no king, the Kalima will have retreated to the rendezvous point in the northern steppes to regroup, and our troops at the battlefront were undoubtedly obliterated when the Zemyans cut their way through to Sagaan.

I imagine the seven sectors of the capital in flames, burning like the Sky Palace. All the beautiful architecture, destroyed. Thousands of years of progress, lost. I picture the people scrambling down the streets like rats before a cat, screaming for help—for warriors who will never come.

And what will become of the Protected Territories? How long will it take for the Zemyans to reach them? I want to believe our remaining troops will stand their ground and guard our holdings, but when I close my eyes, I see them abandoning their posts and fleeing into the night. There's nothing keeping them there without the king to answer to.

Without me to lead them.

Thankfully, I won't have to witness any of it. I'll be long dead.

Perhaps the Kalima did me a favor after all.

We reach Karekemish a week later, and it's nothing like I remember.

When we invaded the Zemyan capital three years ago, I galloped past houses that were nothing more than hovels made of mud and hay. Rudimentary wells had been dug right into the center of the streets, causing massive amounts of flooding. Sad little boats were tipped over on every rocky stretch of beach, and it reeked of fish and sewage. And the people! They looked like the clear white sand scorpions that only emerge in the desert at night.

Now I gape up at towering copper gates. They are as high as any wall in Sagaan and just as beautiful—the copper as green as the sea beyond, the bars formed of sculpted serpents and tiny spiral seashells. Starfish and long, swirling plants crown the top.

Inside the city, the houses are definitely not made of mud and hay. They may be brown, but they're tall and sturdy, with wraparound balconies, windows made of sea glass, and shining abalone roofs. The roads are paved not with cobbles, but an endless slab of sandstone that's so smooth, the wagon feels as if it's floating.

The Zemyans have clearly rebuilt.

Except barbarians could never accomplish all of this so quickly.

"Impressed, Commander?"

I lurch back from the window, and the Zemyan sorcerer laughs. He leers at me through the bars, so close that I choke on the sour tang of his breath.

The deeper we wind into the city, the more the wagon slows. Crowds of Zemyans in golden finery pour from their homes to point and shout. Shrill horns blare and hands pound the wagon's walls like thunder. As if this is a monumental occasion. As if I'm someone important.

The irony isn't lost on me.

My enemies revere me more than my own warriors.

The sun creeps higher and the heat intensifies. I feel like I'm baking inside this blasted box as we plod down the long, thin peninsula. The glaring light shining off the water is so bright, I don't see Empress Danashti's palace, rising out of the sea, until we come to a halt in front of it.

It's the opposite of the Sky Palace in every way.

Where the Sky Palace is dazzling white marble, reaching up into the clouds, Empress Danashti's palace is one sprawling level made from black coral that juts and twists into strange, porous shapes.

I would never call it pretty. This entire country is harsh and austere—devoid of the lush grass, sparkling snow, and tall, spired buildings that make Ashkar beautiful—but it's also not the slum that lives in my memory.

The lock on the wagon doors clanks and harsh sunlight fills the compartment, making it easy for the Zemyans to clamp manacles around my wrists and shove me from the wagon while I squint.

I hit the ground like a flopping fish and the crowd roars louder.

The sticky heat is even more oppressive out here. If my icy core had begun to refreeze, it's a puddle beneath my armor now. Seeping from my skin in buckets of sweat.

"We've brought a gift for the empress!" my captor bellows.

The throng roars, and heralds with long, strange trumpets turn toward the palace. Their music is low and rumbling, buzzing the marrow in my bones, and they do not stop until a water chariot appears from the far side of the coral palace. The chariot is shaped like a cup, with fanning grooves like a seashell, and it's pulled by a team of porpoises. A cluster of people stand inside, but my eyes go immediately to the woman at the front: an enemy I have only seen from across the battlefield.

Empress Danashti is somehow more imposing and more unremarkable up close. I've only ever seen her mounted on her warhorse, and she's much smaller than I realized. Hardly larger than a child. Her features are blunt and unrefined. Dark brows frame her bone-white face and silver-white hair billows behind her like the foam churning from her chariot. She looks too soft and too hard. Too plain and too beautiful to be the ruthless leader of these magic-wielding demons.

The gathered crowd falls onto their faces as she lifts her gauzy skirt and steps onto the sand. It's so quiet, I can hear the jangle of her silver anklets. My captor extends his cape and performs a sweeping, melodramatic bow that would get him laughed out of the Sky Palace. The other Zemyan soldiers do the same.

"Your Most Noble Excellency," he says in Ashkarian, wanting me to understand. I've refused to debase myself by learning their barbaric language.

The ruler of Zemya glances at me and responds in Ashkarian as well, her voice heavily accented. "What have you brought me now, Kartok? You know gifts are unnecessary—you're already Generál Supreme."

"I assure you, my empress, you'll want this gift." He grabs me by the collar, twisting a chunk of my hair in his fist. I yelp as he throws me at the empress's feet. Coarse black sand sticks to my lips and cheeks. "The Sky King is dead. And I've captured the commander of the Kalima warriors."

Danashti peers down at me with a cocked brow. I'm a filthy, bloodstained mess. I don't look like a commander. I don't even look like a warrior. But an exultant smile breaks across her face. "A very desirable gift, indeed. You've outdone yourself, Kartok."

"Which is always my aim, Your Excellence."

Empress Danashti swivels to address the crowd, points at me, and switches to Zemyan. She doesn't shout, but somehow her voice carries. I only understand a handful of words: *Sky King. Dead. Captured. Commander.*

The crowd roars with riotous approval.

Empress Danashti speaks again, and I surmise her question based on the mobs' ferocious answer.

"Kill her!" they scream.

I swallow hard but jut my chin. Refusing to cower.

Empress Danashti waits for her people to settle, then she turns to me and switches back to Ashkarian. "A wise suggestion. But I, being the magnanimous ruler that I am—as different from your grasping king as the ocean is the sky—have another offer, *Commander*. Admit defeat, proclaim your disgrace before my people, swear allegiance to Zemya, and help us dismantle your empire. Then I will spare your—"

"I'd rather die," I growl before she's finished.

Empress Danashti nods. "And so you shall. But not until we've wrung every drop of usefulness from your carcass. You may take her to your laboratory, Generál Supreme."

Kartok flings himself into another ridiculous bow, but before he can rise, one of the men standing behind the empress steps forward. I'd assumed they were all guards and servants. Most are wearing plain smocks or sea-green uniforms. But this man wears an ocean-blue suit embellished with silver braids, and a wreath of sea grass rests atop his ash-white hair—similar to the one the empress wears. He isn't handsome—nothing that so closely resembles a night-crawling worm could be attractive—but the Zemyan girls hoot and call his name: Ivandar. Along with another word: *Prince.*

He touches his mother's arm and murmurs something in Zemyan.

The empress whirls on him, staring at his hand on her sleeve.

He doesn't let go. "Please."

That's a word I know well from interrogating hundreds of Zemyan prisoners.

Danashti barks something at him and points to the water chariot. He scowls but stomps in that direction like a pouting child, though he must be as old as I am. The empress follows. Kartok kicks my backside and forces me to crawl after them on my hands and knees.

The Zemyan throng crows with delight. Every time I attempt to stand, Kartok knocks me down again. I drag myself through the rough sand and broken shells, leaving a trail of blood.

He shoves me into the belly of the water chariot and steps in behind me, purposely grinding his boots on my fingers as we skim toward the coral palace.

The ride is short, and no one says a word.

The moment we dock on the opposite side of the palace, away from the crowd, Kartok grabs my manacles, hefts me onto the landing, and drags me toward a door hidden in the protrusions of coral.

The prince is right on our heels, shouting and gesticulating. He's speaking too quickly for me to pick out many words, but again, only a few are necessary. "Enemy. Suspicion. Plans."

They're arguing over who gets the pleasure of torturing me. How nice.

Kartok growls something over his shoulder. The prince tosses his hands and turns to his mother. Empress Danashti looks between the men for a silent minute before nodding at Kartok.

With a smug grin, the Zemyan general propels me through the hidden door. I can still hear the prince shouting after it bangs shut. Muttering under his breath, Kartok yanks me down a narrow staircase, though I don't understand how we're descending. As far as I could see, there's nothing below the palace but water, which is bad news for me.

I can't swim.

No Ashkarian can. There's no need and nowhere to learn; the Amereti is the only river, and it barely reaches my hips.

My heart drums and my breaths rasp when the stairs empty into a room surrounded entirely by water. Nothing but flimsy walls of glass to hold back the crashing, crushing blue. Water doesn't appear to be seeping in through the walls, but I still hunch inward and step carefully, listening for a crack. A drip.

"Afraid of the water, *Commander*?" Kartok asks with a chuckle. "I'll remember that." An invisible door slides open and he motions me down an even smaller, more suffocating tunnel. I trip through it as fast as my bonds allow and gasp when I emerge on the other end.

It's worse than a prison cell or even another room of glass.

I am standing in the center of the throne room at the Sky Palace.

I gape down the long, vaulted hall. Shake my head at the gradient blue walls and hand-painted clouds. Run a finger along the empty golden throne, and shudder beneath the face molds of our country's greatest warriors, dangling from the ceiling on invisible strings. I always used to think the masks looked down on me with pride. Kinship. Inviting me to one day join their ranks.

Now their eyes are slitted with condemnation. Snarling with hatred.

You failed the Sky King.

I lean over and vomit.

"You don't like it?" Kartok pouts. "But I made it especially for you. I want you to be comfortable."

"Get your poisonous magic out of my head!" I roar.

"Where am I really? What is this place?"

There are no cells. No bars of any kind. No hot pokers or instruments of torture. The lack of anything expected makes my skin prickle with unease.

None of this is possible. None of this is *right*.

I whirl around and dive behind a cluster of chairs where the Council of Elders usually sits. I know furniture won't shield me from Kartok's illusions, since the chairs themselves are an illusion, but I don't know what else to do, so I let my instincts and training take over. Find cover, make a plan, counterattack.

The manacles make it difficult, but I twist my hands around the side of my body and curl my fingers into a fist. Under normal circumstances, my ice would chisel a saber into existence as soon as I imagined it. But the glacier that usually resides in my chest is still the size of a pebble. Sweat slathers my skin as I extract drop after pitiful drop of cold.

I shouldn't have bothered.

The dagger that eventually crystalizes in my hand is the size of a paring knife. And so dull it could barely slice through butter. I throw it at Kartok's head anyway, screaming with frustration.

It flies true—my aim, at least, unaffected by my depleted power—but instead of slamming into his chest, the dagger passes through him. Or maybe it disappeared altogether. I can't tell. All I know is, it's gone. Without a sound or trace of blood.

Kartok should be screaming in agony, but the only cry in this eerie replica of the throne room comes from me.

And it sounds like a whimper.

CHAPTER TEN

ENEBISH

ZIVA RETURNS TO THE CARAVAN WEARING A TRIUMPHANT smile. "They've agreed to give us shelter!"

The Namagaan woman following her looks considerably less pleased. Though, I don't know if that's due to the harsh black makeup she's wearing across both brows, making her look eternally perturbed, or the explosion of cheers and shouts from the shepherds, who raise their hands and collapse into tearful hugs.

My lips pull into a frown because this is not how a group of people who would make formidable allies should react. The Namagaan woman takes note. She's clearly a soldier—tall and muscular in her wood-plated armor, topped with an orange cloak covered in jeweled emblems. Her yellow hair falls in long tufted strands that look like cattails—the traditional Namagaan style—and her skin is as rough and lined as the trees they live in. All Namagaans look as craggy as bark, no matter their age. It's beautiful in a hard, intimidating way.

Her eyes flick over our motley group. "So many of you. How

lovely," she says, but her teeth grind the words. "Follow me."

Another root pathway rises out of the muck and she leads us to one of the behemoth trees. She presses her palm to the trunk, and a panel slides open, revealing a spiral staircase that twists up to the canopy. The shepherds rush in like floodwater and race to the top, dripping all the way. My bad leg slips and twists painfully on the wet stairs.

By the time I finally reach the platform, the Namagaan warrior has been joined by a sizeable contingent of soldiers, all of whom study us with thinly veiled contempt. They haven't brandished weapons, but their fingers hover at the ready.

Our group is so large, we fill the entire platform and spill down several of the interconnecting rope bridges. Serik is on the opposite side of the crowd, and when his gaze finds mine, I try to muster an encouraging grin. Though, it's difficult to look past the squawking shepherds and bleating animals and the soldiers' deepening scowls. The tension is as thick as the muggy swamp air.

When someone screams, I'm certain the Namagaan soldiers have lost their patience and are tossing us over the rope railings, but then a golden-skinned woman from my own country shoves through the crowd and flies across the platform.

"Zivana?"

"Auntie!" Ziva melts to the boards, reminding me, suddenly, that she's only thirteen. It makes my insides squirm. Perhaps I've been *slightly* hard on the girl.

The woman throws her arms around Ziva and they collapse into a tangle of limbs, laughing and crying as she smooths the curls away from Ziva's face. I can't bear to watch. Because that's how familial love should look. *That* is the bond an aunt or mother or sister should share. Unbridled tenderness. Complete trust. They would never betray each other.

"What in the skies happened?" Ziva's aunt asks. I'd place her somewhere near Ghoa's age, though it's hard to tell, as her face has been painted to look as rough as the Namagaans'. It's strange to see someone from Verdenet dressed in the style of the marsh people—her dark hair bound like reeds, thick black makeup joining her brows, and a vibrant crimson dress that wraps and ties across her middle.

I try to imagine being sent to live in an entirely different country, so foreign from your own. A moment passes before I realize that's *exactly* what I did. I learned to live in Ashkar. Learned to dress and speak and fight like them, almost to the point of forgetting my roots. I wonder if it's the same for Ziva's aunt. If she considers herself fully Namagaan now. Or if she misses Verdenet and cares what becomes of it. Does she even know her brother's been removed from the throne? King Minoak has only been a figurehead since relinquishing his sovereignty twenty years ago when Verdenet became a Protected Territory. But he was at least allowed to keep up pretenses and tradition. Until now.

"We were attacked!" Ziva's voice wobbles and she speaks in fast, gasping breaths. "An assassin tried to kill Papa. We escaped the palace, but he was gravely injured. I tried to dress his wounds and nurse him to health, but we were alone in the desert without food or supplies. That's why I started stealing them from these people. They're refugees from Ashkar, and they were kind enough to help us. We couldn't return to Verdenet because an imperial governor has taken the city."

Tears are running down the woman's face, smearing her makeup, and she fans herself with her hand. A long moment passes before she can speak. "My brave girl. And my poor brother. You did the right thing, coming here."

She stands, makes a vain attempt to smooth her rumpled red dress, and finally addresses the rest of us. "I am Yatindra

Yimeni, daughter of Verdenet and wife of Namaag. Thank you for aiding my family. You have my deepest thanks and are welcome to stay for a time to recover from your efforts. May I see my brother?"

The shepherds part. Yatindra passes through our ranks and kneels beside the litter. "It's about time you came to visit me," she chokes out, touching Minoak's face. Her fingers continue down his bloody garments, and she gasps into the back of her hand. He stirs at the sound. Not fully waking, but a subtle change of breath. A tiny sign of life, which makes her cry even harder.

"We must tend these wounds at once." She directs the shepherds responsible for the litter to follow her down one of the swaying bridges, and Ziva trails behind them. Before they disappear into the dense foliage, Yatindra calls back to us, "I'll return for the rest of you once he's settled with the healers."

I want to object. She can't just leave us here, surrounded by soldiers in an unfamiliar land. But she does.

The soldier who escorted us into the city steps forward, looking even more imposing with her orange-cloaked brigade behind her. They're armed with reed-thin spears and small, sleek bows fitted to their wrists. Weapons that can zip easily through the trees.

"Follow us," she barks.

Serik steps forward, his face tight with a forced smile. "Yatindra instructed—"

"I don't serve Yatindra. I serve King Ihsan, who will want to meet you." She jabs her spear at the nearest shepherds. As they wail and stumble down the swaying rope bridge, I want to reach for the night, craving that added protection. But I release the tendrils before they blacken the marsh. If we want to make an alliance with the Namagaans, we cannot present as a threat.

We *also* can't present as a pitiful group of yowling refugees, but there's nothing to be done about that right now.

The soldiers prod us deeper and deeper into the canopy. Chattering voices join the cacophony of birdsong and vibrant colors flash behind the leaves. Curious Namagaans trail us. Watching us. But no one emerges to greet us from the homes and shops crowding every branch. And the common areas they've constructed by connecting the platforms of close-standing trees are newly deserted. Meals left half finished. Riderless swings swaying.

King Ihsan's palace is built around a particularly large tree, each level stacked atop the next, clear to the thinnest branches. I have no idea how they can bear the weight and I have no interest in journeying up there. Just looking at the far-off windows puts me back in the spire salon, crashing against the frozen glass. Leaping from the balcony.

All to save a traitor.

I expect the soldiers to herd us into an extravagant throne room that could rival the Sky King's, but the commander raps on a humble door made of bark with a quaint apple knob. A scrawny man with thinning hair opens it and squints into the morning.

"Ruya? What is the meaning of this?" Sleep lines crisscross the man's cheeks and his voice is still rough.

I wait for her to snap at the servant to run and fetch the king, but she brings her fist to her forehead and bows.

"Pardon the intrusion, Your Majesty."

Your Majesty?

Shocked whispers ripple through our company. What sort of king answers his own door? And in his dressing gown! I take in his scruffy robe and drooping socks. The dim light of the room behind him shows a modest fireplace and a simple desk littered with books.

"These refugees arrived unannounced and wish to seek

asylum in our city," Ruya resumes. "I knew you would want to address the issue yourself, since there are so many of them. It seems overtly suspicious."

"Yes." The Marsh King eyes us. "Especially when they look so . . . menacing." He studies our dirty faces and threadbare clothes and the lambs wriggling in the shepherds' arms.

"Precisely," Ruya says.

King Ihsan bites back a smile and pats Ruya's shoulder. "Excellent work. You may go. I'll determine what's to be done with these intruders."

Ruya hesitates. "Don't think me impertinent, Your Majesty, but—"

"I'd only think you impertinent if you suggest I cannot handle this matter on my own."

"Of course not, my liege. Forgive me." Ruya bows and leads the other soldiers back across the bridge.

King Ihsan leans against the door frame and raises a silver brow at us. "Well?" It's the least formal, most unkingly action I've ever witnessed. "Have you come to lay siege to my kingdom? Or steal my jewels? Or perhaps you plan to attack me with your rabid sheep?" He chuckles at a little lamb, bleating as it totters across a bridge.

Serik steps forward, and a swell of pride fills my chest as he wets his lips and pulls his shoulders back. "We mean you no harm," he says in a practiced, official tone. "We are humble refugees from Ashkar, simple—"

"Wait, let me guess," Ihsan cuts in. "Shepherds?"

"How could you tell?" Serik asks, so focused on impressing the king that he seems to have forgotten the frightened animals literally knocking around our feet.

King Ihsan laughs and slaps Serik on the shoulder. "I like you. You're funny. Come, let's chat in the dining hall. Minerva will fix you all something to eat. It looks as if you've been through a lot."

More than a few of the shepherds break down with tears, and Serik blurts out, "You're receiving us, just like that?"

"Is there a reason I shouldn't?" For the first time, the king's eyes flash with a spark of warning. It's visible only for an instant before a jolly grin takes its place. But it was there, like a leopard crouched in the treetops.

Ever hungry.

Ever ready.

Serik's throat bobs and his eyes flit toward Ruya and the soldiers, standing in rigid lines a few trees over.

"Oh, don't mind Ruya," King Ihsan says. "She's a bit overzealous, but I indulge her. No harm in letting our enemies believe we're fiercer than we are."

His quip is charming and self-deprecating, and it makes Serik and the others laugh. But it makes my hackles rise and my palms grow slick. Because the Namagaans *are* fierce. They must be, to have commanded such respect and independence from the Sky King. We *need* them to be fierce if they're going to be of any help liberating the Protected Territories and defeating Zemya. Yet here we are, speaking to the king in his dressing gown. Receiving a warm welcome without a hint of hesitation or suspicion.

I don't like it.

You're doing it again, Serik's voice cautions. *Creating trouble where there isn't any.*

But being overly kind is its own form of warfare, and while the rest of our entourage cheers and rushes into the palace, I systematically catalog each bridge and platform and ladder. Locating every potential exit—just in case we need it.

CHAPTER ELEVEN

ENEBISH

KING IHSAN'S PALACE IS ENORMOUS, WITH VAULTED CEILINGS that seem to soar higher than the canopy, even though I know there are still dozens of floors above us. We pass sitting rooms hung with garlands of embroidered leaves, the colors changing to mimic the four seasons, and a ballroom made of wood so dark, I can see my awed reflection staring back. It all feels too large and grand to be suspended from branches.

Ihsan proudly points out the armory and the royal gallery, featuring the work of Namaag's most renowned carvers, and he regales the awestruck group with the history of the royal palace and family. At last, we enter a spacious banquet hall with lengthy tables made of split tree trunks, with toadstool cushions for sitting. I sink into the squishy comfort and sigh much louder than I mean to. Thankfully, everyone else is sighing too. And the sighs grow even louder when the food arrives: roasted chestnuts and acorns, spicy blackened alligator and a wide variety of tree fowl and fish I've never tasted before. I eat and eat and eat, wiping my mouth on my sleeve and sloshing sap wine down my front. For weeks I've been telling myself that sacrificing my rations doesn't affect me, but that was a glaring lie.

I glance down the packed table and grin when I spot Serik. He's elbow deep in grease and crumbs, shoveling spoonful after spoonful of huckleberry pudding into his mouth.

Ziva and Yatindra join us halfway through the feast, along with her dour-faced husband, Murtaugh. They look on with horror as we chomp and slurp like animals. "Are you going to devour the table as well?" Yatindra asks.

"Happily if it tastes this fine!" Bultum calls.

Everyone laughs and Ihsan smiles proudly. "Our delicious cuisine is just one of Namaag's many strengths."

A middle-aged woman with flour-dusted cheeks beams as she bustles around replacing the empty platters.

"So, where exactly are you from?" Yatindra asks no one in particular before daintily sipping a spoonful of soup.

"Everywhere and nowhere," Iree says. "We're herders, so we wander the tundra, chasing the best grazing lands and weather."

"Fascinating," Yatindra says, but her pinched lips say otherwise.

"Sounds burdensome to me," Murtaugh adds through a mouthful of stew.

"Where's your sense of adventure?" King Ihsan booms. "Imagine all the places you'd see. All the people you'd meet. The excitement of never knowing where you're going to lay your head next."

Yatindra dabs her lips with a napkin. "So then where will you go when you leave us?"

Serik and I exchange a glance across the table. The timing feels wrong, asking them to join our cause immediately, when they've already taken us in and provided this feast. Plus, we don't exactly look like desirable allies at the moment. I also don't want to get into the specifics with the entire caravan present. There are too many loud voices and strident opinions.

"We're not entirely sure," I start. "It depends on several variables—"

"What do you mean you're not sure?" Ziva interjects, her spoon clattering to the table. "As soon as Papa's well, we're returning to Verdenet to depose the imperial governor and retake the country. That's been the plan all along."

Yatindra chokes on her soup and gawps down at her niece. "You intend to confront the imperial governor with *these* people?"

"Why would you confront the empire at all? They're our allies." Murtaugh glares across the table at us, his tree-bark face suddenly crinkled with twice as many lines.

Serik gives a little cough. "There have been some complicated developments recently. . . ."

But Ziva jumps to her feet, slashing her butter knife like a saber. "The empire is not our ally. Allies don't attempt to murder your king and seize your capital."

"What are you talking about?" King Ihsan's cheery expression flattens.

The tangle of side conversations ceases, and every eye in the banquet hall darts between the Namagaan king and the Verdenese princess.

I want to bang my head against the table—*after* wringing Ziva's neck. I try to shoot her a threatening glare, but of course she won't look at me. Yatindra's eyes, however, flay me open like the fish now languishing on my plate. "You intend to drag my brother and niece back to Lutaar City after they barely escaped with their lives? You're not even soldiers!"

"We're not *dragging* them anywhere," I explain, but King Ihsan shouts over me.

"Who has been assassinated, and why is this the first I've heard of it?"

"You haven't heard anything because the double-crossing empire doesn't want you to know," Ziva cries, as if rousing troops to battle. "Then they can come for you next."

King Ihsan stands, suddenly looking a head taller and far fiercer than he did just minutes before. The entire room goes still, save for old Azamat, who continues gnawing on a pigeon bone. "These are bold accusations," the king mutters.

"Forgive us, Your Majesty." I march down the table, grab a fistful of Ziva's fresh Namagaan tunic—how nice, she got to change while the rest of us remain filthy—and tug her out of her chair.

"What are you doing?" She claws at my arm.

I drag her toward the door. "Our travels have been long and difficult," I plead with King Ihsan. "We're clearly exhausted and raving. Perhaps we can retire and discuss these matters after we've rested?"

He stares at us for a good ten seconds without blinking. Finally he nods and tersely rings a bell. Less than a minute later Ruya arrives with her battalion of grim-faced soldiers.

"Zivana will be staying with me." Yatindra rises and wrenches Ziva from my grip, but I dig my fingers into Ziva's dress. I'm not about to let her leave, not when she's the reason we're being dismissed.

"Let her go," Serik murmurs. "It's better this way. Everyone just needs to calm down."

"But she can't keep her mouth shut," I hiss. It's bad enough that Ziva broke the news about the situation in Verdenet. If she breathes a word about the Shoniin scout, we'll be cast out immediately. Or executed.

Ruya bangs the blunt end of her spear against the floor. "Out. All of you."

"All of us?" Iree cries. "But it isn't our fault Enebish—"

Ruya bangs her spear again and points us out of the dining hall.

The shepherds moan loudly and shoot me murderous glares as the soldiers escort us through the treetops with even more contempt and suspicion than before. Only now, no one intervenes on our behalf: not the Marsh King and definitely not Yatindra or Murtaugh, who are whispering furiously with Ziva in the corner.

The soldiers herd us across several swaying bridges to a series of barracks that will house us for the night. The wooden floors are hard and the woven palm frond blankets are scratchy, but it's so much more comfortable than everything we've endured the past month, the shepherds eventually settle and stop squawking about the disrupted feast.

Serik huffs down beside me with an exhausted groan. "Well, we *were* off to a good start. King Ihsan is much more hospitable than I expected."

"He *was* hospitable," I growl, viciously tugging the strings of my boots. "Ziva ruined everything. Like I knew she would."

Serik reaches over and places a steadying hand atop mine. Then he helps me unknot my laces—my bad arm refuses to cooperate when I'm agitated. "I actually don't think she ruined anything," he says.

"Were you in the same banquet hall as the rest of us? It was a disaster! We were dismissed."

"For now. But surely Ihsan realizes we're tired and scared and emotions are running high. Once we sit down in a more intimate setting and explain the larger picture, I think Ziva's fierceness could be seen as a good thing. As long as her father shares her sentiment when he wakes. Who wouldn't want such passionate allies?"

I let out a disgruntled sigh and lie back on the floor, tugging the itchy blanket over my head. "Passion is only helpful when it's accompanied by levelheadedness."

"Would you classify either of us as levelheaded?" Serik asks, and I can hear the smile in his voice. I grumble incoherently, and he laughs. "Don't give up on Ziva just yet. I think she might surprise us."

"I'm trying," I whisper after a beat.

"I know you are." Serik lies down beside me, close enough for me to see the slightest hint of pink returning beneath his freckles. Close enough I could reach over and gently smooth away the worry lines between his brows. And close enough to feel the balminess of his heat, which he doesn't have to share with anyone.

For the first time in weeks, he can truly rest.

My heart flutters with tenderness as I watch him settle into sleep.

All around us, the shepherds are drifting off or talking quietly, *happily*, about the food and accommodations. Praying we get to stay at least a little longer. Overhead, lightning bugs buzz in jars strung from the ceiling, knocking against the glass like drunkards. Every time they do, the night judders away from the flare of light, and my eyes begin to droop as I watch the playful back-and-forth. The sky deepens, darkens, and the tendrils of night dance down from the ceiling, gliding lower and lower until they settle around me like fog.

I've nearly drifted off to sleep, wrapped in their inky embrace, when the threads are suddenly, and clumsily, sucked away. Shock seizes my lungs—even more abrupt than having your blanket ripped off on a chilly night—and my eyes snap open. I force my body to hold perfectly still as I scan the room for Ziva, who chose not to return with us—until now.

When the entire group is sleeping.

Tingles ignite my throat, but I resist the urge to yank the

darkness out of her hands. Through slitted eyes, I watch her tiptoe between the sleeping shepherds, ducking down every so often. At last, she lifts a parcel, slings it over her shoulder, and makes her way back across the barrack.

The tension knotting my shoulders abates and I finally take a breath. She's just retrieving her belongings. But if that's the case, why creep around? She could have easily come while we were awake.

Suspicion hammers my breastbone as she slinks around the shepherds sleeping near the door. The buzzing in my limbs is intense. Overwhelming. *Get up*, it says. *This isn't right*. But my gaze darts over to Serik, resting peacefully beside me, and guilt weighs me down like a soaked wool blanket. I turn away from the door. Close my eyes. Command myself to go back to sleep and ignore Ziva. I don't care what she's doing. Following her will only stir up more trouble.

But as the door whispers shut, the churning in the pit of my stomach becomes unbearable—like a starving sand cat gnawing at my bones. It reminds me of the monster I was so certain lived inside me. A monster I spent two years hiding from. A monster that turned out to be nothing more than a natural instinct to fight and protect myself. A warning of sorts.

Yes, I need to trust my allies, but I also need to trust my gut. And my gut says Ziva's up to something.

I wiggle out of my itchy blanket and tiptoe to the door, not bothering to conceal myself with the night. First, because Ziva would notice. And second, because I don't need to. She's so focused on being silent and holding the darkness steady, I can trail her like an ordinary shadow.

She scampers across two swinging bridges and up an impossibly tall ladder to one of the largest treetop estates. I lag farther and farther behind, heaving for breath. This skies-forsaken city wasn't made for people with injuries like mine. Thankfully, I manage to keep the princess in my sights, despite my slow, methodical pace. If I push myself too hard, I'll stumble and fall and it will bring Ruya and every Namagaan soldier running. They'll think I'm spying—which I am. But not on them.

My ascent up the ladder is slow and agonizing. The rungs are steep and I have to rest every few steps. By the time I finally reach the top, I'm so out of breath and out of sorts, I don't notice Ziva's round face hovering directly in front of mine.

"Why are you following me?" she demands.

I yelp and nearly tumble down the ladder, dangling for a terrifying moment before my fingernails sink into the wood. "Why are you creeping around like a bandit?" I accuse once I'm nose to nose with Ziva again.

"I just needed to retrieve my bag." She slings the satchel off her shoulder and shakes it. "Is that all right with you?"

"That depends on why you felt the need to retrieve it while everyone was sleeping."

"Because Yatindra said it would be better not to upset the group. She said it would look like I'm abandoning you if I'm seen leaving with all of my things."

"Why would Yatindra care about upsetting us? She wasn't concerned about our feelings in the banquet hall."

Ziva glowers at me. "*She* is the reason we were admitted into Namaag. Show some gratitude. And I'm not the one who announced that we're uncertain where to go and what to do next. If anyone is deceiving the group, it's you." She hefts her pack back onto her shoulder. "Are we done here?"

"I only said that because I didn't want to trouble King Ihsan and seem too demanding when we'd only just arrived. And I don't want to negotiate an alliance in front of the entire caravan. You've seen how they are."

Ziva shakes her head like a disappointed parent. "You still

refuse to trust any of us. Does Serik know you're out here? Spying on me?"

"No. And he doesn't need to know. This is between you and me. Just please, *please*, for the love of the Lady and Father, don't do or say anything foolish. Don't sabotage our negotiations and don't utter a word about the Shoniin scout. No one can know we were spotted. Not even Yatindra."

"Would you like to accompany me inside to make sure I mind my manners?" Ziva points at the mansion towering above us.

I grumble and start back down the ladder.

Once I reach our barracks, I shimmy beneath my blanket and command myself to sleep, but I can't stop tossing and turning. Worrying about Ziva. And the Shoniin scout. And King Ihsan. And all of these shepherds, who look so grateful and content.

When the rustling of blankets finally marks the beginning of a new day, I feel even more exhausted than I did while trekking across the desert. Serik, however, sighs and stretches like a lazy cat—back arched and fingers kneading the blankets.

"I haven't slept that well since I 'accidentally' locked myself in the abba's chamber while cleaning his commode. Naturally, I had no choice but to sleep on his feathered bed while they dismantled the lock." He looks at me with dancing eyes, and I try to summon a scandalized smile, but he recoils with a jerk. "Bleeding skies, En, you look awful."

"Couldn't sleep," I say.

He scoots closer, making my skin prickle with heat. "You don't need to worry so much. Things are finally looking up. For the first time in weeks, the shepherds are calm and hopeful, and I think King Ihsan will be amenable to our proposition with a bit of convincing." He swings an arm around my shoulders and draws me even closer. "We're doing everything right."

Not me. I snuck out and followed Ziva just last night.
That's what I should say.

But I can't. Not when he's looking at me with those soft hazel eyes. Not when I can feel his breath skimming across my face. So I say nothing at all.

An hour later Ruya and her stone-faced comrades escort us back to the Marsh King's study, where we first met him. Today Ihsan has opted to wear a simple leaf-embroidered tunic rather than his dressing gown. A definite improvement, but I'd hardly call it regal. And he sits in a shabby leather armchair, so soft it nearly swallows him. A fire roars in the hearth and an array of honeyed scones and nutty muffins are laid out alongside a pitcher of liquid that smells like sap. Ihsan even smiles good-naturedly, as if we're visiting dignitaries rather than hunted refugees.

The ruse no longer works on me. Not after last night.

"Please, help yourself." Ihsan gestures to the spread, but my eyes immediately stray to the hundreds of framed insects adorning the walls. Creatures I've never seen before with needle-thin noses and long, spindly legs that have been stretched beyond their limits. Delicate, opalescent wings have been punctured and held down with pins. It has the macabre air of a torture chamber, enhanced by the presence of a small white alligator curled up like a cat beside Ihsan. Its pink, milky eyes watch us, and it hisses when we approach the king, showing rows of razor-like teeth.

"Hush, Alamacus," the Marsh King says with an indulgent tut. "These are our *guests*."

The word *guests* has never sounded quite so menacing.

I dart a glance at Serik, but he, of course, is already piling a plate with pastries and asking questions about the alligator as if it's the most fascinating thing in the world.

I give the reptile a wide berth, pluck a roll from the tray, and settle into one of the simple wooden chairs set out for the rest of us. Murtaugh, Yatindra, and Ziva sweep into the room a moment later. Murtaugh arranges himself beside the king like a stone-faced sculpture, but Yatindra and Ziva cross the study to join me. I scour Yatindra's face for any indication that she knows more than she should. Proof that Ziva let our secrets slip. But her face is placid, her smile serene, as they take the chairs across from me.

"I trust you slept well, Enebish?" Ziva asks through a large mouthful of scone.

"Like the dead. A thief could have crept in and robbed us and I wouldn't have known it," I say, even though I can feel Serik's confused gaze from across the room.

King Ihsan stands and clears his throat, motioning for Serik to take the seat beside me. "We have much to discuss, and since King Minoak can't participate in this council, his daughter has volunteered to represent him, under the guidance of her aunt and uncle. I presume you have no objection to this?" The Marsh King looks to us.

Oh, I have plenty of objections. Namely, we have no idea what she and Yatindra discussed last night. This could be a setup. But I shake my head.

"These are most unusual circumstances," King Ihsan continues, pacing slowly through the center of the room—me and Serik on one side, Ziva and Yatindra on the other. Murtaugh and Alamacus stand sentinel at either end. "Never, in the history of Namaag, have refugees from Verdenet and Ashkar appeared in our swamp, seemingly bound together in purpose. My question is, what is that purpose?"

Ziva hurries to swallow an enormous bite and scoots to the edge of her seat, but Ihsan holds up a hand. "I am well aware of your views, Miss Yimeni. You made them quite clear last night. I want to hear from *them*." He turns and peers down at me and Serik.

"I know these are strange circumstances, Your Majesty." Serik stands and smooths his tunic, even though it's wrinkled and soiled beyond hope. "And we shall elucidate on your every concern, but first we'd like to thank you for this munificent reception." He's using that strange, official tone again, and he tries to mimic the complicated bow the Namagaans perform when addressing their king—a combination of elaborate arm waving and crisscrossed legs. When the Namagaans do it, they look like a dove gently touching down on a branch. When Serik does it, he looks like an eagle crashing into a finch's nest.

It's so bumbling, it's kind of adorable. But I'm the only one who thinks so. Ziva, Yatindra, Murtaugh, and even the king himself, look a breath away from laughter. I want to smack the cruel smirks off their faces. At least Serik's making an effort.

You don't have to overcompensate, I want to tell him. *Just be yourself.*

But that, right there, is the problem. In Serik's mind, he has never been good enough.

"It all began with the shepherds freezing and starving on the winter grazing lands outside of Sagaan," Serik resumes. "They usually endure the winter months on those fields with the help of Sun Stokers, but the Sky King withheld the Sun Stokers this year, then refused to provide shelter or aid. So we led the group south, toward Verdenet—where Enebish is from—with the hope we could appeal to King Minoak for refuge, in return for our help retaking Lutaar City from the imperial governor."

"Who attempted to murder my father!" Ziva jumps to her

feet, but Yatindra places a firm hand on the girl's shoulder and pulls her back down.

"How did you know Lutaar City was seized?" Murtaugh asks. "We've heard nothing of it, and our relations are strong." He points to his Verdenese wife.

"There were rumors . . ." I say, hating how flimsy it sounds.

"You dragged hundreds of people across the grasslands during winter based on a rumor?" King Ihsan stares at us, his craggy face pinched with disapproval. But he doesn't understand. I knew it was more than just a rumor. Temujin may have lied about many things—nearly everything—but he wouldn't lie about Verdenet.

"Technically, it isn't a rumor if it's true," Ziva says matter-of-factly, and for the first time since meeting her, I appreciate her infuriating bravado. "The Sky King tried to have my father assassinated."

"How do you know it was the Sky King and not a random mercenary?" King Ihsan demands.

"Because I was there! *I* drove a blade into the assassin's back. I saw his blue-and-gold livery. The imperial governor's voice filled the downstairs hall, for skies' sake! They didn't even attempt to hide their treachery."

King Ihsan appraises the girl with greater interest. "*You* killed your father's assailant?"

Ziva crosses her arms and attempts to scowl, but her lip quivers.

"Even prior to the assassination attempt," I cut in, "the Sky King had been ravaging Verdenet—stripping the people of their culture and customs, forcing them to fight a war they had no stake in and no prayer of winning."

"It's true." Ziva nods at me from across the aisle. "We were never treated with respect or given the protection we were promised."

"And it's the same in Chotgor," I say. "They're more like conquered slaves than imperial citizens."

"Has this 'situation' in Chotgor been confirmed or is this another rumor?" Murtaugh asks archly, which earns him exasperated looks from me and Serik. "And I still don't see how this has anything to do with you and your shepherds."

"It has everything to do with us!" Heat radiates from Serik like the desert sun. "The Sky King exploited and turned his back on the shepherds, just as he's done in Verdenet and Chotgor. And he'll do the same to Namaag, too, if you sit back and do nothing to stop him. Our only prayer of salvaging our independence is together—united. The Imperial Army would lose three-quarters of its strength without the warriors conscripted from the Protected Territories. The empire would face the real possibility of falling to Zemya, putting us in a position to make demands of the Sky King."

There's a good chance we'll fall to Zemya no matter *who* unites, but I don't mention this. It might prompt Ihsan to continue to side with the Sky King. The alliance has kept his people safe in the past.

"How is any of this Namaag's concern?" Murtaugh says. "If the other territories are being mistreated, it's no one's fault but their own. They shouldn't have allowed the Sky King to gain such a firm hold. Make him respect you."

"We didn't *allow* anything!" I think Ziva's going to throw her half-eaten scone at her uncle, but Yatindra grabs her wrist.

"Breathe, Ziva. Remember what we talked about."

"The rest of the continent doesn't have the same bargaining power as Namaag," Serik explains, staying remarkably composed. "The Sky King is dependent on your aqueducts, so he's had to respect you, but don't believe for one second that you're safe. Once he's drained Chotgor and Verdenet of people and resources, the Sky King *will* come for you."

"You cannot scare us into aligning with you based on these unfounded, and frankly ridiculous, claims," Murtaugh says sharply, as if that's the end of the conversation.

But King Ihsan taps his fingers against the side of his face and paces silently for a moment. "I don't mean to sound dismissive," he finally says, "but if your claims are true, do you honestly expect to succeed with an army of ravaged, war-torn people? Greater numbers do not always amount to greater strength."

I force my lips into a smile, but my face feels as if it's fracturing into tiny pieces. Because our situation is even grimmer than he knows. "I know we can succeed," I say, "but only with Namaag's strength and leadership."

Murtaugh shakes his head sternly and leans forward to whisper into the king's ear. Ihsan's dark brow lowers and the tangle of dread in my gut knots tighter. If he doesn't agree, we're finished. Dead at the hands of the Sky King or the Zemyans. It hardly matters which.

Finally Ihsan says, "Allow me to consider it for a time. The Sky King has been slow to respond to my missives. And our shipment of Ashkarian goods hasn't arrived for two weeks. I'd like to make some inquiries."

Murtaugh looks like he's going to crash into the swamp like a felled tree. "Your Majesty!"

Yatindra glares at her husband while Ziva flops back into her chair with a satisfied grin.

King Ihsan ignores all of it. "I also wish to send scouts to ascertain the conditions in the other territories and validate your claims before I make my decision."

Serik nods diplomatically, but I squirm in my chair and blurt, "That will take weeks."

"Is that a problem?" Ihsan turns back to me.

Serik's fingers clamp around my wrist and tighten with

warning. "No, of course not," I whisper, lowering my chin.

"It isn't wise to rush such important decisions," the Marsh King continues. "If we are going to form a tightly knit alliance, I want to know you as well as I know my own kin. So, please, make yourselves at home in the treetops." He holds out his arms as if he's offering us a magnificent gift. But the glint in his bark-brown eyes feels less like an invitation and more like a warning.

Or a threat.

CHAPTER TWELVE

GHΘA

I STARE AT THE ZEMYAN SORCERER, HATING HIS SMUG, thin-lipped smile. How he glances over one shoulder, then the other, making a show of looking for my ice dagger. He even pats the blue papered walls and rustles the elaborate tapestries adorning the throne room, though it's obvious that the blade I forged is gone.

It *vanished*.

But how?

Zemyans can manipulate the weave of the world to conceal things that do exist or to create replicas of things that don't. But never, in twelve years of battle, have I seen a Zemyan stamp out something that I know for a fact was corporeal.

It isn't possible.

Yet, Kartok stands before me, unharmed.

"How did you do that?" I shout.

"How did I do what?" His grin becomes even more oily. "Did you misplace something, Commander?"

I raise my hands and direct every morsel of strength I have

left into my palms, to forge another blade and prove I'm not losing my mind. But my cold is so depleted, steam instead of ice rises from my hands.

Kartok lowers into one of the ornate council chairs and crosses his long legs, hands resting on his knee. "You and your sister are so alike. Rage all you'd like, Ice Herald. It only benefits me."

I scramble to my feet and lunge at him with a furious roar. "I am *nothing* like my sister! I will never use my power for you!" He's so thin and rangy, I should be able to snap him in half, but I'm even slower and clumsier than a magic-barren warrior. He slides his chair a fraction to the left, and I hit the slippery floor. My momentum carries me into the wall. The crunch of my nose reverberates through my skull, and as I curse and writhe, a hanging tapestry rattles loose. It covers me like a death shroud, making me scream even louder, because I'm nose to nose with the Sky King. His face flawlessly rendered in peach and gold threads.

Condemning me. Smothering me.

I fight against the cloth. It's surprisingly heavy, or maybe I've become pitifully weak. Either way, I can't claw my way free. Can't hide from those searing eyes.

You failed me. You failed Ashkar.

Finally Kartok ambles over and peels back the tapestry. He looks down at me, not even attempting to suppress his peevish grin. "All of this flailing is quite unnecessary. I only want to run a few little tests. You'll hardly feel a thing."

"I'd rather skip to the part where you kill me." I'd been so certain he would execute me as soon as we arrived in Kareke-mish—make a spectacle of my death for his empress and the throng of bloodthirsty Zemyans. So when it didn't happen, I was momentarily relieved. But now I see it for the misfortune it is. I don't want to die. But I want to be Kartok's test subject even less.

He circles me like the sharks undoubtedly prowling the water surrounding this prison and retrieves a waterskin from the folds of his robe. "I presume you're familiar with tales of our sacred hot spring?" he asks.

I eye the waterskin swinging like a pendulum from his bony fingers. "If by 'sacred hot spring' you mean 'diabolical pool of unnatural magic,' yes."

Kartok doesn't take the bait. He stands taller and speaks to the ceiling with reverence that borders on fanaticism. "We may not be born with power, but that doesn't make our abilities any less valid. Quite the opposite. Zemya created our powers through persistence and innovation. Characteristics she passed along to her people—we are hungry and hardworking because we have to be. Instead of hoarding Her power and bestowing it on a select few, Zemya gave each of us *equal* opportunity to succeed by transferring Her magic into the hot spring and allowing all to drink. We are the masters of our own fate, depending on how hard we are willing to work."

I snort. "Giving power to all is a recipe for disaster. *Clearly.*" I wave my hand at the general.

"Is it? Or are you afraid of what that would mean for you? How it would feel to be as ordinary as the rest of us? There's no denying the strength that comes from struggle. Tell me, Commander, who is the better warrior: One with natural abilities but a poor work ethic, since they've never had to try, or a naturally weaker warrior who throws everything they have into training, who finds ways to counteract their shortcomings, who has to fight, tooth and nail, for every little success? Who would you rather have at your side in battle?"

When I don't answer, Kartok crouches in front of me. I can smell the dust and sweat of the road on his robes, the overpowering tang of garlic on his breath. I press myself against the wall and turn my head. But that only draws him closer. His face hovers a finger's breadth from mine.

"All 'power' is created by someone or something initially," he says. "What does it matter if it was born of the Lady and Father or one of Their children? In the end, they are one flesh. Zemya's power is Their power. She shouldn't have been condemned and banished."

I look directly into his unsettling blue eyes. "Zemya got what She deserved. And I don't see what any of this has to do with me."

He grabs a fistful of my hair, wrenches my head back, and forces the waterskin into my mouth. The liquid gushes down my throat, thick and warm and sulfuric. Like the sweltering rot that hangs over a battlefield. I cough and heave and spit, suddenly boiling inside my skin. Yet my body twitches and shivers. My tongue is drier than the stale jerky in the disgusting ration sacks reserved for lesser warriors.

Kartok chuckles as I claw at the neckline of my tunic. "Do you feel anything unusual?"

"If your hot-spring water is so precious and powerful," I finally growl through the pain, "why give it to me? Why bestow me with more power?"

Kartok touches the heel of his palm to the bottom of his chin in a strange religious gesture I've seen many times at the war front. "Because I have perfect faith in my goddess. I know that Zemya would never allow Her magic to strengthen you. In fact, I predict it will do the opposite."

"I thought She wants 'all people to be equal,'" I retort.

Kartok slaps my cheek. "Summon your ice."

"Now I don't want to."

"Summon. Your. Power."

"I'd rather die."

The truth is, I don't know if I could summon the ice even if I wanted to. I was hot and depleted and exhausted before Kartok poisoned me with his goddess's magic. But I'm not about to give him the satisfaction of thinking he won. And part of me is terrified to know if it worked—if his hot-spring water can actually strip me of my gift. So I focus on the blue vein bulging in the center of Kartok's forehead, and smirk. I have an insatiable desire to pinch it between my fingers and pop it like a bloated leech.

"You do not want to anger me, Commander," he warns.

"Oh, but I do."

His hands fly toward me, and the same wrenching pain that incapacitated me in the prison wagon grips my tongue. Only now I don't crumple. Because I know it isn't real. If I don't believe his lies, they won't be able to hurt me. Kartok's invisible grip tightens, but the pain doesn't increase. It doesn't lessen, either, but I am slowly gaining ground against the illusion. Learning to fight it.

"Very well." Kartok whips a long double-edge blade from his robes and throws it at my face. It flies faster than I can react, even if I wasn't injured and exhausted, and the razor tip sinks deep into my right eye. Pain detonates through my skull, shooting and stabbing. I scream and clutch the wound, certain it's deep enough to kill me. But blood doesn't wet my fingers. And there's no hilt protruding from my skull.

Another illusion. This one ten times more painful than his trick with my tongue. It almost makes me feel a twinge of guilt for the thousands of icy daggers I've rammed into Zemyan skulls over the years. Except, of course, they deserved them.

"Next time the knife won't be an illusion," Kartok warns, drawing back the folds of his azure robe to reveal an identical weapon. Only, this one rings as the steel leaves the scabbard and the edge is cold and sharp as he jabs it beneath my chin.

I lick my chapped lips and stare into his unnaturally blue eyes. Demon eyes. "We both know you're not going to kill me."

"That doesn't mean I can't make you wish you were dead."

"I have an extremely high tolerance for pain."

Kartok leans against the blade, and drops of blood trickle from my throat. "There's more than one type of pain, Commander." He returns the knife to his hip and fiddles with little knobs hidden in the wall until the glass passageway reappears behind him. "Get some rest."

A dangerous smile steals across his lips, and as the throne room solidifies between us, the low rumble of laughter fills the room.

My stomach lurches into my chest.

Because the laughter isn't Kartok's.

It's the Sky King's.

I'd recognize his voice anywhere.

I *know* he isn't here, but I whip around to check because it sounds so real. So close—wild, unhinged laughter that borders on crying. It seems to be coming from the gilded throne, and as I creep toward it, the Sky King slowly materializes, fading into existence as if through thick fog. Those eyes that miss nothing. The merciless slash of his brows. That thin, unforgiving mouth.

"You." He stands and moves toward me, and that's when I notice the bright strip of gore staining the side of his robe. How his fox fur crown sits askew on his head—the back half of his skull crushed. Blood bubbles from his lips, thick as tar, when he speaks. "You failed me. You failed Ashkar."

I close my eyes and chant, "It isn't real, it isn't real, it isn't real." But it *feels* so real, my body refuses to believe the logic from my brain. I can smell the king's expensive cologne. I can even hear the imperceptible hitch of his step from an old war wound that only I know about.

"How does it feel to be responsible for the fall of an empire?" he prods. "To be the biggest disappointment Ashkar has ever known? What will your parents think?"

I try to fight it off, but the woody scent of Papá's pipe smoke and the citrusy punch of Mamá's orange water perfume drift past my nose. And then they're there, standing before me. Sobbing.

I cough so hard, I vomit.

"Their fall from society will be catastrophic," the Sky King continues. "Not only did I perish under your watch, you were captured during the Zemyan siege—when commanders are *never* captured—because your own soldiers saw your weakness and ineptitude and turned against you. Your parents will be shunned. Humiliated. They'll regret ever having a daughter—*if* they survive the siege, that is. . . ."

His laughter resumes, boring into my brain like a spear tip. I feel my throat closing. My eyes stinging. I have to get away. I throw myself against the walls, pounding and poking, desperate to find the invisible knobs.

After what feels like days, I retreat to the farthest corner of the hall and huddle into a ball. Teeth clenched. Palms over my ears. But that only provides partial relief, because I'm surrounded by eyes. All of those damnable eyes, peering down at me from the dangling masks. Only now they're no longer the eyes of Ashkar's greatest warriors. They're eyes I stared into every day for over a decade. The eyes of my Kalima warriors—stripped of their humanity and every shred of respect, leaving only a reflection of those final, terrible moments on the ice bridge. Varren's regretful but rigid gaze. Weroneka not even bothering to look back. Eshwar's sneer and Karwani's disgust. Even little Reza, my page, who wasn't trapped in Papá's office and who has never looked on me with anything but adoration, blinks round, wet eyes. Bright with betrayal. As if I ran my saber through his gut.

I've never seen magic like this. Not in all my years on the battlefront. I knew the Zemyans could disguise their faces and manipulate their weapons, but I didn't know they could create the illusion of entirely different worlds. And trap me within them.

The painted walls press closer; the king's laughter peals louder. I rock in the corner. Spewing profanities. Praying Kartok's magic will eventually fade. Power always has a limit. But the onslaught continues, and the images filling my head are more horrifying than any amount of bodily torture he could have inflicted.

My anguish is so heavy, it feels like I'm sinking through the floor. Like I couldn't possibly descend any lower. Which is when the specter of Enebish arrives to haunt me. She drags herself toward me through red-stained snow, her right arm nearly severed and her leg flopping bonelessly. "Are you happy?" she croaks, blood burbling from her lips. "You destroyed me—and yourself—for nothing."

"*You* are to blame!" I scream back at her. "You were trying to usurp me, humiliate me. No matter that I saved you and trained you and gave you everything. None of this would have happened if I'd left you to die in Verdenet."

As my mother counseled me to do.

"I'm not certain this is the best idea," she said when I returned with Enebish from the war front. She paced the halls and picked at her nails while our maids scrubbed the soot and dirt from Enebish's skin and scrounged for clothes small enough to fit her emaciated frame. Finally Mamá pulled me into Papá's study and lowered her voice. "We know nothing about this Southerner. Or her family. And we've already endured so many rumors by taking in your cousin. She's not even from Ashkar. . . ."

But I wouldn't take no for an answer. Because I couldn't forget the way Enebish looked at me when I lifted her from the ashes and onto Tabana. How her dark eyes memorized my face, full of wonder and admiration. How her small fingers traced the grooves in my armor. It was nearly as intoxicating as my parents' praise. I wanted everyone in the empire to look at me like that. To need me like that.

But they were all fooling me. Using me. Taking, taking, taking until they bled me dry.

I stagger to my feet and run at the Sky King's throne. I can't bear to look at it any longer. I can't stand *any* of this for another second. With a scream, I thrust my palms forward and a thin layer of frost varnishes the velvet cushion and goldwork of the throne. Not enough to shatter it, but enough to prove Zemya's vile magic didn't taint me. Not fully, anyway. I try again, but the sputter of cold vanishes the moment it leaves my hands. Growling with frustration, I pick up one of the small wooden chairs that line the wall and dash it against the throne. Fragments of wood spray into the air and scrape my face, harming me more than the throne, but it feels good to do *something*. So I grab chair after chair and continue smashing them.

Once they're all obliterated, I take up a fragment of wood, step onto the seat of the throne—grinning savagely at the smudges my boots leave on the indigo cushion—and swing at the hanging masks.

The translucent strings may look flimsy, but they slice my hands like razor wire. Blood falls in bright crimson spots across the floor and the golden arms of the throne. It's horrific. And glorious. I scream louder. Strike harder. Smashing face after face of warriors I once looked up to. Warriors I was certain I would eclipse in greatness.

It isn't until the final mask falls, and the symphony of shattering plaster fades, that I hear a throat clear behind me.

I whip around, fully expecting to find Kartok smirking in the corner, but it's a Zemyan girl with silvery hair bundled into a topknot, a filthy apron strapped around her waist. Her mouth hangs open and her pale eyes gape at me. As if *I'm* the barbarian.

I would be mortified if I had any dignity left. Since I don't, I plunk down on the throne, kick my legs over one armrest, and tilt my head back against the other, face up to the muraled ceiling. Hoping she'll go away if I don't respond. Like the mangy opossums in Namaag that pretend to be dead as a method of self-preservation.

The girl shifts from foot to foot and holds up a steaming tin cup. "I'm Hadassah. I've brought you food." Her Ashkarian is slow and her accent is thick, but she seems proud of her effort.

"You can't possibly think I'd eat or drink anything else," I snap back.

"I'll just leave it here, then. In case you change your mind." With trembling hands, she sets the mug down and steps back. But then she stops and says, "Let me know if you need anything else." As if I'm a guest rather than a prisoner.

"Are you mocking me?" I swing my legs around and lean forward, perched on the edge of the throne like a coiled snake. "Because I definitely *need* several things. I *need* to get out of this prison. I *need* to prove my warriors made the biggest mistake of their lives when they betrayed me, and I *need* to conquer this repellant country to salvage my reputation, but you can't help me with any of that, can you, Hadassah?"

She flinches and looks down at her feet. "No. But if you answer a few questions, I can unlock your manacles."

I make a show of looking her up and down. "*You* have the key?"

She reaches into her apron pocket and procures an old brass key, which she swings back and forth.

My entire body tenses. My mind screams to attack and take it from her, but my battered limbs don't rise to the call. "What questions could *you* possibly have?"

"What is the general trying to accomplish?"

The laughter that explodes from my mouth is sharp and cynical. "He sent you in here to trick me into saying something he can use against me, didn't he?"

Hadassah shakes her head furiously. "He's hurt me, too." She unfastens the tie of her colorless blouse and wiggles one shoulder free. She turns to show me the long, raised scars cutting down her back. As if I care. As if it will foster some sort of camaraderie between us. She could have gotten those scars anywhere. They're probably an illusion! If Kartok did make them, she already knows everything she needs to about him.

"Is it your power he's after?" she presses. "Rumor has it he's been obsessed with capturing a Kalima warrior for years, but it's next to impossible, since they never leave their comrades behind."

"Enough!"

The blood drains from her already pale face. "Sorry if that's a touchy subject, but—"

"Even if I knew his aim, do you think I'd tell you anything? I don't see why any of this matters to a servant."

Her lips pinch into a scowl. As if she honestly expected her sweet-faced simpering to soften me. It wouldn't have worked before, and it certainly won't work now. I'm heartless, soulless, friendless. Nothing but vengeance and fury wrapped in skin.

"Be gone!" I yell, raising my palms. There isn't a breath of cold left within me, but the girl doesn't know that. She cries and sprints for the glass tunnel while I laugh and wish her good riddance.

It's only after she's gone, when the walls of the fabricated throne room are hardening between us, sealing the only exit, that I realize my mistake.

The wasted opportunity.

I didn't try to escape. I didn't even get the key to my manacles.

The Sky King's laughter refills the echoing hall, taunting me, mocking me, driving me closer, every second, toward the cliffs of insanity.

CHAPTER THIRTEEN

ENEBISH

Murtaugh and Yatindra storm out of King Ihsan's study, thin lipped and tight jawed, dragging Ziva behind them. As if the Marsh King's decision to *consider* our proposal personally offends them. Ziva, on the other hand, pumps her fist and throws a triumphant smile at us as they tug her through the door.

"I don't understand why they're so angry," I murmur to Serik as we follow them out into the muggy morning. The sun is already stabbing through the canopy, and a horde of ravenous mosquitos flock to us like the hummingbirds buzzing around the flower boxes. Serik smashes one of the long-legged insects between his palms and proudly opens his hands to show me the mangled carcass. Then he blows it toward Murtaugh's and Yatindra's backs.

"They're like children, throwing a tantrum because they didn't get their way. That vice chancellor, Murtaugh, thinks quite highly of himself. I doubt he's ever supported a plan he didn't come up with. And I doubt the king disagrees with him often. I almost feel sorry for Ziva's aunt, being shackled to such an ornery narcissist."

"Why do you think *she's* so upset? You'd think she'd be grateful that Ihsan is considering lending aid to Minoak and Verdenet. Her brother and her country."

"She's probably just worried and overwhelmed," Serik says as we start down the nearest rope bridge. It sways beneath our feet, and I grip the woven railing, terrified the flimsy thing is going to collapse. "Her brother was nearly assassinated and lies motionless in the infirmary, she must care for her strong-willed niece, and she just learned her home country is in peril."

I nod as we watch the three of them vanish into another mansion several trees over, slamming the door behind them.

"Murtaugh's a lost cause, but I think Yatindra will come around with time—and perhaps a little encouragement." Serik peers over at me.

I narrow my eyes. "What do you want me to do?"

"Nothing much. I just think now would be an excellent time to start training Ziva. Show the Namagaans the strength we have to offer as allies. And our willingness to share those advantages."

I shove past Serik, purposely knocking him against the flimsy railing, and stomp to the next platform.

"Does that mean you'll consider it?" He chases after me.

"It means your suggestion doesn't merit a response. I'm *not* training Ziva. You saw how rash and unpredictable she is, throwing starfire when she doesn't have the slightest idea how to control it. I won't be responsible for that."

"If you trained her, she would know not to do such things."

I spear him with a death glare.

"And if she *did*," he relents, "she would at least know how to do it safely. Just think about it, En. We've nearly accomplished what we set out to do, and this could cement the alliance. King Ihsan has agreed to investigate our claims, but he's much more likely to view the findings in a good light if we appear invested."

I whirl around and poke Serik in the chest. "What happens when the Shoniin and Zemyans show up before Ihsan's scouts return? We both know they're coming; we don't have weeks to wait. And once they attack Namaag, nothing we've said or done will make a sheep's dung worth of difference. So I'd rather not waste my time. Or compromise my integrity."

"Keep your voice down," Serik growls, pulling me away from the homes and shops built into the enormous trunk of the tree we're in. All around us, Namagaans bustle about the day's chores, so he leads me down another bridge, deeper into the canopy, where there are fewer ears to overhear. "We don't know if or when the Shoniin and Zemyans are coming, so we proceed with the plan until then. It's our only option. And you've required so many sacrifices of me and the shepherds, it would be nice if—"

I slam to a halt and gape at Serik, the bridge swinging erratically around us. "You don't think I've made sacrifices?"

"I never said that."

"That's sure how it sounded. . . ."

Serik drags his fingers through his hair and puffs out his freckled cheeks. "Burning skies, En. Of course you've made sacrifices. I just meant . . . Never mind. We should be celebrating the fact that King Ihsan agreed to consider our proposal, not fighting over Ziva. I'm sorry," he adds as I resume limping across the bridge.

"I'm sorry too," I grudgingly admit. "I just hate feeling like I'm disappointing you. I wish I could be the courageous mentor you want me to be. But I can't."

"You're everything I want you to be," Serik insists, reaching for my hand.

But the words sound as hollow as the flute reeds whistling in the swamp below, and I shove my hands into my pockets.

The shepherds don't utter a word of complaint when Serik announces we'll be staying in Namaag for a time. In fact, their joyous cries and jubilant hugs are nearly as excessive as when we first arrived in Uzul. It bothers me—even though I'm just as relieved. We desperately need the rest, and it's a miracle King Ihsan is considering our proposal. But as I watch the shepherds gleefully unpack their trunks, unease burrows beneath my skin, hollowing me out like a brood of termites feeding on these ancient trees.

The need for my Book of Whisperings is bone-deep—a twisting pain in the center of my chest. With it, I could ask the First Gods directly what to do, if we're still on the right path. I'd even be grateful for something as simple as a prayer doll. Anything to soften the razor edges of doubt. But since my Book of Whisperings was lost on the winter grazing lands, and my prayer doll burned in Kartok's *xanav*, I have to find another way to commune with my gods.

"I'm going for a walk," I tell Serik.

"Do you want some company?"

"Do you mind if I go alone? I just need a moment of quiet. . . ." I nod at the shepherds, pressed all around us.

"Go. I'll be here when you get back." He smiles, but it's thin and watery and doesn't reach his eyes.

Guilt nibbles the edges of my heart but not enough to stop me from fleeing the barracks.

Outside, the sun shines directly overhead, and warm light sifts through the canopy of leaves, dappling my skin and shimmering across the wooden platforms. I pull the humid air into my lungs and let it out slowly, feeling instantly lighter as I strike out across the nearest bridge. I don't have a particular destination in mind, and I don't know where anything is located in this treetop kingdom anyway, so I drift from platform to platform, past bustling markets and quieter clusters of homes. The Namagaans eye me curiously. A few offer tentative smiles or nod politely in passing, but no one attempts to talk to me. I'm so grateful for the reprieve—to not be summoned or scolded or shunned—I could cry.

After wandering for a good hour, I find myself standing in front of a long, boxy building that's unremarkable save for the bundle of aloe leaves hanging over the door. The plant is expensive and rare, since it grows only in Namaag, so only the best imperial healers can afford to carry it on the battlefield.

I smile up at the bright green parcel. The Lady and Father always know just what I need. They have led me to the infirmary. To my king.

If Minoak is awake, he can fix all of this. He will be more forceful in his negotiations with King Ihsan and ensure we march on Verdenet before the Shoniin and Zemyans arrive. Seeing him alive and well will remind the shepherds that we never planned to hide out in the marshlands while the rest of the empire crumbles.

I limp up to the door, more eager than ever to see my king, but as I reach for the handle, the door swings inward and I stumble into a sobbing mess of a woman. Her turquoise dress is rumpled, the makeup across her eyebrows is smeared, and she catches herself against the door frame, as if her legs are too weak to support her weight.

She looks so disheveled, a long moment passes before I realize it's Yatindra.

"I'm sorry. I didn't know anyone was leaving," I say.

"Are you okay?"

Is Minoak okay? I try to peer around her into the infirmary.

Yatindra glowers down at me, nearly a full hand taller. "My brother still hasn't stirred, so no, I am not okay."

"Oh." I look away, trying to mask my disappointment. "I was hoping he'd be much improved by now. We all were."

She gives a harsh little laugh. "Don't pretend he matters to you."

"What are you talking about? He's my king. Of course he matters."

"He matters inasmuch as you can use him. You don't care about the actual man beneath the crown."

"Why would you think that?" *We* rescued Minoak. We brought him here to recover. And we're attempting to restore him to the throne of her home country. We're on the same side, yet she swipes beneath her eyes and shoves past me, shaking her head with disgust.

I want to grab her long cattail hair and yank her back. Call out her ingratitude. But as I watch her storm away, I think about what Serik said—how worried and overwhelmed and afraid she must be—so I take a deep breath and limp after her.

I can be the bigger person. I can bridge this gap.

"Wait!" I call.

She hesitates before turning. "What?"

"I recognize how difficult all of this must be for you. We arrived with a lot of somber news. I don't blame you for resenting us."

She waves a dismissive hand. "I'm just grateful my brother and niece are alive. And I'd like to ensure they stay that way."

"We're united in that purpose."

"Are we?" Yatindra challenges.

Her skepticism makes me want to scream. "Yes! And it would be considerably easier if your husband didn't oppose our propositions to King Ihsan."

She scoffs. "You're missing the entire point." Then she turns in a whirl of black hair and turquoise fabric and strides away.

I mumble curses at her back. What more does she expect us to do? She's even more impossible than Ziva.

I stomp back to the infirmary, my bad leg throbbing painfully—and for nothing. I extended an olive branch, I tried to put myself out there, and Yatindra spat in my face.

At least I can tell Serik I tried.

Inside the infirmary, I jump at the sudden surge of darkness. Only two jars of lightning bugs illuminate the space, giving the night plenty of shadowed corners to occupy. The threads welcome me with nips and nuzzles as they usher me down the long hall. Rope beds line the walls and incense sticks burn on little golden plates, filling the air with cinnamon and orange smoke, but it isn't enough to overwhelm the fetid tang of sickness.

A few of the beds are occupied with Namagaans—some resting with their eyes closed, others moaning and tossing with pain—but I make my way to the end of the hall, where two orange-clad sentries stand watch over a bed that's finer than the rest. The frame is made of wood, the mattress is stuffed with feathers, and a sumptuous scarlet blanket covers the gray-haired figure underneath.

The guards jump to attention when they notice me and position themselves between me and King Minoak, spears crossed like bars. "Visitors aren't permitted," one of them says.

"I know for a fact that he just had a visitor." I point to the door Yatindra exited.

"She's the king's sister."

"And I am his subject." I gesture to my dark hair and golden skin and tattooed calves, which indisputably mark me as Verdenese. "I'm the one who rescued him and brought him here."

"Unfortunately, we cannot permit anyone other than the royal family near His Majesty."

"By whose decree?" My voice quickly rises. "I just want to talk to him. It's important. I'm responsible for so many—"

"It isn't possible. He's not even awake."

"I have to see him!" It feels like my head has been shoved into the swamp and my lungs are screaming for air. I hadn't realized how desperately I needed to see my king until now. When it's being denied. The hovering threads of darkness pull taut and shiver against my fingers. Prodding. Ready. "Please!" I beg.

The other patients gape over at us, and the healer bustling between their beds looks ready to throw his instrument tray at my head.

"Go!" The guards thrust their spears at my face. I have to make a choice: concede and retreat or blacken the entire infirmary and do as I please.

I know what I *want* to do, but being belligerent won't foster trust and convince King Ihsan to join us. And there's no reason to force my agenda if King Minoak isn't awake to hear what I have to say.

The agitated tendrils of darkness nip at my cheek. *Why must he be awake to receive your message?*

"Fine," I say to the guards, making a show of tramping back the way I came. After they slam the door behind me, I noiselessly sneak back around the building and situate myself beneath the rear windows of the infirmary, where Minoak rests.

I wrap myself in shadows, perch on a branch near the window—which is open to let in fresh air—and summon the threads of darkness from the room. I may not be able to speak to my king in a traditional sense, but that doesn't mean I can't express my worries and needs. Plant the seeds of our rebellion while he sleeps, so when he finally does wake, he'll think the ideas were his own.

It's exactly what I did to the Sky King all those years ago, when I was lobbying to be named commander of the Kalima warriors. The choice that set so much of this madness into motion. Those same feelings of urgency and need twine through me now, tingeing my voice as I whisper into the darkness.

I sing fragments of old desert songs, relay my plans to free the Protected Territories and unite against the Sky King. I spare no detail about the war front and Temujin and the Zemyans. Anything I can think of to combat the inevitable barrage of opinions he'll be faced with when he does wake.

"Please, let it be soon," I pray as I send the ebony tendrils back through the window. I watch them wash over Minoak's face and settle around him like smoke. Then I ease out of the tree and slowly make my way back to our barracks. Turning everything over in my mind. Begging the First Gods to show me the truth. And the path forward.

"You were gone for an eternity," Serik says when I finally hobble through the door. "I was beginning to think you fell into the swamp. We were just about to send a search party." His tone is playful, but he eyes me expectantly. Waiting for me to tell him where I went. Why it took so long.

For half a second I consider spewing everything. What would he think of Yatindra's coldness—despite my efforts to be kind—and the guards' refusal to let me see Minoak? But, as always, our cabin is crowded to the point of suffocation; anything I tell Serik, the entire caravan will hear. And if I tell him about Yatindra, he'll think I followed her to pick a fight. He'll be frustrated that I angered the guards in the infirmary, who could report the incident to Ihsan.

Nothing good will come from Serik knowing the truth. Not until I figure out if the reasons behind Yatindra's hostility are cause for suspicion, or if I'm just reading into everything because I'm broken. Ruined by the past. Unfit to be trusted because I can't trust in return—not even my allies.

A painful scowl twists my face as I ease onto the floor and painstakingly untie my boots. "I walked farther than I should have, so it was difficult to get back. I ended up going down to water level for a while to soak my leg," I lie.

"I'm sorry again . . . about what I said earlier," Serik says quietly. "I shouldn't have pushed you about Ziva."

"It had nothing to do with that," I assure him, but he still insists on helping me with my boots and lifts me onto my bed. He rubs my feet and brings the food he set aside for me, since I missed our midday meal.

"I'll do better," he promises. Making me feel like the most despicable creature on the continent. Even worse than the bloodsucking mosquitos.

But I paint a smile on my face and murmur, "So will I."

CHAPTER FOURTEEN

GHΘA

I SPEND THE REST OF THE NIGHT INSPECTING THE WALL THAT opens into a passageway. If that mousy little servant has the power and intellect to access it, I should certainly be able to manage it. But no matter how I scrape and claw, no matter how much thick blue paint jams painfully beneath my finger-nails, I find nothing. And now my hands are slick with blood, my wrists rubbed raw from the manacles, making the search even more impossible.

"I'm not surprised," the Sky King's voice drawls from everywhere and nowhere. "You have always been lacking, incompetent."

I shred every window curtain in response. Not that it does any good—the king isn't real and neither are the curtains—but it passes the time and helps to block out the specters hell-bent on driving me mad.

Once I've destroyed everything within reach and yelled myself hoarse at the unrelenting illusions, I crouch beside the invisible door to wait. I don't care who comes through the tunnel next. I'm going to incapacitate them with ice, or the sheer force of my desperation, and get myself out of here. Then I'll assassinate the empress and general supreme and send this hideous palace crashing into the sea. After which the people of Ashkar will gladly welcome me back—the savior of the empire—and the Kalima warriors will spend the rest of their lives wishing they hadn't betrayed me.

After what feels like years, but is probably no more than the length of a night, the door slides into existence. My mind snaps to attention and I lift my hands, practically crowing with relief when Hadassah, rather than Kartok, shuffles into the room.

I launch myself at her like a snow panther at the end of the great freeze—wild and half mad with hunger. My fingers sink into her flesh and I shove every morsel of cold from my core into her body. But her skin only cools a fraction. Her lips part with a scream as she hits the floor. The bowl of sludge she's carrying falls and a lumpy spatter coats the wall, not frozen in the least.

It's hardly the ambush I imagined, but it's good enough. I scramble over her as if she's a bloodied corpse on the battlefield, and lunge for the tunnel.

"Stop!" she shouts.

I run faster, flinging myself through the door as it begins to slide shut. I almost think I've made it, when Hadassah's fingers close around my ankle. She yanks me back with surprising strength and I slam into the ground, unable to catch myself due to the blasted manacles. She tugs me swiftly back into the room, as if I'm the scrawny maid and she's the seasoned warrior.

"Let go!" I kick at her face.

"I'm trying to help you!" she snaps as she dodges my strikes. "He's coming. He'll recapture you immediately. And kill me."

Her warning knocks me so off balance, she's able to snatch the bowl of muck, vault over me, and disappear down the passageway before I can recover.

The door clicks shut behind her, and Kartok appears less than a minute later. "Good morning, Commander. How are you feeling this fine day?" he asks, even though the answer is clear.

I look like death. And worse, I *feel* like death. But I bare my teeth and say, "These accommodations are most restful. I feel stronger than ever." I wag my fingers and a flurry of frost spirals between us. Just a trace, and it melts immediately, but enough to prove I'm not powerless. That his goddess wasn't strong enough to rip the ice from me. Not even when it's already depleted.

Kartok's expression darkens. Before I can blink, he's on top of me, knees jabbing into my shoulders, hands forcing another waterskin between my lips, tipping more of the scalding hot-spring water down my throat. He pours until the vessel is empty and water dribbles down my chin. Then he looms over me, breathing hard. "How do you feel *now*?"

The burning sensation invades my body faster and hotter and stronger than before. I feel like I'm spitting flames. But I can still feel the ice nestled deep within my chest. It's shrunken— a tiny stone that used to be a boulder—but it's there. Proof that Zemyans have never been and will never be as strong as Ashkarians. Not even their goddess.

"Well?" Kartok digs his pointy knees into my shoulders.

I reach out with shaking fingers and touch the toe of Kartok's slipper. His stubbled cheeks redden as a beautiful lacy crusting of frost overtakes the beadwork. I want to gloat, but only a rasp of breath escapes my scalded throat. Finally I manage to wheeze, "Do you still have *perfect faith* in Zemya?"

"Do not speak ill of the goddess!" Kartok flings his arms to the sides and the sky-blue walls of the throne room splinter like broken glass. I close my eyes and take a final, gasping breath, waiting for seawater to rush in and pummel me. But the deluge doesn't come. Not a single drop of blue-black water seeps through the cracks. Instead I see moving shadows and refracted light. I hear low murmurs and dragging chains. I *knew* I couldn't be the only prisoner, but the replica of the throne room is so convincing, I had almost started to believe the sorcerer's lies.

Now I see the truth: I am surrounded by dozens of identical glass cells, most of which are occupied by Ashkarian warriors. Though, I do spy a few gray-clad Shoniin and even some Zemyans. They are always pale, sickly looking people, but these Zemyans' veins glow blue beneath their translucent skin—like the jellyfish that glide through the water beyond—as if they haven't seen the sun in half a lifetime.

Most shocking of all, however, is the sound of far-off singing. The melody is distorted by the water and the glass, but it's a song I know by heart: the music of my childhood. Every night, Papá would croon the soothing lullaby at my bedside until I drifted off to sleep. The words are different, of course— strange Zemyan lyrics that are too smooth and menacing—but the tune wraps around me like a sheath around a sword. Snug and protective.

The singer is a Zemyan woman, kneeling with her hands pressed against the glass. On the other side, an imperial warrior, who looks as small as our youngest recruits, kneels in the same manner, palms held up to the woman's. The child's slim shoulders shake in their unmistakable blue and gold, and the louder they cry, the louder the woman sings. Her voice rings out, strong and clear, and pops of color burst from her fingers and spread through the glass between them like a watercolor painting.

The colors form the fuzzy image of a dove and a lion, the characters from the song, and they twist in a dizzying whirl that's both haunting and mesmerizing.

Beautiful. It's the only word to describe it. But it *can't* be beautiful because Zemyan magic is vile. *Wrong.*

With a loud clap from Kartok, the cracks in the throne room knit back together, blotting out the other prisoners.

"You can't leave me here to rot like them," I say, my voice gaining conviction. "My power *will* rebuild—there's nothing you can do to stop it—and when it does, I'll obliterate this prison."

"Impossible," Kartok says, but his reply is a second too slow. A note too high. "Even if you managed to break the barriers, you'll never survive the sea."

I flash a vicious grin. "That's fine, because neither will you."

Kartok's nostrils flare. He makes his way over to the wall, fiddling with the knobs I can't for the life of me find. "This can be as simple or as difficult as you choose," he says as he pulls a lever. Instead of opening the glass passageway, a panel in the floor slides and an unremarkable tub rises into the room. Water sloshes over the edges and the bitter stench of Zemyan magic is overwhelming. It reminds me of wet horses and moldy tents. "You can cooperate and avoid further pain. Or you can suffer." He points to the tub. "Either way, I'll extract the information I need."

"Is this the only method of torture in Zemya? Or are you that unimaginative? The hot-spring water doesn't even suppress my ice."

"But it does affect your body. And a weakened body cannot wield volatile power."

"To what end? Why not kill me and be done with it?" I don't actually want to die, nor do I plan to, but if I can't worm my way out of here, I'd rather a quick death than weeks of suffering as the hot-spring water slowly melts me from the inside out.

"I need your help. And if the hot spring is not effective, we must explore other options."

"I won't help you with anything," I retort.

"You don't have a choice," Kartok says. "Where will the Kalima warriors go now that Sagaan has fallen?"

I shake my head and smirk at him. "Hunting them is a waste of time. Your hot spring won't strip their powers either. They may not be as strong as I am, but they're not as weak as you—or your goddess."

I brace for a livid slap, but after a tense moment, Kartok settles back on his haunches and appraises me with unnerving amusement. "I never pegged you as the noble and forgiving type. . . ."

"What are you talking about?"

"You have no reason to protect the Kalima. In fact, you should want to punish them for abandoning you. This could be your revenge. Show them what happens when they cross you."

"They did what needed to be done for the well-being of Ashkar," I grind out, even though abandoning me was *not* in the country's best interest, and I'd love nothing more than to see every one of them thrown into this Zemyan prison pit. But unlike those double-crossing cowards, I am actually thinking about the empire. And, like it or not, Ashkar needs their powers. If the Kalima are captured and killed, we won't have a prayer of ousting the Zemyans.

"Give me the rendezvous point," Kartok insists.

"*Clearly*, the Kalima don't want me to join them." I hold out my arms for emphasis. "Do you honestly think they'd meet anywhere I'd know about?"

Kartok's scruffy jaw tightens. He scowls down at me as if I'm a cockroach in the rice bin. "How pitiful—to be so thoroughly despised by your own soldiers."

"Every commander is despised. You're delusional if you think you're any different. No one likes being told what to do. And no one will follow a lenient, indecisive leader. We must be brutal. Exacting. Your soldiers wouldn't hesitate to leave you on the steps of the Sky Palace, wrapped in ribbons for King Tyberion, if that's what suited them best."

"You forget your Sky King is *dead*."

The word zings through me like a bolt of Eshwar's lightning.

"Wasn't it your duty to protect him, Commander?" Kartok prods. "You should have seen his body . . . mutilated on the frosty cobblestones."

Those final, terrible moments in the treasury flicker in and out: Varren helping the Sky King onto the buttress. The excruciating slowness of his steps. The chunk of marble careening through the charcoal sky. The haunting sound of his scream.

"Stop!" I shout.

"Cooperate!" Kartok shouts back. "How many Kalima warriors are there in total?"

I say the first number that pops into my head. "Ten thousand."

"Lies!" Kartok stomps closer, forcing me to retreat until my back is literally against the wall. "There aren't half so many! You would have ended the war long ago."

"If you're so certain of our numbers, why ask me?"

"Do not test me, girl."

"Or what? What else could you possibly take from me?"

Kartok holds out his arms, palms up, and two forms rise into being, like the plumes of dust created by thousands of marching warriors. The particles shift and gather and slowly form the faces of a man and a woman. He has shiny waxed hair and a pipe clenched between his teeth. She wears soft curls and a proud smile. My parents say my name and reach for me.

Unaware of a third form looming behind them. The hooded figure raises a blade—*the* blade strapped to Kartok's hip.

"Look out!" I scream. But it's too late. The steel has already bitten through their necks.

"Your parents live in Sagaan, do they not?" Kartok shouts over my wails. "A city now occupied by Zemya. . . ."

"If you harm a single hair on their heads—"

"Where will the Kalima go?" Kartok roars.

My eyes are still glued to the severed heads of my parents, rolling around my feet. I nearly concede and relay every potential rendezvous point I can think of, but thankfully, my tongue knows better. It sits heavy and thick in my mouth. My teeth clench tighter; Kartok won't spare them, not even if I cooperate.

Before I can comprehend what's happening, Kartok's bony fingers close around my neck and he drags me across the throne room. I don't even have time to fill my lungs before he shoves my head into the overflowing tub.

He plunges me in and out. Harder and faster. Until I don't know if the burning in my chest is from the scalding hot-spring water or lack of air.

At last, Kartok flings me to the floor. "I *will* find a way to defeat you. I *will* see Zemya exalted. Ashkar's reign of terror over the continent ends *now*. With me."

When I try to respond, I cough up mouthfuls of putrid water and howl at the horrendous pain. My body heaves and sweats. It was bad enough having the Zemyan poison searing down my throat and gnawing through my organs. But now it assaults me from the outside as well. Drenching me. Overtaking me.

Enebish once told me how they burned their dead in Verdenet—a crass, disrespectful tradition we eradicated as soon as the Southerners joined the Protected Territories—and

I imagine this is how that must have felt. Except even worse, since I'm still alive.

"Where can I find the Kalima?" Kartok demands again.

"Finding them will do no good. Our powers cannot be suppressed or taken. You'd have to stop us from receiving power in the first place."

I expect my declaration to deflate him. Infuriate him. Because it's impossible. Our Kalima powers are born within us, like a heart or lungs. It's not something that can be removed. But a slow grin spreads across Kartok's face, chilling me so completely, for an instant I feel cold. Even with the hot-spring water dripping off my nose.

"Finally, Commander, you've said something useful," he says, his eyes practically sparkling. Then he turns without another word and vanishes into the tunnel.

I lie in the puddle of hot-spring water, groaning and tossing, unsure what hurts most—the agonizing heat or my pride. The Zemyan has bested me at every turn. Made a complete and utter fool of me.

"Pathetic." The Sky King's voice pelts me like shrapnel.

"Nobody asked you!" I snap at him, sitting smugly on his throne. If I have to endure another day with his vengeful ghost, I'll lose my mind.

"Haven't you lost it already?"

"Get. Out. Of. My. Head." I say every word like a threat, but that only makes him laugh harder.

"I can't 'get out' of your head. I'm a projection from your own mind. A personification of your guilt. You're not angry with me; you despise yourself. You failed yourself, Ghoa."

I try to push up—I have to get out of here; I'll fight my way out or die trying—but my arms are so weak, I barely manage to roll over. It isn't far enough, but at least I don't have to look at the Sky King anymore. Unfortunately, his poison is already in my head, under my skin. Every bit as painful as the hot-spring water.

Tears pool in the corners of my eyes, and I finally let myself cry. Weep, even.

Which is exactly how that nosy little servant, Hadassah, finds me.

"Merciful seas!" She drops the tin of gruel she's carrying and hurries to where I lie. She even has the audacity to kneel at my side. As if she cares whether I live or die. I expect her to smell of sweat and foul lye soap like the servants in the Sky Palace, but the rich scents of bergamot and jasmine envelope me as she dabs my face with her filthy skirt.

"What happened? What did he do now?" she asks. "Is that hot-spring water?"

"Get your scorching fingers off me!" I roar. Every brush of fabric stings like embers burrowing into my skin.

"Sorry! Sorry!" She retracts her hands and appraises them for a long moment. Then she flutters back across the room, fetches the tin bowl off the floor, and holds it between her hands. She whispers something in Zemyan and the metal liquifies, spreading into a hovering puddle of silver.

"Do you honestly think you need to forge a weapon right now?" I growl. "I can't even stand up."

"Hold still." She returns to my side, brings the metal to my face, and drapes it gently across my forehead like a wet cloth.

"Get that off me!" I shout, but it's too late. The metal is already dripping down my face, coursing down my neck and chest, expanding to cover every inch of me until I'm entombed in tin. I pull in a breath to scream, but it quickly becomes a sigh. Somehow the pain and heat are fading. Draining out of my body like blood from a corpse.

"How?" I ask, my voice soft and dreamy. I've never felt such overwhelming relief. My eyelids flutter shut and I feel as if I'm floating away. So light and cool and weightless.

"It's a simple manipulation. Metal conducts heat better than flesh, so given the choice, heat will always choose metal."

The sound of Hadassah's voice breaks the spell, and I remember where I am. And what she is. "Why would you help me?" I bark with derision, frantically swiping at the strange metal coating. But it continues to course over me, spilling over the edges of my body and pooling on the ground like syrup.

"Because we can help each other. I need to know what Kartok is doing and—"

"Won't he punish you?" I interrupt. I want to glower at her, but it's difficult to do anything but sigh as the pain continues to slough away.

Hadassah gives a little shrug. "He can only punish me if he catches me."

"Do you truly mistrust the general enough to risk his wrath? And to strengthen your enemy? I thought he was the lauded hero of your country?"

"He's been the bane of my existence since the day I was born," she mutters darkly. "I told you—he's hurt me, too. And worse, his scheming and power-mongering will hurt Zemya. So if he wants you injured or dead, I want you alive and kicking. If he demands answers, I'm going to ensure your lips remain sealed tight. Whatever it takes to undermine him."

I appraise her, my eyebrows knitting. *Why does it matter to you?*

The lowborn servants in Ashkar couldn't care less about the state of our government or leadership. They're just trying to survive the great freeze. But I say none of this because

Hadassah's jewel-blue eyes are glittering with animosity. Contempt emanates from her pores the way ice seeps from mine, and it fills me with a frigid rush of hope. It doesn't matter why she's angry and desperate. Only that she is.

Hatred is something I can use; desperation makes her someone I can use.

"If you really want to anger him, release me," I dare her.

"So you can kill me and every living soul in this palace, then bring your bloodthirsty warriors back to vanquish the country? I think not."

"Ah, there it is—your true opinion of me. I knew all of this congeniality was a sham."

"You act as if my animosity isn't merited," she snaps. "You've been attacking us for centuries!"

"*Your* ancestors are the ones who started this endless war— attacking Ashkar even after they were banished for practicing wicked magic."

The laughter that bursts from Hadassah is surprisingly low and cynical. "Is that the lie your king told you?"

"It's what hundreds of years of records have told me. Zemya has always been the aggressor."

"Wrong!" Hadassah's vehemence makes me jump. "Ashkar attacked *us*. We had already been cast out, but that wasn't enough. You wanted to utterly destroy us. To ensure we never cultivated our magic or thrived in this arid land. Our ancestors had to defend themselves. We are *still* defending ourselves."

I glower at Hadassah and shake my head. The ancient Ashkarians had no reason to attack after the Zemyans were banished. All we've ever wanted is to be left alone, but the Zemyans couldn't abandon their bitter grudges. "How must it feel," I ask, "to be so thoroughly brainwashed? The entire foundation of your country is built on lies."

"How can you be certain the lies weren't shoved down

your throat?" she volleys back.

"Because I know my people. I know my king."

"And I know my empress."

"What could a serving girl know of an empress?" I sneer.

Hadassah stands with a huff. "More than you'd think." She stomps away, murmuring indignantly about how she's never met anyone so thankless and arrogant and infuriating. I smile as her insults settle around my shoulders and warm me like the finest compliments.

"I'm trying to *help* you!" she shouts. "All I want in return is information on a man we both despise. You'd think that you would—"

"What?" I cut her off. "What did you honestly think? That I'd fall on your feet in gratitude? That we'd suddenly become bosom friends and trade secrets while brushing each other's hair?" Pink floods her cheeks, encouraging me. "I didn't ask for your help. That was your own poor decision. I owe you nothing. And I don't give a damn about anyone or anything in this wretched country. Especially not the gallant ambitions of a prison servant."

She halts in the center of the hall, rumpling the extravagant floor runner as she wheels back around. Her expression is desperate, her eyes pleading, but that stopped working on me years ago. I've run my saber through thousands of soldiers with pleading eyes.

"Don't you have a scrap of honor?" she spits.

"No," I say. And I mean it. Honor and integrity are what drive people to make selfless choices and irrational sacrifices. I have drive. Ambition. Pride.

"Well, doesn't it bother you to be indebted to me?"

"No," I say again, even though that's the one thing that does, in fact, bother me.

"Don't you care that you were healed by Zemyan magic?

And that you *liked* it? I saw your face. I heard your moans. Is that something you can live with? You're a hypocrite. Shackled to me. Haunted by this debt."

Discomfort lifts the hairs down my neck, and I shiver now that the unnatural heat is no longer blazing through me. I'm not interested in being haunted by anyone or anything else after enduring Kartok's specters, but I can't let the girl know she hit a nerve. I harden my features and hold out my hands. "Unlock the shackles and I'll tell you everything he's said and done."

"I already healed you!"

"*Voluntarily.* This is *my* price for the information." I shake my hands and the iron rattles.

Hadassah mutters furiously but inserts the key into the lock. I groan as the shackles fall away, and gently massage my wrists.

"Well?" She puts her hands on her hips.

"Kartok attempted to nullify my Kalima power by forcing me to drink your hot-spring water, but it isn't strong enough. Your unnatural magic never has been and never will be."

Hadassah sighs with exasperation. "Did he try anything else?"

"Other than attempting to drown me in it? No. The water seemed to be his only plan."

"If he thinks nullifying your powers is the key to winning the war, he won't stop until he's found a way. Did he make threats or say anything that points to what he might try next?"

"No. He didn't give me a torture itinerary, unfortunately," I say. Hadassah rolls her eyes. "He just asked about the Kalima's numbers and rendezvous points—as if finding them will do any good. Then he scowled and repeated all of the tired old platitudes your people love about ensuring everyone has an equal opportunity in magic. Avenging and exalting Zemya. On and on and on."

Hadassah deflates. "That's all?"

I almost lie and say yes. I don't want to believe I gave Kartok anything remotely helpful. But if I did, perhaps this Zemyan girl will understand his train of thought.

I force the words out. "There's one more thing. Before Kartok left, I said the only way to thwart our Kalima powers would be to stop us from receiving them. I meant it as a taunt. So he'd see the futility of his quest. But he thanked me for finally saying 'something useful.'"

"How could he sever your ability to receive power . . . ?" Hadassah's voice trails off.

"He obviously can't. It's impossible," I say. Because it has to be.

But I don't like the way the Zemyan girl's forehead crumples, or how she worries her lip and mutters to herself as she leaves the throne room. As if she thinks it's something he could actually accomplish.

CHAPTER FIFTEEN

ENEBISH

THERE'S NOTHING TO DO BUT WAIT. . . .

For King Ihsan's scouts to return and confirm our reports of Verdenet and Chotgor.

For Minoak to wake and regain his strength.

For the Zemyans and Shoniin to arrive and ruin everything.

And I am the only one who seems worried or impatient.

In an unexpected show of generosity, the Namagaans allow us to construct pens on the root pathways below the city, to house the goats and sheep. It feels entirely too permanent, but up the makeshift bars go, and the shepherds fall into the routine of this strange forest world. Every morning, a group of shepherds lead the animals from the pens to a clearing of swamp grass, with the help of Namagaan guides. The animals spend the day there grazing, then the shepherds bring them back into the swamp at sunset—so they can keep a close eye on them overnight, to ensure congregations of alligators or yellow-eyed reed panthers don't attack.

The process is inconvenient and unsustainable, but no matter how many hints I drop, reminding the shepherds of the beauty of the open grasslands and that traveling is their way of life, they wave away my remarks and assure me their animals are resilient. And that they themselves are not averse to change.

"After the suffering we've endured these past months, our mindset has shifted," Bultum explains when he returns from bringing in the sheep. "I finally see the appeal of having a permanent home and putting down roots." He pats one of the large tree trunks and smiles. As if Namaag is that home and these trees are his roots.

The other shepherds nod their agreement, and it leaves me so flabbergasted, I babble in starts and stops as I follow them back up to the canopy.

"Doesn't it bother you that the Namagaans plainly don't want us here?" I ask Emani and Lalyne, along with several other shepherdesses, the next day as they sit at their wheels, spinning wool. "I hate how they stare at us through their windows and spy on us from behind branches but never offer greetings or help. I'll be relieved when King Minoak recovers and we can return to a more normal existence, somewhere we won't feel like burdensome outcasts."

"Where will that be?" Lalyne demands. "Where will we ever be welcome? *You* may be from Verdenet, but the rest of us aren't. They may not be any more hospitable."

I have nothing to say to that.

A week later I'm forced to swallow more complaints when the Namagaans finally venture down from their tree houses and become *too* friendly: showing us how to make button-bush pastes and sea oat poultices to dress our wounds, how to mend holes in our tunics and tents with fibrous pondweed that's stronger than cloth, and how to work the wonderous aqueducts. With the turn of a knob, water streams from above, as if summoned by a Rain Maker, washing away the day's sweat and grime. With the lift of a lever, you can fill waterskins or wash dishes, accomplishing tasks in one tenth the amount of time it takes in Ashkar.

In return, the shepherds roast lamb each day in the clearing, where it's safe to build a fire, and the Namagaans happily feast on the new delicacies. They're equally excited about the balls of raw wool that the weavers "magically" transform into yarn.

I relay it all to King Minoak as I perch outside his window in a cocoon of darkness, praying one of these reports will be troubling enough to wake him. But he remains in a fitful, fevered sleep.

"Doesn't this *concern* you?" I finally break down and ask Serik at the close of our second week in the marshlands. We're sitting on the edge of a platform, legs dangling through the rope railing, watching the marketplace below—where the shepherds are wearing colorful Namagaan head wraps and eagerly gathering chokeberries and hickory nuts. Some even help to prepare tree fowl and alligator for supper—things they will never cook again once we leave Namaag.

Serik chuckles and gives me a puzzled look. "Why would this concern me? It's exactly what we hoped for—kinship and camaraderie. When the scouts return and verify our claims, the Namagaans will be more likely to stand with us."

"But we're getting too comfortable!" I wave at the disturbing scene below. "Just look at them. They practically look Namagaan. They'll never agree to leave."

"First off, I think they've earned a little comfort after everything they've endured. And of course we'll leave. If we don't stand up to the Sky King and Zemyans, Namaag will be overtaken too. The shepherds know we can't stay. We just have to hope the Namagaans will join us when we return to

Verdenet. Try to relax and enjoy this small victory. We've had so few. Hopefully morale will be high when we do leave."

I mumble something that could pass for agreement, even though I'm more agitated than ever. Of course Serik doesn't see the problem; like the shepherds, he's settled into Namagaan life with frightening ease. He's either rubbing elbows with their soldiers and groveling before King Ihsan, or down at water level with the fisherman, armed with a double-pronged spear. Turns out, his power is most useful for spotlighting the black speckled manta rays that swim through the water after dark.

I am the only one who doesn't fit here. The only one who isn't being lulled into complacency. How many times must I remind them that Kartok and Temujin are coming? They could arrive any day!

I invent an excuse about promising to help Azamat weave a palm-frond mat, but as soon as I'm out of Serik's view, I head toward Yatindra and Murtaugh's mansion. Ziva will share my restlessness. She never stops talking about marching to Verdenet—when she's around. Disquiet dances down my spine when I realize I haven't seen her in days. Well over a week. It's almost as unsettling as the shepherds' contentment. If even Ziva has lost her urgency, I might as well start unpacking.

With twitching hands, I climb the treacherous ladder and practically run to the extravagant mansion. I tug on a braided rope dangling in the entry, so desperate to find Ziva, I foolishly assumed she would answer the door. My smile falters at the sight of Yatindra. Her smile flattens too, and it makes me feel instantly vindicated. Re-centered. There's no need to put on pretenses here.

"What do you want?" Yatindra asks, already closing the door. Despite her heavy Namagaan makeup, dark circles ring her eyes and she looks thinner than when we first arrived. She's avoided us, but I've still seen her coming and going from the infirmary, dutifully visiting her brother. When she's not perched at his bedside, she flutters about the treetops to luncheons or scrawls invitations to tea or dinner on little yellow note cards that she personally delivers. As if the entire continent isn't on the verge of collapse.

"I'm looking for Ziva," I say.

Yatindra clucks her tongue. "So impudent, referring to the princess of your realm so casually."

"Ziva doesn't care."

"Have you asked her?"

"Fetch her now and I will."

She shakes her head and tuts again. "I'm afraid my niece is busy."

"Doing what? Why do I never see her? Are you purposely keeping her from us?"

Yatindra sighs heavily. "That would require me to actually think about you and your misfit caravan. Believe it or not, you aren't a pressing concern of mine."

"Liar," I accuse.

Yatindra pretends not to hear me. "Zivana is a princess. She has many studies to attend to. Not to mention caring for her father, whom you failed to heal and protect while traveling here. I wouldn't expect someone such as yourself to understand the demands put upon the leaders of a country."

"What do you have against us?" I finally blurt with exasperation. "We are here to help!"

"Is it true you were allied with the rebel Temujin?" she fires back.

The sound of his name knocks me so off balance, I have to catch myself against the door frame. "Where did you hear that name?" I demand. Even though there's only one logical explanation: Ziva told her about the scout.

"I see I've hit a nerve." Yatindra grins. "Ihsan isn't the only

172

one with spies. Nor is he the only one who's keen to know more about your claims and your 'cause.'"

I turn and walk away. I don't have the energy to fight with her. And she's no longer the main source of my fury.

I walk until I find a quiet bridge, then I sit down and pluck the emerging threads of darkness out of the indigo and claret sky. Once I've gathered a fistful, I give them a fierce tug. I haven't communicated with another Night Spinner through the darkness since Tuva died, and it feels like part of me has been trapped in a small, windowless room, screaming at the top of my voice. But now, finally, someone is there to listen.

Even if it's only Ziva.

When she doesn't respond immediately, I tug again and again and again, which might be slightly unfair—she doesn't know how to reply. She probably didn't even know it was possible to communicate through the darkness, but her ignorance isn't my problem. I keep pulling and prodding until she finally responds with a disgruntled jerk.

What?

Her agitation makes me smile. It's also gratifying to know that Yatindra didn't win. She can't keep me from talking to her niece.

I want to interrogate Ziva about Temujin and, specifically, what she told her aunt, but I'll get nowhere if I burst in with my sword brandished. So I form the darkness into an image of Yatindra slamming the door in my face and send it Ziva.

It takes her an eternity to respond, and when she does, the image is crude and disjointed—like a child learning their letters. Though, I'm impressed she managed at all.

She's strong. Stronger than I'd like, if I'm honest.

Her darkness expands above my face, forming a picture of her narrowed eyes and shaking head. *Why did you visit Yatindra?*

I murmur my answer into the darkness. *I was looking for you, but she refused to admit me. Do you know why?*

Ziva's answer comes much quicker this time. *Why were you looking for me?*

Because I haven't seen you in days—

And you missed me?

I grumble at her cheeky retort, forgetting that the night's still listening—and relaying my frustration.

The tendrils shiver around me with Ziva's laughter, and the single thread of patience I had snaps. *Did you tell Yatindra about the Shoniin scout?*

The laughter stops abruptly. *Why would you think that? Did you honestly seek me out to accuse me?*

Not originally. I wanted your help with keeping the shepherds from becoming too complacent, but then Yatindra mentioned Temujin. How would she know that name if you didn't tell her?

Ziva's answers pelt me one after the next, like the blow darts the Namagaans use to hunt birds. *How in the skies should I know? Rumors are always flying. Isn't that the explanation you gave King Ihsan for knowing about the Protected Territories? But thanks for assuming the worst of me.*

I close my eyes and count to ten before responding. Trying to stay patient. *If you haven't told Yatindra about the scout, why is she investigating us?*

Maybe because she's an intelligent woman who wants to know more about the strangers who arrived in her kingdom seeking an alliance. Wouldn't you do the same?

Yes, but I wouldn't be so hostile about it. It's almost like she wants us to fail.

Just like the rest of us, right? Ziva doesn't even try to disguise her accusation. *According to you, we're all untrustworthy.*

I squirm with discomfort, glad Ziva can't actually see me

through the threads of night.

Yatindra is my family, Ziva continues with such ardent hope, I feel sorry for her.

That doesn't always mean as much as it should, I warn.

Maybe not in your family, but it means something in mine. Yatindra is with us. Stop meddling.

But—

Good night, Enebish.

Ziva releases the darkness and the threads of night collapse, pouring over me like a bucket of filthy brown swamp water.

At long last, King Minoak wakes.

Though, I don't know if or when we would've been informed had I not been dutifully keeping watch from the branch outside the infirmary window.

The moment I climb into the tree, I hear voices. And not just the bored chatter of the guards. There's an entire choir's worth of noise, ranging from sobbing to laughing to shrieking and giving thanks.

Minoak is propped up in bed, haggard and dull-eyed, but alert enough to brush Yatindra's fussing hands away. "Enough! You're my sister, not my mother," he says, voice scratchy with disuse and tinged with annoyance. Though, a broad smile overtakes his bearded face.

"We both know Mother would have wrapped you head to toe in eucalyptus leaves and forced the entire country to kneel in prayer until you arose. My ministrations are mild by comparison." Yatindra reaches out and smooths a lock of graying hair behind his ear. Minoak grumbles but his smile grows.

"The Namagaan look suits you." He tugs on one of her

long cattail braids. "I've always meant to visit."

"Don't lie. Ziva had to drag you here—literally."

"When did you get so strong?" He turns to Ziva, who's sitting on the bed beside him, tucked beneath his arm. Minoak's gaze is the definition of tenderness, and tears glisten in his eyes as he gazes down at his daughter. "You saved me, my brave, beautiful girl."

Ziva bursts into tears and lays her head in his lap. The jostling makes him flinch, but when Ziva tries to pull away, he holds her there. His big, weathered fingers skim across her cheek.

"On behalf of Namaag, welcome back to the land of the living," King Ihsan says. He stands at the foot of the bed with Murtaugh. Behind them, Ruya and five soldiers, as well as a handful of dignitaries, line the wall.

So much for only permitting the royal family to visit.

"We have much to discuss," the Marsh King continues. "I've received some very interesting reports from my scouts."

My stomach drops as if the branch snapped beneath my feet. When did his scouts return? What did they report? And why weren't we informed? It takes all of my restraint not to fling myself through the window and interrogate him.

"King Ihsan is going to help us seize Lutaar City from the imperial governor," Ziva cuts in.

Murtaugh turns so pale, it looks like he should be laid out on one of the sickbeds, but Ihsan laughs heartily. "Your daughter is quite the politician, Minoak."

"Skies, Zivana!" Yatindra scolds. "Don't pester your father about marching into battle when he isn't even well enough to stand. There will be plenty of time for our kings to discuss these things and form a plan. You needn't worry yourself over such heavy matters any longer."

Her smooth dismissal of Ziva makes me bristle, but I don't know if it's because her comments warrant suspicion, because

I simply don't like Yatindra, or because *I* am suspicious and distrustful, looking for betrayal in every little word.

Ziva doesn't seem troubled in the slightest. She smiles and rolls her eyes as Yatindra ruffles her curls. Making me doubt myself more than ever. Prompting me not to breathe a word about Minoak's revival to Serik or the shepherds, lest I look like a paranoid spy. Which is feeling more accurate every minute.

When King Ihsan finally announces the good news two days later, I act as surprised and overjoyed as the rest of the shepherds—hugging and toasting with sap wine at the celebration held in Minoak's honor. The cooks prepare both Namagaan and Verdenese delicacies, and a trio of our very own shepherds, including Serik, play lively dance songs on fiddles.

Halfway through the revelry, King Minoak shuffles out onto a high platform overlooking the chaos. He still requires the aid of two healers and a cane, but when he takes his place beside Ihsan, you'd think he was an illustrious warrior marching across the battlefield, the way the crowd roars.

"We are celebrating more than the recovery of this great man," Ihsan booms. "Today also marks the birth of an even deeper alliance between Namaag and Verdenet."

Serik takes my hand and squeezes, his eyes as bright as the lightning bugs buzzing in the jars overhead. "It's really happening."

I squeeze back, finally letting myself smile. Finally releasing the breath I've been holding since we left Sagaan. I hadn't realized how close I was to suffocating until the rush of fresh air hits my lungs. It's so light and invigorating, I tilt my head back and yell at the top of my voice. I stomp my feet and chant with the writhing mass of shepherds.

The Marsh King waits for the crowd to settle before continuing. "The very empire that vowed to protect and strengthen us has turned their backs on the Protected

Territories. An imperial governor sits on the throne of Verden-et, the Chotgori people are imprisoned in the ore mines, and the scout we sent to Sagaan never returned. We must assume the worst of the Sky King."

Serik and I exchange a worried glance. There's no way of knowing whether the scout was silenced by the Sky King or the Zemyans. If Sagaan still stands or if it fell to Kartok and Temujin as easily as they'd predicted.

If it did fall, how much time do we have?

All around us, the Namagaans roar their outrage and disbelief. This time, King Ihsan stokes the flame until the canopy quivers and every bird takes flight. "Together, we will stand against the deceitful Sky King and free the Protected Territories!" he cries.

I'm gripped by the feeling I expected to have when I found Minoak. For the first time since leaving Sagaan, I allow myself to truly hope. To let go of my doubt and distrust and completely believe.

We begin preparations, and I assign Iree and Bultum to procure and organize provisions for our return journey to Verdenet however they see fit. When Azamat volunteers to scout ahead and sneak into Lutaar City to raise the portcullis for our arrival, not only do I give him my blessing, I refute Murtaugh's arguments that Azamat is too old and frail until the Namagaan chancellor finally tosses his hands in the air and storms out of King Ihsan's study. I check in regularly with Ziva through the darkness, to receive the latest reports on Minoak's progress—which has been astounding, thanks to the Namagaans' riverweed salve. I even give her a few pointers on how to coax the threads of darkness so they're more coopera-tive when delivering her messages.

It's a small trick. Harmless enough.

With every passing day, and every proud grin from Serik, I

feel more certain and confident. So much so that when Yatindra approaches me at lunch the day before we're scheduled to leave for Verdenet, I manage to nod politely and even smile. She's been nothing but supportive since her brother announced his decision to retake his throne. She even intervened during some of Murtaugh's more disagreeable moments and has worked tirelessly as a scribe for King Ihsan, sending hundreds of missives to the war front in an attempt to rally support from the warriors who were conscripted from the Protected Territories.

Yatindra slides onto the stool opposite me. "I want to apologize," she says without preamble. It catches me so off guard, a forkful of chestnut cream misses my mouth and plops onto my tunic.

"*What?*" I shout. Serik stomps my foot beneath the table, so I quickly add, "I mean . . . thank you. Me too. I let past betrayals haunt me, which wasn't fair to you and many others."

She nods and fiddles with the orange tassels on her dress. "I was so distraught over my brother, and terrified of the unrest in Verdenet, I needed to lash out at something, and you and your shepherds were the most convenient target."

"I would have done the same," I say, realizing the truth of the words as they leave my lips. "We're all just trying to survive and protect the people and places we love."

"Thank you for being gracious, but I'd still like to make it up to you." She procures one of her embossed yellow cards and slides it across the table. I cock a brow at her as I pick it up.

"Is now really the time for one of your banquets?"

"Enebish!" Serik barks, but Yatindra laughs.

"It's a fair assumption, but I'm not hosting a banquet. Ziva and I plan to kneel in prayer tonight, to ask the Lady and Father to bless our journey, and we thought three Verdenese prayers would be stronger than two. I even have an extra prayer doll. . . . I couldn't help but notice you don't seem to have one, and I can't imagine how much you miss it."

I'm so overcome with emotion, my voice is too breathy for words. I blink at the table until I'm certain tears won't escape. Part of me hates that Yatindra is the one to break me down to this rawest, barest version of myself. But it also feels right. Balanced, somehow.

"Well? Will you join us?" Yatindra asks.

I smile at the note card. "I'd be honored."

After sunset, I pull on a clean tunic and weave my hair into a long braid—how the priestesses at Sawtooth Mesa wore their hair. Then I kneel and offer up my own silent prayer so I'm prepared to join my faith with Ziva's and Yatindra's.

"Do an extra oblation for me," Serik says before I leave.

"Words I never expected to hear from you." I flash him a teasing smile.

"I never thought you'd assimilate with the shepherds or mend things with Ziva and Yatindra. Miracles are all around us."

I chuckle as I make my way across the bustling platforms and bridges, where the Namagaans are gathering supplies and loading baskets for our journey. I still can't believe they're coming to Verdenet. That they're with us. Miracles truly are all around us.

When I reach Yatindra's door and pull the cord, I'm greeted by a serving girl who informs me that Yatindra and Ziva are down at water level.

I frown and hold up the marigold card. "But they invited

me to join them here."

"Miss Yatindra sends her deepest apologies. She planned to host your prayer circle here, but as she and Miss Zivana were preparing, it didn't feel right. She said you needed to be out there, in the open. Where you can touch the earth and see the skies."

I huff out an exhausted breath. I understand her reasoning—I agree, even—but it would have been nice if they'd told me to meet at water level *before* I limped across Uzul and scaled the impossibly steep ladder to the mansion. "Why didn't she send word?"

"They just made the decision, so the missive wouldn't have reached you."

"In that case, why didn't they wait for me?"

The maid glances at my leg, then quickly averts her eyes. "There was much to carry, with the candles and vorkhi and prayer dolls. They instructed me to assist you to the swamp, if you'd like?"

"No, I can manage." I force a smile to ease the maid's anxious bumbling. It isn't her fault they presumed to know my own abilities. I tell myself it came from a place of kindness, but the twinge in my leg and the tugging in my arm feel more prominent than ever as I descend to the swamp.

"Ziva? Yatindra?" I call once I reach the root pathways. I don't know where they set up, but it must be farther down the path, since I can't see a flicker of light. Only the sheep jostling in their pen bleat in answer.

I pick my way along the bumpy pathway, trying not to choke on the foul swamp air and the stench of soggy wool. The animals are huddled together in the center of their ramshackle pen, blowing and stamping as if I'm a predator.

Every night, one of the shepherds keeps watch, and tonight Iree is on duty. He leans against a tree on the other side of the pen, his head bobbing closer and closer to his chest before it snaps back up and the pattern starts again.

"Iree!" I shout, but he doesn't stir. "*Iree!*" I try again. Nothing. If I were a reed panther, the entire flock would be dead. Bultum would have a heyday if he knew his nemesis was sleeping on duty. I consider walking around the pen to wake him, but I save myself the trouble. It's a long way, and Iree wouldn't have seen Ziva and Yatindra.

After muttering a curse, I continue edging along the fence line, collecting threads of night to sharpen my vision. Would it have been that difficult to wait for me once they got down here? Or at least make themselves easier to locate?

Unless they don't want you to find them. . . .

My feet hesitate and unease grips me. For half a second I consider turning back. I can pray by myself. I don't need to traipse around the marsh for them, especially if they can't be bothered with basic consideration. But then I spot a flash of movement up ahead, just beyond the sheep pen, and I banish my worries with a shake of my head. Yatindra's apology was sincere. Even if it wasn't, she wouldn't use the Lady and Father to bait me. No one is that blasphemous. I won't be ruled by suspicion and fear any longer.

"Ziva? Yatindra?"

"Over here!" Yatindra answers, and I exhale with relief. "Ziva is cloaking us in darkness for privacy."

I frown down at the filaments of night in my hand and give them a little yank. There's no resistance on the other end. And no matter how I twist the tendrils, Ziva and Yatindra don't shimmer into focus.

"Where are you?" I demand, stumbling in the direction of Yatindra's voice.

Without warning, my feet drop out from under me and my shout becomes a scream. My good leg sinks into a hole that's been hacked into the root pathway, and when I try to catch myself, my bad leg wrenches painfully. I scream even louder as I crash into the lowest rung of the fence.

The plank immediately snaps, and the adjoining posts wobble and groan—the wood too wet and bent, and the construction too quick and shoddy, to withstand the blow. One by one, the posts tumble, the cross-planks falling with them. In the space of a breath, the entire structure collapses.

The frightened herd stampedes past me, charging down the pathway and into the murky night.

Burning skies!

"What have you done?" Iree shouts. He's wide awake now and on his feet, gaping at me as if I released the animals on purpose.

"It was a t-trap!" I stammer. "Yatindra cut a hole in the pathway, knowing I'd hit the fence!" I gesture to the thigh-deep hole still swallowing my leg.

Iree looks like he wants to murder me as he unties a bullhorn from his hip and fills the sleeping marshlands with three trumpeting blasts.

Lights flare in our barracks. Within seconds, a swarm of shepherds barrel across the platforms toward the call. Sleepy-eyed Namagaans pull back their drapes and squint at the waterfall of frenzied shepherds, but none of them leave their homes or offer help—despite the "goodwill" and "unity" we've supposedly been currying.

"Enebish destroyed the fence and the animals escaped!" Iree announces as the first of the reinforcements arrive.

"I didn't *destroy* the fence!" I counter. Even though, technically, I did. But "destroy" makes it sound like I demolished the fence on purpose. "It was a setup!"

No one hears me over panicked shouts and thundering hooves.

Serik stumbles onto the walkway with the rest of the shepherds, and his eyes immediately widen when they land on me in the hole. "What happened? What are you doing down here? Aren't you supposed to be with Ziva and Yatindra?"

"They lured me into a trap!"

Serik stares at me for an excruciating moment.

"You have to believe me. I swear to you—"

"*Not now.*" He summons an orb of light, which he holds overhead like a torch, and pulls me out of the hole. Then he jogs into the sticky darkness. "We should head toward the saw-grass clearing," he calls to the shepherds. "It's the first place the animals will go—their food source."

With a nod of agreement, the shepherds fall in behind Serik, splashing frantically through the muck. I follow, my steps slow and stumbling, made worse by the hot tears pulsing in my eyes.

Why would Yatindra and Ziva do this now? When we were finally unified?

"Did you hear that?" Serik slams to a halt, causing the shepherds behind him to collide.

"The only thing I hear is my brain rattling around in my skull," Lalyne grumbles.

Serik holds up his hand. "Shhhh!"

I have a hard time believing he can hear anything over the shepherds' hysterical moans, but then he turns and plunges into the nearest thicket. We follow, stopping every few minutes while he listens and readjusts course. To my astonishment, the sound of far-off bleating grows steadily louder until we reach a small clearing. Unlike the saw-grass clearing, where the flocks graze, this field is made of mud, and long, twisting plants undulate on top of the water like snakes. Shadows move on the far side of the meadow. Most of the group freezes or scrambles backward, but Serik snatches a bucket of feed from the nearest shepherd and shakes it while clucking his tongue.

A tiny black lamb stumbles into view through the murk and trots happily toward the feed bucket. The shepherds weep and hug as they call for the rest of the herd. But as more sheep emerge from the trees, the threads of darkness resting in my fist pull taut, flailing and lashing like a banner in a windstorm.

A second later blackness engulfs the marshlands.

"Enebish!" Serik roars, trying, and failing, to summon an orb of light.

"It isn't me!" I insist.

"What do you mean it isn't you?"

"I didn't blacken the sky!" My fingers tremble as I attempt to reel in the darkness, but the threads pull back, more stubborn than an ornery camel.

Ziva isn't strong enough to hold the night with such a firm grip, which can only mean one thing: It isn't Ziva's darkness. It's mine—the darkness Kartok stole in the *xanav*.

I wind the smoky shadows around my palm faster. Faster. Heart pulsing in my throat as my vision sharpens, revealing a hunter far deadlier than a reed panther or an alligator. A wolf, hidden among the sheep.

Temujin strides into the clearing, flanked by a pack of Shoniin, wearing a predatory smile on his lips.

CHAPTER SIXTEEN

GHӨA

WHEN KARTOK RETURNS TO THE THRONE ROOM THE FOLLOW-
ing day, I'm ready—crouched at the far end of the hall,
barricaded behind the pile of smashed chairs like a frightened
animal.

He methodically scans the room, and when his eyes alight
on me, my teeth automatically clench. I cower lower and gag
on the putrid taste of hot-spring water rising up my throat
like vomit—my body reminding me to stay as far from him as
possible. I'd be disgusted with myself if the response weren't
useful. And calculated.

When a dog sees a frightened cat, they can't help but chase
it. They're too gripped by the scent of fear, and the thrill of the
hunt, to consider where the cat might lead them.

And whether it has claws.

"Retreating so soon, Commander?" Kartok laughs. It's
exactly what I would do if our roles were reversed and I had
him trapped in an Ashkarian prison cell, cowering and pissing
himself in the corner. We're alike, the generál and I. A fact that

would rattle me—if I let it. But I choose to lean into it. To sink into his mind like a thief and steal the upper hand.

He weaves through the mess of broken wood, gliding toward me like the specters he conjures. The little copper discs sewn into the hem of his cobalt robe tinkle as he stalks nearer. My nerves jangle with them.

"Surely you can put up a better fight than this?" he jeers.

I say nothing and hunker lower. Vibrating with readiness. Gathering up the cold and channeling it into my fists.

Thanks to Hadassah's ministrations, I feel better than I have since leaving Sagaan. Which is a boon—it would have taken months for my body to recover on its own. But when I let myself think too much about her magic swirling around inside me, defiling me, my skin pinches like ill-fitting armor.

I don't like it, but my body must be strong to wield my power.

That's why the ice dagger I threw at Kartok that first day vanished. And why the bursts of frost I've managed to summon melt so quickly. My power has been slowly rebuilding, but my body has been too weak to wield it properly. It's the only logical explanation. The Zemyan would never be able to manipulate my ice at its full strength. Or even half strength—which I'm inching toward now. Last night I jolted from the depths of sleep to a glorious crackling in my joints—like the song of a slow-moving glacier.

And Kartok is completely unaware.

He stops directly in front of me and peers through the barricade of broken chairs like a fox staring into a rabbit warren. I want to pounce immediately and unleash my fury. Punish him for every gasp of pain he's caused. But I must wait for the perfect moment. When I'm in a position to inflict the most damage.

I'll only have one shot.

He reaches into his robe. I force myself to make a tiny whimper, even though it kills me to give him that satisfaction. "Please, no more hot-spring water," I beg.

"Oh, water's at the ready, if we need it, but thanks to your brilliant suggestion, I've decided to tackle this quandary from a different angle." He flicks his wrist and shards of wood rise from the floor and reform into a chair. His attention to detail is so meticulous, there isn't a single fracture to show it was ever broken. Once he's settled, he produces a thick leather volume from his vestment. The book is old and ragged, and the stale smell of dust tickles my nose as he thumbs through the pages.

"Can you tell me what this is, Commander?" Kartok angles the book toward me and taps on a picture of a tall, helter-skelter pile of stones. It looks like it could topple over at any second, with all of the ribbons and bottles and trash stuffed into the cracks. It's ugly *and* blasphemous—one of the shrines to the First Gods where travelers used to pray and worship. They're unmistakable and, thankfully, gone. The Sky King tore them down, making the grasslands far more beautiful.

I'm not about to cooperate, though, so I hum and cock my head. "Rocks?" I say after a long moment.

"Don't toy with me, girl." Kartok scoots closer and wags the book in my face. Like I knew he would.

I squint at the picture for another long moment. "Some sort of religious relic?"

"Legends claim it's a gateway to the land of the First Gods. Have you ever seen one?"

"I don't know. . . . Maybe a long time ago? But you can't honestly believe—"

"Where?" He leans even closer, perched on the edge of his seat. Almost close enough.

"I don't remember. I was a child. And they've long since been destroyed."

"*All* of them?"

"Yes, all of them. We haven't worshipped the First Gods in generations."

Kartok blinks as if I just pronounced myself empress of Zemya. "If you don't believe in the gods, how do you explain your powers? It's like denying the hand attached to your arm."

I don't know why he's so upset about this—he doesn't worship the Lady of the Sky and Father Guzan either—but the reason doesn't matter. When I see an angry purple bruise, I jab my fingers into it.

"For someone who has dedicated their life to fighting Ashkarians, you know nothing about our beliefs," I say calmly. "We stopped worshiping the First Gods when we realized they weren't dead or ignoring us—they never existed to begin with. My Kalima power comes from within me. *I* am a god. Which is why there's nothing you can do to take or diminish my powers."

The long lines of Kartok's body pull taut and he leaps from his chair. Diving at me.

Finally.

I thrust my hands forward and heave against the ice block in my chest, pressing harder than I ever have before. Digging deeper than I did on the icy buttress. Raging even harder than I did on the plains of Nariin, when I summoned Standing Death. I have to account for my body's lingering weakness. And it doesn't matter if I burn completely through my power. Kartok will kill me if I remain here.

The surge of ice that explodes from my palms is spectacular. Horrifying. Thousands of razor-sharp spikes careen toward the generál, and for an instant his face slackens with shock. Fear glazes his demon eyes. His hands move to shield his face, and I scream with murderous glee. But then the spears inexplicably sail past him—*through* him—evaporating into mist. Just as they did the first time I attacked him.

No.

It isn't possible. Kalima powers have always been stronger than Zemyan magic. *Always.*

I reach into my core again, grappling frantically for more ice. But I am a quiver without arrows. Completely magic-barren until my power rebuilds.

If it ever does.

Kartok squats in front of me, his face rearranged into a smirk, as if he knew my attack was futile. But I saw the pulse of shock and fear in his eyes.

"What did you do to my power?" I demand. "And how?"

"I may not be able to strip your power, but if you use it freely, there's nothing stopping me from collecting it and repurposing it."

"That isn't possible."

"Isn't it?" Kartok's iceberg eyes practically glitter. "This prison cell is a *xanav*—a pocket world of my creation, in which I'm able to collect and store your power. Since you're not feeling cooperative, I have no choice but to proceed without you. If the stone gateways are destroyed, I must forge another path to the home of the First Gods. Your power will be most useful for that. Just as Enebish's power was key to taking Sagaan."

My reeling mind slowly untangles his words—and the meaning behind them. The only reason a general advances into enemy territory is to conquer it—to dethrone the current ruler and place your own ruler in their stead. But Kartok can't honestly believe he can depose gods. And he said Enebish's power was key to taking Sagaan . . . not Enebish herself.

My ribs expand, as if a suffocating cord has been severed, and the gasp of air that fills my lungs feels almost like relief. Except that's absurd. In order to feel relief, I would have to care about Enebish. And I don't. I stopped caring when she chose that deserter over me. Again and again and again.

While my mind grapples for footing in this new, unsteady terrain, Kartok returns to his chair and flips through the ancient book, humming to himself.

Humming!

"Whose book is that?" I demand, eyeing it with growing unease.

Kartok grins. "Zemya had so many thoughts after she was unjustly banished from the Lady and Father's presence. So many interesting theories and strategies. Plans to make her parents and brother pay for the harm they'd caused. She was quite brilliant, you know. And she could be quite vengeful, too." He licks his finger and turns another page. "With good reason. But the timing wasn't right, then, to wage war against the Lady and Father."

"But it is now?" I shout.

"Careful, Commander. It almost sounds as if you're scared. As if you believe . . ."

"I believe that you're wicked and depraved."

"For wanting to right centuries of persecution and injustice? For mistrusting powerful people who consider themselves gods? For wanting to restore the balance of power so all have an equal opportunity? Yes, that's the height of depravity."

I clench my hair, which would be hard with frost if a morsel of my power remained. "Stop twisting the truth to make yourself out to be a hero!"

"Stop *denying* the truth and accept that you're not a hero either. You never have been."

I need to stay calm. If I let him drive me to hysterics, he wins. But my head has never ached this badly. My brain feels seconds away from exploding. "I never asked for power!" I finally erupt. "It was given to me. For a reason. And you're jealous. Your people have always been jealous. That's the entire genesis of this war."

"No. The genesis of the war is fear. Zemya discovered something unexpected and powerful, but instead of embracing her innovation and achievement, the foolish Ashkarian gods despised it because they couldn't control it. They tried to squash it rather than understand it."

"So you plan to repay us by instilling fear? By striking back cut for cut?"

Kartok shakes his head and turns another page of the book. "You're so narrow-minded. I couldn't care less about Ashkar. I plan to exalt my goddess and promote the reign of my empress, both of which will be much easier once . . . Ah, here we are. I knew Zemya would provide another way. Tell me, Commander, how many disparate powers do the Kalima warriors possess?"

My brows crumple. Why in the sacred name of the Sky King would he care about the distribution of power within the Kalima? "Shouldn't you know? If you've spent your whole life fighting us?"

"How many?" he demands. "And how are they distributed throughout the battalion?"

"There isn't a weak link among us, if that's what you're looking for."

"Your warriors *are* the link!" Kartok roars, slamming the book. "I've never met anyone so infuriating. Your comrades' decision to abandon you makes more sense every minute." He pulls the long, curved blade from his robes and advances toward me.

I stiffen—I don't know if the weapon is real or an illusion—but I don't retreat. I refuse to retreat. "You're finally going to kill me?"

"If you're not going to be helpful, I see no reason not to."

In less time than it takes to draw breath, Kartok is on top of me—the sleeves of his blue robe swirling, his knife flashing. It skims across my throat, the line so thin and delicate that I think he only nicked me. Then I feel the warm curtain of blood pour down my chest. I gargle and gag as pain consumes me. My eyes bulge beyond their limit, turning everything white. It's oddly peaceful. Like an untouched field of snow.

Death. I pluck the word from my gasping, oxygen-starved brain, and for half a second I wonder if this might be preferable. I won't have to live in a world without the Sky King. I won't have to bear the disappointment and ridicule. Or be subject to Zemyans.

The pain ratchets higher. The whiteness blares brighter. But as I swallow my last, rasping breath, the agony abruptly vanishes. So does the glaring whiteness. I'm enfolded in a gentle embrace, like the soft, restful swaying of a hammock. Free from even the remembrance of pain. I feel lighter than I have in years. Since my childhood. Before my Kalima power presented.

My lashes part and I peer through the bleariness, trying to make out the details of my final resting place—this next phase of my existence. But I can't see anything through a cloud of swirling purple smoke. When I try to speak, I choke on a metallic, bitter tang—like corroding steel and wet earth.

My pulse flutters faster, and I wave my hands to clear the haze. I never gave much thought to the afterlife, but I always assumed it would be better than this. I was the highest-ranking commander in the Imperial Army, for skies' sake!

Until they rejected you.

I wave my arms more frantically, and my fingertips brush something warm. Something smooth and soft—like flesh. I scream as Kartok's grizzled face materializes through the smoke, less than a hand's breadth from mine.

"Welcome back, Commander," he says.

I scream again. "What happened? I don't understand. . . . Am I dead?"

A wide, toothy grin crinkles Kartok's face. "Not quite yet."

Without a word of explanation, he opens the tunnel and sweeps out of my cell, leaving me on the floor in a lake of my own blood.

My hands drift cautiously to my neck, but there's no jagged wound. No scar, even. My fingers quickly peruse the rest of me, but there isn't a single new scratch.

Was it all an illusion?

I clutch my throbbing forehead and shut my eyes.

I no longer know what's real. I can't trust my own body.

With a growl, I slam my fists against the ground and gasp when they splash into the pool of blood. Slowly, I bring my dripping hands up to my face and lick a finger, just to make sure.

My throat may be intact, but my blood is undeniably real.

Why would Kartok slit my throat then heal the wound?

And how in the name of the Sky King is it possible?

CHAPTER SEVENTEEN

ENEBISH

"I THOUGHT YOU'D BE MORE EXCITED TO SEE ME," Temujin calls in a wounded voice.

I stumble back before my mind can command my body to stand tall and strong. To meet Temujin as an equal.

"Perhaps you were hoping to be greeted by a *different* friend?" He whistles and Orbai dives from the canopy, streaking toward me and the shepherds, who scream and cover their heads. I stand my ground, willing her to *see* me, begging the Lady and Father to open Orbai's eyes. But she tucks her wings and bares her talons, ripping out a clump of my hair when I don't duck fast enough. My fingers touch the throbbing wound as she circles back to Temujin.

"How strange . . ." he marvels. "It doesn't appear she missed you at all. . . ."

Chanar and Oyunna chuckle on either side of Temujin, and the laughter spreads through the rest of the battalion—at least a hundred deep. So many faces I once considered friends. And even more I don't recognize, with pale hair and eyes and skin.

The true faces of the Zemyans who masqueraded as Ashkarian warriors.

"Stay back!" Pillars of flame rise from Serik's palms, and he takes a bold step forward.

"Ah, Serik, my favorite monk," Temujin drawls. "Such a relief to see you alive. I believe I already had the pleasure of experiencing your new abilities when you set fire to the *xanav*." His voice takes on an edge, and that's when I notice the angry burn marring his neck, and his ragged hair, singed shorter on one side.

"That was just a *taste* of what I'll do if you come any closer," Serik warns.

"I see you and Enebish have the same policy when it comes to your powers," Chanar yells. "Attack first, ask questions later. Spare no mind for the innocent."

"None of you are innocent!" I shout back. *And neither was Inkar*, I remind myself as her visage rises to haunt me: the metal from the obliterated Sky Palace gouging her side, her smiling eyes and warm praise, defending me even as she died.

"That may be true, but there's no denying these people's innocence." Temujin motions to the shepherds, who have retreated several steps. "It's a pity you dragged them through so much needless suffering. They would have been safe and well had you stayed in Sagaan."

The shepherds look from me and Serik to Temujin and his Shoniin. As if there's any question who they should trust.

"He invaded Sagaan with the Zemyans—our *enemies*!" I bark at them over my shoulder.

"You're much safer here than in a fallen city or freezing and starving on the grazing lands," Serik adds.

Temujin clucks his tongue and ventures closer, winding through the panicked sheep. "*Enemies* is such a polarizing term. Just because people have opposing goals doesn't make one side noble and the other inherently evil. Time passes, circumstances change. Someday you may find your goals suddenly align, as ours and the Zemyans' do now—we wish to be freed from the tyranny of the Sky King, and so do they. We wish to coexist peaceably, with freedom to worship as we please, and so do they. I like to think that we're all allies instead."

"Just because we all oppose the Sky King does not make you an ally," I say. "If you're a friend rather than foe, why did you come for us? Did Yatindra coordinate this with you?"

"I don't know anyone named Yatindra. I simply received an anonymous note informing us that something we'd lost was hiding in the marshlands. And if we waited patiently, it would deliver itself into our hands. Look, here you are."

I scoff. Yatindra never accepted King Minoak's decision, and she never intended to pray with me. She feigned an apology to lure me down to the sheep pens, knowing I'd fall into the hole she'd gouged. Knowing the animals would escape and lead us to the waiting Shoniin. The worst part is, she'll get away with it. I've been so suspicious and distrustful, the shepherds and Namagaans are much more likely to believe I'm casting undue blame than to deem the supportive sister of King Minoak and devoted wife of the vice chancellor capable of such treachery.

I want to strangle her. Or obliterate her with starfire. Yatindra may think she's protecting her family by keeping them here, but it's maddeningly shortsighted. We'll all be squashed by the Zemyans.

"We don't want to make trouble with Namaag," Temujin continues.

"Since when is helping Zemya invade Namaag 'not making trouble'?" I challenge.

Temujin ignores me. "We have a very generous proposal."

"Generous for *you*, I'm sure," Serik snarls.

Temujin shoots him an annoyed look. "How many times must I tell you this has nothing to do with me? I am fighting for the people. I want justice for the persecuted"—he gestures to the shepherds—"and freedom for the Protected Territories. How could you possibly condemn me for that?"

"Because of your methods! You'll never accomplish any of it with your current 'allies.' The Zemyans are using you—as you used me," I spit out.

Temujin releases a drawn-out sigh. "I had hoped we could settle this civilly, but we won't allow you to jeopardize the well-being of these good people or to threaten the stability of the entire continent with a needless, slapdash rebellion. Sagaan has fallen. The Sky King is dead. A new dawn is rising, and you can either wake up and rise with it or be left to perish in the dark."

"The Sky King is dead?" I croak.

There was no love lost between me and King Tyberion, so this news should come as a relief—we were going to have to face him eventually, and now there's one less obstacle between us and liberating the Protected Territories. King Ihsan has no one to fall back on now, nowhere to turn but to us and our alliance. But my feet feel like they're sinking deeper into the boggy ground. Like the entire swamp is going to swallow me. Because the Zemyans are that much closer to seizing the continent. Despite Temujin's grand promises, I know Empress Danashti, and Kartok, will be even more ruthless than the Sky King.

"How? When? What's happening in Sagaan?" The words pour from my mouth like vomit. "Was it destroyed? What about the people?"

And Ghoa.

I don't want to think about her—I don't care what happened

to her—but there she is, battling across the stage of my mind. Did she perish alongside the king? She must have. There isn't a single scenario I can imagine in which she would be alive if he isn't. And despite everything, the thought of her cold and vacant-eyed on the ground with a Zemyan blade through her chest makes it suddenly hard to breathe.

"Zemya possesses all of Ashkar's major cities." Temujin ignores my questions. "The only task that remains is quelling what's left of the Imperial Army, which will be simple and peaceable as long as no one attempts to intervene." His amber eyes flick deliberately to me. "If you abandon this doomed rebellion, and you and Serik return with us to Sagaan, we will allow the rest of your party to retreat to the safety of Uzul with their flocks. We will not attempt to 'invade' or 'conquer' Namaag. That has never been our goal."

The shepherds guzzle down his lies like sap wine, and there's an immediate shift in the air. Their feet scuffle restlessly. My ears ring with their unspoken pleas: Go. *Leave us.* I'm fairly certain they would grab me and Serik and physically throw us at Temujin's feet if they weren't frightened of our Kalima powers.

The even more outrageous part is I would let them—I would go with Temujin willingly if I truly believed the Zemyans would let the Protected Territories be. But they won't. The shepherds don't know Temujin like I do. They don't know how he twists the truth to make it smell like honey-sweet sapota fruit on the outside, when it's rotten and festering beneath the skin. And they don't know Kartok, who siphoned my power. Who created an entire world within our own.

I raise my chin. "And if we refuse?"

"Then you'll be responsible for even more destruction."

The shepherds moan behind us, but I look to Serik. Just a flick of my gaze. It's enough. He thrusts his arms forward and a pillar of white fire races toward the Shoniin. They leap back to avoid the inferno, and as soon as Orbai vaults from Temujin's shoulder, I reach into the heavens, harness a ball of starfire, and aim it directly at his chest.

My body tenses with morbid anticipation as the starfire hurtles through the pitch black and slashes through the leaves—a furious streak of incandescent red. Just before it obliterates the Shoniin, another streak of light appears—this one flaming blue. The two balls of starfire collide, just as they did in the desert when I stopped Ziva from killing Orbai. Only this explosion is ten times larger, ten times hotter, since Temujin's starfire wasn't summoned by Ziva's novice hand.

They were both summoned by me.

A pulse of violet light fills the sky, then millions of sparks sizzle down from the heavens, leaving trails of smoke. As the embers settle atop the canopy, pricks of light spatter the foliage—like the fireflies the Namagaans use to light their homes. Only these fireflies grow and multiply and spread.

In what feels like an instant, the leaves are no longer green but burning red and gold. Fire drips down the ancient tree trunks like wax from a candlestick, racing from leaf to leaf, branch to branch. Spreading toward the city of Uzul, less than half a league behind us.

Fear grips my stomach tighter than the vines encircling the trees. The shepherds scream and scatter, dodging the burning debris as they sprint back toward the city. Serik shouts curses. And I stand still, gazing up. The fire will devour the entire marsh if we don't find a way to put it out. But the canopy is too high. And our powers are of little use: Serik's heat will only feed it, and my power birthed it in the first place.

So I do the only thing I can. "I thought you didn't want trouble with Namaag!" I whirl on Temujin and his Shoniin, who don't appear the least bit rattled. Chanar even has the nerve to smile. "Don't you care that Uzul will burn? The capital of one of the Protected Territories, which you're *supposedly* fighting for?"

"Of course we care," Temujin answers, "and we'll do everything in our power to help them rebuild after this devastating fire caused by Enebish the Destroyer. It will be the foundation of our union, in fact. The thing that solidifies their ties with the Shoniin and Zemya."

My heart leaps faster with every awful word. Temujin manipulated me. Again. Even when I know that's his aim, he still manages to be three steps ahead. I run my trembling fingers through my hair. "You're just as responsible as I am," I babble. "You threw the second ball of starfire."

"I'm afraid you're mistaken. I'm not a Night Spinner. I can't wield starfire."

"I'll explain the syphoning to King Ihsan! The shepherds witnessed the entire confrontation!"

"By all means, explain to King Ihsan until you're blue in the face. I doubt he'll be willing to listen to a word you say after his capital is reduced to ashes. You leave fire and destruction everywhere you go, Enebish: Nariin, Sagaan, and now Uzul. This is just another deadly outburst, and I will be the savior who arrives to clean up your mess."

I want to reach for another ball of starfire. I want to incinerate Temujin and every last one of his traitorous Shoniin. But Serik grips my hand and tugs me back toward Uzul. "Arguing is pointless. We have to stop the blaze. Warn the people."

I look over at Serik as we trip through the undergrowth—at his determined, stalwart expression and his hand, locked tight with mine—and sobs fill my smoke-filled throat. He could have turned on me like the shepherds. He could have blamed me for the broken fence and the stampede. He could have scolded me for falling prey to Yatindra's betrayal or refused to believe me at all. But here he is. At my side. Charging with me into battle.

"We'll never get there fast enough," Serik pants.

"There's another way to warn them." I don't know if Ziva helped Yatindra sabotage me, but right now it hardly matters. I shove my smarting ego aside and yank on the perpetual undercurrent of darkness connecting us, snapping the night like a whip until she responds with a groggy tug. I immediately send her an image of the fire raging toward Uzul and the Shoniin.

The tendrils pull taut. Ziva sends back so many frantic messages, they bleed into an indecipherable jumble of black. A distant scream rises over the roar of the inferno. Lights flash, winking like stars through the leaves and thickening smoke.

"Everything will be fine," I chant as we run. The Namagaans must have a way to combat fire. They live in trees, for skies' sake.

The flames snap behind us, consuming the leaves like an oiled wick. My mouth feels dry and blistered and tastes of burning sap. We stumble past the demolished sheep pen and Uzul sprawls above us, overrun with absolute mayhem. Bridges swing precariously as far too many Namagaans shove across, burdened by clothing and jewelry, paintings and tapestries and fine china. Everything they can possibly carry.

Meanwhile, Ruya and her orange-clad soldiers wheel carts bearing massive brass fittings across the platforms. Men and women crowd around them, helping to lift the fixtures and fasten them to the brass pipes running beneath the limbs.

With a shout from Ruya, and a creak like the turn of an ancient knob, silty-brown swamp water explodes from each nozzle. The torrent that blasts through the canopy is even more violent than the geysers in the Ondor Mountains. Just the runoff pelting my head feels stronger than a Rain Maker in battle. Limbs tear from the ancient trunks, and the holes that riddle the canopy look like they were made by actual cannons.

In order to douse the fire, the Namagaans have to decimate their forest.

I stand in shivering, dripping silence with Serik and the shepherds, who gradually emerge from the trees with their animals and gather around a different tree—noticeably apart from me and Serik.

We watch the water cannons beat back the blaze. After what feels like a hundred days of battle, the last of the embers die and the water cannons peter to a trickle. The Namagaans drop the hoses and wilt into soaking heaps, crying and coughing and hugging. The shepherds scratch at the doors hidden in the tree trunks like hungry strays, but the Namagaans don't hear. Or they've chosen not to respond.

King Ihsan appears on a platform overhead and moves among his people. Once again, he's wearing his dressing gown, and he looks as exhausted and worn down as everyone else, but he still manages to clasp hands and pat shoulders, offering quiet words of comfort to his people.

Murtaugh and Yatindra trail the Marsh King, and the sight of her teary eyes and quivering hands makes me see red.

"Breathe, En," Serik whispers in my ear. "Lashing out now will only make things worse."

Things can't get any worse! I want to scream. I pull several deep breaths through my nose, waiting for King Minoak and Ziva to appear at the end of the royal procession, but they're nowhere to be seen.

It immediately strikes me as odd.

"Where are Ziva and Minoak?" I mutter.

Serik shrugs one shoulder. "Who knows? They're not Namagaan. There's probably little they could do to help."

"King Minoak isn't the type to sit back if his allies are in danger."

"Maybe he felt he needed to prioritize his safety for the sake of Verdenet?"

"What about Ziva?" She would never hide away and avoid trouble. Especially not after the frantic images I sent through the darkness. I reach for the night to compose another message, but the sound of sloshing boots makes me whirl around.

Temujin and his Shoniin trudge into the clearing, looking eerily clean and composed compared to the rest of us.

The shepherds wail and throw themselves at the hidden doors, pounding even harder.

The Namagaans peer down at us through the rope railings, as if suddenly remembering we exist. But still the doors don't slide open.

The night buzzes around me in agitated circles. "Let us up!" I beg. "They are dangerous traitors!"

Temujin's voice fills the swamp like another cannon blast. "If anyone is going to be labeled a traitor, shouldn't it be the Night Spinner who set fire to your forest?" He points an accusatory finger at me.

"He's equally to blame!" I shout back as every Namagaan eye fixes on me with horror. "He's using my siphoned power!"

"Do you think these people are fools?" Temujin waves an arm at the crowded platforms. "Lies will get you nowhere, Enebish. Stop trying to manipulate them. We are advocates for the Protected Territories. We have no quarrel with Namaag. We wouldn't have ventured into the marshlands at all if you and Serik hadn't betrayed us and fled. We even attempted to treat with them in the desert," he calls up to the crowd, "but Enebish attacked—like always."

"*He* is the one trying to manipulate you!" I insist. "They are allied with the Zemyans! They helped them take Sagaan! They're going to seize the entire continent!"

King Ihsan approaches the rail and glares down at me,

a ruthless frown on his face. "You knew they were following you, yet you came to Uzul anyway? You took advantage of our kindness, knowing full well you were putting my people in danger?"

"W-we had no choice," I stammer. "King Minoak—"

"Silence!" Ihsan cuts me off. "You failed to mention the Zemyans had taken Sagaan. You led me to believe the Sky King was our common enemy. Why?"

"Because we didn't know for certain . . ." Serik tries to explain.

The shepherds shout over him: "We had no part in this! The Shoniin only want Enebish and Serik and vowed to leave Namaag in peace if we hand them over!"

Ihsan appraises us all with distaste. He shouts something in Namagaan and the people manning the water cannons retake their posts, hefting the bulky nozzles back over the railing.

We freeze. Even the sheep fall silent as we stare down potential death.

"This is a misunderstanding!" I cry. "We are friends. Allies."

The Marsh King draws out the moment until it's agonizing, maddening. "We are not allies," he counters. Then he slashes his right arm downward. The Namagaans manning the water cannons angle the nozzles higher. Temujin and his Shoniin don't even have time to turn before the deluge knocks them off their feet and sweeps them into the forest, dashing them against trees and fallen logs like debris in an avalanche.

I fall to my knees and begin to offer up my heartfelt thanks, when King Ihsan slashes his other arm. And the water cannons turn on us.

CHAPTER EIGHTEEN

GHΘA

I LIE ON THE FLOOR FOR HOURS, FINGERING MY NECK. Growing more furious every second.

Having the sorcerer's illusions in my head and hot-spring water in my gut was bad enough. Knowing that his magic is the only reason I still draw breath is maddening. Unbearable. I want to open my veins and drain every tainted drop of blood. But that's what Kartok wants: frenzy, desperation. He expects me to yield and crumble. But I haven't descended that low. Not yet.

I still have one potential iron in the fire, one possible way to break free: Hadassah. She is the fault line—the fracture. If I can wedge my chisel into her, I can shatter the walls of this prison. She already despises and distrusts Kartok, and she doesn't even know the extent of his ambition.

To attack and depose the First Gods.

I laugh because the notion is so absurd. How does one even go about killing a god? It doesn't seem possible. And what would the repercussions be? Not that it matters, since they don't exist. But Hadassah believes, and I have a feeling she'll be willing to pay dearly for this information. It's the precise sort of nefarious scheme she's been desperate to uncover—the kind of revelation that's worthy of drastic action.

If killing the Lady and Father were an acceptable way to end this war, Kartok would use his legions of magic-wielding soldiers to accomplish the task. But he's skittering around this prison like a weaselly flea-bitten rat, which means he doesn't have the empress's blessing. If I wield this information correctly, I *might* be able to convince Hadassah to strike a bargain in exchange for my freedom.

I consider remaining sprawled on the floor in a hysterical, writhing heap so Hadassah is compelled to "help" me again when she comes. It clearly makes her feel useful and important. But I need the debt to fall in my favor this time, so I arrange myself in Kartok's newly reconstructed chair—in the center of the throne room, atop spatters of gore and the splintered wreckage of the other chairs. It paints a striking scene—poetic, even. The chair and I were both obliterated and brought back together. Given new life through the generál's unnatural magic.

"Merciful seas!" Hadassah cries as soon as she enters the room. "What happened now? Where did that chair come from?" She rushes to where I sit. I'd thought she might be squeamish, but she stares at the smears of blood and even drags a finger across a dried splotch on my arm.

"The generál and I had a most enlightening discussion," I say.

Hadassah's eyes widen. "About what?"

"I know what he intends to do."

"What?" She waits expectantly, and I laugh.

"Knowledge is power. Knowledge is *currency*. And this information came at a high price. I won't breathe a word of what I know unless you prove it will be worth my while."

A dark cloud passes over her glacial blue eyes. "You know I can't free you."

"So don't *free* me. Accidentally leave a door or two unlocked. Ensure the halls are clear for a moment. It could be an honest mistake."

"An honest mistake that would ruin me! It would invalidate the trust and approval I'm trying to gain by exposing Kartok in the first place."

"Why are you so concerned with trust and approval? You're a servant!"

"Wrong!" The sliding door slams open, and Kartok blazes into the chamber, faster than the starfire Enebish threw at my chest. He seizes Hadassah's upper arm and shakes her violently while he shouts in Zemyan.

I have a sudden, inexplicable urge to throw myself between them. Except that would be ridiculous. I owe Hadassah nothing.

"Did you honestly think I wouldn't catch you? Or see through this pitiful disguise?" Kartok shakes Hadassah harder and skin sags from her arms like melting cream. Her cheeks slough off in a long, thin coil that resembles the skin of a snake. I watch in horror as piece after piece of her pools into a clump on the floor until a young man stands in Hadassah's place. And not just any young man.

The Zemyan prince, Ivandar.

Nausea grips my throat. I gasp, then immediately hate myself for betraying how well the prince's deception worked. How stupid and gullible I am.

Fury rages through me, hotter than an entire cask of hot-spring water.

It's all so glaringly obvious now: why Hadassah smelled of expensive perfume and had the courage to speak so boldly. How she had the physical strength to drag me back from the tunnel, and why she was so obsessed with uncovering Kartok's plans. A servant could never have a prayer of intervening, but a *prince* does.

And I helped him. I knew better than to let my guard down—I didn't tell Hadassah much. But I wouldn't have shared *anything* with the Zemyan heir—not even to save my own life.

I appraise Ivandar again—his gauzy shirt the color of the sea and his fine linen pants, his harshly chiseled features and his towering height. He is the opposite of Hadassah in every way, except for those clear, icy blue eyes, which are currently fixed on Kartok with loathing.

The only thing he and I have in common.

Ivandar wriggles free from Kartok's grip and whirls on him. "I know you've been experimenting on the commander with hot-spring water. I know you're trying to stop the First Gods from bestowing power on the Kalima warriors. Why?"

Kartok's eyes cut to me for an instant. A flash of annoyance. But his voice remains even. He folds his arms and leans against the wall. "Why do you think? It will be much easier to win the war if we don't have to contend with a snow squall or ice storm every time we face the Ashkarians in battle."

"If that's the case, why experiment down here in secret? Why not flaunt your ingenious plans before my mother and the people? The only logical answer is ambition. My throne will be easier to seize if you're the hero who vanquished the Kalima. But it can't look intentional."

Kartok quietly clucks his tongue. "Oh, Your Highness, you're so ignorant and oblivious. I couldn't care less about sitting on any throne. My only goal is to serve and honor Zemya. It's sad, really, that your insecurity has driven you to consort with prisoners. What would your mother say?"

"What would my mother say about all of *this*?" The prince

gestures wildly around the replicated throne room.

They're so caught up in their argument, they've completely forgotten me, huddled in my chair. I rise with excruciating slowness and creep toward the wall.

"The empress would say I'm doing my duty," Kartok replies. "*You* are the only one with unfounded—"

"Why do you have *that*?" Ivandar points at the tattered book tucked under Kartok's arm. While both of them scowl at it, I slink closer. Closer. Focused on the long, curved blade hanging from Kartok's hip. "The Psalms of Zemya are never to leave the sanctuary!" Ivandar exclaims. "Never to be touched by anyone other than the current ruler. This is an act of treason!"

Ivandar lunges for the book, but Kartok easily whisks it out of reach. "The empress gave me permission. We're so close to achieving—"

"My mother would never do such a thing," Ivandar argues. But his voice has lost its hard edge of certainty. It's thick and warbling with hurt. "If you're following my mother's orders with exactness, why not tell me your plans? Let me help. Prove that I can trust you."

I hold my breath and shuffle the final few steps—stopping just behind Kartok. My hands tremble with anticipation. If escape is out of the question, I'm going to bring this vile palace crashing into the sea and take both of these idiots with me. I even have the means: Kartok's dagger is forged of Zemyan steel. Imbued with his magic. If anything is strong enough to break the enchantment on these prison walls, it's this weapon, born of the same creator.

I know I won't survive the aftermath—if the enchanted steel doesn't impale me, I'll be swept into the raging sea and drowned. But the Zemyan heir and the empress's foremost advisor won't survive either, not even if they can swim, because I intend to freeze the water and entomb them beneath the surface. Thanks to Kartok's strange healing magic, ice is once again crackling through my fingertips. Not much, but hopefully enough to perform this one, final act.

To claim this one, final victory.

Even if the Zemyan army continues to advance and take the continent, the destruction of these prominent men will be irrefutable evidence that I was the strongest Kalima warrior. Proof that my comrades were wrong to turn their backs on me. Even if Ashkar falls, everyone will tell stories of the last commander of the Kalima warriors, who killed two-thirds of Zemya's rulers from within the dungeon.

I picture my parents, hearing the news. Receiving condolences that are actually declarations of praise. Commissioning a concerto in my name that will play forever after.

I'll die knowing I made them proud.

That thought gives me the courage to leap.

I dive into the back of Kartok's knees and my fingers dart through the folds of his cloak like a snake, coiling around the hilt of the sword. He's heavier than I anticipated, but I manage to bring him to the ground. The impact knocks the breath from his lungs, giving me time to free the sword and roll away.

Kartok shouts something, but I can't hear it over the roar of my pulse. It drums in my head. Faster every second. He reaches for me, his long, knobby fingers tangling in my hair. I swing the blade behind my head and sever my ponytail with a swish. Hoping Kartok's fingers came off with it.

"What are you doing?" Ivandar cries. He looks completely bewildered. Like he honestly believed I'd perish without a fight.

With a roar that explodes from the depths of my gut—the place where I stored every hope and dream and ambition I had for my life—I drive Kartok's blade into the wall.

The generál slams to a halt and clutches his stomach, as if I buried the knife in his flesh. Our eyes meet, and I expect to find fury, outrage, perhaps even fear, but he looks contemplative. Almost amused. He lifts a finger, and I flinch, expecting the enchanted blade to retract through the hilt and lodge in my chest. But it remains buried in the throne room wall. A second later there's a monstrous crackle and the murals splinter into fragments, revealing the actual wall of glass behind the illusion.

Slowly, as if in a dream, spiderweb fractures spread through the pane. Beads of water race down the cracks and drip from the ceiling. The smells of brine and sand and victory fill my nose as the frothy green sea bears down on us.

Ivandar's jaw drops.

Kartok is close enough and quick enough to tackle me, but he remains perfectly still and watches as I throw my weight against the splintered glass.

There isn't time to contemplate why.

The wall explodes with a *pop*, and I laugh as the waves rush over me.

CHAPTER NINETEEN

ENEBISH

The blasts from the water cannons slam into our stomachs and fling us across the marsh like twigs in a raging current. I crash through the cypress trees, battered by their jabbing roots, and tumble through the wreckage of the sheep pen, colliding with too many shepherds and animals to count. My vision darkens with every impact. Pain detonates through my rag-doll body—crushing and suffocating and endless.

When the floodwater finally slows, the city of Uzul is no longer visible. Only a dripping expanse of trees and mud. Catching hold of a vine with my good arm—though neither arm feels "good" anymore—I drag myself onto a cluster of roots. As I cough up mouthful after mouthful of brown sludge, the current continues to swirl around me, littered with broken branches and leaves. Scattered with floating satchels and shoes and shawls. And strewn with battered, motionless bodies.

Sheep lie on their sides, mangled and soggy, their wool stained red and brown. Goats are bent and broken against the trees. And, most horrifying of all, are the people. The corpse of a shepherdess glides past, her eyes staring vacantly, her face bruised and bloated. Her long dark hair waves around her like the swamp reeds, and her hand is outstretched, fingers interlaced with those of a small boy, who is just as waterlogged and still.

My stomach turns itself inside out. I fling myself off the roots, desperate to get away from the woman and the child, but as I claw through the puddles in the opposite direction, another body floats around the bend. Then another. They move silently through the cypress trees—three gray-clad Shoniin and four shepherds. And these are just the bodies I can see. I'm sure there are dozens more scattered across the marsh.

So many lives taken because of Yatindra's selfish deception. And my stupidity.

I never should have accepted her invitation. I *knew* she couldn't be trusted, but I was trying to "make an effort." I wanted to prove I wasn't too damaged to unite the Protected Territories and lead them against the Sky King and Zemyans. My doubt and mistrust had already ostracized and endangered so many. I wanted to be better and braver and stronger, but burying the past and moving forward proved even more disastrous.

There's no winning.

Not for me.

"Serik?" I cry into the eerie silence. There isn't a single note of birdsong. Even the relentless cicadas have stopped chirping, leaving only the gurgle of mud and the far-off sound of weeping. "Serik?" I shout louder.

Still no answer. Panic seeps into my pores. He was right beside me before the blast. Hands intertwined. Now he could be anywhere—crushed beneath a broken branch, dashed against a rock, the next corpse to drift downstream. . . .

"Serik!" I stagger to my feet and wade through the slough. I don't have a clue where I'm going—I could be stumbling in the wrong direction, wandering deeper into the maze of trees.

My bad leg buckles every few steps, but I scrape off the grime and forge on.

He's alive. I'll find him. I refuse to accept anything else.

After what feels like years, my ears prick with the hum of voices, one louder than the rest. It doesn't sound like Serik, but I follow it into a thicket of reeds, where the mud is even heavier and the plants jut from the ground like spikes. As I hack through the shoots, my legs give out for good. I lie there for a moment, the grime cold and stodgy against my cheeks, tempted to let the bog devour me. But I dig my elbows into the mire and continue to drag myself forward, length by torturous length, until I reach a cluster of people.

Several dozen shepherds stand in a huddle, keening—tortured sounds I haven't heard since my days on the battlefield. I try to stand, but my body is too caked with the viscous mud. I feel so inhuman, it isn't a surprise when several of them point at me and cry, "Alligator!"

The rest of the group screams and retreats.

I manage to lift a hand and force out a single word: "Serik?"

The shepherds' screams abate, but their horrified expressions remain firmly in place.

"Enebish?" Old Azamat squints as he ventures forward.

Lalyne scoffs. "Of course she would survive! Of all the wretched creatures under the sun!"

"And only concerned for Serik. To hell with the rest of us," Iree snaps.

"That's not true," I wheeze. But I can hardly hear my rasping voice. There's no way it reaches the shepherds.

"We never should have followed you!" an unseen voice grumbles.

"We've lost everything!" several more proclaim.

"We're going to die."

"So many are dead already!"

Suddenly I'm surrounded by seething faces. Everywhere I turn, there's more. Shouting and snarling and spitting. A boot strikes my lower back. Another jabs my chest. I gasp, like the fish flopping vainly in the muck, washed from their streams by the raging cannon water.

"I was trying to help," I babble incoherently. "I was trying to trust—"

"We should kill her and drag her body back to Uzul," Emani proclaims.

"Maybe the Namagaans will reconsider admitting us if she's no longer a threat," Bultum adds.

Tears tumble down my face, and my fingers itch to swipe them away. To hide every vestige of weakness and put on a brave face—the face of a warrior. But I ball my fists and let the drops slide off my chin. I let the shepherds see them—see *me*—for the first time since we met: ashamed and terrified, but trying.

It's useless.

The mob comes at me with twice as much fervor. Hands shackle my wrists and stretch them painfully to either side. Someone presses on the back of my head, forcing my face deeper into the squelching mud. When I try to scream, sludge fills my mouth and clogs my nose. I feel like I'm back at Ikh Zuree, beset by the hateful monks. Only, this is even worse because Serik and the abba aren't here to stop them.

I squirm and kick as white spots burst behind my eyelids. My head feels like it's going to explode. I spread my fingers, grasping for the darkness, but my hands are too full of mud. My body is too frantic for air to work properly.

I am going to die—at the hands of my allies.

My flopping becomes weaker and weaker. "I'm sorry," I say with my last gasp of breath.

All at once, the pressure releases. My body feels as light as the floating lanterns in Sagaan, and as the distorted bursts of light recede, Serik's perfect freckled face takes shape. He's standing over me, arms outstretched, heat billowing from his palms.

"Stand aside!" Lalyne booms.

Serik shakes his head.

"Don't make us turn on you," Iree warns.

"Because we will!" Bultum joins Iree, standing shoulder to shoulder.

"You have no reason to turn on either of us!" Serik argues, but the shepherds' bitter laughter cuts him off.

"We have every reason!" Azamat jumps into the fray. "People are dead! Our animals are dead! We've been cast from Uzul without clothing or supplies, which means we'll all perish soon, thanks to her erratic actions." He points emphatically at me. "She will never be content. She can't stop meddling and lurking and spying, and look where it's led us!"

"Enebish has made mistakes," Serik agrees, and even though his voice is diplomatic, it stings. Because it's true. I've made so many mistakes, *too* many, but it's no longer out of suspicion and stubbornness. I'm trying to learn and change— it's just always at the wrong time.

"But we've all made mistakes," Serik continues. "Her actions weren't erratic. She did exactly as we asked and put her trust in the Namagaans, and they betrayed her. *We* are the ones who didn't listen this time. *We* are the ones who forced her to doubt her intuition, stay silent, and fall prey to another trap when her concerns were more than justified." He gestures to the flooded swamp.

"How do you know she didn't plan this?" someone demands.

"Why would I?" The words bubble up on a surge of indignation. I even manage to hoist myself onto my elbows. "That's absurd!"

"Because we weren't heeding your plan," Azamat accuses. "You could sense we didn't want to leave the marshlands to fight against the entire skies-forsaken continent, so you decided to force our hand."

"I didn't!" I cry at the same moment Serik proclaims, "She wouldn't."

I glance up at his fierce expression, those blazing eyes, and my heart squeezes with gratitude. I have never loved him more.

"What proof do you have?" Bultum asks. "How are you so certain that she was betrayed by the Namagaans?"

"I was there when she received the invitation to pray with Yatindra."

"Yet, she wasn't with Yatindra when the sheep escaped. . . ."

"Because she and Ziva changed plans and left without me!" I interject, though no one is interested in what I have to say. "When I arrived at Yatindra's house, her maid told me to meet them down at the water. Where the trap was waiting."

"Did you escort her to Yatindra's home?" Iree looms over Serik. "To ensure that's where she actually went?"

"Well, no—"

"So how do you know she didn't make up the bit about Yatindra changing the meeting location? How do you know she didn't go directly down to water level to meddle with the sheep pens?"

"Because I know Enebish!" Serik barks.

"And she's never lied to you before?" The harsh angles of Lalyne's face contract into a piercing scowl. "She's always been perfectly forthcoming and trustworthy?"

Serik hesitates and his gaze darts to me, filled with agony and frustration. I have to look away. He can say nothing in my defense. *I* can say nothing in my defense. The shepherds have been with us for weeks: they've seen me lash out and sneak around and ignore so many of Serik's pleaded instructions.

"If you want to forgive her because you're in love with her, that's your prerogative," Lalyne sneers. "But the rest of us are under no obligation to do the same. Stand aside, Serik. We must do what's best for those who are left, and if that means eliminating Enebish to be readmitted into King Ihsan's good graces, so be it."

Serik looks from one hostile face to the next, then he drops to his knees between me and the shepherds, closes his eyes, and stretches his hands skyward. It's the epitome of helplessness, of vulnerability, and it feels so much braver, and so much more powerful, than drawing a sword. If you'd told me a few short months ago that this would be Serik's reaction—the final stand in the fight for my life—I would have laughed myself hoarse. But there he is, swinging at our assailants with patience and faith rather than fists.

"*Please*," he says in a small voice, "after everything we've been through, do you honestly think I'd endanger you? If I truly believed Enebish was to blame, I'd let justice take its course. But I'm asking you to believe me, to trust me. I've given you everything—all I could possibly give and more. All I ask is this one thing in return."

The shepherds are quiet. Too quiet. The kind of quiet that leaves no room for deliberation.

Iree takes a decisive step backward. Away from us. Bultum and Lalyne and Azamat and at least twenty others do the same, spreading out to encircle us.

Serik raises his hands and fire pours from his fingers, streaming skyward. The blazing pillars almost remind me of the gateway to Kartok's false Eternal Blue. "You're certain you want to do this?" he asks, trying to mask the quaver in his voice.

The shepherds don't answer, but the air is charged with the hair-raising buzz before a lightning storm. I reach for the night, prepared to fight alongside Serik, but before we unleash the sky, a voice drifts through the reeds, shocking in its high pitch but ferocious in its conviction.

"If you refuse to believe Serik, perhaps you'll believe me!"

The tension shatters, and the shepherds part, sweeping to either side like window curtains. Sandals slosh into view, and dark, slender hands reach down and take my chin, forcing me to look up.

"You were right," Ziva proclaims.

I gape at her for several seconds, waiting for her to wash away like the runoff from the water cannons. "What are you doing here?" I finally say. "Isn't it enough that we were cast from the city? That innocent people lost their lives? Do you also have to gloat? Do you expect me to congratulate you and Yatindra on your little trick?"

"Didn't you hear what I said? You. Were. Right." Ziva enunciates each word. "I had nothing to do with that fiasco. I didn't even know Yatindra had invited you to 'pray.' Yes, I was resistant to your claims, but in this case, they were justified. Yatindra was conspiring against our alliance. She wrote to the Zemyans, telling them to come for you, instead of sending missives to our soldiers at the war front. I found their correspondences when she locked me and my father in her powder room as soon as the confrontation began—'to protect us,' she said. But I'm not interested in cowering in a closet while my country crumbles. Nor will I waste time trying to convince King Ihsan to change his mind about marching to Verdenet. Not if there are people who are willing to act now."

Shock ties my tongue. I can't remember how to form a single word. If the shepherds had fallen on my feet and showered them with kisses, I wouldn't have been more astonished.

"Well?" Ziva crosses her arms and looks around the group. "Aren't you going to say something? I made a rather horrifying scene in Uzul and trudged all the way out here. I'll be furious if it was for nothing."

I shake my head and laugh. Because, in that moment, I have

no trouble picturing her as a queen.

As *my* queen.

"From the moment you arrived in the caves, I knew you were the key to everything!" Serik crows and slaps Ziva on the back.

The shepherds slowly nod. A few even clap.

"Did your father come as well?" Serik leans around the princess, scanning the marsh for King Minoak, but Ziva shakes her head.

The group falls instantly silent.

Ziva squirms, but only for a moment. "My father still thinks this is a misunderstanding. He doesn't wish to sever ties with King Ihsan by joining you. But maybe it's for the best. He's too weak to travel or invade Lutaar City anyway. He would only slow us down."

Bultum chokes with surprise. "But he allowed you to come to us?"

"He doesn't *allow* me to do anything," Ziva retorts. "I am perfectly capable of making my own choices. My father encourages it, in fact. I will be queen someday."

Serik's nod is slow and shallow. "So we proceed with our initial plan, then, and march on the imperial governor in Lutaar City?" It sounds like he's trying to convince himself along with the rest of us.

"I hate to be the naysayer," Azamat interjects, which is laughable because he *loves* to be the naysayer, "and I mean no offense, Your Highness"—he sketches a little bow at Ziva—"but we can't invade Verdenet and expect to unseat the imperial governor when led by a princess who's hardly more than a child. It won't rally the citizens of Lutaar City. Plus, we have no food. Or supplies. Or weapons."

Ziva glares at Azamat, and I feel the darkness shiver as her fists tighten. My fingers tense—ready to step in—but Ziva blows out a breath and rearranges her sneer into a saccharine smile. "No need to worry about supplies, old man."

Ziva turns and, with a wave over her shoulder, a handful of Namagaans emerge from the trees pulling wagons piled with food and blankets and tarps and furs, as well as everything that was left behind in the barracks during our rush to recapture the herds.

The shepherds shriek and clap. A large majority break into heaving sobs, while the rest hug one another and Ziva and Serik. A few even embrace me, which is when I know the tide has well and truly shifted.

"How did you convince King Ihsan to give us these supplies after everything?" Serik gestures to the floodwater below and the scorched canopy above.

"I didn't need to." Ziva flips her curls away from her face. "While he was consoling his people, I commandeered several wagons that were loaded for the journey to Verdenet, which the Namagaans will no longer be needing, and made it clear to the people guarding them that they could either follow me or be obliterated by starfire." She turns to the Namagaans now and shoos them away with a flick of her fingers. "You may go."

"As for where to journey next . . ." Ziva continues. "Verdenet isn't the only territory that needs freeing." Her eyes meet mine over the carts, and a thoughtful grin climbs my cheeks. Once again, I was so focused on freeing Verdenet, I didn't allow myself to consider other options—a different order of events.

"We go to Chotgor." My voice rises with excitement. "If they're unaware of the Sky King's death, we can deliver the news, which will give them the strength they need to rise up in rebellion. If they've already heard, there's no reason they shouldn't join with us. We'll be stronger against the Zemyans, united. And they needn't fear reprisal from the imperial guards if the foundation of the empire is crumbling."

The group explodes with chatter—whether it's about our plan or the supplies, it's hard to say. It doesn't matter at this point. There's a path forward. A clear way to navigate this disaster. And I know what I need to do to play my part in it. Something I should have agreed to from the beginning. A small way to show my commitment and, hopefully, begin to regain the shepherds' trust.

"I'll train you as we travel," I tell Ziva. "We need every bit of strength the Lady and Father have given us. I was wrong to deny you before. Scared and doubtful and threatened, which is a shameful way to live."

She blinks at me for a long moment. So long, I expect her to fling a retort back at me and insist she doesn't need or want my help anymore. But then she bounds through the mud, throws her arms around my neck, and hugs me tightly.

After a few shocked breaths, I lightly pat her back, silently praising the Lady and Father for this miracle, and so many others.

"To Chotgor," I say, looking to the filthy but smiling shepherds.

"To Chotgor!" they agree.

We leave at once, traipsing northward through the flooded marshlands with a surge of newfound energy. The shepherds pass out food and dry clothes with minimal bickering, and more than enough people volunteer to pull the heavy wagons. It's amazing, what a little bit of hope can do.

"Can you believe this?" I ask Serik, who walks beside me. "I thought we were finished."

I expect a proud, moon-eyed grin, but he shrugs and drags

the toes of his boots through the mud.

I reach for his arm. "What's wrong? Everything's coming together. It's nothing short of miraculous."

He looks at my hand instead of my face. "Chotgor is so far north, and so cold. Even colder than Ashkar. And I'm already exhausted. It will be *miraculous* if we don't freeze to death."

The strain in his voice makes my heart squeeze. Our new plan may have lifted the weight from the rest of our shoulders, but it's settled squarely on Serik's. He's been so strong and unflappable since we left Sagaan—the steady hands reaching down to lift me and the shepherds out of every pothole.

It's about time someone eased his burden.

"Keep going. We'll catch up in a minute," I tell Ziva. Then I lace my fingers through Serik's and guide him into the forest. Out of sight of Ziva and the shepherds, where the air is thicker and bullfrogs welcome us with throaty croaks.

"Where are we going? We should stay with the group." He tries to turn back, but I tighten my fingers on his sunburst cloak, drag him around an enormous tree, and tug him closer. So the entire length of our bodies touch—arms, legs, and chests fitted together as if chiseled from the same mold. "What are you doing?" he whispers, hazel eyes wide.

"Thanking you. For refusing to back down and never giving up on me. For standing beside me when no one else would. For believing me, even though I gave you every reason not to. You're the strongest, bravest, most loyal person I know, and I don't know what I did to deserve you, but I thank the Lady and Father every day for their kindness. I figured it was about time I thanked *you*, too." I lean up on my toes, eyes locked with his, and gently tilt forward until our lips touch.

His mouth is warm and soft, and tingles explode in my stomach. It shouldn't be possible for such a small touch to make my body flare with heat, but I am burning, blazing, bubbling with need . . . until I realize Serik isn't kissing me back.

I pull away, cheeks flaming. "I'm sorry! I shouldn't have—"

He reaches out and takes my face in his hands, his thumb trailing over my scars. "Yes, you most definitely should have. I should have been ready, considering I've spent half my life imagining this moment."

"Only half?" I say with a breathy laugh.

Then his lips are on mine and his hands are in my hair, and even though our clothes are muddy and dripping, I feel like I'm sprawled across the sand, baking beneath the desert heat. My mouth presses harder against his, somehow knowing what to do despite never having kissed anything other than Orbai's beak. I've never felt anything like this. It's like the euphoria at the height of my Kalima power combined with the comfort of a heavy wool blanket. I am completely exposed yet completely understood.

I break away to catch my breath, and Serik plants tiny kisses down my jawline, making me shiver. "Where did you learn to kiss like this?" I demand. "It definitely isn't something they teach at Ikh Zuree."

"I lived plenty of years before being banished to Ikh Zuree. . . ."

"And I was there for most of them! Who else have you kissed?" I swat his chest playfully. "It was Rhona, wasn't it? The cook's girl. Don't think I didn't notice how you made eyes at her."

He shakes his head adamantly. "My eyes have always been on you."

I melt back into him, our lips moving in a rhythm that feels effortless but ravenous. Smiling against his mouth because I'm kissing Serik.

Finally.

He backs me up against the tree and my fingers curl into his collar, pulling him even closer. I want to stay like this forever—two blades soldered together—but a long, agonized moan makes us freeze.

"What was that?" I whisper.

"Probably just the shepherds." Serik leans back in, but I shake my head and hold up my hand.

"It's coming from the opposite direction. It almost sounds like crying. . . . Do you think there are other survivors still out there?" I squirm free of Serik's arms and cast off in the direction of the weeping. The closer we draw, the louder and more animalistic the screams become. My toes curl inside my boots, and I have to force my feet to keep moving. I don't want to find anyone else suffering because of my mistakes. But not finding them would be even worse.

I crash through a particularly thick jumble of undergrowth. "We're coming!"

"Hurry! Please!" a shattered voice calls.

My legs wheel. My heart thunders.

I hack through the thicket and stop dead in my tracks. *"You!"*

Serik skids to a stop beside me and we stare up at a figure dressed in Shoniin gray, dangling from the gnarled branches like a broken kite. Golden hoops glint in his ears and jagged black hair flops across his face.

"I didn't think you were the type to 'hang around' after a battle . . ." Serik laughs wickedly.

Temujin's tiger eyes find us, and the horrified expression that twists his face is the most beautiful thing I've seen in weeks. A ray of golden sunshine, slicing through the oppressive clouds.

"Can't I catch a skies-forsaken break?" he mumbles up to the heavens.

But the Lady and Father ignore him.

As well they should.

CHAPTER TWENTY

GHθA

THE ZEMYAN SEA IS MORE VIOLENT THAN ANY OPPONENT I'VE faced on the battlefield. More forceful than every Kalima power combined. The water advances in terrible, crashing waves that fling me back and turn me over. Every time I open my mouth to scream, salt water invades my lungs. When I try to get my bearings, it gouges my stinging eyes.

I have never encountered water like this.

And I have never felt so miniscule. So powerless.

The current sucks me out into the expanse of terrifying blue and green. My lungs sputter as the water smashes me lower and lower. My heart rate increases with the pressure—pounding in my wrists and throat and head. Booming against my temples.

Air, air, air! it screams.

But air won't bring me glory. Only ice can do that.

I spread my fingers, reach into my glacial center, and pour all of my remaining strength into the swirling water. But the salty surge refuses to cooperate. It's slow to freeze, and when I do manage to forge a branch of ice, the swells rip it from my fingers. Before I can fully freeze one wave, the next one dashes it to pieces. There isn't enough ice in the entire world to harden this much water.

My knees sink into the soft, silty bottom, where I droop and sway like seaweed. The sand cradles my face like a pillow, and as my vision blurs, my parents appear in the rippling waves. They gaze at me from across the music room, their sorrowful faces begging me to lift my voice and sing. *Sing, Ghoa!* But there's no music in this place. And singing will help nothing.

I see Enebish, too, with black pearl eyes and seafoam scars. I hate her and love her. I miss her and despise her. She is my greatest accomplishment and biggest failure.

It doesn't have to end like this, her voice swirls and gurgles.

How else can it end? I'm trapped beneath the sea. Don't pretend you care.

You could ask for help. . . .

From who? I snap. Though, of course I know the answer. Enebish and her fool gods.

Those old stories may comfort her, but I refuse to believe some nebulous lady of clouds and sunlight will swoop down from the heavens and rescue me. What's more, I don't want her to. I don't want anything from anyone.

The burning in my chest and the pressure in my head disagree, and as the agony mounts, the raw, primal part of me takes over. The most vital, inner self that refuses to die a failure. To leave my parents in humiliation and disgrace. To let my honorless warriors defeat me like this.

"Please." The word slips out—the last bubble of air in my lungs.

As it rises to the surface, just before I'm sucked into oblivion, a hand clamps around my bicep and drags me upward.

I wake to sand beneath my fingers, water in my nose, and lips on my mouth. Cold, thin lips that are as slimy as a dead fish.

When my eyes pop open, and I see the ashen face hovering a hairsbreadth from mine, I wish it were a fish.

I vomit up a bucketful of seawater straight into the Zemyan prince's lap.

"Honestly? You couldn't have retched in the other direction?" Ivandar gags as he crawls away from me, his woven shirt now plastered to his chest with water *and* vomit.

"What are you *doing*?" I demand.

"What does it look like? Would you rather I didn't resuscitate you?"

"Yes!"

His dripping face twists with outrage. "Are you really going to disparage me? I could have swum directly to shore and let you drown, but instead I tugged you three leagues through rough seas so you wouldn't be found." He gestures to the long stretch of beach surrounding us. It's completely deserted, hemmed in with gnarled foliage that creeps up to a distant mountain peak. "What were you thinking, destroying the prison like that? You were never going to escape."

"Maybe I wasn't trying to escape." I peel tentacles of seaweed off the side of my face and spit sand from my teeth. The only thing worse, the only thing more horrifying, than being betrayed by my warriors, captured by Zemyans, and dying in a sea I couldn't freeze, is not dying and being saved by the Zemyan heir.

Of course this would be the outcome of my first prayer.

Technically, it was *answered, was it not? You survived.*

I close my eyes and groan. If the gods do exist, they're clearly punishing me for having the audacity to call on them. If they don't exist, the universe is ridiculing me for considering the possibility.

"What were you doing if you weren't trying to escape?" Ivandar demands.

"Reclaiming my honor. If I had managed to kill you and the generál supreme, I would have died with glory. I'd be revered in Ashkar for generations to come. But thanks to your senseless heroics, I now owe a life debt to the Zemyan heir and must live in a world where I failed my king and country."

The weight of it hits me then, pummeling me even more violently than the sea. I may be free from Kartok's prison, but I have nowhere to go. No battalion to command. Even if my power rebuilds, I could never contend with the entire Kalima to reclaim my position. And without my position, I can't show my face in Ashkar—especially not after my failures in the treasury. I can't even go home; I won't smear my parents with my disgrace—assuming they're still alive.

Which leaves only one option: I fall back on the gritty sand, spread my arms wide, and beg the buzzards to devour me.

"You can't just lie there and give up!" Ivandar says. "Not after I risked everything for you. You're indebted to me. You said so yourself."

"I didn't ask you to save me. And I honestly can't fathom why you did. If you're trying to convince your mother to trust you over Kartok, cavorting with the commander of the Kalima warriors isn't the way to go about it."

Ivandar waves a dismissive hand, but I see the furrows between his brows, the tightness in his jaw. "She may be disappointed initially, but she'll thank me when I uncover Kartok's true motives. Despite his noble claims, I know he's scheming and vying for power. Which is precisely why I saved you. *You* know his plans," he adds when I stare at him dubiously.

I laugh. I can't help it. "Did you honestly risk your life, and potentially your crown, on a little carrot of information I dangled in front of your nose? How do you know I was telling the truth? Prisoners spin all sorts of lies to save their necks."

"I saw your face the last time I came to your cell—when you were covered in blood. You were ready to work with Hadassah."

"Unfortunately, Hadassah doesn't exist."

"Maybe not in that incarnation, but she and I want the same things. I *am* Hadassah."

"What you are is a fool." I close my eyes and focus on the blazing heat of the Zemyan sun. It's even more punishing than a suit of lamellar armor in high summer, steaming my flesh like overcooked potatoes. Sweat collects beneath my arms and runs down the sides of my face, and the worst part is, I can't summon a single puff of cold to cool my burning skin.

The gods and universe are definitely mocking me. The circumstances are too targeted to be a coincidence—the girl forged of ice, melting into nothing.

Ivandar huffs out several long breaths before asking, "Does it make you feel powerful, being so cruel?"

"I'm not cruel. This is just who I am."

"Or is it the armor you hide behind?"

I bristle. My fingers automatically move to tighten my ponytail, but the slashed pieces are too short to tie back. "I don't hide behind anything," I growl. "I framed my sister for a massacre. I sentenced my cousin to prison. I methodically removed every person who stood in the way of my promotion, as if they were a burr clinging to my cloak. Would you call any of that an act?"

"No," Ivandar admits, "but it's never too late. We can always change our course, set our sails to a different wind."

"Spare me your inspirational drivel," I groan.

That finally shuts the prince up.

For a moment.

I feel his shadow pass over me. Feel his eyes bearing down on me, as hot as the merciless sun.

This is pathetic. Get up.

"Don't tell me what to do." I shoot up from my back and glare at the Zemyan prince.

"What are you talking about? I didn't say anything," Ivandar retorts, sitting precisely where he was before—slumped and shivering in the sand like a drowned cat—but I know better than to buy into his illusions. I felt him there, looming over me.

"Don't toy with me, Prince."

"I haven't said or done anything," he insists. "The salt water has gone to your head."

"Speaking of going . . . shouldn't you be running back to Karekemish? You have quite a lot to straighten out."

"You know I can't return. Not until I have damning evidence against Kartok. And in order to find that, I need you to tell me what you know."

I fold my arms, prepared to ignore him until he either leaves or perishes beside me, when the voice comes again. Louder and more adamant than before. Only now that I'm paying attention, I don't know how I ever thought it was Ivandar. Because it sounds like me—only sharper. The surest, most unflinching version of myself. The commander still buried deep within me—revealing what my tortured, water-addled mind couldn't piece together.

Open your eyes, Ghoa. The answer to everything is literally sitting in front of you.

My gaze flicks again to Ivandar—filthy and dripping but unmistakably Zemyan. His clothes may be soaked and slashed, but the material is luxurious and the royal sea green marks him as someone of consequence. He's the type of prisoner who would guarantee respect for the captor. Maybe even merit reinstatement. Especially if the prince can be used to turn the tide of the war.

Empress Danashti may have sided with Kartok regarding my torture, but I have a feeling her choice would be different if her son's life were at stake. I can use Ivandar to drive the Zemyan troops out of Ashkar, then I'll celebrate my victory by thoroughly punishing every last one of my double-crossing warriors.

"Why are you looking at me like that?" Ivandar demands, bringing me back to the beach.

"Like what?"

"With that disturbing smile."

A dozen snappy remarks dance on the tip of my tongue, but I blow them out on a long, weary breath. This will only work if he doesn't suspect my motives. Which means I can't change my tune too quickly. The shift must feel natural, logical, and, most of all, like his doing.

"You're right. I don't want to sit here." I stand, brush off my tunic, and shield my eyes from the sun. I survey the coarse pink sand and craggy cliffs as if deciding which way to go. Zemya truly is an inhospitable wasteland. All rough edges and prickly briars.

Without another word to Ivandar, I turn and march up the beach. Where I'm going, I haven't a clue. The only thing that matters is that the prince follows me.

Which he does.

"You can't leave without telling me what you know!" He scrambles to his feet and gives chase.

I walk faster.

"You don't know your way out of Zemya, and you look nothing like us. Without my help, you'll be recaptured in half a day. Probably less. You'll still die disgraced and forgotten in a Zemyan prison. Is that what you want?"

No. But I rub the prickles assaulting my arms and screw on a determined, stalwart face.

"Why are you being so stubborn?" he cries. "We can help each other. I'll guide you to Ashkar—even though, technically, you're indebted to me since I already saved your life—but I'm willing to overlook that."

I study him, tapping my finger against the side of my face. "Aren't you worried I'll kill you the moment we reach Ashkar?"

Ivandar snorts and steps closer so we're nose to nose. "You're welcome to try to kill me anytime you'd like, Commander, but I don't think you're battle ready. . . ."

"You'll regret making that challenge."

"And you'll regret not taking my offer."

I frown and grind my teeth. As if the prospect of this arrangement is galling rather than exactly what I want. "I'll reveal a piece of information at the end of each day's travel," I finally say.

"But that could take—"

"Weeks?" I give him my most winning grin. "That's the point. Like you said, this arrangement only works if we need each other."

In theory, traipsing across Zemya while gaslighting the prince seemed like a simple operation. But I failed to take into consideration the hellish landscape. And Ivandar himself.

"Everything in this country is barbed and sadistic," I announce as the sun finally sets on our first day of travel. We've spent the entire day hacking through the bramble between the beach and the mountain, and my arms are riddled with more holes than a sieve.

"You are *choosing* to trudge through the gauntlet." Ivandar holds out his own arms, which are free from a single scratch. He uses his devil magic to rearrange the branches into an archway, which he ducks through.

Before I can follow, the branches snap back and drag their thorny claws across my face. But I don't give in. It's a matter of principle. I won't willingly use the magic I've spent my life fighting against. I won't be further indebted to him.

"This spot looks as good as any." Ivandar stops in a tiny break in the undergrowth. It can't be more than a length or two across, but he sweeps away the twigs and rocks with his boots and plunks down.

"You expect us both to sleep here?" I demand, eyeing the miniscule space. If either of us rolls over, we'll be touching.

"We won't find a larger space, not in a thicket this tight, but you're welcome to find your own clearing. Though, the thorn-nosed demons are more likely to attack a lone camper. Easier prey."

I haven't a clue what a thorn-nosed demon is, but my skin crawls at the mere thought of unseen eyes and scales and claws. It seems unfathomable, but the prince is the lesser evil. So I ease down, putting as much distance between us as possible.

"Well?" He looks at me expectantly.

"You're not even going to give me a moment to catch my breath?"

"You're not out of breath."

I heave an exaggerated sigh as I slowly untie my boots. "Fine. Kartok showed me drawings of stone mounds in that ancient book and asked if I had ever seen them in Ashkar. And if I know what they're used for."

"Well, have you? Do you?"

"Skies, I'm exhausted." I stretch my arms overhead and pretend to yawn as I curl into a ball on my side. It takes everything within me not to laugh while he sputters.

"That's really all you're going to give me? The security of my country depends on this information. I swear I'll see you safely to the border—you have my word."

Little does he know he'll be joining me well beyond the border. Once he knows the full extent of Kartok's plans, he'll be begging to tag along. "First of all, there is no we," I say gruffly. "And the word of a Zemyan, especially Danashti's heir, means nothing to me."

"But—"

"If our roles were reversed, would you reveal your hand so soon?"

He grumbles something indecipherable and rolls to face the other direction.

I let him stew for a good ten minutes, listening to the foreign croaks and chitters playing around us like a symphony, trying not to imagine the horrid creatures they must belong to. Then I finally put him out of his misery and take the first step toward my miraculous "change of heart."

"The stone mounds were monuments to the First Gods," I murmur into the quiet.

Ivandar sucks in a breath and holds it, as if afraid I won't continue if I remember he's listening.

I smile. "Several generations ago they populated the plains of Ashkar like globeflowers. Travelers would stop to pray and pay tribute to them—until the Sky King denounced the old gods and destroyed the mounds."

Ivandar hmms and mumbles, then says, "If the monuments have already been eradicated, why would Kartok ask about them? We know he wanted to nullify your Kalima power. Did he plan on using a prayer mound to ask the Lady of the Sky and Father Guzan to strip Their own children of power? They would never listen."

Because they don't exist. I grunt and hum a few times, so I appear cooperative.

When we resume our trek the next morning, Ivandar is still lost in thought, puzzling over what little information I gave him. Apparently, it was enough to curry favor, because he holds a few branches aside for me with his hands instead of his magic. He also plucks hard green berries from the vines and offers me a handful, even showing me how to peel them.

We make camp that night in another miniscule clearing, even smaller than the first, and as we're sweeping the ground of debris, I toss him another bread crumb: "Kartok had a rather shocking theory about the stone mounds. . . ."

Ivandar whirls around, dropping a rock on his foot. We both laugh as he kicks it away. He thinks I am laughing with him, but I am most definitely laughing at him. I could say anything, make up all sorts of lies, and he'd hungrily devour them. But the best deceptions parallel the truth—like two paths winding through a forest, so similar, it's easy to mistake one for the other, until you're lost.

"He thought the mounds were gateways to the land of the First Gods," I offer, shaking my head as if the theory is ridiculous. Because it is.

Ivandar's icy blue eyes widen. I swear I can feel him trembling as he settles on the ground, quietly repeating the word *gateway*. "Do you think it's possible?" he finally asks, lying on his side so he's facing me instead of the briars.

"I don't know. I've never worshiped the First Gods, so I've never had any desire to reach them. Kartok shouldn't either, by the same logic. Your goddess doesn't dwell with the Lady and Father, right?"

"No, but She used to. Maybe he feels Zemya's entitled to a portion of the sky, since it's Her homeland too. Maybe he sees reclaiming it as a sort of recompense for casting Her out? He's always been zealous in his devotion."

"How do you think the Lady and Father would feel about relinquishing part of their kingdom to Zemya?" I ask, tempted to pat the poor, witless prince on the head. "After hundreds of years of war and animosity, do you honestly think they could live together peaceably?"

"Well, no . . ." Ivandar's brow furrows.

"So Kartok would have to wage *war* against the Lady and Father and depose them."

"That's absurd!" Ivandar cries. "And undoubtedly impossible. They're *gods*."

I shrug and lie down. "You're probably right. I don't worship any of your fool gods, so I haven't a clue what's possible. I've just been ruminating, from the viewpoint of a fellow commander. But it doesn't matter. All of the stone mounds have been demolished."

"You're certain they're all gone?"

"I haven't scoured the continent, if that's what you're asking." I close my eyes, as if settling into sleep. I wait ten seconds before saying, "Don't think me insolent, but why would you care if Kartok infiltrated the realm of the gods and waged war against the Lady and Father? They betrayed your goddess. Shouldn't you want to see Zemya restored and exalted?"

Ivandar stares at me across the dark, the pale blue of his irises blending into the whites, making his eyes look too large, too empty. "Of course I want that. But I also want my kingdom and my birthright. Who do you think my people would choose to follow? The prince whose own mother doubts and overlooks him? Or the generál supreme, who defeated the First Gods and restored all glory to Zemya? If this is truly Kartok's aim and he succeeds, I might as well never return to Karekemish. There may not be anything to return to, depending on the consequences of his actions. Waging war against the gods could break the sky itself."

"What do you mean 'break the sky'?"

"Exactly that. Zemya was born of the Lady and Father. They created *all* things. There's no telling what would happen to us, and everything under the sun, if the Lady and Father were overthrown or killed."

Ivandar's looking at me as if he expects a horrified reaction, but it's difficult to fear fallout from the death of gods you've never believed in. For the sake of my plans, I manage to purse my lips in concern. "Surely Kartok would have considered such things? He may be grasping for your throne, but he couldn't be desperate enough to shatter the sky. I'm sure you have nothing to worry about." I smile gently, knowing my misplaced certainty will make him doubt the sorcerer more than ever.

The higher we climb up the mountain, the thinner the trees become until we finally break free of the briars. After which, we spend the better part of three days trudging back and forth across the narrow switchbacks leading up the mountainside. My feet ache and the thin air refuses to fill my lungs. When at last we reach the pass and begin our descent down the other side, I want to skip with joy. It can only be easier. But I quickly discover the leeward side is even steeper and more difficult to navigate. The path is hardly wider than my foot and it gives way to sheer cliffs that vanish into thick curls of fog.

About halfway down the switchbacks, buildings appear through the mist, built on plateaus carved into the mountainside. The houses and shops cling inexplicably to ledges like lichen, following the shape of the rocks from one level to the next.

"We have to pass through the village—it's the only way down," Ivandar announces. "Which means I'll need to disguise us."

"That is *not* a village!" I point to the impressive watchtowers and the fine houses made of gleaming orange and yellow stone. Delicate, arced staircases cascade from one plateau to the next like a fountain. It's expansive. And breathtaking. And, once again, nothing like the Zemya I remember from our siege. "Why would you hide such an impressive city in the mountains? The cities I saw when we invaded three years ago—"

"Torinth is smaller than most of our cities, so yes, it's a village. And all of our villages and cities are impressive if you truly look at them. We are masters of illusion, remember? Things are rarely as they seem." He lets his words hang in the air, rife with deeper meaning—his *people* and their *magic* aren't what they seem. "It's safer if our enemies think our land is barbaric and not worth conquering."

Ivandar pauses before we round the final bend, then passes a hand over himself from top to bottom. His royal visage ripples, like a blurred reflection in a pond, and transforms into a gangly, pig-nosed messenger boy.

When he raises his hand toward me, I shield my face with my arms and lurch back. "Under no circumstances will you touch me with your devil magic."

"You do realize you look nothing like us?" He glares specifically at my chestnut hair and sun-freckled cheeks.

"I'll turn my hair white with frost. And conceal my freckles with ice," I announce. But when I reach into my core, there isn't enough cold to cover a fingernail, let alone make myself look even partially Zemyan. "I don't understand why you need to be disguised at all," I say, preferring to argue over accepting the inevitable.

Ivandar peers around the bend at the guards in the

watchtowers. "Kartok will have sent soldiers to look for me. He'll pretend it's out of concern, of course. But I have no doubt he's instructed them to push me off a cliff and never breathe a word of it to my mother."

"Why are you in this position?" I ask, genuinely curious. "Why would your mother side with an advisor over her own son when you're seemingly capable and devoted to your country? I can understand why Kartok would be jealous and wish to undermine you, but I don't understand why Danashti would allow it."

Ivandar pulls his fingers through hair that's now chopped short and in the shape of a bowl. "Kartok saved my mother's life eight years ago, and she's bowed to his whims ever since. She was gravely ill with the sweating sickness, and none of the royal healers could do a thing. The entire nation was prepared to enter mourning, and I, at twelve years old, was being whisked to council meetings and tugged down dark corridors by members of the nobility. All of them trying to prey on my youth and inexperience.

"But then Kartok appeared. He was one of the many royal sorcerers serving at the war front, creating illusions and enchanting weapons. But he claimed his father had been a healer, and asked for a chance to see if there was anything he could do for my mother. The royal healers agreed—there was no reason to object at that point. Kartok entered her chambers alone, and when he emerged not an hour later, she was sitting up in bed, groggy and weak but considerably better. He told us he had bled her and administered poultices, things the other healers had attempted a thousand times.

"The entire country celebrated his astonishing work, and my mother named him Generál Supreme for his efforts. Then she never looked my way again."

My hand jumps to my throat, where Kartok carved me

open and erased the scar entirely. Disquiet settles on my skin like the heavy mountain mist. I don't know if it's because I experienced Kartok's unnatural healing firsthand. Or if it's because I can't imagine having your own parent cast you aside like that. As horrible as it is to imagine my parents' horror and disappointment when they learn of my disgrace, at least I had their pride and adoration to begin with. I can't fathom losing it without reason. Especially so young. I would have been completely unmoored. Not to mention jaded. How exhausting must it be, and how resilient must Ivandar be, to continue striving to prove himself, year after year, when it's obviously fruitless?

"That must have been difficult," I say without meaning to.

He looks at me askance. "Don't mock me."

"I wasn't—"

"We need to be through Torinth before nightfall. I'm not strong enough to hold both of our illusions longer than that. Are you ready to cooperate?"

He raises his hand again and I start to shake my head, but the stern voice of reason I first heard at the beach reprimands me again. *Put your arrogance and prejudice aside and do what you must. Focus on the greater goal. Get to the Kalima.*

The thoughts feel so visceral—like fingers clamping around my shoulders, shoving me forward—that I reach out to steady myself against the rocks, even though I haven't actually moved. My thoughts have never been so adamant. But then I've also never been on the run with a Zemyan prince.

Of course my subconscious is screaming.

I take three deep breaths and crack my neck from side to side. "Fine. Do it." I hold out my arms and squeeze my eyes shut. I don't want to see the color leach from my skin. I don't want to feel my bones fracture and reform.

Ivandar's hand passes over me, and I brace for the

bone-wrenching pain of the hot-spring water, for fire to ignite in my belly and melt what little of my power has returned. But I feel tingling instead. A slow, steady trickle that seeps into my bones and gently expands. Almost like water transforming into ice.

"Oh!" I gasp as coolness floods me.

"Not what you expected?" Ivandar asks with a bemused chuckle.

Ignoring him, I open my eyes and survey my body. My tanned, muscular arms are thinner and paler. My legs feel withered and wobbly inside scratchy wool tights. In place of my shredded tunic, I'm wearing a brown messenger's uniform, like Ivandar's, and platinum hair pokes out from my cap.

"How is this possible?"

Ivandar clutches his chest. "The commander of the Kalima warriors wants to learn about our magic?"

"I *want* to ensure it isn't permanent."

"Why? Zemyan skin suits you."

I swat at the prince, but he catches my wrist and turns my hand over. His finger traces up the inside of my forearm, following the vivid blue veins beneath this skin. "It's like a coat," he explains as the illusion bunches up toward my elbows, revealing my freckled complexion beneath. "I rearrange the weave of the world, bending the colors and textures to conceal what I want to hide and create what I want to be seen instead. Satisfied?" The sleeve of Zemyan skin falls back into place.

I nod numbly, holding my arms away from my body as I follow him around the bend. As if I can somehow keep from touching myself.

"Stop walking like that," Ivandar barks back at me. "And don't say anything. Your Zemyan is terrible."

"I've never spoken a word of Zemyan!"

"Exactly."

I have an overwhelming desire to snatch a rock from the path and throw it at the back of his head. "Not because I couldn't, but because I have no interest in speaking your barbaric language."

"You always have to have the final word, don't you?" He shakes his head as he collects a handful of sticks, which he transforms into scrolls stamped with the royal seal. He shoves a few into my arms, then tucks the rest against his side.

When we reach the sentries guarding the gates, Ivandar says something in a high, pre-pubescent voice and waves a scroll excitedly. The sentries admit us with a bored sweep of their blades.

The inside of the mountainside city is just as impressive as its façade. Colorful drapes hang from the open-air storefronts, connecting one shop to the next, and carts with pretty offerings—from amber resin pendants to sea-salt foot scrubs—trundle past. I sit on a bench in a shadowed corner of a plaza while Ivandar goes to collect supplies for the rest of our journey.

I watch a girl selling fresh goat's milk and a group of boys playing with a small silver ball and hoops. When one of the boys overshoots the target, the ball lands in the bucket of goat's milk, drenching the girl. She bursts into tears as the boys laugh and point, but I only hear a single sob before there's a flash of movement and the girl and bucket vanish. I watch the empty space, skin crawling to think what's being done to her now, behind the cloak of magic. But when she reappears several minutes later, her tears are dried, a colorful shawl covers her soiled dress, and an old woman offers her a piece of candy before walking off.

While I gape, a man holding a fussy baby crosses the square, conjuring tiny fireworks over the infant's head and making silly faces.

It seems so ridiculous now, but I have only seen Zemyans at the war front—or in Karekemish, calling for my execution. It never occurred to me that they would live in normal cities and do normal things like sell food and jewelry and chat with friends. That they would calm their babies and console crying children. If I closed my eyes, I'd almost think I was in Sagaan—without the abhorrent magic, of course.

"You look perplexed," Ivandar says, walking up with a full satchel slung over his shoulder. "Ready to go?"

I say nothing. I don't remember how to form words. At least not coherent ones. The thoughts jumbling around my brain are disturbing. And ludicrous.

"Let me guess . . . You're disappointed to discover we don't spend our days weaving deception and eating raw meat and sacrificing Ashkarian virgins?" he asks with a goading smile.

"Something like that," I mumble as we descend from plateau to plateau. A headache is drilling into the center of my forehead and this irritating Zemyan skin is too tight. That's why I feel like I'm suffocating.

I need it off.

I need out of this godforsaken country.

I need to reach the Kalima as quickly as possible and reclaim my title. Regain my footing. And re-center my mind.

Which means it's time to speed this deception along.

"I wasn't completely honest with you about the stone mounds," I say as soon as we're alone on a dirt path, cutting through fields that look to be weeds, but who knows—maybe they're bursting with fruit more abundant than the vineyards of Ashkar and this is all an illusion. The reality the Zemyans want me to see.

I don't know how I'm supposed to decipher what's real and what isn't when *nothing* feels real. I was abandoned by the Kalima and tortured by Zemyan magic. I am traveling with

Danashti's heir and currently wearing Zemyan skin.

Ivandar slams to a halt and towers over me, somehow still intimidating despite his pig-nosed disguise. "What do you mean you weren't honest?"

"I didn't lie," I quickly explain. "Kartok *did* tell me the mounds are gateways. And I haven't seen one in years. However, I withheld what happened afterward—to ensure I had leverage to force you to take me to Ashkar. But after everything you told me about the danger Kartok poses to the entire continent, I'm worried we don't have time to waste."

"Why?"

"Kartok continued thumbing through that book, insisting Zemya would provide a way to accomplish his task without the stone mounds. Then he seemed to find something promising and demanded to know how many different Kalima powers there are, and how they are distributed throughout the battalion. When I said none of my warriors were a weak link, he said *they* are *the link* and demanded to know where the Kalima would go."

Ivandar stares at me without blinking. "What exactly are you saying?"

"I'm saying, Kartok knows how to access the land of the gods through the Kalima. I think he's looking for them. Which means the Lady and Father, and all of us, are in real danger."

"Why would you suddenly care? You don't believe in any of this."

"I don't . . . know what I believe anymore," I say, treading carefully. Admitting just enough to lure him but not enough to entangle myself in lies. "I just know Kartok is determined to strip me of my power, and if there's even a miniscule chance he'll succeed, I have to stop it. But I don't know enough about the gods to warn them or protect them. And your mother is the only person who has a prayer of reasoning with Kartok, but we'll need proof of his corruption, proof that the entire continent is in danger, to convince her to turn against him."

"What are you suggesting?"

"Come with me into Ashkar. Help me find the Kalima. And let's save your fool gods."

"You're serious?" he demands.

"No, I'm stirring up all of this trouble for fun. Yes, I'm serious! We each have something the other needs. You've been begging for answers and aid all this time. Well, now I'm offering it."

"I don't know if I can trust you," he says, searching my gaze.

"I don't know if you have a choice."

CHAPTER
TWENTY-ONE

ENEBISH

"For the love of the Lady and Father! Don't just stand there," Temujin groans. He's dangling from the branches of a tree, as if every bone in his body has crumbled. "Either cut me down and do what you will with me, or kill me here and put me out of my misery. Despite my impressive fortitude and high tolerance for pain, being partially impaled on a broken limb is rather uncomfortable."

"We'd *hate* for you to be uncomfortable," Serik says as he hoists himself into the tree. A branch the width of my arm is, indeed, buried in Temujin's side. The jagged shards stab him like the pronged spears used by ice fishermen in Sagaan.

"Remove the debris first," Temujin pants through his teeth when Serik reaches him. "It will be horrendous otherwise."

Serik reaches over, but instead of extracting the shards, he frees Temujin's saber from its sheath and hacks through the branch nestled in Temujin's flesh, conveniently obliterating the limbs beneath him too.

Temujin groans as he crashes to the ground.

"Oops." Serik hops down beside Temujin, who's writhing in agony. "Guess I don't know my own strength."

We move to grab Temujin—me from one side and Serik from the other—but as our fingers close around his thrashing arms, a shadow streaks from the top of the tree and a deafening screech fills my ears.

This time, I know to jump away from Orbai's talons before they gouge me. That doesn't make the attack any less painful, though. Tears spring to my eyes as she banks around a tree and circles back. My mind *knows* she's under Kartok's influence, but my heart still refuses to accept it. The core of my soul is so entwined with hers, I can't believe there's a power in this world—or any other—that could sever our bond.

"Give me your cloak," I shout at Serik. *"Quickly!"*

He unfastens the clasp and tosses me the heavy bundle. I manage to wrangle it into position and fling it into the air, just as Orbai dives. She lets out another screech but doesn't have time to veer before the fabric swallows her, entangling her wings. She crashes into the mud and I jump on top of the wriggling cloak.

"I'm sorry," I murmur, imagining her pain and terror, wishing I could stroke her feathers rather than pin her wings.

"You didn't bother apologizing to me," Temujin says sardonically.

"That's because we aren't sorry." Serik snaps a vine from a nearby tree and winds it around Temujin's wrists. "Any pain you feel is deserved. And of your own making." Then, without a word of warning, he wrenches the shard of wood from Temujin's side.

Temujin's cries are so loud and horrific, Ziva and the shepherds come crashing through the forest, all wide-eyed and panting, certain we'd been attacked by animals—or worse.

"We found a little parting gift for the road," Serik announces, dragging Temujin through the muck and displaying him like a goat in an auction ring.

I watch the shepherds' reactions closely, looking for the slightest hint of compassion, the smallest flicker of sympathy. They were ready to hand me and Serik over to him before the fire. And I know how persuasive Temujin can be. How he makes you feel so essential and respected—right up until the moment he slits your throat. We must tread carefully. I can't have the shepherds secretly aiding him because he gave them a few stolen ration sacks back on the grazing lands.

Thankfully, everyone is still so distraught from the fire and water cannons, no one makes a move to defend Temujin. We bind him with proper ropes and start our journey north to Chotgor. Serik leads the wagon train, keeping us on track and the shepherds in check, and also heating the air so it's slightly warmer as we pass through. I, on the other hand, hang back and keep a close watch on Temujin, knowing it's only a matter of time before he starts weaving his carefully crafted lies.

"I meant what I said," I overhear him telling Iree the next day, when the mugginess fades and the first hint of a chilly breeze rustles the leaves. "All of this traipsing across the continent is unnecessary. You're in no danger. You have no reason to bustle about recruiting allies or whatever it is Enebish has convinced you to do."

Temujin chose this moment with care, hoping Iree would be weak and pliable, dreading the punishing wind and cold to come, but Temujin doesn't know how stubborn and grudging this particular shepherd can be.

Iree tugs sharply on Temujin's rope, sending the rebel sprawling. "Half of my flock perished because of you."

I tilt my face up to the heavens and praise the Lady and Father. After which I immediately ask Them to help me stay vigilant. Iree won't always be holding Temujin's rope, and there are many others, like Emani or Lalyne, who will lap up Temujin's lies like cream atop fresh milk.

I debate sending them all ahead, insisting I be the one to manage Temujin, but that's what I would have done before. I don't want to be that wary and untrusting person anymore. I can't be. I refuse to let Ghoa and Temujin and Kartok continue to win, and the best way to thwart them is to trust the shepherds and show I'm capable of working as a team.

On our third night of travel, Temujin makes a grab for the darkness. I knew it was only a matter of time. I just didn't know how much of my power Kartok had siphoned, or how much Temujin could access—or even *how* he accesses it, for that matter. But it must have dwindled considerably, since he doesn't reach for starfire.

It happens as we're breaking down camp at sunset, the group still in fairly high spirits, despite the ever-thinning trees and the snow beginning to crust the grass. One moment, the midnight tendrils are gliding around my neck and cooing in my ears, preparing to shield our caravan, and the next they're clumsily yanked away. Like a child holding a quill with so much concentration, it stabs through the sheet of parchment.

I could easily snatch the darkness out of his untrained grip and be done with it, but since he's considerably weaker than before, I decide to use it as a teaching opportunity. I've been showing Ziva something new every day—how to coax the ribbons into flat stitches to form the netting that conceals our caravan. How to nudge those tendrils along in the direction you want them to go. How to toss a cluster of darkness to incapacitate a person. And now, how to disable a halfwit. I don't know where in the skies Temujin thinks he'll go, or how he's going to get there, considering Ziva and I can still see him plain as day, but I make a point not to think about the inner workings of his dubious mind.

"Ziva!" I call.

"It isn't me!" she insists as she scrambles to where I'm folding my bedroll.

"I know. Not even you're this pathetic." I shoot her a teasing grin and she shoves my shoulder. "It appears our aspiring Night Spinner has taken a handful of darkness. . . . How would you react?"

"By taking it back." She lifts her hand, but I drape my fingers over hers.

"You *could* . . . but consider our enemy. Temujin acts like a spoiled, entitled child. That would only start a tug-of-war."

"You don't think I'm strong enough to best him?" Ziva's thick brows flatten into a familiar scowl.

"Don't look at me like that. Of course you are. But it's a needless waste of energy."

"So what do I do?"

"If he wants the darkness, give it to him."

Ziva cocks her head in confusion. "But—"

"*All* of it."

The corner of her mouth curls. With a flick of her wrists, she gathers the night in her arms and thrusts the bundle across the encampment at Temujin, who's attempting to blend into the shadow of a rock. The oily darkness pummels him like a waterfall, knocking him flat on his back. He gulps and sputters as if he's truly drowning, and I encourage Ziva to keep the tendrils flowing perhaps a tad longer than necessary.

Two nights later Temujin attempts to steal the darkness again while we're wading through the deepening snow. This time, the inky weave barely snags and he collapses with a frustrated roar.

I snicker and yank him back to his feet, pleased to be holding the rope tonight, to witness this failure. "I thought Kartok promised you access to Zemyan magic?"

"He did! I drank the hot-spring water. That's how I was able to wield your siphoned starfire! I don't know why—"

"You don't know why the *enemy* lied to you?" I say with a needling grin.

"He didn't lie. I'm sure there's a logical explanation."

"The logical explanation is, you're pitifully naïve."

"Just kill me and be done with it."

"Not until you give me what I want," I say for what must be the hundredth time.

"I *can't* give you any information."

"You mean you *won't*," I correct him. "If Kartok discovers you relayed his plans, he won't appoint you governor of Sagaan. All of your treasonous scheming would have been for nothing."

"No, I mean I *can't*. I don't have a choice."

"'We always have a choice,'" I parrot the seemingly valiant proclamation he spewed at me back in the false realm of the Eternal Blue. "'It's no fault of mine if you can't bear the alternative. . . .'"

"*Fine.* Yes. Initially, there is always a choice. But sometimes we make mistakes that limit our options, cinching them into a funnel, until every choice has been stripped away and we're shackled to the path of that original misstep."

I resume marching without warning, forcing him to stumble to keep up.

"Why don't you ask Orbai if she *can't* or *won't* stop trying to return to Kartok?" Temujin gestures up ahead, to the shepherd tasked with transporting my eagle. She's trapped inside a cage originally intended for a dog, still attacking the wooden bars as if they're the carcass of a rabbit.

I've visited her every day of our journey. Begging her to come back to me. Whispering happy memories of our years together. Reaching out to gently stroke her golden feathers.

But her eyes continue to dart with a wild intensity I haven't seen since the day she arrived at Ikh Zuree, just hours after being snatched from the tundra. Every time my fingers get close, she lunges to snap them off.

There has to be a way to reverse the binding. I will *find* a way to reverse the binding—or spend the rest of my life trying.

"So quick to forgive your eagle, but so quick to condemn me . . ." Temujin muses into the silence.

"Orbai is a *bird*," I retort. "She doesn't have agency or a conscience. She can't be held accountable."

"Do you think the binding magic cares if you're bird or human? I'm doing my best within the parameters I've been given." Temujin's voice hitches, and it makes my gaze flit back. I watch him totter through the knee-deep snow, battered and bloodstained. The last time I saw Kartok in the Temple of Serenity, he tried to slit my throat in order to heal me with Loridium—to bind my will to his, as he'd done with Orbai.

And, supposedly, Temujin.

How much of the rebel's treachery has been intentional and how much is Kartok's pull? I wonder before I catch Temujin watching me with those mournful golden eyes. Willing these thoughts into existence.

Thankfully, I'm immune to his charms this time. In fact, I revel in his moans over the next two weeks as we trudge toward the Chotgori steppes, where the wind blows sideways and frost gnaws at your fingers and toes—even with the help of Serik's heat.

"Please kill me and reap your revenge," he begs me every day.

And every day I smile and say, "But this is so much more satisfying than killing you."

We arrive in Arisilon City three weeks to the day from the time we left Namaag. Even though I knew we wouldn't be greeted by a welcoming party and whisked away for hot baths and a feast, and even though Temujin claimed the Chotgori were living in squalor and forced to work in the mines, the sight of their ravaged capital still grinds my heart like the heel of a boot.

Just get to Chotgor, I'd chanted through every grueling league of our trek. As if making it this far north was the ultimate goal rather than the first rung on an incredibly high and rickety ladder.

It seems the shepherds had the same misguided hopes. Their eyes grow rounder than shields as we pass through the wreckage. Iree's youngest daughter, who can't be more than five, reaches for her father's hand. "It's worse than the grazing lands," she whispers.

He nods solemnly and pulls her closer.

The riverside city is even bleaker than it was five years ago, directly following the Battle of a Hundred Nights, when Ashkar finally brought Chotgor into the Protected Territories. Unlike Namaag, I was present for this siege. I helped topple the quaint snow houses stippling the outskirts of the city. I aided Tuva, lending what I could of my novice Night Spinning, to help her drench the sky with a blackness so oppressive, all vestiges of everyday life ceased.

It was always under the assumption—nay, *promise*—that it would all be restored to even greater glory than before. That was the entire purpose of forming the Protected Territories— to offer these struggling people a better way of life. Yet here we are, half a decade later, and the charming little pubs and fisheries are still boarded up. Not a single ice barge floats in the frozen river, and the once great Castle of the Clans, which burst from the earth like fountains of cascading ice, lies in shattered ruin across the square. Above it all, a thick layer of charcoal smoke presses down like rain clouds.

It looks like chimney smoke, but every hearth in the city couldn't produce billows so thick.

"Bleeding skies. I don't have the strength for this," Serik mutters as we pick our way through debris. "This is hardly better than the grasslands!" He waves at the ice-crusted buildings surrounding us and the leagues and leagues of windswept snow behind us. He's spent every waking hour either clearing a pathway through the snow or hunkered beside a sputtering fire, collecting the wavering bands of heat and redistributing them over the caravan. His face is so gaunt and his skin so sallow, it takes on a greenish pallor against the starkness of his freckles.

"Where is everyone?" a shepherd boy asks, his voice echoing like a cannon down the empty street.

Not a single soul has peeked their head into the cold to investigate our passing. They wouldn't be able to see us, of course, not through the cloak of darkness Ziva and I have stretched over the group, but surely a few people should be bustling down the road on errands.

"They're mining the ice fields. Just as I told you," Temujin says, shooting me a frigid look.

"Do you expect me to congratulate you for telling the truth this once?"

"It looks like a graveyard," Lalyne says solemnly.

"That's because it *is* a graveyard," Temujin interjects again before I can respond. "The imperial troops blew through these streets like a snow squall, destroying everything in their path."

He isn't wrong, but at the time it felt justified. Provoked, even. The Sky King had attempted to treat with the leaders of each clan several times to draft an alliance agreement, but not only did the Chotgori spit on his offer, they organized against us, attacking our encampment on the steppes in the middle of the night, armed with fishing spears and clubs, looking for all the world like snarling bears in their grizzled furs. The Chotgori clanspeople were more ferocious warriors than the citizens of Namaag and Verdenet combined—that's how we lost Tuva, and so many others. We had to respond.

Or so I thought.

We had no right to ride into their city and expect them to thank us for offering "protection" in the form of chains. We had no right to assume the Ashkarian way of life was superior or would suit them better than their own traditions and beliefs.

We lumber past the obliterated palace, which is where we spot the first of the imperial guards. The majority of the shepherds remain hidden in the debris, while a group of us sneak closer, pressed along the walls beneath a blanket of darkness.

There are several dozen soldiers milling between the outbuildings at the rear of the royal estate—an entire little city of barns and barracks and guesthouses that avoided destruction during the siege. Except now I'm not ignorant enough to believe their "survival" was coincidental.

The Sky King had this planned all along.

"Do you think they know about the Sky King? And Sagaan?" Serik asks.

I watch them, smoking their lichen pipes and drinking their steaming ale. They certainly don't look like warriors who've recently learned of the fall of their empire. But they could be keeping up pretenses to fool the Chotgori, until instructions and reinforcements arrive.

Beyond the outbuildings, heaps of dark earth, taller than any building in Sagaan—including the Sky Palace—pepper the snowy expanse. At the base of every mound, a gorge is cut into the earth, wide and deep enough to hold an entire battalion of warriors. Never-ending lines of Chotgori workers file in and out of the pits, some pulling carts loaded with rubble. Others stoop beneath the weight of enormous boulders, which they unload into a massive circular furnace—the source of the oppressive black smoke. The Chotgori workers are so caked with dirt and soot, their vibrant red-and-gold hair is the color of clay and dried mud. Their skin is almost as dark as mine and Temujin's, when they're naturally almost as pale as the Zemyans.

A host of imperial guards hang over the railings and patrol the rims of the mines. Their numbers may be fewer than ours, but they are trained and well-fed and haven't been traipsing through the bitter cold for weeks.

"How do we even begin to stop this?" Bultum asks when we rejoin the group and describe the conditions. "We'll never be able to contend with that many imperial warriors."

"Which is why you need the help of the Shoniin and Zemyans," Temujin declares, earning him a swat across the head from Serik.

"If your 'allies' are so honorable and dependable, why haven't they come for you?" Serik asks.

"I'm certain they've sent search parties," Temujin fires back, but the defensiveness in his voice hardly suggests certainty. "They're coming."

Serik laughs. "Whatever you need to tell yourself, deserter. As for a way to take out the guards . . . that furnace is all the ammunition we need. We escort the workers from the mines under the cover of darkness, as Enebish did at the war front, then lure the guards close to the refinery and I'll blow it to pieces. *Boom!* Laborers freed, adversaries vanquished, mines collapsed, all in one explosion."

I slap my palm to my forehead. "Why do your plans always

involve blowing things up?"

"Because it's effective," Serik proclaims. "And because I'm a Sun Stoker. It all makes so much sense now."

I roll my eyes and give him a tender, but firm, shove. "The guards will notice if there's suddenly only a trickle of prisoners carting rocks back and forth. We'll be much better off entering the mines beneath the cover of darkness and rallying the laborers to rise against the imperial warriors with us, as planned."

The group is quiet, fidgeting. Most of them won't even look at me, and the few who do are shaking their heads.

"I know it seems more daunting now that we're here, but with the Chotgori workers, we'll outnumber the imperial warriors at least three to one. And they're already armed with shovels and picks."

"If it were only about numbers, the Chotgori would have risen against the imperial warriors long ago," Iree exclaims.

"Maybe not." I force my voice to stay strong with conviction. "Maybe they haven't attempted to rebel because they feared they would just be recaptured and punished if they tried. But once they learn the empire has fallen, once they see all of us—"

"They'll know there's no hope!" Azamat calls, which earns several hysterical laughs and a death glare from me.

"*Once they see all of us,*" I repeat, "they'll have no reason not to rise. It's the best opportunity they could hope for."

I twist my tunic through my fingers and hold my breath, waiting for at least one person to nod with reluctant agreement. To be the pebble that starts the ripple through the pond.

But it's Emani who eventually speaks. "We're going to die, aren't we?" she wails.

And the group devolves into chaos.

CHAPTER TWENTY-TWO

GHӨA

Five exhausting days later we finally cross from Zemya into Ashkar.

There's no jarring shift in the landscape to delineate one country from the other. In fact, the transition between the rocky, weed-littered fields to the lush, sprawling grasslands is almost seamless. As if the earth is somehow blissfully unaware of the chasm that exists between our people—the centuries of endless war. There aren't even any sentries patrolling the border, since there's no border to speak of. Not with the Zemyans occupying Sagaan and a good majority of our cities.

But I sense the change immediately—the welcoming tug of my country. My boots sink deeper into the dark soil. My spine straightens, lengthening toward the infinite sky. And the icy core in my chest, which has been steadily hardening since my escape, crackles with recognition.

I glance over at Ivandar, curious to see if he felt the shift. If his love for his country runs as deeply as mine.

But of course it doesn't.

He's plodding along, more concerned with rubbing his shivering arms and moaning through his chattering teeth than noticing the terrain—and it isn't even cold enough to snow yet! I smirk and shake my head. It would be impossible for him to possess the same level of devotion when the foundations of Zemya are so inherently flawed. Yet a small, bewildering droplet of unease trickles down my neck because I can't deny the quiet moments of humanity I saw in Torinth. Or how Ivandar's healing ministrations eased the effects of the hot-spring water. Or the Zemyan prisoner who comforted the young Ashkarian warrior with her illusions.

Their magic is vile. I *know* this. But what I know and what I've seen aren't adding up. I can't reconcile the Zemyans I've battled for the past twelve years with the Zemyans I've seen these past twelve days.

I stop abruptly, refusing to carry even an inkling of doubt into my country. "If Ashkar attacked first and your people were only acting in self-defense, as you claim, why did they *continue* to attack Ashkar after the initial battle?"

Ivandar trips and blinks at me with his pale demon eyes. The only facet of his appearance he didn't change with his messenger-boy disguise. "What are you talking about?"

"For centuries, the Zemyans have been crossing our border and sacking our villages. How could you possibly condone those actions?"

The prince continues gaping as if I've sprouted a second head. Finally he says, "We had to defend ourselves. Ashkar was always hammering at our border, and when that didn't work, you swept into Namaag then Verdenet and Chotgor, forcing them to align with you."

"We didn't *force* anyone into an alliance! The induction of every Protected Territory into the Unified Empire was voluntary. We needed soldiers and resources, and they needed aid and protection—from *you*. It's an equal partnership."

"Is an alliance voluntary if one party is so desperate for relief they *can't* refuse 'aid,' no matter the terms? Zemya had to make a stand or we knew we'd be next. We had to choose to be the hunter or the hunted. And, yes, there was spite and animosity, too," he adds. "How could there not be when the Lady and Father cast Zemya from Their presence, refused to acknowledge Her innovative magic, then tried to squash Her and Her power altogether?"

"None of that is true!" I insist.

"It doesn't matter which version of history is true!" Ivandar shouts over me. "That's the entire point. All of this fighting is needless. And while we're locked in this endless conflict, Kartok's waging a completely different kind of war."

I have nothing to say to that. Whatever Kartok's up to—whether he's laying siege to the heavens, stripping the Kalima of our powers, or something else entirely—none of it results in my glory and reinstatement.

I stare at the prince and force a small nod.

He dramatically brings a hand to his chest. "Have we finally found something we agree on?"

"I don't *agree* with you," I retort. "But I don't entirely disagree, either."

"You realize that makes no sense?"

"It doesn't have to. And since we're back in my country, we play by my rules. Please remove this horrid Zemyan skin suit at once."

"Only because you said please," Ivandar taunts as he passes his hand over me from top to bottom. The warmth of his skin raises goose bumps down my arms and legs. Or perhaps the involuntary shudders are from the chunks of ghost-white flesh dripping down my limbs. "Though, I still say the Zemyan form suits you . . ." he says with a peevish grin.

"Do you know what suits you? My fist. In your face." With a flutter of my fingers, I chisel a small clenched fist out of ice and send it flying at his nose. It's the largest weapon I've been able to conjure since I drained my power in the sea, and I smile proudly as it flies toward the slack-jawed prince, who, unfortunately, ducks at the last moment.

"Merciful seas, Ghoa! It was a joke!" he sputters. "You could have taken off my head."

Now I'm the one sputtering. Not because I'm worried for his fool head but because he called me by name. The sound of it crashes against my temple like the hilt of a sword. Swift and jarring.

"This is no time for jokes," I finally manage to bark. "And don't address me so lightly."

"*Really?*" He stomps closer as his own Zemyan disguise melts away. "We've been traveling together for nearly two weeks. Don't you think we've reached a certain level of familiarity?" He slashes his hands downward with quick, broad strokes, painting his skin the color of linen and his hair and eyes a deep, syrupy brown. Seeing him like that—looking like me and my people—is even more unnerving than his natural form.

"No," I say without further explanation. "And under no circumstances are you permitted to do more of *that*"—I wave an agitated hand at his unfamiliar features—"without my express consent."

"I wouldn't dream of doing anything without your consent." He stalks past me, even though he doesn't have the slightest idea where he's going. "I'm guessing you don't know where the Kalima will be, since Kartok wasn't able to torture it out of you? And because they clearly want nothing to do with you," he adds.

"You guessed wrong." I surge forward, matching him stride for stride.

"Why would they go anywhere you could find them?"

"Because they'd never expect me to escape from my Zemyan captors—which is their second biggest mistake."

He rolls his eyes. "So where will they be?"

"Sequestered at our rendezvous point, trying to regroup and form a plan of attack."

"*Where* is the rendezvous point?"

I laugh in the prince's face. No one beyond the Sky King and his most trusted warriors know about the ice caves hidden beneath the plains just north of Chotgor. I'm not about to tell the Zemyan heir, traveling companion or not.

"You're really not going to tell me?" He sounds as if I owe him this. As if we're truly partners on this quest. "You do realize you're taking me there?"

"Precisely. You'll find out soon enough. All you need to know is that you'd freeze to death if you tried to get there without my assistance. So don't get any ideas."

"Of course it's somewhere colder," Ivandar grumbles, hugging himself.

"The coldest," I affirm with a devilish grin, eager to finally seize the upper hand.

It takes us three days to reach the old pelt smugglers' tunnels that run between Sagaan and Chotgor. The underground highway shaves weeks off the journey. Which means even if Kartok somehow learned of the Kalima's hideout, it would take him twice as long to reach the caves. Giving me time to prepare the Kalima to meet him.

Just before we reach the outskirts of Sagaan, I lead Ivandar down a hidden pathway that branches off the main trail, and use my power to heave an enormous boulder of ice aside.

"We're going underground?" Ivandar balks at the top of the wet stone staircase, squinting down into the frigid dark.

"Is that a problem?" I ask sweetly. "It's sheltered from the wind and snow. You should be thanking me."

"Do you feel that draft? It's colder and damper than a grave!" His teeth chatter harder and he hunches his shoulders.

"Zemyans are truly the least resilient people on the planet. We should have defeated you centuries ago," I say as I trot down the stairs.

Ivandar curses and follows me into the tunnel, which I'll admit, feels almost chilly and looks like a rodent's burrow—a long, squat shaft completely devoid of light, save a torch at the base of the stairs. I light it and venture into the murk. Ivandar follows, already complaining about the wet and dark, disparaging Ashkar for its differences from Zemya, even though he doesn't have the context to appreciate those differences.

It's precisely what you did when you arrived in Zemya. . . .

I smash the irritating thought beneath my boot like I do the worms slithering through the mud. Zemya *is* a barren wasteland. Ashkar, however, is a beautiful, discerning mistress—kind only to those who are strong enough to endure her perils. A trial of worthiness, of sorts.

And the Zemyan prince is far from worthy.

Whenever we stop to rest, he shivers and whimpers pathetically—even in his sleep. Making it impossible for *me* to sleep. But no matter how many times I tell him he's welcome to return to the warmth of Zemya—which is a bald-faced lie—he bravely soldiers on. Forcing me to acknowledge the risks he's taking and the sacrifices he's making. All in the name of his country and goddess.

After four long nights I can't stand the sound of his sniveling for another second. I glance over at him, curled up like a dead roach. I could leave him. Leave all of this behind. Forget the Kalima and start anew.

Listen to yourself! The internal reprimand feels like a slap to the face—one I probably deserve. But still, my cheek burns so acutely, my fingers peruse it for damage.

This isn't right, a tiny instinctual voice in my brain counters.

What isn't right is quitting. Allowing traitorous warriors to tarnish your name, sound logic intervenes. *Where would you even go? Using the prince is the only way to reclaim your position.*

Of course, I'm right—it's impossible to be wrong when you're arguing with yourself.

Again, I peer at the shivering prince. I have to do something to shut him up, and since leaving him behind isn't an option, I close my eyes, place my hands on my ankles, and turn all of my focus to the frozen ground beneath me. It's hard and sharp, and I silently invite it to join me. Taking it in instead of forcing it out, as I do when I attack.

The frigid mud and frosty air funnel into my body, storing ice inside my flesh the way marmots gather barleynuts for winter. Within minutes my skin is colder than the ground. My eyelashes crystalize with frost. My legs are so numb, I can't feel the weight of my hands, and it makes me laugh with giddy triumph. Ice cuts most people down to the smallest shivering fragment of themselves, but it chisels me into a saber. Hardens me into a weapon. I haven't felt this strong, or deadly, since my capture.

It won't last long. Soon enough, the balance will shift and the ice will overwhelm me. My body will become slow and stiff and heavy—flesh wasn't meant to hold infinite, raw power—but I intend to revel in every second of limitless strength while I can.

"Why are you laughing?" Ivandar groans through chattering teeth. He cracks one eye open and instantly scrambles to his knees. Pleading and babbling. I can only imagine how I must look—every inch of me covered in frost, like the ice sculptures carved in my honor at the Kalima's celebratory feasts. "Whatever you're doing, stop," he begs. "You still need me!"

"Quit blathering. I'm not going to freeze you to death."

"Then what are you doing?"

"Shutting you up so I can sleep."

"You can freeze my voice?"

I probably could—I don't know why I didn't consider that possibility first—but I don't have the energy to goad him. My head already feels like a boulder of ice, cleaved in half by a pickax, and my arms are so stiff, I can no longer bend my elbows. "I can ease the chill by siphoning the cold from the air into me."

Ivandar glowers at me, even as his teeth stop chattering. "Have you always been able to do this?"

"Yes."

"And you only decided to use it now?"

"Yes," I say again without a hint of remorse.

"You're unbelievable!" His face is a smear of angry shadows in the torchlight. He tries to climb to his feet but slips in the mud, which is looser thanks to the pocket of warmth surrounding us. He lands with a splash on his backside. The dark brown sludge spatters his unearthly white skin, which he doesn't have to disguise belowground. "How could you just sit there and watch me suffer for so many days? After everything I've done for you!"

I settle gingerly onto my side, my muscles crackling like a frozen pond, and close my eyes. "First of all, I owe you nothing. I don't know how many times I have to remind you of this. Second, Kartok made it nearly impossible for me to wield the ice at all. And third, taking the cold into my body requires even more energy than pushing it out. I've never even helped my own warriors this way, so I don't know why I'd do it for you."

"Why are you then?"

"I'm not," I say, refusing to open my eyes, even though I can feel his gaze boring into my face. "I couldn't care less about you. It's for me. To shut you up—like I said."

"Well, I'm grateful, no matter the reason," he says after a long pause.

I groan so he knows exactly what I think of his *gratitude*, then I pull the cold around me like a blanket and command myself to sleep.

But the hours pass, and rest refuses to come. And I can't even blame the prince and his whimpering anymore. I tell myself it must be the increased ice flooding my bones or the anticipation of what awaits when we reach the Kalima's rendezvous point. My restlessness has nothing to do with the prince or his softly murmured thanks.

"Stay close and stay silent," I instruct Ivandar as we edge around the icy boulders concealing the tunnel's entrance. Daylight filters through the cracks, making my eyes squint and my pulse pound. I haven't a clue what to expect in Chotgor—if the imperial warriors abandoned their posts when they heard news of the Sky King's death, or if the Chotgori workers caught wind and rose up in rebellion. Or maybe the Zemyans have already claimed this territory?

Thankfully, the state of Chotgor makes little difference to

me, so long as the prince and I can pass through Arisilon City and into the ice fields without being seen.

I flex my fingers, press them against the craggy surface of the nearest boulder, and channel its unyielding cold. My ice is always strongest in winter, and stronger still in Chotgor.

The entrance to the smugglers' tunnel is in the animal market, concealed behind a stall that sells muskox pelts—or *used* to sell muskox pelts. No one's sold much of anything since the Chotgori refused to enter the Protected Territories peaceably. I don't come to Chotgor very often anymore, but the markets haven't been open the last few times I visited, so I don't expect them to be now. Still, I peer carefully around the dirty boulder of ice—just in case.

"Where is everyone?" Ivandar's voice is right in my ear, his breath hot on my cheek, and I nearly jump out of my skin.

"Get back!" I stab my elbow into his ribs. "I told you to stay behind me!"

"No, you told me to stay close," he wheezes.

"Not *that* close! Instead of poking your nose where it doesn't belong, make yourself useful and clothe us in blue and gold. We need to blend in with the imperial warriors." I look expectantly at Ivandar.

He grumbles under his breath but complies, manipulating the colors and textures to change his face and to conceal our filthy tunics with spotless Ashkarian uniforms. "Happy?"

"It isn't so fun when you have to dress like the enemy, is it?" I taunt, smoothing my fingers down the pressed uniform. I wait for relief to wash over me, but the fabric doesn't feel as crisp as I remember. Nor does it fill me with the same pride and confidence.

That's because it's an illusion. The fault is with the prince's magic.

Shaking my head, I emerge from the tunnel and strike

out into the hazy orange light. The sun never rises high in Chotgor, circling the horizon like a ruby-studded belt, even at midday. Normally, I despise the dim half dark and perpetual gloom—and Arisilon City seems even darker than I recall from previous visits—but today I thank the shroud for the added cover.

I jog through the silent, shadowed market. The prince follows, his breath heavy, though he doesn't seem to be struggling to keep up. "Where is everyone?" he asks again. "The streets and stalls are so snow-covered. There isn't a single footprint. . . ."

I ignore him and dart into a residential neighborhood, where doors hang lopsided on their hinges, slamming open and closed with every gust of snow. Broken carts spill decaying goods across the road, but I vault over them with ease. Focused on the ice fields waiting on the other side of this quarter.

"Nearly there," I whisper.

But as I hurdle a low stone wall, Ivandar's bony fingers close around my elbow. His grip is so tight and unexpected, my body jerks to a halt and I crash into the wall. A long, piercing cry explodes from my lips and rattles through the empty homes and shops.

"Are you trying to get us caught?" I whip around and fling the prince off. My eyes dart up and down the road and I drop into a crouch, waiting for a storm of imperial warriors.

"What happened here?" Ivandar demands. "Where are the people? Aren't you perturbed by these abysmal conditions?" His face is crumpled with an expression that looks like concern. Which is ridiculous.

"Don't act as if you give a piss about Chotgor."

"What about you, Ghoa? Do *you* give a piss? You don't seem the slightest bit disturbed. Almost as if you knew . . ." Ivandar buries his hands in his hair, and the dark brown illusion trickles down his face—like paint smeared in the rain.

I should ignore him. I don't owe him any sort of explanation. But for some inexplicable reason, I feel compelled to defend myself and my empire: "The Chotgori chose this. We tried to negotiate with the clans, but they *attacked* us."

"Maybe because you invaded their land . . ."

"Just as *your* people are invading our land?" I shove my palms into his chest. Forcing him away. Commanding him to stop.

"These are *your* people, Ghoa. . . . At least they're supposed to be. Doesn't that bother you?"

"What bothers me is being harangued by a Zemyan! Why do you care? Chotgor's weakness will make seizing the continent easier for you."

"I don't want the continent! And I care because you're better than this!"

"No. I'm not," I snap.

"You are! You sacrificed yourself to save your entire battalion. Then you endured Kartok's torture without betraying the very people who left you to die. You were willing to work with Hadassah—and *me*! Not only are you leading me across your country, but you kept me from freezing to death."

The longer his list grows, the more nauseous I become. I clamp my palms over my ears. "Enough! You know that wasn't for your benefit."

"I know that you're fiercely dedicated to your position," Ivandar counters. "You would do anything for Ashkar."

"I would do anything to further my *standing* in Ashkar!" The confession flies from my lips, and I can't stop myself from flinching when disappointment fills Ivandar's eyes. Which enrages me more. "Where is this even coming from? Who cares about Chotgor when the gods themselves are in danger?"

When Ivandar says nothing, I step closer. Puff my chest higher, preening with triumph. But it isn't as satisfying as I thought it would be. The prince stares past me, his pale eyes wide and blinking. He points over my shoulder with a thin white finger, which is when I realize his disguise melted away in his agitation.

Mine did too.

"*We* care about the Chotgori," a familiar voice pelts me from behind. A voice that hounded me every day in Kartok's prison. The last voice I heard when I was drowning in the Zemyan Sea.

"Enebish?" I gasp as I turn.

For a moment I see nothing but a flash of blinding white. It isn't uncommon for my power to flare during battle, but it usually spirals outward, spitting ice at my enemies. It's never clouded my vision like this. But then, I've never crammed myself full of so much additional cold.

As my vision clears, I see Enebish flanked by scores of people, who must be the shepherds she led from the grazing lands. They're old and young, fierce and fragile. All of them unfamiliar and unimpressive on their own, but oddly unnerving as they pour from the abandoned houses and spread across the road like a massive herd of sheep.

Blocking our path.

Strands of long black hair whip across Enebish's honey-brown eyes. Her expression teems with loathing. And as she aims her palms at my chest, I know she won't hesitate to kill me this time.

CHAPTER TWENTY-THREE

GHΘA

OVER THE COURSE OF MY TRAVELS, I HAD TIME TO PLAN MY revenge, down to the smallest detail. So I'd be prepared and unflinching when I came nose to nose with every traitor who stabbed me in the back. I've pictured this reunion with Enebish more times than I can count. I gleefully imagined how terrified and remorseful she would look—and how ardently I wouldn't care. How I'd crow with delight as I flung blades of ice at her chest. Shooting her down, just like her irritating eagle.

But now that she's here, her traitor's mark standing out starkly against her bloodless cheek, I can't remember a single point of my battle plan. Gritty uncertainty fills the hollows the hot-spring water burned into my heart.

I *knew* Enebish despised me. She made that abundantly clear when she nearly killed me at Temujin's execution. I've been plagued by phantoms of her snarling face for weeks. But for some reason, seeing the curl of her lips and the ruthlessness of her stare is more painful than I anticipated.

Probably because it's the opposite of how she looked at me

all those years ago when I pulled her from the wreckage of her hut in Verdenet.

Stop being so sentimental. So weak! that firm inner voice commands. Now I'm grateful for its sharp certainty.

"What are you doing here? With one of *them*?" Enebish growls.

"The better question is, what are *you* doing here?" I fire back.

"We came to free the Chotgori laborers, who the empire, apparently, enslaved." Enebish laughs bitterly. "But you knew that, didn't you? Just as you knew about these shepherds suffering on the winter grazing lands." She gestures to the filthy people surrounding her, many of whom are bickering. "But you chose to ignore it. Because it didn't benefit you. It's always about *you*. The empire is in shambles, yet here you are, hunting me and a caravan of shepherds for the sake of your pride and reputation. There isn't a single drop of honor left in your bones, is there? No bottom to the well of your selfish desperation? First you betray me. Now your country." She waves a trembling hand at Ivandar. "You're no better than Temujin!"

Frost consumes my hair and continues hungrily down my neck and arms. My fingers twitch, eager to fling the icicles dangling from nearby storefronts at the lies spilling from her lips. "I am *nothing* like Temujin."

"Prove it." Enebish squeezes her fist, and the dim arctic light fades even further, darkening into twilit blues and purples, enough to play tricks on my eyes and throw me off balance.

"I don't owe you proof of anything, and I certainly don't owe *them*." I gather the snow and ice from the road with a flick of my wrists and send it spiraling around Enebish and her rebels.

The shepherds scream and scatter, but not Enebish. She stands her ground, her dark eyes drilling into mine through the blizzard, flashing with warning. But her bravado is wasted on me. She's never had the necessary fierceness to be a truly great warrior. Or maybe the problem is, she has too much heart. Either way, that hesitance, that *weakness*, is how I've always managed to stay one step ahead of her. It's how I claimed the title of Commander of the Kalima warriors and it's how I'll reclaim that title too.

"We won't go without a fight!" Serik appears at Enebish's side, and his presence is like a saber cleaving into my skull. I *knew* he would be here, but I forgot how the mere sight of his infuriating face makes me want to scream.

Unlike Enebish, I have no doubt he would kill me—if he could.

"Do your worst, cousin," I taunt him.

The shepherds yowl even louder. Some fall to their knees, begging for mercy.

"They're your *family*?" Ivandar looks at me, completely flabbergasted.

But I keep my eyes on Serik, who deliberately raises his hands. I chuckle. I can't help it. It's such a ludicrous fantasy. So Serik. "Still clinging to hope?"

Columns of fire burst from Serik's palms, snapping the tip of my nose. I stumble back and crash into Ivandar, who catches me. But I'm too horrified and confused to care.

"H-how—" I gawk at Serik.

It shouldn't be possible. He's far too old, not to mention too disagreeable, to have proven himself worthy of power. Yet the angry welt on my nose says otherwise.

I laugh even harder. Only now I'm laughing at myself—at the irony of life. The Kalima betrayed me, Serik is a Sun Stoker, and I'm traveling with the Zemyan prince.

The world has truly gone mad.

There's nothing left to do but join in.

"Well, this is an interesting development." I crack my

knuckles one by one and stretch my head from side to side. Readying for the fight Serik and I have been spoiling for the better half of our lives.

"Stop, Ghoa." Ivandar grabs my arm and hauls me back for a second time, and I swear on the memory of the Sky King, I'm going to kill him. Slowly.

"Remove your hand!" I growl.

"We didn't come to fight!" he calls out to the group. "We're just passing through! We need to reach the Kalima."

"I'm sure you do," Serik spits. "You don't stand a chance against us without them. Not when we have three Kalima warriors."

Three? I stop straining against Ivandar to squint at their sorry group. *Who is the third?*

"Varren! Cirina!" Enebish turns a slow circle in the middle of the street, calling for my warriors, as if they're lying in wait behind the boarded-up homes and shops. "We know you're here!"

"It's honestly just the two of us," I say.

The beginning of another piercing headache is tapping at my temples. Lacy frost edges my vision, and for a moment I consider freezing the entire street. That would simplify everything.

That would also be a terrible waste. Think of your reception at the rendezvous point if you arrive, not only with the Zemyan prince, but with Enebish and Serik. The Kalima will be forced to acknowledge you. No one in the empire will be able to refute your worthiness.

I drop my hands and take a deep breath. Patient. Calm. Whatever it takes. "I'm not hunting you, and I haven't *abandoned* or *betrayed* my country by aligning with Zemya."

"Then what is he doing here?" Enebish glares at Ivandar. "What are you *both* doing here?"

"We've formed a temporary truce to address a more

pressing issue," I say carefully.

"What could be more pressing than the Zemyans taking the entire empire?" a nameless shepherd calls from the back of Enebish's sorry group. As if they're part of this conversation and have any business addressing me.

"Tell your 'followers' to stay out of it," I bark.

Ivandar's fingers slide around my neck and squeeze. I nearly scream before I realize it's an illusion. He releases his invisible grip, shoots me a warning look, and steps forward. "While your commander was imprisoned in Zemya, it was revealed, through her torture, that the generál supreme has ambitions far beyond Ashkar and the continent. We believe he's attempting to infiltrate the land of the First Gods, as some sort of reckoning on behalf of Zemya—to strip the Kalima of their powers and restore our goddess to Her rightful home. Needless to say, the Lady of the Sky and Father Guzan will be in grave danger if he succeeds, so we're trying to intercede. Kartok seems to think he needs Kalima warriors to access the gateway, so we are determined to reach the Kalima first. You must stand aside and let us pass."

No one utters a word when Ivandar finishes. The way the entire group is gaping at him—at both of us—makes me wonder if he was actually speaking Zemyan, if all that time in his abhorrent country infected me more than I realized.

"*You* were imprisoned in Zemya?" Serik says at last, looking at me with a dramatically cocked brow. "How did they capture you? Where were your loyal minions?"

Of course he's the first to respond, and of course that's the detail he latches onto.

Enebish remains much more focused. "You honestly couldn't concoct a more believable lie? Neither of you care about the Lady and Father! You don't believe They exist"— she points at me, then asks Ivandar—"and shouldn't you *want*

Kartok to succeed in avenging Zemya?"

"I don't have to believe in your gods to want revenge," I say curtly. "Kartok tortured me for weeks. And he's trying to seize my power."

It's near enough to the truth. I may not plan on thwarting Kartok by protecting their old gods, but if that's what'll convince Enebish and Serik to follow me to the Kalima, so I can reclaim my position, so be it.

Ivandar shoots me an irritated look, as if he expected me to press my face to the earth and grovel at their feet.

Which is precisely what he does.

He bows his fair head, presses his palms together at his chest, and kneels as if praying. Or pleading. As if my cousin and former sister outrank us both. "Just because I worship Zemya doesn't mean I want to see the Lady and Father deposed. They *created* Zemya—They created everything. Surely there would be consequences if They perished. Please, don't slow us any further by forcing us to engage with you."

The shepherds murmur among themselves. I haven't a clue if they're believers like Enebish or if they're loyal to the New Order, as the law decrees. And I suppose it doesn't matter, now that the Sky King is gone. I try not to think about what it means, that a god on earth perished without consequence. Without a breath of acknowledgment from his land or people. Almost as if he were as ordinary as any one of these shepherds.

"You're actually serious," Serik guffaws, seconds away from laughter.

Enebish, on the other hand, looks skyward, and even though her lips don't move, I know she's praying for guidance.

The shepherds murmur and jostle, and it's all a waste of time.

"Stand aside and let us pass," I order. "Or . . . if you truly wish to be heroic . . . help us warn the gods and defend the continent from Kartok. What good will freeing the Chotgori do if the sorcerer brings the heavens crashing down on all of us?"

Several shepherds actually nod, but then a weak voice rasps from the rear of the group, "They're lying!"

The low, cocky timbre makes every hair on my body bristle with contempt. But at the same time, it's music to my ears. Another piece of the puzzle to restore my honor. The *final* piece.

Temujin.

The crowd of shepherds parts and everyone glances back at him, sitting in the snow. He looks utterly wrecked—hands bound to his feet, bruises mottling his face, and a burn blazing down his neck.

I love it.

I haven't a clue what created this rift between Enebish and the Shoniin leader—the last time I saw them, she was willing to risk her life and destroy Sagaan to save him—but I'm positive I can use this fracture. Deepen it to suit my purposes. Just as I did with Ivandar and Kartok.

"I've been allied with Kartok for years." Temujin's voice gains strength now that he has an audience. "And he's never mentioned anything about infiltrating the actual realm of the Eternal Blue or deposing any gods. Do you think I would have allied with him if any of these lies were true? I am a devout follower of the Lady and Father. Kartok wants equality. Magic for all. Which is in Ashkar's best interest. There will be no more exploitation of the magic-barren. No reason to send warriors into battle at all. . . . Don't forget who helped me raid the supply wagons to deliver you rations. And he was responsible for saving so many young, mistreated soldiers from the war front."

"Spare us your lies. You're anything but devout," Enebish snaps back at him, her voice teeming with even more hatred than when she addressed me. It fills me with the tiniest flicker of satisfaction. Pride, even. She knows I was right about the deserter. "How *is* that magic he 'gifted' you?" she continues, limping back to loom over Temujin. "Why don't you demonstrate your power? Use it to escape?"

Temujin's eyes narrow, but he says nothing. It's Ivandar, beside me, who speaks.

"Kartok offered you our magic?" He sounds amused rather than incensed. "And you actually believed he'd follow through?"

"He did! I drank your hot-spring water! I wielded her siphoned darkness and starfire!" Temujin juts his chin at Enebish. "Kartok vowed to give it to everyone who aligned with him."

"Except you haven't been able to access the magic again, have you?" Ivandar asks. Then he waits like a disapproving parent for Temujin to shake his head. "Zemya formulated Her magic to be incompatible with your bodies. It's toxic to any Ashkarian who possesses Kalima powers and all but useless to the magic-barren. Partaking once doesn't open the floodgates to Zemya, as it does for Her children. You must continually take it into your system, each time you wish to use Zemya's power. But Kartok didn't tell you that, did he?"

Temujin stares ahead at nothing, blinking furiously. "Why don't you tell everyone the real reason you're here, *Prince Ivandar?*" he finally explodes. "You're not worried about the gods or the continent, are you? You're here for your throne. Because your mother favors Kartok."

"*He's* the Zemyan prince?" Enebish whips back around and blackness consumes the entire street, broken only by the wavering heat that rises like a fiery blade in Serik's hands.

His control is impressive for a warrior so new to his power. It feels like something or *someone* is openly mocking me.

"You're right. I don't want my country in Kartok's hands,"

Ivandar begins, but a flood of furious accusations drown him out. The darkness abruptly recedes to reveal Serik, Enebish, and every shepherd on the street surging toward us.

Icy white explodes across my vision, twice as bright as before, and I feel the distinct impression of unseen hands on my back. Shoving me forward.

Fix this. Force them to comply. Get to the Kalima.

Again, I consider reaching for the ice. It wouldn't be the first time I've immobilized a group this large. They deserve it for supporting Enebish—a traitor. But as I look into the eyes of the raging, terrified people rushing toward me, my hands refuse to rise. I can't dredge up even half of the staggering amount of fury I'd need to entomb them all in ice.

I tell myself it's exhaustion from torture and travel. The strength I recklessly forfeited, taking the ice into myself to ease the cold. I could still obliterate them all, if I wanted to.

But that's the strangest part: I don't want to.

And I don't know what that means.

Serik and several other wild-eyed shepherds are nearly on top of me, spitting war cries, but for the first time in my life, I'm not thirsty for battle. Instead of rushing to meet them, I drop to my knees, pressed down, again, by the weight of unseen hands on my shoulders.

I have never felt so weak—cowering and covering my head. But it's the last thing they'd expect. The only thing that might work.

"*Please*, En!" I don't consciously choose to cry her name. The plea is just there, on my tongue.

Still, my assailants come, blades flashing and arms swinging.

She's going to let me die. At *their* hands. After all of the impressive battles I've won, Serik and these misfit shepherds will be the ones who finally cut me down.

At the last second my resolve wavers and I make a desperate

grab for the cold, but my ice-filled muscles are too slow. My mind is so white and frost-covered, it's like a clouded window-pane. I can't see or hear anything other than one word.

Wait.

The command is stern. Inarguable. So I raise my chin and glare defiantly at my cousin.

Right before Serik lays my throat open with his fiery saber, blackness slams down around me, more crushing than the Zemyan Sea.

I flatten my body against the frozen dirt as blades whistle over my head and hands whoosh past my sides, all of them missing their target, thanks to Enebish and her shield of darkness.

CHAPTER TWENTY-FOUR

ENEBISH

I watch Ghoa dodge Serik's blade through the sudden mist of darkness.

Ziva's darkness.

"Do you have any idea what you've done?" I scream at the girl.

At the exact same moment, Serik yells at me. "Why'd you intervene? Ghoa deserves this! She's never going to change."

I, of course, know that.

But Ziva, apparently, doesn't.

"You've ruined everything!" I shout at her, hiding like a coward behind a cluster of shepherds. I'd thought it was strange, how quiet she was during the confrontation. How little she had to say when she *always* has too much to say. "I never would've trained you if I knew you were going to sabotage us!"

I curl my fingers around the threads of darkness and try to yank them from Ziva's grip. Serik and the others need their sight if they're going to gain the upper hand. But Ziva refuses to let go, and she's much stronger than she used to be—thanks to my training.

"Stop!" I bellow.

"This isn't sabotage!" Her face is set with determination, her eyes aflame with scorching desert heat. "I think they're telling the truth about Kartok and the gods and the Kalima."

Of all the things I expected her to say, that was at the bottom of the list.

Why? How? What would possibly make you think that? But there isn't time for questions. I have to make a decision. Ghoa and the Zemyan are stumbling their way across the street. Out of our reach. Either I side with Serik and my fury—backed by a lifetime of evidence against Ghoa and the Zemyans. Or I choose Ziva and her audacious but earnest declaration. Yes, she's young, but she's fiercely devoted to Verdenet. She wouldn't have made such a bold claim, or backed it with equally bold actions, unless she had good reason.

The shattered part of me that's been betrayed too many times to count insists it's all a lie. *Don't make the same mistake again.* But I can't get the image of Ghoa, dropping to her knees, out of my head. My heart and gut clench.

Serik's going to kill me.

I drop the threads of darkness, allowing Ziva to maintain the cover of night, and mutter, "You'd better be right."

"Enebish! Stop this!" Serik and dozens of irate shepherds beg, but they're easy to avoid, since they can't see.

Once we've isolated Ghoa and the prince, Ziva and I tackle them to the ground and secure their arms and legs with rope we stole from the flailing shepherds.

"Cooperate and we'll spare you," I hiss. *For now.*

Ghoa stops thrashing at the sound of my voice and the Zemyan follows suit. "You came," she marvels. Either her relief is truly genuine or she's gotten much better at feigning gratitude.

"*Ziva* believed you. She is to thank for the darkness," I say, tightening Ghoa's rope with a merciless jerk. Hearing Ziva out is very different from siding with Ghoa. Or forgiving her. And I want to make sure she knows the difference.

Serik's skin is so hot, it pulses with eerie orange light. He refuses to speak to me, or even look at me, as we drag Ghoa and the Zemyan prince into the abandoned home we've been squatting in. He stomps down the narrow hallway and up the stairs. I let him go. He needs space if we're ever going to have a civil conversation.

I lead the rest of the group into the kitchen, where we stuff Ghoa and the prince into a windowless pantry. Neither of them fights or attempts to retaliate, and it sets my teeth on edge. Ghoa could have frozen us all where we stood, just as she did to the caravan of traders at Nariin. But she didn't. And I need to know why. Even if their warnings about Kartok prove to be true, Ghoa could have an ulterior motive.

Once several guards are posted outside the pantry door, Ziva and I slowly ascend the stairs. Several rooms branch off either side of the hallway, but it's easy to tell where Serik went. Billows of heat pour out from beneath the farthest door on the right.

"Your reasoning had better be sound," I say to Ziva before I open the door.

She swallows hard, tucks her wild curls behind her ears, and shoves inside ahead of me.

Serik paces back and forth along the far wall, looking for all the world like a prowling sand cat, and it transports me back to the day Ghoa returned to Ikh Zuree. When she offered to let us take the Sky King's eagles into Sagaan. The day that set all of this in motion.

The rest of our makeshift council is already here: Iree and Bultum sit on opposite sides of the room—one on a bed that's still neatly made, the other leaning against a chest of drawers. Lalyne stands between them with her arms crossed. And old Azamat sits on the bearskin rug on the floor, grinning fiendishly, as if this is the most fun he's had in years.

Before I can even part my lips, Serik erupts and the flare of heat is so intense, I half expect him to spit actual flames. "Why in the skies would you spare them? You know they're going to ruin us. Ruin everything. This was our chance to gain a true advantage!"

"*I* didn't spare them." My voice comes out twice as loud and ten times more defensive than planned. "At least not initially . . ." I add softly. I need to douse Serik's rage, not stoke it. "Ziva is the one who called the night."

Serik stops abruptly and laughs. "You're telling me you didn't have the power to stop her?"

"I'm getting stronger every day," Ziva interjects.

I give her arm a threatening squeeze. "That isn't the point—"

"The point is, we never should have trusted you," Lalyne interrupts. "You lead us from one disaster to the next."

It hasn't all been a disaster. You're alive, aren't you?

But arguing will get us nowhere. I pull a deep, balmy breath into my nose and calmly say, "Ziva believes that Ghoa and the prince are telling the truth about Kartok."

"And you believe her?" Iree demands.

Ziva's fingers clench. The light in the room wavers, and I quickly jump in to steady the threads of darkness. "I believe her enough to hear her out," I say. "She hasn't given us any reason to doubt. She wouldn't risk—"

"Ghoa and the prince don't care about the Lady and Father.

Or any of us," Serik says, pacing even faster.

"I know it seems improbable, but you've been begging me to trust, to listen to our allies. . . ."

"Not in place of using your head!" Bultum barks.

Serik shoots the shepherd a blistering look. "You will *not* speak to Enebish like that."

It might just be the suffocating heat, but his rush to defend me makes me feel like I'm basking in the desert sun.

"This isn't an attack against Ziva," Serik continues with a nod in her direction. "It's accepting the truth about our enemies. That's the Zemyan heir down there. And Ghoa, who framed you for a massacre, En."

"I have a profound idea." Azamat lies back on the bearskin rug and props his head up with his hands. "Why don't we let the girl speak and save the arguing for when we know what we're actually arguing about?"

Most of the time I want to strangle the old man, but right now I could kiss his stubbled cheeks. "Thank you for the sound advice, Azamat." I turn to Ziva, trying to convey with a single, searing look how serious this is. *Do not make me regret putting my faith in you.*

She rolls her shoulders back. "I will happily explain if I'm allowed to speak." She glares at Iree, Bultum, and Lalyne in turn. "As you know, I spent a good deal of time hiding with my father in the Temple of the Kings at Sawtooth Mesa. It's where every king of Verdenet is brought for their Awakening, before ascending to the throne. The temple is the size of an entire city, with rooms and halls branching out for leagues beneath the plateau. Before the Sky King invaded, it housed priestesses and scribes—"

"I'm sorry, but what does this have to do with Zemyan sorcerers infiltrating the land of the First Gods?" Iree interjects.

"Everything!" Ziva snaps back. "I wandered those halls

for hours on end, day after day, studying the walls, which generations of scribes had painted with murals of Verdenese life and beliefs. They were beautiful, of course, but nothing groundbreaking. Stories I had heard a thousand times before. Except for one, though I didn't realize it at the time.

"I had been on my knees for hours that day, praying to heal my father's wounds and for deliverance from starvation and assassins, when the Lady put a distinct image into my mind of a mural I'd never seen before. For three days, I scoured the temple until I found it.

"The Lady of the Sky and Father Guzan were depicted high up in the sky, walking through what looked to be a floating garden, surrounded by high, jagged mountains. Their son, Ashkar, stood at the base of the mountains, where numerous people waited in line. One by one, they approached Ashkar and were turned away, until a group came forward, bearing a key. Ashkar inspected the key, counting the sigils of ice and snow and wind emblazoned on its head. Then he inserted the key into the mountainside, and when a tunnel appeared, he permitted the group to enter."

"Were those people the Kalima?" Iree asks.

"I assumed they were the Goddess-touched—the select few who have proven themselves worthy to enter the realm of the Eternal Blue—and I was furious at the Lady and Father for leading me to something so unhelpful. But now I know what I am and what those symbols of the sky mean. The Lady of the Sky didn't deliver us from Sawtooth Mesa then because She knew you would find me. She knew you would help me save my father and bring me to this point." Ziva links her arm through mine, and an overwhelming flood of peace courses through me. A feeling I've only ever experienced while writing in my Book of Whisperings. Quiet confidence. Complete stillness. "The Lady gave me the key and the answers that would deliver us all—Herself included."

Silence fills the room. There isn't a word, not in Verdenese or Ashkarian, that's weighty enough to describe the tightness in my throat or the lightness in my chest. The tremendous surge of gratitude and love I feel toward the Lady and Father. For guiding our feet and placing us exactly where we needed to be to find each other. To help each other.

"I believe you," I say, a sob more than words.

Ziva's laughter is full of tears. She looks up and wraps her arms around me. We bump into the wall, my trembling body suddenly unable to support our weight. We laugh harder as we regain our balance.

I don't know what the shepherds believe about the First Gods. They weren't in the habit of discussing anything with me, and to claim any god other than the Sky King was heresy. So I never mentioned the Lady and Father, and our quest wasn't about Them anyway. But the expressions on each of the shepherds' faces makes their stance perfectly clear: Azamat's mouth lolls open so wide, I can see the gray, rotting tooth at the back; Lalyne lowers slowly to the floor, her hands clutched to her chest; Iree and Bultum, on the other hand, cross their arms and shake their heads, becoming even more disgruntled when they look across the room and realize they're in agreement with each other.

Serik is the only one whose expression is unreadable. He stops pacing, and his anger ebbs enough that sweat no longer pours down my cheeks, but his face is completely blank.

"Can you give us a moment?" I ask the others.

Ziva, Lalyne, and Azamat go without complaint. Bultum and Iree eventually leave, but only after insisting on further discussion. Finally it's just me and Serik, staring at each other, and I can't tell if we're standing on the same side of a battlefield or the opposite.

Since he is apparently incapable of movement or speech, I cross the space and lean against the wall beside him. The room is tiny—it has to be, with the thick walls built to keep out the cold—and it smells faintly of salt and cedar. Trinkets sit neatly on the dresser—a silver spoon, a pot of powder, and a bone hair-comb—as if the owner had every intention of returning. "Say something," I finally plead.

"What am I supposed to say to all of *that?*" Serik tosses his hands, then drags them through his hair. It reminds me so much of our days at Ikh Zuree, I can't help but laugh.

"Why are you laughing?" he demands. "This isn't funny. So many lives—"

"I'm not laughing at you, Serik. Not in the way you think, anyway. I just love you."

"You *love* me? And *this* is the moment you decide to declare it? When my thoughts are scrambling around my head like whisked eggs, and I don't know what in the skies is true?"

I grab his wrist before he can resume pacing, and tug him close. "*This* is true. Me and you. Let's start with that." I tap his nose gently.

"You really love me?" A wicked grin crinkles his freckled face.

"How many times are you going to make me say it before you say it back?"

"You know I love you! I've been telling you for years."

"Not in those exact words."

"Because words aren't the only way. Nor are they necessarily the best way."

"Agreed." I twine our fingers together and fit my head beneath his chin. We sit in quiet for a long moment, feeling the drum of the other's heart. "Why did Ziva's story upset you so much?" I finally ask.

Serik plunks down on the bed and buries his hands in his

hair. "It didn't upset me. It's just . . . a lot. A few months ago I was certain the First Gods despised me. Or had *overlooked* me," he amends when I give him a stern look. "How am I supposed to accept that the Lady and Father orchestrated all of this? That They know where we'll be and what we'll need, when They couldn't acknowledge me or what I needed for *nineteen* years?"

"Better late than never," I say in an attempt to lighten the mood. "They act according to Their timing, not ours. Maybe you wouldn't be as strong as you are now if you hadn't endured those years at Ikh Zuree. It made you resilient. It taught you to question authority and never back down. Maybe you couldn't be the warrior They needed until this moment."

"Maybe," he mumbles, "but why would the Lady and Father have our most hated enemies deliver this information about Kartok? Why force us to work with people who don't even believe in Them? It doesn't make sense."

"Maybe They're ready to forgive Zemya? And maybe They're telling us we need to do the same. That it's time to mend these old, bitter grudges and finally move on. Ghoa fell to her knees when you attacked, Serik. I never thought I'd live to see the day—"

"It was a trick, En."

I sigh and sit beside him on the bed. It's stiffer than I expected, and a plume of rancid dust rises from the quilt. I wait until it settles before speaking. "We've both grown so much over the last few months. . . . Why not Ghoa? She was held prisoner in Zemya. There's no telling how that changes a person."

"*Why not Ghoa?* Are you serious?" Serik tilts his head back and groans. "She's doing what she always does to you. Reeling you in with promises of love and acceptance and greatness only to use you as a stepping stone and cast you aside. Because of her, you've spent *months* mistrusting the people who actually care for you. And now, when you're finally rebuilding that confidence, she immediately shows up to snatch it away again. And you're ready to let her. Ghoa is toxic, En. She always has been and she always will be. She arrived with the Zemyan prince, for skies' sake!"

"But I felt the rightness of Ziva's story—which aligns with Ghoa's claims about Kartok."

"Are you sure it isn't just your heart wishing for something that will never be?"

"Or is it your heart refusing to accept something that *is*?" I ask, glancing over at Serik. "We could pray to the Lady and Father and ask for confirmation. . . ."

"*Here?* Right now?" Serik looks all around, as if an empty, quiet room isn't the perfect place to pray.

"I can teach you how," I offer, already sliding to the floor. "It's simple. We don't have prayer dolls, but you just kneel facing east and—"

"No, thanks." Serik stands abruptly and moves toward the door.

"How do you still have doubts?" I accuse, unable to keep my voice from quavering. "Even now that you have a Kalima power? I thought . . ."

"Just because I don't view the gods the same way you do doesn't mean I don't worship in my own way."

"Of c-course not," I stammer. Why didn't that ever occur to me? Just because I don't see him communing with the gods doesn't mean he isn't. "How *do* you view Them?"

He blows his hair out of his eyes. "I don't know. I'm still figuring it out. I know there's *something* up there, something more powerful than us all. But I have a hard time believing They're physical beings I can have a conversation with. Not when They ignored me for so long. It feels disingenuous that They suddenly 'care' when They need me. And I feel insincere, suddenly pouring out my heart to Them now that I have what I want."

"So how *do* you worship?"

Serik's cheeks redden and he can't stop fiddling with his hands. "It's still new. . . . I'm not even sure—"

"*Please*, Serik. I want to understand."

He bites his lip. "I burn things."

"Of course that would be spiritual for you." I laugh and shake my head.

"Not like you're thinking. I don't blow things up. When I was frustrated during the early days of our trek from the winter grazing lands, I started burning notches in the side of a cart, to mark the days. But every time I cut a notch, I felt something—something I couldn't describe. Not a voice talking to me. More like a weight being lifted. Like I put my fears and grievances into the fire, and they were scorched away."

"That's . . . beautiful, Serik. Will you show me?"

He starts to nod, but then hesitates, his expression almost shy. "It's weird to know you're just sitting there, watching me."

"Let's worship together, each in our own way." I kneel, clasp my hands, and imagine the soft felt body of my prayer doll nestled between them. I press my forehead to the ground, and after a silent minute or two the smell of smoke fills my nose.

I peek. I can't help myself.

Serik stands before the dresser, eyes closed, as he draws his finger along the top of the polished willow. The marks instantly blacken like a brand, and as the smoke hisses up, his body sways forward. Bending as he unburdens himself. When he straightens again, he stands a little taller than before.

I get so caught up in the rhythm, I lose track of the words whispering from my own lips. But there's no denying we are two instruments playing in harmony, even more beautiful and complementary because of our differences.

When we finally finish and he helps me up, I don't have to ask what his higher power told him. It's burned across the surface of the dresser—the ten sigils of the Kalima that Ziva described. Symbols Serik couldn't have known.

"Incredible." I trail my fingers through the still-warm grooves.

Serik's hand covers mine, tracing the image of the Sun Stoker with me. "We should let Ghoa and the prince warn the Kalima, but it'd be unwise to send them alone."

I nod. "We could escort them to the rendezvous point, but we can't just leave the Chotgori. . . ." The words Ghoa screamed at the prince replay in my head: *Who cares about the Chotgori when the gods themselves are in danger?*

But she *should* care. We all should. The Kalima will be far more likely to heed our warning and consider an alliance if at least part of the Protected Territories are present and committed. Otherwise, we'll look like exactly what we are—a band of homeless, wandering shepherds led by Enebish the Destroyer and two fledgling Kalima warriors.

Even if the Chotgori decide they want nothing to do with us, I can't bring myself to leave them. Not after seeing them suffering in the mines. Not when we're right here. And not when Ghoa could make freeing them so much easier. With her help, it won't be nearly as dangerous.

Serik catches my eye, and the grin that lifts the corners of his lips confirms he's thinking the same thing. "Ghoa can't expect our help without offering something in return," he says. "As Commander of the Kalima warriors, she should know all good treaties require compromise."

CHAPTER TWENTY-FIVE

GHΘA

"YOU EXPECT ME TO DO *WHAT*?"

I laugh so hard, I inhale the spices strewn across the shelves of the otherwise empty pantry where they've "imprisoned" us. Pepper and cinnamon invade my nostrils, which is exactly as unpleasant as it sounds. Three violent sneezes grip me, and Enebish and Serik wait for me to stop heaving before they speak.

"Help us free the Chotgori laborers and we'll allow you to continue on to the Kalima," Serik says again, as if the problem is with my hearing.

"Oh, you'll *allow* me to go, will you?" I say with a cutting laugh.

Ivandar repositions abruptly, slamming my side into the shelving. "It sounds like a reasonable request."

"It's not," I snap. "We don't have time, and those workers won't help us protect the gods."

"But they will!" Enebish delves into an impassioned speech, but I stop listening. The Chotgori won't help me reclaim my position. They'll be nothing but a nuisance. And I'm done doing favors. Ivandar's list of my "noble" actions has been looping in my head for the better part of the day, cynical and taunting.

I stab my filthy nails into my thigh, my mind sharpening with the pain. "You realize I could leave this sorry prison anytime I want to?"

Enebish and Serik fold their arms and press their sides together in the doorway. As if that will stop me from barreling through them.

"If you could escape so easily, why haven't you?" Enebish demands.

Because I want the glory of capturing all of you. Except that isn't entirely true. When I first saw Enebish, I wasn't thinking about capturing or annihilating anyone. There was only that voice deep inside me—that *feeling*—forcing me to my knees. Commanding me to stay my hand.

But I'm obviously not about to admit any of that.

"I exercised restraint for the greater good of Ashkar," I say instead. "Our journey will be safer and faster under the cover of darkness."

"You expect me to assist you freely after everything you've done?" Enebish slams her palm against the door frame.

Ivandar jumps. I don't.

"Your gods are in danger, and you could save them," I say, my voice as sweet as the honey crusted on the floor. "You're the one who'll have to live with the consequences if you choose not to help."

"We're not foolish enough to release you," Serik cuts in. "So the only way you're getting to the Kalima is if you cooperate. Help us free the Chotgori workers, and we'll take you to the rendezvous point."

"That's exactly what I *don't* need—a parade of rebels and shepherds and slaves announcing my arrival to the Kalima." I blurt before I can stop myself.

Serik steps into the pantry, flooding the tiny space with his insufferable heat. "Why don't you want the Kalima to know you're coming?"

Bleeding skies.

"It has nothing to do with not wanting them to know I'm coming," I lie, "and everything to do with counterattacking swiftly to have a prayer of reclaiming our land from the Zemyans. Which will be impossible with such a big unwieldy group. But you wouldn't know that, since you've never had a mind for battle. You're not a *true* Kalima warrior. Just a monk with powers you can't control."

Fire bursts to life in Serik's palm and he slashes it past my face. "I'll happily display my control anytime you wish."

I will never, *ever* get used to that.

Ivandar elbows me as we lurch away from the flare of heat. "It's our best option. And the Chotgori are *your* people too," he tacks on. As if I need another reminder.

They're as much my people as a stray cat that curls up under your porch is a pet. But I groan and nod. There's no other way that doesn't involve fighting my way out of this pantry killing hundreds of people. Which, to my embarrassment, I don't have the stomach for. And maybe arriving with a large group will be of some benefit. It will at least look impressive—from afar.

"Fine. I'll help you free the workers. Though, it will be an interesting battle if *they* are my 'warriors.'" I fling a dismissive hand at the roomful of shepherds. "I'll basically be fighting singlehandedly."

"Which is why we have a different plan in mind," Enebish says.

The next morning, I march down the streets of Arisilon City exactly as I did five years ago, clad in gleaming lamellar armor with a pair of twin blades strapped across my back. My objective is even the same: overthrow the current ruler and seize control of the people.

The only difference is the warriors behind me.

Instead of the Kalima, I'm flanked by a battalion of shepherds—though the imperial guards won't know that thanks to Ivandar's magic. Their rags have been transformed into perfectly pressed blue-and-gold uniforms. Their staffs and crooks look like sabers and spears. We march loudly down the street, as if we have nothing to fear and no one to answer to, and I send blasts of arctic air at the outbuildings and tents as we near the imperial encampment. So they know precisely who they're dealing with.

I spot a cluster of imperial warriors leaning against a barn, puffing on long, curled pipes that emit purple smoke. They pass them back and forth, chatting and laughing, until I roll out a slab of chiseled ice that looks like the intricate floor runners in the Sky King's throne room. When it bumps against their boots, they immediately fall silent.

Temujin isn't the only one who knows how to make an entrance.

"So, this is what happens in my absence?" I frown at each of the five warriors. Then with a flick of my wrist, I shatter their pipes with cold. Soot covers their faces and two of them scream as plaster shreds their cheeks.

"Commander Ghoa!" several of them cry.

"We heard you were captured by the Zemyans," another says, gaping as if I'm an apparition.

They scramble forward, then immediately shrink back.

Intimidated. Terrified.

I've always reveled in these moments, believed my fierceness was fueled by their panic and fear. But something changed in Kartok's prison. Maybe it was seeing so much of myself in the sorcerer. Realizing his mocking and threatening didn't make me respect him at all. I am fierce in my own right—*I* shattered the walls of that prison. No one else's perception of me gave me that strength.

"Well, you obviously heard wrong," I say, holding out my arms and gesturing to myself.

"What happened in Sagaan? Where are the rest of the Kalima? What's happening at the war front?" Their questions pelt me like hail. Their lack of information almost makes me feel sorry for them—so secluded up here on the steppes, cut off from the rest of the continent—but I lacquer my voice with ice and peer at them with unbridled disgust.

"Why would I share any information with lazy magic-barren warriors?" The jibe comes easily, naturally, only now I *feel* it leave my tongue—or rather, the grittiness it leaves behind in my mouth.

They all look down and curl into themselves. "You're right. You owe us nothing."

"Forgive us."

"We are honored by your presence."

Instead of bolstering me like the icy breeze, their words—and this entire pretense—feels exhausting. Beneath me, somehow.

You're better than this.

I glance back at Ivandar. He didn't say it out loud this time, but I feel certain he knows it's haunting me.

"I don't *feel* honored. This place looks worse than the grazing lands." I point to the broken pipes and soot at their feet. "And since when do imperial warriors stand around gossiping? You're a disgrace."

"We're on break. It isn't our r-rotation," one of them stammers.

"And it will never be your rotation again," I respond sharply.

They step back, shaking their heads frantically, as if I'm going to cast them from the army with a dishonorable discharge. Or kill them. Even though I've rarely killed anyone for such a small offense.

"This battalion has come to relieve you of your post," I continue. "Your regiment has been recalled to Sagaan to aid in the fight against the Zemyan invaders. Go, gather your comrades, and return to the bunkhouses to pack your belongings immediately. I'll explain your orders in detail as you prepare to leave."

They stare at me, faces paler than the snowdrifts piled almost as high as the roofs.

"Have you been up here so long that your ears froze?" I bellow. "*Go!* Be ready to march within the hour."

"Within the hour?" one of them squeals.

"We'll perish if we cross the grasslands now," another says.

"*We* somehow managed the trek." I wave at the disguised shepherds behind me.

"Please, Commander. There's no need to punish us. We've done our duty. The Chotgori miners know nothing about the Sky King or Sagaan—"

"*I* will be the one who judges whether or not you've done your duty." With a slash of my hand, gleaming spears of ice burst from the snowdrifts and fly toward the inane warriors. The ice isn't all that sharp, or terribly quick, but the soldiers dash off toward the other outbuildings, screaming with absolute terror.

As soon as they're out of sight, I release a long breath and lean against the very wall I chastised them for slouching against.

Being myself has never been this draining.

"You can't be tired already, oh great Commander," Serik

jeers from his place in the ranks. "You're just getting started."

"Do you honestly treat people like that?" Ivandar asks softly.

Enebish laughs. "That was Ghoa being kind. . . ."

"It's what my position requires," I grumble. "I don't have a choice." But my voice fades away completely. Because I *do* have a choice. "Enough chitter-chatter," I snap. "You're the ones who wanted me to lead you as the commander. Now keep up. And keep quiet."

I lead my battalion of "warriors" into the center of the outbuildings, where we watch the actual imperial warriors hustle between barracks, collecting their belongings and supplies. Every few seconds, they steal anxious glances at me, which I make sure to answer with stern scowls of disapproval.

"You're supposed to be prepared to march at a moment's notice!" I yell. "What if the Zemyans had arrived before I did? You'd be dead. We would have ceded even more ground to the enemy. *Hurry!*"

"We have to pack in turns." A panting warrior points to the mines. "To ensure the workers remain compliant."

"What do you think this *entire* battalion is for?" I shoot a furtive look at Enebish and wave them on. She starts to march ahead, but Serik grabs her arm and holds her back, glowering at me as if he's not going to cooperate, even though this song and dance was *his* idea.

I can't hear him, but I don't need to. The words are as plain as day on his lips: *She could betray us.*

The very same thought has been circling my mind like a prowling wolf. It would be so easy to turn on them. Once they're down in the mines "freeing" the Chotgori, I could join with the imperial warriors. Tell them everything. They would happily help me entrap these rebels alongside the Chotgori. I could storm into the Kalima's stronghold flanked by actual soldiers, rather than shepherds.

301

Enebish glances back at me. Her dark eyes search mine—desperate, imploring.

I stare back, freezing my face into an expressionless mask, giving nothing away because there's nothing to give away—not yet.

After a long second, Enebish starts toward the mines and the others follow, marching in swift straight lines, as instructed. A few minutes later, streams of actual soldiers pour into the encampment from the mines. I fold my arms and watch them scramble to pack.

Cold. Aloof. Without a speck of compassion.

But on the inside, another wave of exhaustion pummels me.

"What is the meaning of this, Commander?" A lined and graying warrior storms up to me, face livid. I should definitely know his name, as he's one of the highest-ranking magic-barren generals, but I never bothered to learn it. "You can't just *cast* us into the tundra in the middle of winter!"

The bustle of packing slows. Frost varnishes the hairs on my arms as the other warriors turn to watch, gauging my reaction, as if it never occurred to them to question me.

Part of me wants to react how I would have a few short months ago—to let ice consume my hair and cascade down my arms to my fingertips. To chisel a dagger, hold it against his throat, and ask him in a dangerous whisper if he's certain he wants to go down this path.

But I set my teeth into what I hope looks like a smile and say, "I'm not *casting* you into the tundra. You've done such an impressive job up here, holding Arisilon City, we need your battalions' strength in the capital. We need your leadership and experience. I know the journey won't be easy, but I have every confidence your warriors will manage it."

The man furrows his brow even lower, trying to hide the

pleased smile tugging at his lips, but it has already crept into his eyes. "I just didn't expect to see you up here, Commander. There are rumors—"

"You know better than to believe rumors," I cut him off.

"I assume you'll be leading us back?" he asks.

Tell him everything. Now is your chance.

But the words don't come. They *won't* come. My lips part, but my mind is slow and sluggish, almost as if it's frozen. Patterns of frost embroider my vision.

Stay the course. It will serve you better in the end.

As improbable as that seems, I decide to trust myself. Trust my instincts. They're the only thing that hasn't abandoned or betrayed me.

"You assume incorrectly," I finally answer. "I'm not returning to Sagaan quite yet."

That makes the old man's frown return. "Where will you go? If the capital is in such dire straits, shouldn't you—"

"Do everything in my power to defend it. I assure you, I am. In the absence of the Sky King, I must coordinate the many arms of this war. I go where I'm needed most, which is everywhere at present. If you do not wish to accept this honor and promotion, I'll find another general who's more loyal to Ashkar. General Akiba would already be halfway across the steppes by now."

General Akiba is the only magic-barren general whose name I do remember, and I only remember it because he's a fool. Always bumbling and smiling merrily, as if he's leading a dance troupe rather than a cadre of warriors. The idea that someone like Akiba could be more competent and dedicated to Ashkar rankles this grizzled warrior precisely as much as I hoped it would.

"We'll be ready to march in ten minutes," he barks.

That gives me ten minutes to change my mind. Ten minutes

to slip over to the mines and assess the strength and numbers of the Chotgori. There *are* enough of them to outnumber these imperial warriors; Enebish was right about that. What I don't know is how many miners and shepherds are equal to one trained warrior. At what point would the balance tip in their favor? I'm not about to start a battle I can't win.

I nod at the general and raise my fist in the Kalima salute. "For the Sky King."

"For the Sky King," he repeats with a thump of his chest.

The ore mines are as quiet as I've ever seen them. Instead of the slow, thick trudge of Chotgori workers—staggering beneath the weight of their loads like the world's slowest mudslide—only a trickle of people remain. They shuffle back down into the pit, where I assume Enebish and the others have taken up their "posts."

I duck behind the refinery and smear the orange soot and dust all over my hair and face and chest to blend in. So I can see what my "new allies" are saying about me when they think I'm not there. And so I can slip away to rejoin the imperial warriors if that's my best option.

The mine looks like an arena of sorts—crude steps made of red dirt and rock that narrow toward a bottomless central shaft. Like a sunken bull's-eye, the size of a battlefield. I fall in line behind the workers, the air growing colder and wetter and the light growing dimmer and dimmer as we descend. Enebish and her little fledgling Night Spinner must be loving this.

The mine is twice as sprawling as the last time I visited, and the Chotgori workers are twice as slow. It takes us an eternity to spiral down one revolution. Long enough that I have no choice but to look at the people ahead of me—backs hunched and broken, arms and legs mottled with bruises. A little girl who can't be much older than Enebish when I rescued her in Verdenet drags a mutilated foot behind her. She can hardly walk, yet the leather boulder straps are still fastened tight around her scrawny body.

It's their contribution to the Unified Empire, I tell myself. *We all must sacrifice. If they would have cooperated when we initially proposed an alliance, things wouldn't be like this.* But now these perfectly reasonable explanations leave me cold—and not in a good way. The maddening voice of the Zemyan prince won't stop whispering in my ear, telling me the Chotgori were always going to be used like this, whether they resisted or not.

It doesn't matter. They're in no shape to retaliate. Not even if they outnumber the actual imperial warriors ten to one. Go back. You've seen what you needed to.

Before I can turn, Enebish's voice echoes up from the depths of the pit. I don't want to listen, but I have no choice. It's like a splinter you can't stop picking, even though you know you're only driving the shard in deeper. How can she always sound so noble and impassioned? It makes my skin crawl with irritation—and jealousy, if I'm honest. People have always flocked to her earnestness. They happily followed her unassuming lead. She's never had to resort to threats and coercion and terror to command respect, so she doesn't know how hard it is for the rest of us. For those of us who have never been seen as anything but hard and heartless for simply going after what we want. For being ambitious.

"You can trust us," she continues, her voice filled with certainty and hope. "We are citizens of the empire who were used and exploited like you. We've come to free you—from the mines and from Ashkar. We just have to wait for the actual warriors to leave Chotgor."

"Spare us your lies. We'll never be free!"

"The Sky King is dead. Sagaan has fallen!" Serik's voice joins Enebish's. "There's nothing keeping you here anymore."

Voices ping around the massive pit, and I don't understand most of them. Chotgor was the last territory to join the Unified Empire, so fewer of them speak Ashkarian, but there are enough who understand. Judging by their tone, they're not buying Enebish and Serik's claims.

I chuff out a laugh. They were daft to think the Chotgori would drop their tools, cry tears of relief, and pledge their allegiance.

But then gasps sound like battle horns. Followed by a few actual screams—of shock, not fear. And I know what's happening. What Ivandar is doing—peeling away their imperial disguises to reveal the true faces of the shepherds.

I reach the lowest level of the mine in time to behold the end of Enebish's speech.

"You're free to leave the mines and return to your homes. Or you can join in our fight. We're headed north, to the Kalima's rendezvous point, to warn the First Gods of the Zemyan threat. Then we'll continue on—"

"The threat isn't from Zemya!" Ivandar takes a bold step forward. "It's from the generál supreme, Kartok, who doesn't represent our entire country. Most of us want what you want—to retake our land and reclaim our lives. We are capable of working together—I used my Zemyan magic to free you. Let's free the rest of the continent together!"

The whoops and tearful shouts start gradually, but soon it's as deafening as one of Varren's downpours. Everyone is hugging and kissing and praising the First Gods.

I could easily slip away. Sprint up the shaft and inform the imperial warriors. Lead them back to stifle this nonsense.

Instead I retreat into the shadows and lean against the wall, hands pressed to my thumping chest. My eyes won't look away from the celebration—this group of people who never should have come together but did—and I can't fathom betraying them. Even if it would be in my best interest.

I don't know what that says about my loyalty.

Or my heart.

CHAPTER TWENTY-SIX

ENEBISH

GHOA DID EXACTLY WHAT SHE SAID SHE WOULD. SHE SENT the imperial warriors marching off into the tundra, and I don't know who's more shocked: me, Serik, or Ghoa herself.

I spotted her, watching me deliver my speech. Her face was pale, despite a thick smearing of dirt. Her jaw was rigid and her eyes were pinched into slits. For a second I assumed the worst—the imperial warriors would appear from behind her and come crashing down on us. But then she leaned heavily against the wall, like a satchel held together by a thread.

She let me finish speaking. She watched, expressionless, as the Chotgori miners celebrated. And now she's unnervingly quiet as we help the jubilant and tearful workers climb out of the ore mines. She even carries an armful of picks and doesn't issue a single command as she plods along in the middle of the pack.

She always makes a point to lead. *Always.*

"I don't like it," Serik mutters in my ear. "It isn't right. *Look* at her." He waves at Ghoa, a good twenty paces ahead of us. Her face and hair are so caked with red-orange dirt, she must have rolled around in it. Or purposely smeared it all over herself.

"Maybe she's trying to blend in? Maybe she didn't want to frighten or intimidate the workers and make our task more difficult?" I say.

Serik's frown is immediate. And incredulous. "Ghoa has known about their suffering for years. She obviously doesn't care about upsetting them. And intimidating people is her primary goal in life."

"I know, but she's been through a lot these past months—" I start to say.

"No amount of torture could change her nature," Serik cuts me off. "Selfishness is the foundation of who she is."

I bite my lip and take several silent steps. "I just know how discouraging it is . . . to fight and struggle to free yourself from the past, only to have everyone sneer at your efforts and insist it's impossible."

"Except there's one *teeny, tiny* difference between you and Ghoa: *You* never did any of the things you were imprisoned for. Ghoa did. Then she blamed you. You should doubt and despise her more than anyone."

"I know," I mumble again, kicking a rock. "It just feels wrong to be so critical when she actually upheld her end of our compromise."

Serik stares at his cousin's back, grinding his teeth as the Zemyan prince sidles up beside her. "Or *maybe* she has a secret agenda and we're helping it along."

"What could she possibly gain from taking in another horde of weak, traumatized people? Or by helping the Zemyan prince warn the First Gods? None of it benefits her."

"*Everything* benefits her." Serik stops and grips my shoulders tight, prompting curious looks from the Chotgori workers who stream around us. "Every choice she makes is for herself and no one else. Never forget that. She wants you to question and doubt and *hope*. Just enough to keep you clinging, so she can string you along and use you."

Ziva appears out of nowhere, like she always seems to these days. My little shadow. She motions toward Ghoa and Ivandar and reaches for a swathe of darkness. "I can sneak up there and listen to their conversation, if you'd like?"

"Yes," Serik insists.

But I reach out and disrupt Ziva's grip on the shadows. "Not yet." Serik may think Ghoa hasn't changed, but something about her expression and demeanor feel so familiar to me.

It isn't until we ascend into the frigid wind and the shepherds immediately resume moaning that I realize Ghoa reminds me of myself. When I first arrived in the winter grazing lands outside of Sagaan—the day I began to wonder if everything I'd stood for and fought for was a lie.

The temperature plummets with the setting sun. By the time the moon rises, the tendrils of night are the stillest I've ever seen them. Entombed in ice. It would take every Sun Stoker in the Kalima to make conditions even somewhat comfortable, and we're headed even farther north. Beyond the shelter of the city.

Thankfully, the Chotgori are far more capable and prepared to withstand the cold. They raid the imperial barracks—or reclaim them, I should say, since the empire did the raiding. The buildings and everything inside them were the Chotgori's to begin with. Methodically, they hand out jackets and hats and cloaks and load blankets and furs and sacks of salted cod and seal meat onto a fleet of sleds recovered from a nearby barn.

We lend our help, even Ghoa, and as the supplies dwindle, the gnawing in my stomach threatens to devour me. What if none of it's for us? The Chotgori could be grateful for their freedom but too exhausted to aid us. I said they were under no obligation to join our cause, but I obviously didn't mean it.

Once each sled is packed, seven women make their way to the front of the crowd. Most are gray and stooped with age, but two are tall and broad-shouldered with copper hair down to their waists and faces that look no older than mine.

They're the seven chieftains of the Chotgori clans, and even though they're as dirt-caked and haggard as the rest of the mine workers, I recognize them in an instant thanks to the silver bands soldered around their necks. They're each given one when they become chieftain, and they acquire additional bands for heroic deeds.

The oldest woman, whose entire neck is covered in silver, raises her hands and mumbles in their melodious tongue.

One of the younger chieftains interprets: "You have done us an extraordinary service. As a token of our thanks, we offer you a sled of provisions, but we must stay and rebuild—" The girl stops translating and says something to the eldest chieftain in Chotgori.

The old woman gives her head a terse shake, as if that's the end of the discussion. My heart falls into an abyss even deeper than the ore mines.

When we first left Sagaan, I was so sure the other Protected Territories would rally to our cause. It never occurred to me that convincing people to fight for their freedom would be even more difficult than traversing the continent with the shepherds.

Yet here we are. About to be turned away. Again.

Serik shifts with discomfort, and the side of my body burns like I'm standing too close to a fire. Ziva keeps shooting me worried glances, as if I have the slightest clue how to change their minds.

I want to lie down in the street and let the snowdrifts bury me, but I tilt my head back and send an exhausted prayer up to the heavens.

Before I've even uttered two words, the other young chieftain steps forward, links arms with the first, and says something to the matriarch, respectful but stern. As they debate, the other chieftains join one side or the other, and the clanspeople bustle around to follow their respective leaders.

I feel like I haven't breathed in well over a minute. Serik reaches for my hand and our fingers tangle, squeezing hard.

Finally the matriarch stands alone on one side of the street with a good third of the Chotgori surrounding her. The other chieftains stand together on the opposite side of the road, their people flooding the space behind them. The matriarch waves her gnarled hands and snaps something.

Our original supporter turns to us with a smile. "The sick and elderly, as well as their caretakers, will stay to recover and rebuild. The rest of us will happily join you on your quest to save the First Gods and free the territories. We will not sit back and be enslaved again."

The eldest chieftain looks anything but happy, but I bow at the waist and murmur a heartfelt thanks. Because it's the pledge we've been waiting to hear since the start of our journey, when we left the winter grazing lands in search of allies. Our path has been riddled with more potholes and hills than flat stretches of easy road, but we got here eventually. Surely the rest will be downhill.

Between the shepherds and the Chotgori, our group is several thousand strong. We may not be the most fearsome or battle-trained, but there are warriors from our countries on the front lines who are. Citizens from the Protected Territories that the Sky King ripped from their homes and forced into service. When they hear of the union and uprising, they'll defect to our side. Hopefully the Kalima will lend their aid too, once they realize Kartok is trying to strip them of their powers. We all must ban together against the Zemyan generál or there might not be any continent left to fight over.

"You're wasting your time and energy!" Temujin says as several Chotgori men dump him into the back of a sled. He's still bound, and apparently in need of a gag, too. "You needn't fear Kartok. He would never endanger the continent. He's committed to justice and equality for all."

Surprisingly, Ghoa is the first to respond. With every armload of supplies she carried from the barracks to the sleds, her spine grew a little taller, her expression a little harder, morphing from bewilderment into resolve. She leans over the side of the sled and blows wisps of icy breath in Temujin's face. "Tell me, deserter, if Kartok is such a devoted ally, why hasn't he come for you?"

Temujin's tiger eyes flash with hatred. "You know it isn't that simple. We're at war. He'll come for me when he can."

"So you're expendable?"

"No! That's not—"

"How does it feel to know you've been played? Beaten at your own game?"

A smile overtakes my face as Temujin squirms and spits. I'd forgotten how utterly delightful Ghoa's ruthless candor can be when she's fighting *with* you, rather than against you.

She catches me watching her, and for an instant we're both smiling. Almost laughing. Then we jolt and look away.

Shared hatred for Temujin hardly makes us allies. But as our growing caravan strikes out across the tundra toward the Kalima's rendezvous point, I'm unable to shake the moment. That *look*. It was like falling back through time. The girls who laughed and conspired like that are long gone, I know that. But for a second I almost missed them.

Serik shoots me a stern look. *Don't fall prey to her deception.*

I roll my eyes and break away to check on Orbai, who's secured in a cage on the back of the nearest sled. "What do you think of all this?" I ask her.

She beats her golden wings and slashes at me with her talons, even though I didn't raise a finger to the bars.

Sighing, I sidestep to give her a wider berth, though I continue walking alongside the sled. So she knows she can't get rid of me that easily. I will never stop trying to reverse Kartok's hold.

With nothing else to do, I observe the lumbering caravan, marveling again at the unified shepherds and Chotgori. Inevitably, my gaze slides back to Ghoa, who ambles along beside the Zemyan prince. Their presence, and the fact that they haven't done a single thing to invite suspicion, are the most unbelievable of all. They're even taking turns pulling the heavy sleds, and it could be the blistering wind getting to me, but I swear the snow grows firmer and harder as we walk. The sleds suddenly seem to glide faster and my boots don't sink nearly as deep into the snow.

You're imagining things. Ghoa would never contribute more than the bare minimum. And you're well beyond that.

But the snowpack is undeniably thicker. When I can't stand speculating any longer, I limp up beside Ghoa. "Are you doing this?" I wince at how snappish and accusatory I sound. It's just been so long since I've spoken to Ghoa without flinging ire or blame.

"Doing what?" she says without glancing over at me. She looks so different without her sleek ponytail, gleaming armor, and rattling sabers.

"You *know* what," I insist.

"No. I don't."

I gesture to the slick snow beneath us. "The ground is notably harder than before."

"Probably because we're traveling *north*. Where it's colder." Her voice is clipped, but a mischievous twinkle lights her eyes.

Or am I imagining it?

"You're not helping us by freezing the ground?" I ask.

"Why would I do that?"

That *isn't* an answer, but she expects me to interpret it as one. "Do you remember when you froze the Amereti River when we returned to Sagaan after quelling Chotgor? The entire city celebrated on the ice that day instead of the royal complex. There was skating and races and flavored ice desserts."

Ivandar smiles. "How lovely."

I'd almost forgotten he was there, on Ghoa's other side.

She shoves the prince's shoulder and looks at me through slitted eyes. "Of course I remember . . . but I don't see what it has to do with anything."

I shrug and say, "Maybe it doesn't." Knowing Ghoa will hear: *Maybe it does. Maybe you had no reason to do something kind for the common people. But you did.*

"Do you remember when I framed you for Nariin?" she says in response, blasting it at me like a cannonball. "Or when I was prepared to execute you alongside Temujin?"

She's doing it to throw me off balance, to regain the offensive. I don't bite. "But you didn't."

"Momentary weakness."

"You seem to be having a lot of 'moments' these days . . . taking pity on Zemyan princes, saving gods you don't believe in, betraying your own warriors to free people you enslaved."

"Why does everyone insist on reminding me of my bad choices?" Ghoa growls, and now there's no denying the ground is harder. "Trust me, if I had other options, I'd be pursuing them."

"Why come at all? Why bother saving the First Gods? That's what I can't understand," I press.

"I told you. I have no interest in being stripped of my power."

"Except you've always believed your power is born within *you* . . . so eliminating the First Gods should have no bearing on that, right?"

"I don't know what I believe anymore. Is that what you want me to say?" she bites back, prompting the shepherds and Chotgori within hearing distance to stare.

She drags her fingers through the uneven ends of her short hair, looking more distressed than I've ever seen her. Like the most grueling battle of her life is waging inside her head and, somehow, she's losing, despite commanding both sides.

"I want you to say what's true. Not what you think I want to hear," I say once everyone's looked away.

"Okay, I believe I'm losing my mind. *Happy?*"

"Maybe a little. I'm not used to seeing you this off-kilter."

"And I'm not used to seeing you so assured. You always did want to be a leader, though, didn't you?" she jabs, alluding to my ambitions. When she claimed I'd tried to take her position as commander, even though it wasn't yet hers.

I laugh—long, bitter chuckles that make my belly ache. That quarrel feels like so long ago. "I only wanted to be a leader until I discovered how exhausting and terrible it is. If I could go back, I would do so many things differently."

Ghoa holds out her palm, catching the tiny snowflakes spiraling down from the low-hanging clouds, and stares at them indignantly. I presume it means she's done talking to me, so I'm surprised when she says, "Me too."

It isn't an apology, and I don't expect one. Nor would I accept it. Far too much has happened to mend the rift between us. But the divide doesn't have to be filled with hatred.

"Why is your eagle in that cage?" Ghoa nods at Orbai, who's screeching and flapping as wildly as ever. "She clearly doesn't like it."

Stabbing pain drills into my chest again. "It's the only way to keep her here," I admit.

"Trouble in paradise?" Ghoa taunts, which earns her a reproving look from Ivandar.

I don't think I'll ever get used to the fact that the Zemyan prince is here, with us. Every time he speaks, I hear Kartok in his voice. When he removes his shirt, I flinch at the jarring whiteness of his torso. Though, he's not without his uses. His scowls and nudges do miraculously seem to penetrate Ghoa's iron-thick skin.

"Orbai's just going through a difficult phase," I mutter.

"Perhaps she's smarter than I gave her credit for." Ghoa watches my eagle. "Even she can see the folly of your mission."

"Heading to the Kalima's rendezvous point is *your* mission," I remind her. "And Orbai doesn't doubt me. She doesn't have a choice."

"Why is that?" she asks dubiously.

I don't owe Ghoa any sort of explanation, but the words gush from me like a geyser: "Orbai had to be healed with Loridium in Kartok's *xanav* after you nearly killed her. Now she's tainted with his magic. Bound to him—until I find a way to reverse it."

I don't know how I expected Ghoa to react—to scoff and scorn like always, I suppose—but her brows pinch together and her hand slowly drifts up to her throat.

It's Ivandar who eventually speaks. "What in the name of the Goddess is Loridium?"

"Medicine. Kartok keeps it in a small cedar chest. It's black and green and smells of steel and soil. I figured it was common Zemyan magic. . . ."

Ivandar shakes his head. "I've never seen or heard of anything of the sort."

From what I've heard of his standing, this is probably because he was purposely left in the dark. Before I can think of a kind way to point this out, the sled in front of us skids to a halt, causing the sled behind it to ram into its runners. A series of collisions ripple through the tail of the caravan, and shouts of outrage flare up behind us. Though, they're quickly overwhelmed by screams coming from the head of the group.

Serik's at my side in an instant, boosting me up onto the nearest sled to get a better view.

I immediately wish I hadn't seen.

Silhouettes speckle the horizon—an army of imposing shadows, framed by the eerie red sunlight. The shepherds naïvely ask if it's the Kalima, eager for our trek to be over—wouldn't that be convenient? But even at a distance, I can tell there are far too many of them.

Which means it must be the Zemyans. Not the battalions from the war front—they couldn't have marched so quickly. These are the Zemyans who invaded Sagaan. The ones *I* brought into Ashkar.

"Blazing, burning skies," Serik whispers. "Why would they come this far north? They couldn't have known the Kalima would be up here. Or us. Could they?"

The same panicked thoughts are whirring around my head. So loud, I can no longer hear the shepherds and Chotgori screaming.

I clench my fists, pulling the tendrils of darkness around our group, even though it's likely too late.

"Is this your doing?" I glare down at Ivandar. "Was this your plan all along?"

He shakes his too-pale face. "No! I swear I had nothing to do with it."

I give the night a firm tug to alert Ziva, who's been walking with the other children. Instantly she joins her efforts with mine, thickening the walls of our defense.

"What do we do?" Serik murmurs low.

We knew we'd have to face Kartok and the Zemyans

eventually, but I had hoped it would be *after* we warned the Kalima about the threat to the First Gods and convinced them to fight with us. *After* we gained the support of all three Protected Territories. This ragtag jumble was never supposed to go to battle. We could try to retreat, but we have nowhere to go. The Zemyan soldiers will easily overtake us.

"Stand your ground and prepare to meet them," I command. "Ready any weapon you can find."

The shepherds wail. The Chotgori exchange grim looks. And Serik gives a firm nod and raises his hands.

I don't notice Ghoa climbing the sled until she's suddenly there, beside me, hands poised to fight. It's somehow fitting to have her on my right and Serik on my left. Facing our very possible end together—just as we began.

The Zemyans march closer.

My blood teems faster.

Give us strength, I beg the Lady and Father.

The Zemyans soldiers are mostly shadows, backlit by the sunset, but even still, we should be able to see the menacing white of their skin, the billowing strands of their silver-white hair. But they remain a smudge of unbroken brown no matter how I squint.

Because that's the reality they want us to see.

"Flood the air with cold and strip them of their disguises," I tell Ghoa.

"Gladly." She flexes her fingers, but before the air fills with cold, a horn blares—a low, humming drone that's unmistakable.

A kuzu horn. Used only in Verdenet—to summon soldiers to battle.

Goose bumps sweep over my entire body as it blares again.

Ziva drops the darkness. The ribbons slide through my fingers as well as she shoves through our caravan, screaming King Minoak's name.

CHAPTER TWENTY-SEVEN

GHθA

NOTHING SHOULD SURPRISE ME ANYMORE. BUT THE UNIVERSE or the First Gods or whatever force is commanding this continent saw fit to upend my world.

Again.

I stare, dumbfounded, as the kings of Verdenet and Namaag stride toward us, flanked by scores of Namagaan soldiers in vibrant orange uniforms.

"They came." Enebish's voice is a warbling tremor.

"They came!" Serik whoops and flings his arms in his loud, irritating manner. After which, he kisses Enebish's scarred cheek and lifts her into an embrace that nearly sends them both tumbling over the side of the sled.

It's overblown and exasperating, but Enebish smiles up at him—her cheeks flushed, her gaze tender—and reaches for his hand. Their feelings for each other have been nauseatingly obvious since we were children, which is precisely why I made a point to wedge myself between them. I wasn't about to be the odd one out. Not when I brought them together in the first place.

But there isn't a sliver of room left between them anymore, and not because they pushed me out. *I* pushed *them* away.

I push everyone away.

"What's happening?" Ivandar asks. "What does this mean?"

"It means we did it!" Enebish exclaims. "Before coming to Chotgor, we tried to convince the Namagaans to rise with us against the empire and Zemya, but there was an unfortunate incident with Temujin and we were cast from the marshlands."

"It's *always* Temujin's fault," I mutter automatically, and the others laugh. The sound is surprisingly satisfying.

"Between Chotgor, Namaag, the shepherds, and hopefully the Kalima," Enebish continues, "we'll easily oust the imperial governor from Verdenet. We can reclaim our independence and rally against Zemya."

Enebish is still holding tight to Serik. I can't look away from their interlocked hands. Can't stop myself from wondering how it'd feel to have someone standing by you through your darkest moments. Especially if that someone wasn't commanded to be there, but *chose* to be there. Chose *you*.

Ivandar awkwardly clears his throat. "You mean, your plan will stand a chance *if* Kartok doesn't succeed in obliterating the gods. . . ."

The jubilant mood dies like the quick slash of a saber through the neck.

"Thanks for that," Serik spits. "You couldn't let us enjoy this *tiny* moment of success?"

"We can't lose sight of the greater threat," Ivandar insists.

It's such a backward scenario, the Zemyan heir warning us about his own generál supreme, I laugh. Everyone stares at me, but I can't stop. It feels like the permafrost and the glaciers beneath it are melting under my feet. The entire world is sliding, and I can't get my footing.

"Do you think the kings will agree to join us to the Kalima's rendezvous point?" Ivandar asks.

"They'll have no choice." Enebish tugs Serik toward the advancing kings.

I want to run in the opposite direction. I personally ousted these men from their thrones, I systematically exploited their countries, and now they're joining with people I knowingly enslaved and forsook. I am the common enemy. The one thing they all share.

It reminds me of a joke that warriors tell at the war front—if you can't pinpoint who's smelling up the encampment, it's you.

I am the stench. A fact I've always known but refused to acknowledge. Because acknowledgment requires responsibility. And responsibility requires change.

Enebish glances back, and her dark eyes flicker with warning: *Don't ruin this. Don't make me regret trusting you.*

I want to roll my eyes. Or walk away, to prove she doesn't command me. But the longer Enebish stares, the more the fist crushing my chest tightens. With a bone-weary sigh, I follow.

The reunion is gallingly sweet.

The little Verdenese princess clings to King Minoak's waist and cries, "You came, you came, you came, you came." She can't stop repeating herself. Nor can she stop burying her face in his side. But I'm more drawn to his reaction: the tenderness in his eyes and the fierce pride he exudes as he pats her back.

It's all so achingly familiar—the smiles and whispers of encouragement that always left me hungry for more. Pushed me to aspire. Would my parents be as proud of me for establishing peace as they were when I conquered? Would the people of Ashkar revere me more for defending them in battle or for calling a cease-fire?

Focus, Ghoa. White sprays the edges of my vision, bringing me back to the moment. The throbbing in my head resumes, punctuating a stern reprimand: *Don't forget the Kalima. Your revenge and rebirth. Nothing else matters.*

But if it doesn't matter, how do I explain the restlessness in my fingers when I accidentally look at the shepherds? Or the swelling in my chest when Ivandar gives me a small nod of approval?

Enebish bows to her king and the Namagaan ruler. "Our apologies for the hostile greeting, but we assumed you were Zemyans. After our expulsion from the marshlands, we had no reason to believe you would join us."

"The weather was too foul to send word, even by eagle." The desert king gestures across the frozen steppes.

It's no longer snowing, but everything is glittering white and the wind claws at our cloaks. I'm the only one who isn't hunched into a coat or cowering behind a sled, but with the amount of ice I've been collecting to lessen the chill and harden the path beneath the sleds, even I will be shivering before the day is through. Though, I'll die before I admit this to anyone. I still don't know how or why Enebish suspected my involvement. She should know me better than that.

Evidently, she knows you better than anyone.

"We followed your tracks and prayed we'd catch up before we were too late to help," King Minoak continues. "But you managed to liberate the Chotgori without our assistance." He admires the large hodgepodge group.

His approval feels like a targeted jab. The Unified Empire was never meant to be "unified" by anything other than Ashkar's rule.

"Why come at all?" Serik blurts. "What changed?"

"You discovered I was right, didn't you?" The little Night Spinner jabs a finger into her father's chest. "Yatindra was lying. She betrayed Enebish to the enemy!"

The girl is self-assured and spirited—the type of warrior I would have welcomed into the Kalima.

Minoak places a loving but firm hand on her shoulder. "My sister was trying to protect us the best way she knew how. But yes. I discovered her hand in casting these people from Namaag and decided to make amends. I should have followed my brave daughter into the swamp the day you left. But I'm here now. And King Ihsan generously decided to join us."

"With my forest in shambles, we're in no position to defend against Zemya without aid. This is the only way forward—for everyone." His gaze sweeps across the crowd, halting abruptly on me and Ivandar. His craggy face turns as red as his frostbitten nose.

Apparently, "everyone" doesn't apply to the commander of the Kalima warriors or the Zemyan prince.

"What is the meaning of this?" he demands. "What are *they* doing here?"

The entire group turns to gape at us, including the shepherds and Chotgori, who are well aware of our presence and have been more than happy to accept our help.

"They weren't with you before. Or part of your proposed alliance," King Minoak barks.

"We didn't seek them out," Enebish responds carefully. "We ran into them outside of Chotgor. They were headed to warn the Kalima about a threat to the First Gods from the Zemyan generál, Kartok."

The rulers exchange a dubious look. "And you believed them? Why would a Zemyan conspire against his own general?" King Ihsan inquires.

"Because he's corrupt," Ivandar says over Ihsan.

Both kings, and all of the Namagaan soldiers, glare at Ivandar. Then at me.

"You can't possibly trust them," Minoak says.

"We don't," Serik affirms. "Which is why we're escorting them to the Kalima's rendezvous point ourselves—to ensure they do exactly as they claim. That way, we'll have done everything in our power to protect the gods and, hopefully, we can secure the Kalima's support against Kartok."

"You're mad," King Ihsan says.

"You're wasting your time," King Minoak agrees. "They're deceiving you."

"Maybe. But would you be able to live with yourselves if the First Gods perished and you could have prevented it?" Enebish asks, respectful but unflinching.

Once again I'm struck by her newfound confidence. By her willingness to trust and hope despite everything that's happened.

Neither king responds. Their soldiers stand at attention, as if waiting for the signal to turn on us.

Go! the wind howls in my ears, urging me toward the Kalima and the promise of vindication. *Say whatever you must to move them along.*

Except now an inconvenient seedling of conscience whispers back. *Are you certain that's still what you want?*

The headache I've been nursing since we left Zemya pummels my temples.

No matter what I choose, I have nothing to gain by standing here, hesitating.

"We're nearly there, for skies' sake!" I point at the blue-quartz ice caves less than half a league away. "It would be foolish to turn back now."

I vowed on pain of death to never reveal the Kalima's hidden refuge. But my warriors also vowed to never stab me in the back, and they had no problem doing that.

Anything's fair in war. Whatever it takes to restore my honor.

The trouble is, I'm not entirely sure what constitutes as honorable anymore.

With a terse shake of my head, I lead the rebels to an enormous ice boulder and watch as a dozen men heave it to the side. I could have easily crumbled the boulder, but I won't expend a drop of my power. I'm saving it for the glorious reunion with my warriors.

The image of their horrified faces as I burst into their stronghold has lulled me to sleep every night for weeks. It's kept me focused and resilient and hungry. Finally, *finally*, I'm here.

The entrance to the cave resembles a fox's den. It requires crawling on hands and knees through a short stretch of tunnel before it opens into a vaulted cavern that's a gradient swirl of blues. Its grandeur could rival any palace, but I opt not to share this information. I prefer to watch the shepherds balk and cry at the entrance. Half of them choose to stay behind with the sleds and Enebish's noisy eagle. The Chotgori, on the other hand, crowd closer to the entrance, marveling that the Kalima's rendezvous point was hidden so close.

Ivandar babbles with excitement beside me, staring into the ice as if it holds the answers to all of his problems. I sneak a glance at his harsh-cut profile. What if all of this has been a ruse: The feud with Kartok? Rescuing me from the sea? His seemingly noble ambitions? The prince and sorcerer could easily be working together. Ivandar could be plotting to access the realm of the gods to carry out the very plans he's so intent on "stopping."

You don't care, I remind myself. *The Lady and Father aren't your gods.*

He'll never succeed anyway. You're turning him over to the Kalima.

You're acknowledging them as gods now?

The back-and-forth is enough to give me whiplash.

"Is there a reason we're waiting?" Serik calls from behind me. "Shall I go first? I know coming here must be difficult after your warriors rejected you. . . ."

"Nothing about this is difficult," I lie as I wriggle into the tunnel. The deeper I crawl, the more the ice calls to me. Its energy is intense and feverish, whisking away my anger and filling me with a giddy rush of joy. An immediate influx of certainty.

Whatever waits at the tunnel's end, I am strong enough to face it.

I *will* emerge victorious.

The group follows me through the twisting blue quartz tunnels, past stalactites so clear, they look like chandeliers, and down slopes of ice as black as the roads in Sagaan. The swift-moving meltwater that carved the tunnels rushes along beside us, providing drinking water and serving as our guide.

As we walk, I run my fingers along the wavy turquoise walls. I stare up at the ceiling, which rolls like the Zemyan Sea. I've only been here a handful of times—there was no need when Ashkar had a firm hold on the continent—and I'm immediately overcome by the beauty of this place and the power it stirs in me. This feeling in my chest that's both warm and cold. Perfect wholeness and stillness, like the arms of my parents wrapping around me.

Welcome home, it whispers.

But where is home: With the Kalima? With these rebels? With the ice? Or whatever created it?

My feet move faster as we round another bend. The frozen walls are too thick to see or hear through, but thanks to my power, I can *feel* the body heat of the Kalima warriors in the adjacent chamber. So close.

"How do you want to approach this?" someone asks. It could be Serik or Enebish or Ivandar. Or the kings, who are still naysaying. Or one of Enebish's outcasts. They're all talking at once, but I hear none of it. Because none of it matters.

I know exactly how I want to approach.

I raise my hands, inhale a frigid breath through my nostrils, and slam every morsel of hate and hurt and frustration against the block of ice in my chest. Frozen spears hurtle from my palms and obliterate the wall separating me from the Kalima.

The ice shatters as it hits the cave floor, throwing prisms of light across the crystalline walls. Everyone behind me screams, but I hardly hear them over the satisfying *plink-plink-plink*— the final obstacle between me and victory falling away.

I arc my hands overhead to reinforce the walls so that the entire ice cavern doesn't come crashing down on us. Then I step through the hole I blasted with a vicious grin on my lips.

There are so many things I want to say. So many quips I imagined crowing as I paraded into this den of traitors:

Surprised to see me?

Did you honestly think the Zemyans could hold me?

You knew I would come for my revenge.

But as the debris clears and their wretched faces come into view, I am once again left speechless.

Despite his mountains of muscles, Varren lies with his head

in Cirina's lap, a bloody bandage wrapped around his chest. Cirina drags a wet rag across his forehead, even though she's in hardly better shape—gaunt and pale and emaciated. They all are. The Kalima warriors who are present, that is. There are less than twenty of them, and right away I notice Iska, Eshwar, and Bastian are nowhere to be seen. They could be out on a mission or procuring food, but judging from the sorry state of the rest of the battalion, none of them are in any condition to go on missions. Or mount any sort of counterattack.

We stare at one another in horrified silence, and the most absurd thought fills my mind: *Perhaps it was a blessing to be abandoned at the treasury. Perhaps there is justice in the world after all.*

But if this is justice, shouldn't it fill me with satisfaction?

"Ghoa?" Varren's voice is a crackle, and it cleaves my rib cage in two. We've rarely left each other's side for eight years, and now he looks a breath away from death.

Finish him. He deserves it.

Save him. He deserves it.

The war in my mind rages as fierce as ever.

"Did you come to help?" Varren rasps.

"What do you think? She arrived with an army!" Weroneka's voice is hysterical. She points at the rebels behind me, all of whom have fallen silent. And still. "Of course you'd be the one to thrive in all of this," she snarls at me.

My arms drop to my sides. The words that crawl from my inflamed throat aren't the bitter accusations I'd planned but a simple question. "What in the skies happened?"

"The Zemyans happened! They were everywhere when we emerged in the Grand Courtyard after leaving you," Weroneka continues. "They were on us so quickly—they beheaded Bastian before I could even think to forge a blade of fire. With Enebish fighting on their side, we couldn't call upon the power of the sky with any accuracy. We lost Eshwar and Iska before we were even out of the square. And Lizbet went back for her sisters in Sagaan and never returned."

It feels like I've been stuffed into a chest plate five sizes too small. My lungs threaten to collapse. I can't even summon a morsel of satisfaction over Bastian's gruesome death, despite the insolent things he said to me in the treasury.

My entire body deflates. I tell myself it's disappointment to have traveled so far and suffered so long for *this*—there's nothing gratifying about punishing warriors who have already been so thoroughly beaten.

Finally Enebish breaks the silence. "I wasn't with the Zemyans when they invaded Sagaan." She limps forward to stand by my side. The eyes of the Kalima grow wide, but none of them leap to attack. "The generál supreme, Kartok, tricked me and siphoned my power, which *he* wielded during the siege. Think what you will of me, but I would never align with the Zemyans."

"Then why is a Zemyan among you?" Cirina levels an accusatory finger at Ivandar.

"And why have you brought the Chotgori and Namagaans with you?" Weroneka asks.

On and on their questions pepper me, all boiling down to one. *If you haven't come to punish us, why have you come? Why have you come, Ghoa?*

This is my final chance. I could forge twin blades of ice and force Ivandar and Enebish and Temujin to the ground. An indisputable show of my greatness. Proof I should be leading the Kalima—if there isn't proof enough already.

But I glance at Enebish, standing beside me as she used to, my sister in arms and of heart. And at the kings and people from the Protected Territories surrounding me, lending their strength despite the freedoms I stripped from them. And at

Ivandar's bright eyes, brimming with something that looks like pride, even though my success is directly tied to his country's failure. And I know I can't betray them.

I've known it for a long time, if I'm honest.

I wait for the pounding in my head to flare. For rime to coat my vision. For the ruthless commander I've always been to make a final stand.

But there's nothing.

Just peace. And frosty resolve.

I link one arm through Enebish's and reach back with the other to take Ivandar's hand. Ready to lay down my pride— the last of my weapons.

Before I can speak, laughter filters through the tunnels—as soft as the drip of an icicle. The louder it grows, the more it sharpens into an unmistakable voice. Echoing and everywhere. The same susurrating voice that hounded me in the fabricated throne room. The voice that's haunted my dreams ever since.

"Ghoa came because I told her to," Kartok proclaims.

CHAPTER TWENTY-EIGHT

GHΘA

HORRIFIED SCREAMS FILL THE CAVERN, SHAKING THE WALLS like the behemoth gongs that hung in the Sky King's throne room. The ceiling groans and crackles. Fractures carve through the ice, so eerily similar to the glass walls of Kartok's prison—right before they burst. I extend my hand and fortify the ceiling with another layer of frost, but the majority of the shepherds and Chotgori and even some of the Namagaan soldiers are already fleeing back through the caves. Abandoning the fight before we've even *seen* a Zemyan.

I knew building an army of outcasts was never going to work.

"Show yourself!" I turn in a frantic circle, scanning the icy chamber for the sorcerer. But I knock into Enebish and Ivandar instead. They stare at me, appalled, as if they believe Kartok's claim. "It's obviously a lie!" I shout.

Apparently, that isn't so obvious to Enebish.

"Did you betray me *again*? After everything?" Her lips curl into a snarl, but like a fickle Zemyan blade, the words retract and clog her throat, making her sound small and pathetic.

"I don't know how you live with yourself. Sacrificing *more* lives—"

"Open your eyes!" I thunder. "*Yes*, I was furious with you and your rebels for turning against Ashkar and making me look like an incompetent fool. *Yes*, I wanted to punish the Kalima for abandoning me. But even my ruthlessness has its limits. I would never lead him anywhere!"

"Maybe not knowingly . . ." Kartok bleeds into view, his long, lithe form crystalizing in the wall of ice directly in front of me. "But the bond between us is strong, Commander. You've been very receptive to my promptings." He looks like an apparition, blending almost seamlessly into this frozen place: blue robes, pale skin, and smiling, bloodless lips.

"You're here! Thank the Goddess," Temujin mewls from where he lies, tied up like a hog at the back of the cavern. Abandoned by the shepherds who fled. "Release me and I'll help you take them down."

Kartok doesn't even look in the deserter's direction. "I have all the help I need." The sorcerer snaps his fingers and hundreds of replicas appear all around him, as if he's being reflected by dozens of mirrors. We're completely surrounded by the generál supreme.

Another horde of our reinforcements flee, leaving only Enebish, Serik, Ivandar, Ziva, the kings, and a handful of shepherds and Namagaan warriors.

"We are allies!" Temujin bellows. "Equal partners! Release me so I can help you!"

Kartok shoots the deserter a pitying look.

The Kalima clamber to their feet, back into a circle, and raise their hands. Prepared to fight the Zemyans to the death, which will be swift and pitiful in their current state.

"Stand aside!" I run at the original visage of Kartok. If I were going to lie down and die, I would have done it when

I first arrived in Zemya—before I endured Kartok's torture and traipsed across the continent with my enemies. Before my mind became contaminated with these seeds of sympathy that rooted in my heart and grew into suffocating weeds.

The Kalima dive out of my way, covering their heads as I slam my frost-covered fist into the wall. Ice chips spray my face, and my knuckles carve out a cannonball-sized gouge. But there's no man inside the ice. With a roar of outrage, I lash out at the wall to my left. Then my right. Swinging with wild, reckless hatred at the illusions. One of them is real.

"Stop, Ghoa." Ivandar catches my arm and holds me against his chest. "This is what Kartok wants. Stay calm."

How can I stay calm when he's surrounding us? When he's making these horrendous claims about me?

"There's no bond between us! I would never allow it!" I yell at the sorcerer. My hair is so stiff with frost, the chin-length strands slice my cheeks. Red blood spatters the immaculate ice as I thrash against Ivandar's hold.

"I'm afraid you didn't have much say in the matter," the battalion of Kartoks reply, calm as ever as they prowl behind the frozen walls. Just out of reach. I have never despised Zemyan magic more. "You wouldn't have survived without my healing ministrations. . . ."

"What are you talking about?" I start to spit, but then my hands leap to my throat, feeling for the invisible scar. I think of what Enebish told me about Orbai. How Kartok healed her and, by so doing, turned her allegiance. Stole her agency. "You inflicted this wound. I'd hardly consider *that* healing."

"What wound?" Ivandar interjects.

Kartok shrugs lazily. "The magic doesn't know or care how the wound was made. It knows only that healing demands a price. And I've come to collect."

"What is he talking about, Ghoa?" Ivandar's voice rises.

"He slit my throat in his prison, then healed me with Loridium," I grind out.

Behind me, Enebish and Serik gasp.

Ivandar slams his palm against the cavern wall. "What in the merciful seas is this magical elixir and where did it come from?"

"You didn't think it was important to tell us that Kartok had infiltrated your *mind*?" Serik yells at me.

"I didn't know!" I shout. "And it doesn't matter because he isn't in my mind!"

The hiss of Kartok's voice tiptoes across my shoulders. "Tell me, Commander, have your thoughts been a bit fuzzy lately? Snowy around the edges? Consumed by flashes of white?"

"No," I lie—too slow.

Kartok chuckles. "I never dreamed when I siphoned your power that the bond between us would be so strong. Imagine my surprise when I discovered, not only could I whisper instructions into your mind, I could freeze your thoughts if you seemed resistant. Such a useful little trick."

"I don't believe you," I say, even as I think of the constant headaches, those strange flares of whiteness, and the sudden forcefulness of my thoughts. I clutch my head and frantically sift through every impression and prompting I've had since leaving Zemya—every example of "goodness" Ivandar insisted on pointing out. This strange inward transformation I've been undergoing. Was none of that me? "I would know if my thoughts weren't my own," I insist, but it sounds as if I'm trying to convince myself.

"That's the ingenuity of it all." Kartok claps. "They *are* your thoughts. Loridium bends your very will to mine. Until we are one and the same. Isn't that right, Temujin?"

The deserter's head jerks awkwardly, as if he's being forced to nod. I *feel* Kartok's fingers pinch my cheeks too, just like the times he held my tongue. Attempting to move my head in the same manner.

I dig my nails into my scalp and drag them down my face, carving fiery lines through my skin. Desperate to extract Kartok like a parasite.

I think of the moment right before I drove his blade into the prison wall. How he hesitated. He could have stopped me from smashing the glass, but he didn't. The enchanted steel didn't turn against me as it should have. I'd told myself he'd been too stunned by my attack to react, that I'd been lucky with the blade.

But there's no such thing as luck.

Kartok knew exactly what I was doing.

A shiver overtakes me. Cold like I've never felt. "You wanted me to escape."

Kartok's snake lips curl into a grin. "You clearly weren't going to cooperate—though Goddess only knows why you'd protect these traitors." He waves dismissively at the Kalima. "Thankfully, you're just like me. So I stopped wasting my time with questions. I knew you wouldn't be able to resist punishing your warriors and reclaiming your position once you were free. And look, here we are. I should also thank you for getting the prince out of my way. It's been so blessedly quiet without his meddling. Though, all of this inner turmoil and angst over what you believe is getting rather tiresome."

He rubs his temples and my entire body shivers with rage.

Ivandar explodes before I can. "This is how you healed my mother from the sweating sickness!" he cries. "How you always seem to have her ear. Why she continually chooses you over me."

"Or maybe I'm simply more competent," Kartok jeers. "You're a pathetic child, searching for reasons to justify your parent's neglect, while I am a generál—a true patriot—putting an end to this war and glorifying Zemya."

Every incarnation of the sorcerer raises his hands, presses his spider-leg fingers against the ice, and steps into being as the walls shatter and crumble.

In an instant the cave fills with thousands of Kartoks. All of them rushing toward us.

My mind screams orders, but I can't move because I don't know what's real—if Kartok truly shattered the walls and the ice cave is collapsing on top of us. Or if he was never waiting in the ice at all and this is an elaborate illusion. Are his replicas actually Zemyan soldiers? Or is he working alone but wants to create the appearance of support?

"Blazing skies!" Heat explodes from Serik's hands in a long spiraling tube. If the ice wasn't already collapsing, it is now. He slashes his fiery lance from side to side, slicing a barrage of advancing Kartoks straight through the middle.

None of them scream. None of them fall.

One by one, the other Kalima warriors follow Serik's lead. Weroneka adds her heat to Serik's. Cirina's wind tears at the multitude of blue robes. The Snow Conjurers attempt to bury the Kartoks beneath an avalanche. Tanaz, our Hail Forger, summons sheets of stinging rain, and Enebish and Ziva toss a netting of darkness over us.

But I stand there, frozen.

The cold is ready—screaming and thrashing inside me. I can hardly see through the frost encasing my eyelashes. I can hardly move beneath the ice glazing my skin and hardening my muscles. My hands shake in front of me, poised to unleash the ice. Yet nothing comes. And I don't know if it's because I *can't* use my power or because I *won't*. If Kartok is bending my will and suppressing my ice or if *I* am the one holding back.

The ring of steel and painful cries of battle sound real, but no one from either side has fallen. The imitation Kartoks swing their sabers at our arms and legs, never aiming to kill.

337

The powers of the sky rage and swirl around us—the most violent storm I've ever seen—but none of the Kalima's strikes hit their target. Which is too improbable to be a coincidence. Kartok's soldiers are either an illusion, or the Kalima's powers are vanishing before they make contact—just like my ice did in Kartok's prison. When he was siphoning my power. Not to use against me, but for some other purpose.

Tell me, Commander, how many disparate powers do the Kalima warriors possess?

How are they distributed?

Where will they be hidden?

His questions fire at me in quick succession, and I suddenly can't breathe—my chest is too riddled with wounds from spear tips and daggers I failed to see coming, despite Kartok hurling them at me, plain as day.

He doesn't need to kill my warriors or eradicate our powers to reach the First Gods.

He needs to *collect* our powers.

Your warriors are *the link!*

"Stop!" I scream. "Stop using your powers!"

The glares the Kalima throw at me are more blistering than Serik and Weroneka's combined heat.

"Why in the skies would we do that?" Serik snaps as he forges yet another flaming saber, just to spite me.

"He's using us! We're giving him exactly what he wants!"

"Why would he *want* us to attack him?" Karwani demands.

"Because he needs our powers!" I'm speaking so fast, the words tumble and trip from my lips. "It's the reason he tracked me here! He needs the full strength of the sky to access the realm of the gods."

Cirina laughs. "What gods?"

"Why would we believe you?"

"You're bound to him!"

338

"He's probably whispering these lies into your ear!"

I can't tell who's yelling anymore. There are too many voices pelting me, silencing me. The only person who isn't screaming is Enebish.

She's fallen perfectly still and watches, horror stricken, as wind and lightning and snow and fog crash and swirl around the brigade of sorcerers, never inflicting a scratch. She looks down at her hands, then at me, and flings off the cover of darkness. The little Night Spinner, Ziva, tries to protest, but Enebish easily wrestles the invisible threads from the girl's hands—as strong and determined as I've ever seen her.

"It's true!" Enebish's gaze darts from one Kalima warrior to the next, taking inventory.

"*What?*" Serik cries.

"He siphoned my darkness in his *xanav!*" Enebish yells, as if that should explain everything.

But the Zemyan term means nothing to the Kalima.

And Enebish's word means even less than mine.

We are the last two people on the continent they would listen to.

"We'll finish this the way we were born to!" Cirina yells, and the wind picks up, slashing my face and stinging my eyes. Bitter cold and burning heat fill the cave in equal measure as the other Ice Heralds and Sun Stokers redouble their efforts. One by one, my former warriors unleash the full fury of the sky on Kartok.

Varren, the sole surviving Rain Maker, is the only one not fighting. And not out of loyalty to me, but because he's sprawled out on the ground, overcome with pain. His eyes are closed, his teeth are clenched, yet still he tries to raise his hand.

"Please don't summon the rain, Varren," I beg as I slip across the ice. "I'm telling the truth. *Look!* Our powers have no effect on the sorcerer!"

Varren's eyes slit a fraction. "Ghoa?" He coughs.

"Listen to me—" I start, but he shakes his head, the bulging cords in his neck distorting his tattoos.

"No. *You* listen to *me* for once."

"I know I should have shown you more gratitude and appreciation—"

"I chose you again and again and again," he rasps over me. "I set aside my own ambitions because I thought eventually you'd repay the favor. Raise me up the way I raised you. But you never let me be anything but second."

"I should have! I *will*! I'm just begging you to listen to me this final time."

Varren stares at me, and I stare back. Pleading. Hoping.

"Do you remember when Lazare and Feymir said we'd never last a year in the Kalima?" I blurt. "How we coordinated our revenge without even meaning to? You summoned that mist of rain and I froze it across the pavement, and those pompous idiots slipped and tripped all the way across the Grand Courtyard."

A hint of a wistful smile tugs Varren's cheek.

"I almost wish they were still alive so they could see us now. So they could see everything we've accomplished *together*. Everyone knows I'd be nothing without you. But I'll proclaim it. I'll scream it from the top of the Sky Palace, if you'd like. I need you, Varren, and more important, Ashkar needs you— needs *us*."

He hesitates so long, I think he's going to relent. Then a flash of silver-white hair and cobalt robes breaks rank from the throng of identical sorcerers and charges at the Kalima.

Cirina screams as Kartok wrestles her to the ground.

The true Kartok.

Purposely revealing his location to force the Kalima's hand.

"Fall back!" I cry.

But every member of the Kalima has already redirected their fury onto him. Including Varren, who raises a shaky hand and adds his rain to Kartok's collection.

The result is instantaneous.

Cerulean light explodes from where Kartok lies—brighter than the reflection of sunlight on snow. More excruciating than the frost Kartok seared through my mind. It leaves me momentarily sightless, suspended, screaming as the walls of ice shatter and the cave collapses around us. Or maybe it's the sky itself that's breaking—slashing down like vicious shards of glass.

CHAPTER TWENTY-NINE

ENEBISH

THERE IS NO SHIMMERING GATEWAY. NO FLASHY RIVER OF fire that carries us up into the realm of the Eternal Blue, as there was during Temujin's absurd ritual to enter Kartok's *xanav*.

I should have known the true pathway would be quieter than that.

Everything about the Lady and Father is softness, calmness, stillness. Even now, when Kartok has deceitfully forged a key using our siphoned Kalima powers, They welcome us into Their realm with grace.

A halo of brilliant blue replaces the ceiling of the ice cave, and the face of a man appears as if looking through a window. He's both old and young, both handsome and plain. I have never seen Him before, yet I know Him intimately. From the lines on His face to the rings adorning His fingers, each one stamped with a sigil of the Kalima warriors.

It is Ashkar, the father of our nations and guardian of the realm of the Eternal Blue, according to the mural Ziva saw at Sawtooth Mesa.

One by one, the sigils on His rings glow and, with a nod, a chasm opens behind Him. It's blacker than a moonless night—not even I can see through the murk—but I swear I feel hands on my shoulders and fingers interlocking with mine, guiding me, pulling me, urging me forward until we erupt into sunlight and collapse into grass that's softer than Orbai's down feathers.

That's one element Temujin and Kartok got right in their fraudulent world of Zemyan magic: the grass—luscious and long and green. And the sky, too. It's a rich, saturated blue of every shade and gradient. From darkest midnight to the palest smudge of ice. But that's where the similarities between the two worlds end. The terrain in the true Eternal Blue doesn't resemble Ashkar or Sagaan in the slightest. Instead of leagues and leagues of endless grass and a river that looks like the Amereti, we're situated in an expansive walled garden with bushes bearing gemstones rather than fruit—emerald leaves and ruby berries with creamy pearl seedpods. Pathways of gold dust meander through the garden, and trees made of bright orange coral drip garlands of diamonds. The air is damp and dewy and smells like the cardamom incense my mother used to burn in our hut.

I squint toward the center of the garden, where the pathways intersect. The greenery is too dense to see it, but according to every Verdenese prayer and song, the original Book of Whisperings, where the Lady and Father inscribe Their answers, should rest atop a grand pedestal.

Surrounding the garden are seven towering mountains, as desolate and craggy as the garden is lush and beautiful—almost as if representing Zemya and Ashkar, respectively. The summit of each mountain gleams with a brightness beyond the glory of the sun. When the legends spoke of journeying through the seven levels of heaven to reach the Lady and Father's presence, it never occurred to me it would be an actual journey. A *climb* to salvation.

I could marvel over every tiny detail of this realm, cataloging all the ways it's superior to the *xanav*. I don't know how I ever believed Kartok's cheap illusions could be the home of the First Gods. And these physical disparities aren't even what truly matters. The true difference is the *feeling* this place invokes. While the *xanav* teemed with frantic, ravenous energy, extracting every speck of vitality, the Eternal Blue *gives*. It pours strength into your soul like sweet honey wine and warms your belly like winterberry pies fresh from the oven. Filling you to bursting.

The sensation is so overpowering, everyone is momentarily awestruck, including Kartok, who lies on his back, taking in this realm with the giddy, wide-eyed excitement of a child. Scattered around him, a handful of Shoniin and Zemyan warriors—who are, in fact, real—mutter curses and shake their heads. Not half as pleased as their general. Maybe even perturbed. As if they were just as clueless about his true ambitions.

The Kalima warriors stumble into formation to confront the Zemyans, but their faces are drawn, their eyes frightened, and they don't unleash the power of the sky on Kartok and his warriors. It could be because Kartok used their powers to open the gateway—what's stopping him from using them again? Or their fear could run even deeper than that. If the realm of the Eternal Blue exists, it means the First Gods are alive and well. And if They have always been present, it means Kalima warriors are not gods and never have been. Our Kalima powers may not even work here—why would they? The Lady and Father can wield the sky Themselves in this realm.

Off to my right, King Ihsan cries softly. Beside him, King Minoak sings a Verdenese hymn of praise, his arm wrapped tight around Ziva. Ghoa, on my other side, methodically scans the space, eyes shifting from landmark to landmark, not admiring or appreciating, but plotting. Creating a battle plan and mapping her escape route.

Serik scrubs his hand over his hair and murmurs, "Burning skies, it's real."

At the exact same moment, the Zemyan prince mutters, "Merciful seas, it's real."

They look at each other askance. Their words may reflect their opposite heritage, but the reaction itself, and the emotions behind it, are the same. I'm sure there's an allegory in there somewhere about how our people really aren't so different. We never have been. But there's no time to unpack it.

Kartok regains his feet and strides toward us, a new and enlivened verve to his step. "Does this make me Goddess-touched?" he asks in a mocking tone. "I accomplished what only three Ashkarians have managed since the beginning of time, and I'm not even one of you."

His soldiers snicker as they fall into formation behind him. Now that they've shed their disguises, I spot several familiar faces: Chanar and Oyunna and Borte, the Bone Reader. She must have been devout to the Lady and Father once, in order to successfully imitate bone readings, but no longer. I'm sure she has a heart-wrenching story like Chanar's or Oyunna's or Temujin's—how the empire wronged and ruined her. How she deserves to reap this vengeance.

Except this is no longer a vendetta against a mortal king! I want to scream. *Look where we are! While you were focused on taking down the Sky King, Kartok changed the point of attack! Thrust you into an entirely different battle!*

But I save my breath because it won't make a difference. People see only what they want to. Believe the version of the truth that suits them best. Not so long ago, I was just as blinded by Kartok's schemes.

"Where are the Lady and Father?" Kartok snaps at me. "Why haven't they come?" He glances all around with agitation.

"They don't owe you a reception or acknowledgment," I snap back. "Breaking into a home is not the same as being invited inside."

"Precisely! Shouldn't They defend Their realm?"

I cross my arms and stare into his soulless eyes. "I would never presume to tell the First Gods what They should or shouldn't do. . . . Perhaps you're not a large enough threat to acknowledge," I add, unable to stop myself.

Serik looks at me as if I've lost my mind. "Why in the skies would you provoke him?"

"Because we don't cower before weak, frightened men," Ghoa answers, smiling at me proudly. As she did when I was young.

Kartok's cheeks shudder with rage. He raises his hands and spreads his bony fingers. I want to believe it's impossible for him to summon his illusions here—that the First Gods banished Zemyan magic along with Zemya herself—but the only reason They feared Zemya's magic was because They couldn't control it. Couldn't control *Her*.

"You can't harm me. Or my allies!" I blurt before he unleashes his magic.

"And why is that?" Kartok demands.

"Because I know how to find the Lady and Father. You need me or you'll spend an eternity searching this realm."

Kartok chuckles. "We both know you'll never assist me, which is why I brought a devout ally of my own." He nods at Chanar, who easily slips past the shell-shocked Kalima to where Temujin lies, hidden behind a cluster of flowers with amethyst petals. Temujin has been so quiet, I'd forgotten he was in the ice cave with us.

Chanar severs Temujin's ropes, but he doesn't stir. His eyes are wide but vacant, taking in everything and nothing. He's so still, for a second I wonder if the shock of being betrayed—

instead of perpetrating the betrayal—killed him. Or maybe it's guilt, knowing he's ultimately to blame for Kartok's infiltration of the realm of the Eternal Blue.

It isn't so fun to be on the receiving end of deceit, is it? I want to call over my shoulder.

But Kartok speaks first: "Pull yourself together and rise, boy."

Temujin's golden eyes flick to Kartok, filling with the fiery determination that initially drew me to the rebel leader. The same unflinching bravery and commitment that convinced me fighting with him was the right choice. The only choice. Except now that compelling defiance is directed at Kartok rather than the Sky King.

"Was this your plan all along . . . to attack the *gods*?" he explodes.

Kartok rolls his eyes. "My plan has never changed. I intend to end the war, restore balance and equality, and glorify Zemya by any means necessary. I knew eradicating the Kalima was key, but it wasn't until recently—with the help of the commander"—he gestures at Ghoa—"that I realized it would be more efficient to cut off the source of their power than to eliminate each warrior individually."

"You knew I would never agree to this!" Temujin vaults to his feet.

"Which is precisely why I didn't tell you. Now, come. We've wasted enough time." Kartok claps at Temujin as if he's a dog. "Take me to the Lady and Father."

Temujin's nostrils flare. He crosses his arms over his chest and widens his stance.

"The time for defiance has long since passed," Kartok says with a weary sigh. "We both know you're going to cooperate, whether you wish to or not."

"You can't just *kill* gods!" It's strange to hear Temujin voice the same fears he so readily dismissed when we revealed

Kartok's plans in Chotgor. "There will be consequences. Consequences that will affect *you*. Are you willing to risk that?"

"I'm willing to do *anything*." Kartok claps again, and this time Temujin's right leg judders forward. Then his left. He walks with herky-jerky movements that remind me of my own limping gate. With every step, Temujin's teeth clench tighter. His arms thrash harder, as if trying to pry himself free from invisible vines looping around his torso. Sweat trails down his face and neck.

It's horrifying to watch—even if he deserves it.

From out of nowhere, the Zemyan prince moves in front of Temujin and physically shoves him back. "Enough, Generál!" Ivandar snaps at Kartok. "There's no need to hunt the First Gods or strip anyone of power."

It could be my imagination, but I swear the breeze in the Eternal Blue stirs in response—warm and fragrant.

"That mentality is precisely why you'll never be emperor," Kartok says.

"My *humanity* is why I'll be a far better emperor than you could ever be," Ivandar growls as he continues to struggle against Temujin. "This is unnecessary. We can end this war without bloodshed or stripping anyone of power."

Kartok sneers. "If you believe that, you're even more delusional than I thought."

"I'm not! We're capable of working together peaceably with the Ashkarians. I saved the life of the Kalima's commander. Then we traveled together for weeks, working in tandem to survive. She took additional ice into herself to ease the cold on my behalf."

I spin to look at Ghoa. I *knew* it. I knew she'd been manipulating the cold for our benefit. She's done several things for our benefit now. Things I never would have imagined her capable of. Yet still she refuses to acknowledge her part, standing with her arms akimbo and shaking her head as if Ivandar revealed a mortifying secret.

"There's more than one way to end this war," the prince continues. "Look at all of the people who came—"

"But there's only one way to ensure equality!" Kartok thunders over him. "If the Ashkarians have access to power, they *will* use it against us. They've proven that time and time again. And if I have the means to stop them, I owe that to my people. Something *you* would understand if you were worthy of being their emperor. Now move, or I'll force you to."

"How? You've never revived me with your poison!" Ivandar shoves even more of his weight against Temujin, the two of them clashing like rams.

Kartok looks to Chanar and the other Zemyan warriors. "Kill them all except the prince. I want the commander to dispatch of him."

Ghoa gasps as her sword arm twitches, moving in fits and starts like Temujin's legs. Despite how she struggles, she takes a saber from one of Kartok's soldiers and stomps toward Ivandar. He looks at her with beseeching eyes, but she continues to advance with ruthless vigor. Slashing and striking. Swinging for his head. The rest of the Zemyan soldiers fall into formation behind her, closing in on us.

Temujin calls my name as Kartok forces him down the nearest golden pathway. The bitter, smarting part of me wants to laugh. Or send Temujin off with a mocking salute. After so many betrayals, he can't honestly believe I care what becomes of him. But he's the only person, other than myself, who might know where to search for the First Gods. Which means I can't just let them go.

"Enebish!" Temujin calls again. He writhes and bucks against Kartok's magic. "Write!"

Write? About what? His honor and prowess? So he can be fondly remembered by generations to come? *Ha!* If I'm writing his story, it will be filled with the truth. And our children's children will despise him for it.

Only when Temujin's gaze darts toward the center of the garden, where the original Book of Whisperings should rest, do I understand.

I have less than a second to react. The Zemyans are nearly upon us.

"Ziva!" I shout. Our eyes meet and we grasp for threads of darkness. I need to blind our enemies, or render myself invisible, in order to follow Kartok and Temujin. But there isn't a single tendril of night slithering through the sky in this realm. Another detail Kartok unfortunately guessed correctly in his *xanav*. Only bright, cheery blue—Eternal Blue. Which means there are also no clouds to summon, no rain or snow or hail or sleet. No wind to whip into a frenzy or to carry in a covering of fog. No ice to throw like daggers, or lighting to sever like swords. Those elements are created by the Lady and Father—for our use and protection down below. The only element that exists of itself is warmth, light, heat.

"Serik!" I cry, praying he understands.

He raises his hands and fire blazes from his palms, forcing the Zemyans to leap back and shield their faces. Weroneka and the other two Sun Stokers add their heat to Serik's, buying everyone a second—except for Ivandar. Ghoa anticipates the strike and rolls beneath the fire, knocking the prince's feet out from under him. She climbs atop him and stares down, sword arm raised.

Ivandar says something and falls still, eyes closed.

She won't do it. She'll fight Kartok's magic. She can't kill Ivandar after everything they've endured together.

But Ghoa's arm moves with forceful certainty.

I drop to the ground and roll beneath the nearest hedgerow as the prince's wails fill the sky.

I don't want to watch. And if I don't move, I'll be next.

My bad arm objects as I drag myself through the leaves and onto one of the winding golden pathways. As I run, I listen for Temujin's babbling voice and Kartok's clipped steps, keeping my eyes focused on the pedestal rising from the center of the garden like a fountain. I refuse to look away from it, not even when more agonized screams ring out behind me. If I see my friends fighting for their lives, I'll be tempted to go back. But the only way to help them, the only way to save them, is to ensure Kartok never reaches the First Gods. And the best way to warn Them is through the Book of Whisperings—writing side by side with Temujin to forge the strongest connection possible, as we did so long ago in his family's book.

The closer we draw to the pedestal, the louder my anxiety screams. Doubt clings to me like burs, begging me not to trust Temujin. Not after everything. But if the shepherds can trust me after I blazed my starfire through Sagaan, and if the Zemyan prince can align with Ghoa, who savagely attacked his country for over a decade, perhaps I should give Temujin one more chance.

I swear I hear the Goddess in the tinkle of the gemstone leaves: *Don't we all deserve another chance?*

"Where are They?" Kartok's voice is just up ahead, on the other side of the flowering hedge. "Shouldn't we be able to see Them by now? If you're leading me astray—"

"I can't lead you astray," Temujin says meekly.

The rebel is wickedly clever, as always. Bending the truth so you think you're getting precisely what you want, only to discover it twisted into what *he* wants. Technically, Temujin *is* leading Kartok toward the Lady and Father—the pieces of Them that live within the Book of Whisperings—which isn't what Kartok wants, but it's close enough to fool the binding magic.

With every step, my racing heartbeat pulses through my injured leg. My lungs seize as the golden pathways merge from every corner of the garden, twisting into an opulent floor runner that ends at the pedestal. It's as grand as I imagined—made of polished onyx etched with silver moons and golden stars. The base is impossibly narrow and it widens as it rises, unfolding into a perch that resembles the wings of an eagle. Atop the wings rests the original Book of Whisperings. It's twice as large as any book I've seen, with an azure cover and gold-leaf pages.

Kartok and Temujin emerge from the pathway adjacent to mine and I skid to a stop just in time. Heaving for breath, I plaster myself against the leaves and wait for the perfect moment to move. Temujin and I will have just seconds to scrawl our warning—to tell the Lady and Father to stay away, to cast Kartok from their presence before he unleashes his Zemyan magic.

"You brought me to a *book*?" Kartok rages as he scans the clearing, looking for gods who clearly aren't present.

"We have to announce ourselves by writing in the Book of Whisperings," Temujin explains. "Otherwise, we could spend years scaling each mountain in search of the Lady and Father. This is the fastest way to learn Their location. They'll tell me where to go."

"Fine. Do it quickly." Kartok herds Temujin toward the open book.

I can smell the pages from here—the comforting aroma of old, brittle parchment. I want to lay my cheek on the careworn cover and lovingly trail my fingers down the broken spine. I want to cherish the feel of Their quills in my fingers, knowing they're the same instruments the Lady and Father use to answer my prayers.

But there isn't time to be sentimental.

Temujin lifts one of the solid gold quills with a flourish.

My fingers twitch, grappling again for the darkness. This would be so much easier if I could conceal myself in shadows. Or blindfold Kartok with the night while I raced to the pedestal.

You don't need the darkness, a firm reminder elbows into my mind. *You slunk around Ikh Zuree for two years without power, relying on nothing but your wits, determination, and a constant unwavering faith in the Lady and Father. That's all you've ever needed. Your gods and yourself.*

Picking a handful of weighty pewter berries from a nearby bush, I crouch at the edge of the hedgerow and whisper a prayer as I lob them at a tree on the opposite side of the clearing. This particular tree has orange leaves the size of my head that look to be made of blown glass. Much to my relief, they shatter like blown glass too.

Kartok whips around as they crackle and crash.

I burst from the cover of the hedgerow, channeling Orbai's speed and strength as I fly toward Temujin and the Book of Whisperings. I only make it halfway before Kartok turns back to the pedestal and spots me. He waves his hands and shouts in Zemyan, attempting to manipulate the appearance of the terrain to trip me. When that fails, he makes it look as if he slid the pedestal to opposite ends of the garden, but I don't need to see the Book of Whisperings to know where it is. Its energy calls to me like outstretched arms.

Temujin hands me the other quill as I crash into his side.

The tips scratch across the page, and Kartok keens as if our words are blades in his flesh.

Temujin and I didn't discuss what to write. I haven't a clue if we're even scrawling the same message. Or if we're only making everything more confusing for the Lady and Father. I barely have time to scribble a single word—*stay*—before an image rises in my mind. A mountaintop ensconced in pink mist with a crescent moon hanging in the sky on the right side.

"Do you see that?" I breathe.

Instead of answering, Temujin shoves me to the ground.

My skull cracks against a granite boulder, and the quill skitters out of my fingers and under a bush. My vision doubles. My head throbs with pain, worsened by the undeniable fact that I'm a fool.

This was another trick. Another trap.

"How could you?" I scream up at Temujin. Which is when I notice how wide his amber eyes are. How he seems to be choking on the air itself. And how a bloodstained edge of steel protrudes through the center of his chest.

A sword that would have impaled *my* chest if he hadn't pushed me aside.

Kartok removes his blade with a vicious jerk, sending Temujin sprawling forward. He collapses on top of me, his shuddering body pinning me to the ground. Blood gushes across my lap and wets the grass. A spreading pool of scarlet black.

"I do . . . believe . . . in the First Gods," Temujin rasps. "I was only trying . . . to help. . . ."

I don't tell him it's okay. Or that his intentions justify his poor decisions. That this final sacrifice erases his prior betrayals. Because it doesn't. Nor am I in any position to make such decrees. I'll leave his final judgment to the Lady and Father. But I do clutch him tight against my chest as he gasps and sobs and twitches. This confused, passionate boy from my country who was so desperate to make a difference and implement positive changes in Ashkar, he ended up changing himself, betraying himself little by little.

After another round of rattling coughs, Temujin falls still

in my arms. His tiger eyes stare straight ahead, but they've lost their signature luster, dimming until the golden rings climbing his ear are the only part of him that glimmers.

I wanted him dead. I wanted to kill him myself. But nothing about his body, limp in my arms, feels gratifying.

It is only a waste.

Kartok doesn't even blink at his former ally. He comes for me, hands a blur, his curved sword slashing. I was grateful for his inhuman speed during our missions to ferry new recruits to the false Eternal Blue. Now I curse that speed as I struggle to free myself from Temujin's dead weight. In a breath, Kartok's blade is poised at the base of my neck, where the moonstone used to sit. Temujin's warm blood drips from Kartok's sword, spattering my chest.

"Take me to Them," Kartok insists.

"I'd rather die," I spit.

"But would you rather watch *him* die?" Kartok points his knife to the nearest pathway where Ghoa emerges, dragging Serik behind her. A Zemyan blade pressed against his throat.

CHAPTER THIRTY

GHӨA

I AM DRENCHED IN THE ZEMYAN PRINCE'S BLOOD.

A fact that would have pleased me not so long ago.

I've imagined killing him ever since I joined the Kalima. Eager to be the commander to put an end to Empress Danashti's line. But that was before—when he was a faceless, nameless heir. Not Ivandar, my grudging accomplice. Ivandar, my unlikely ally.

Ivandar, my loyal friend.

He didn't even put up a fight.

One moment I was standing beside him, ready to face down Kartok and his soldiers. Then my mind flared with frosty whiteness and my body was no longer my own. Kartok could still manipulate the ice in my mind, since our link was forged through Zemyan magic, which the First Gods can't control.

My captive sword arm swung at Ivandar with lethal skill, slashing closer and closer as his energy flagged. When Serik tried to intervene with fire, I dove at the prince's knees and brought him to the ground.

"It's okay, Ghoa," he panted. His strange blue eyes met mine, and I realized for the first time that they were the exact same shade as a newly formed ice dagger. So familiar and safe. Maybe even beautiful.

"I'm sorry," I sobbed, helpless as my blade tore through him.

Ivandar folded in half with a groan. "Don't be. It isn't your choice."

Hysterical, heaving laughter spilled from my lips as swiftly as his blood. He was right, and I couldn't decide what was worse: the fact that I wanted to save him, or the fact that I couldn't.

And now that same bloody knife is jammed against Serik's throat.

After killing Ivandar, Kartok forced me to turn on my cousin next. But instead of killing him, my hands bound Serik's palms together, to protect myself from the worst of his heat. My feet marched him into the hedge maze, never making a wrong turn. Leading him toward the sorcerer as obediently as a horse on a lead.

"What are you waiting for?" Serik growls. His throat knocks against the blade as he thrashes, wetting my fingers with even more blood. "We both know you've always wanted to kill me, so do it. You even have the perfect justification to murder me in cold blood: Kartok is controlling you."

"In cold blood?" I spit back at him. *He* has always been the instigator of our feuds, blaming me for every problem in his life when it's hardly my fault his father was a weapons dealer sentenced to Gazar. Nor is it my fault his mother fell to pieces in the aftermath. Or that Serik didn't develop a Kalima power sooner. Or that my parents are caring and influential enough to keep him away from the war front.

Most people in his position would have recognized their good fortune and been overflowing with thanks.

But not Serik.

He has always been ungrateful, unreasonable.

Or have you been uncaring, unseeing? a quiet voice pushes back. A voice I want to blame on Kartok's hold, but these memories are from long before the sorcerer's influence. Only now they're colored with new understanding. Lit from a different angle.

You turned your back on Serik when his power didn't present. Not on purpose, not at first. You were off on missions. Training. Marching from battle to battle. But that's not how Serik saw it. You left him, forgot him. Just like the rest of the world. Confirming his greatest fear: if you are powerless, you are nothing.

"Didn't you hear me?" he growls, leaning into the blade.

I release a long, weary sigh, finally willing to accept my part. Finally ready to let this bitter animosity die. We will never defeat the Zemyans if we're always wounding each other.

"I don't want to kill you, Serik," I say softly.

He, of course, responds with spiteful laughter. "Blazing skies, you're loving this, aren't you? Now that I'm asking for death, it's the one thing you won't give me."

With an exhausted groan, I drag him deeper through the hedge maze. Even with the brunt of his power contained, Serik's skin is too hot to touch. My hands blister, and the pain is so agonizing, all I can focus on is the overwhelming need to pull away. Every time I grow frantic enough to rebel against Kartok's hold, though, another surge of ice climbs the walls of my mind and my fingers remain clenched.

Holding me captive in my own skin.

Kartok waits for us by a pedestal, on top of which rests a large blue book. Both Enebish and Temujin lie in the grass in front of the pedestal, covered in blood. I can't tell who it's coming from, and I tell myself I don't care, but the rebel leader isn't moving and Enebish is, and the relief that overwhelms me is enough to steal my breath. I already lost Ivandar. I couldn't bear to lose her, too. To have their blood staining my clothes *and* my conscience.

We halt before Kartok, and Enebish scrambles to her feet. "Release Serik," she says in a low, dangerous growl. I don't know if she's talking to me or Kartok; I don't think it matters either way.

Kartok threads his fingers together in front of his waist and smiles. "Take me to the Lady of the Sky and Father Guzan, and I'll order the commander to release the boy," he says to Enebish.

"Don't lead him anywhere, En," Serik interjects.

"You do realize there's only one other option. . . ." Kartok nudges Temujin's corpse with his toe. "Are you truly willing to die defending gods who overlooked you? Who saw fit to bless you with power only when They needed you?" Kartok clucks his tongue with disapproval. "After so many years of yearning and suffering, I thought you would be wiser. Wouldn't a fair, predictable goddess better suit both of our people? Removing two underhanded gods is much simpler than leading people to battle. But you already know that, don't you?"

Serik swallows hard against the edge of the knife. I can feel his heartbeat thundering in his rib cage. I have no doubt he's entertained these thoughts before—not specifically about supporting Zemya, but wishing there were no First Gods. Wishing everyone was equal so he would have a chance of achieving greatness.

"You'd be willing to die to defend the First Gods?" Enebish's voice is scratchy, her eyes wet as she blinks up at Serik.

Serik nods after only the slightest hesitation. "I would."

I want to laugh. Or maybe vomit. I don't have the slightest idea what he's decided to believe now that he possesses a Kalima power, but I do know he doesn't have the same unshakable love and faith in the gods as Enebish. If this were only about Them, he would probably stand aside and let Kartok pass. Let the gods reap the consequences of the injustice They sowed. But there has always been one thing Serik loves more than the allure of power and greatness. One person he's worshiped in place of a goddess. And if Enebish wants to defend the Lady and Father, my cousin will let me slit his throat before he fails her.

Some would say that's the highest form of bravery and love. They'd claim his devotion is noble, maybe even endearing. Part of me secretly wishes someone would stand with me so completely. Believe in me so fiercely. But then I remind myself it's *Serik*. And this sacrifice, and his baffling new desire to believe, are a waste.

If the Lady of the Sky and Father Guzan are powerful enough to create this realm and the entire continent below, and wise enough to instill the power of the sky into worthy warriors, shouldn't They be strong enough to oust this Zemyan from Their presence? Shouldn't They know he's coming and be prepared to face him without our intervention? How am I supposed to worship gods who are too weak to defend Themselves? If They expect me to admit I'm not a god, I need Them to prove They are stronger. Give me a reason to put my faith in something other than myself.

"Make your choice, Night Spinner, or I'll make it for you," Kartok barks at Enebish. "Your gods or this boy?"

"The Lady and Father would never force me to make such a choice!" Enebish cries.

"But I would. And since They've decided not to grace us with Their presence, my agenda is the only one that matters." His fingers twist viciously.

So do mine.

A second later Serik cries out as fresh blood wets my hand.

Enebish's teeth sink into her lower lip. Her gaze flits to the mountains on her left and she tilts her head back, muttering a warbling prayer. Asking her gods what to do while Kartok's eyes trail her sight line—sharp and hungry.

"Follow me," she finally says, limping toward the encircling peaks.

"Don't do this, En," Serik pleads as we wind through the neatly trimmed hedges—first Enebish, followed by me and Serik, with Kartok taking up the rear. Keeping us all in line. "I am willing to make this sacrifice. I *want* to make this sacrifice."

Enebish shakes her head firmly. "The Lady and Father will show us another way."

"What if They don't? Or can't?" Serik squirms against my hold. The harder he struggles, the hotter he becomes. And the hotter he becomes, the more my hands blister. And the sharper the pain, the more I begin to panic. It's finally in that panic that the icy walls encasing my mind begin to melt and shrink. For a brief moment I'm overwhelmed by clarity and autonomy—almost enough to let go of Serik. But Kartok is right there, hovering over my shoulder, forcing the frost to rise and reform. Starting the process all over again.

As we walk, the sounds of battle fade until I no longer hear fighting at all. Either the Kalima, the little Night Spinner, and the kings were defeated by the Zemyans or this garden is even larger than I realized. I find myself silently hoping for the latter. Not because I agree with their rebellion or their gods, but because the thought of the Kalima and the kings of Verdenet and Namaag falling to the Zemyans is infuriating and insulting.

At last, the garden spits us out onto hard, cracked dirt that's not quite brown and not quite gray—a wash of rocky desolation that surrounds the garden like a moat. The ground slopes sharply upward to towering mountains that would be adequate fortification for anyone trying to enter from the opposite side. For people less zealous than Kartok, who found a way to bypass the range entirely and battered into the garden itself.

The rocky ground diverges into trails that climb each peak. Enebish shields her eyes and squints up at the fog-shrouded summits. "That one," she says reverently, even though they all look the same.

Kartok frowns as his eyes follow the switchbacks, rising up, up, up. "Why would your gods be up there when They have this magnificent garden? If you're purposely leading me astray, girl, I'll—"

"Perhaps They enjoy the view," Enebish interrupts, looking fierce and unflinching. Like the warrior who fought by my side in the Kalima. I'd foolishly thought I could weaken and control her by cutting her down at Nariin, but being thrust into the forger's fire has only made her stronger. "Or maybe They knew you were coming. Maybe They want to watch you suffer and sweat before shoving you from the mountaintop."

"Enough!" Kartok brings his palms together, and my sword arm jerks in response. Before I can comprehend what's happening, I've cut a gash across Serik's bicep—deep enough to reveal bone. The knife is back at his throat before he even starts screaming.

"If you refuse to cooperate, the boy will suffer," Kartok says to Enebish.

"Don't help him," Serik sputters through his clenched teeth.

"You picked a terrible time to become so devout," Enebish says as she marches forward, up the rocky trail.

We climb for hours, sweating in the unbearable heat. Between Serik and the sun, which is far too bright and close in this realm, I'm certain I will never be able to wield the ice again. My frozen core is nothing but a puddle, escaping through my skin and evaporating into the thinning air.

After what feels like days, we ascend into a veil of blush-pink fog—the precise color of the pear trees that blossom in the springtime on my parents' estate. The mist is heavy and cool on my skin and shields us slightly from the harsh sunlight, which hasn't faded, even slightly, since our arrival. Though, a crescent moon as risen up from behind the peaks and hangs in the sky beside the sun. Proof that this is the Eternal Blue in the most literal sense.

The fog grows thicker and thicker as we climb until I can hardly see Serik, who's trapped in my arms. Which means Kartok might not be able to see me. I wiggle my fingers to gauge his awareness, focusing all of my energy into one finger. It feels like I'm lifting a warhorse, but I manage to pry my pinky away from the dagger. I'm straining to lift my ring finger when the fog falls away abruptly and, with it, all thoughts of escape.

It was a fool's notion anyway. Where would I even escape to? I don't know how to leave this place. Nor do I have the slightest clue what awaits back in Ashkar. And, most horrifying of all, my mind quails at the thought of leaving Enebish and Serik here with Kartok.

The summit of the mountain is no larger than a common parlor, though far more extravagant, with blue-and-white checkered floors, midnight velvet lounges, and cloud-white chaises arranged around a towering mound of rocks, like the cairn Kartok showed me in his book. Tiny twinkling lights and thick swathes of blue silk drape from the apex of the rock tower and form extravagant tentlike walls that rustle in the breeze.

On the opposite side of the terrace, the fabric is pulled aside to reveal a balcony overlooking an infinite expanse of sky and rock. There two figures sit. I can't see their faces, but one wears a gown the precise shade of a star-riddled sky and the other a robe of the greenest leaves.

My mouth drops open, and I blink as if They'll disappear. I'm hallucinating—I have to be. I was so certain we'd find nothing up here but additional gray dirt and scattered rocks. Yet here is undeniable proof of more.

Just as you requested.

Air refuses to fill my lungs. I tell myself it's the altitude. Or the exertion from the climb.

It's one thing to consider that your views on life and power and the gods could be wrong. It's something else entirely to have those fears confirmed—and with all the subtlety of a fist to the jaw.

Enebish falls to her knees. Garbled praises and frantic warnings pour from her lips in an indecipherable stream as she crawls closer to the Lady and Father. Serik is so still in my arms, I can't even feel him breathing. Behind us, Kartok whispers something in Zemyan, then charges past me and Serik and kicks Enebish aside like a cat underfoot.

"I've come on behalf of Zemya! The daughter you so callously forsook!" His voice carries on the wind like a clap of thunder, but the Lady of the Sky and Father Guzan do not acknowledge him. They continue looking out, nodding or pointing occasionally. Absorbed in Their own conversation.

"I tried to warn you!" Enebish cries out. "I wrote in the Book of Whisperings!"

Kartok turns and raises a hand toward Enebish, who immediately falls silent. She thrashes and clutches her face, just as I did when Kartok used his sorcery to twist my tongue.

"It isn't real!" I try to go to her, but my legs have turned to stone. Frozen—just like my useless arms. I can do nothing but watch as the sorcerer advances across the room, his robes billowing, his white hair whipping. He looks so colorless and out of place in this sumptuous palace. Like a stain that was blotted from existence.

"Your reign of injustice has ended!" he cries emphatically. "You can abdicate your power, declare your sins, and give Zemya the glory and birthright She deserves, or I will forcibly remove you."

Still the First Gods pay him no mind. I can't tell if it's intentional. Maybe They simply can't hear him. Or maybe this is proof of Their supremacy: They do not cower before invaders. They do not shrink. They are omnipotent. Maybe even deserving of my respect.

With a growl that originates in the depths of his chest, Kartok brandishes his curved sword and swings it into the mound of rocks supporting the tent. "Zemya will not be ignored any longer!" he cries as the boulders topple like soldiers cut down in battle.

I gasp, somehow feeling the force of Kartok's blow in my side. Serik groans as well. And Enebish clutches her stomach, still on her hands and knees. The backlash of Kartok's attack ripples through all of us—and through the realm itself. The mountain shudders as the stones hit the blue and white tiles.

Finally the Lady of the Sky turns, peering at us through the falling rocks and collapsing walls of satin, and I gasp even louder. An overwhelming ache skewers me like a saber through the heart.

I've never had any reason to wonder or imagine what the Lady of the Sky would look like. Even if I had, never in my wildest dreams would I have expected to see the face of my mother staring back at me. The Lady of the Sky is her perfect likeness, down to her bowstring lips, always colored with rose paint, and soft auburn curls. She even has my mother's eyes—kind but fierce, gazing at me with pride.

"M-Mother?" I stammer.

As soon as I say her name, the Lady's face changes, morphing into the likeness of Shoshanna, the Ice Herald who mentored me when I first joined the Kalima. She perished during the siege of Verdenet, and I cried silently in my bedroll every night for an entire year after. Yet here she is, her warm eyes smiling, her lips quirked into their signature smirk.

"I don't understand." Tears soak my cheeks, but I'm unable to remove my hand from the blade at Serik's throat to wipe them away. "What do you see?" I ask him.

He answers with a warbling grunt followed by a stream of whispered pleas, *"Get up. Wake up."*

Enebish rises from the ground and slowly looks from the Lady of the Sky to me, her expression full of wonder and awe, hurt and outrage. And then I'm crying even harder because I finally understand. She sees *me* in the face of the goddess. The Lady has cared for all of us. She *resides* in all of us. She is every incarnation of a mother.

I don't know what Kartok sees, but whoever or whatever it is, the visage doesn't deter him. He raises his sword and charges toward the Lady and Father, bellowing a Zemyan war cry.

Enebish starts after him, her injured leg moving faster than I thought possible.

The Lady and Father stand tall and unflinching on their balcony, watching the sorcerer come. Unlike the Lady of the Sky, Father Guzan's face isn't one I know, but his arching brows and peach-blossom cheeks invoke a familiar feeling—memories of places I've felt happy and safe and loved: running through the sprawling vineyards on my parents' estate; sitting astride Tabana while her hooves churn up the grasslands; kneeling in the throne room at the Sky Palace, surrounded by my warriors.

Kartok is just steps away from the First Gods when Enebish catches the back of his robe in her good hand. The fabric pulls taut, collaring Kartok like a leashed dog. He coughs and his arms flail, grappling for balance. Enebish pounces again, diving into his waist and tackling the sorcerer to the ground. Then they're rolling, snatching, struggling, the blade slashing between them, hungry for blood.

Bile rises up my throat. My ears ring with screams. With every swing, Kartok comes closer to flaying Enebish open.

"We have to do something!" Serik's skin flares hotter than ever, and I pull away with a curse.

I gape at my hands. My fingers actually moved. Not much, but enough to bring the knife a hairsbreadth from Serik's throat. Thanks to his skirmish with Enebish, Kartok doesn't immediately refill my mind with ice.

"Burn me," I say urgently to Serik. "Raise your hands to my knife, cut the ropes, and burn me with the full strength of your power."

Serik is so perplexed, he outright laughs. "Why in the skies would I do that?"

"It will weaken my bond with Kartok! We're connected through Loridium *and* through my siphoned power. If we break that link, I might be able to resist him enough to set you free."

Serik says nothing. I can't see his face, since I'm standing behind him, but I can *feel* him rolling his eyes.

"Neither of us can help Enebish if I'm holding you hostage," I hiss in his ear. "I don't know why you're hesitating. We both know you've dreamed of setting me aflame long before you ever had a Kalima power."

"I'm hesitating because I know this is a trick," Serik says. "Some sly way to get the upper hand. You'll probably charge up there and assist the Zemyan."

Enebish cries out as Kartok's sword skims her cheek. Another scar to add to the others. The sight of her cherry-red blood detonates a cannon in my chest. An explosion of fear and outrage.

"Do you honestly think I'd do that?" I try to snap, but my throat is too raw, too tight. "I know I've wronged you both. I know I've committed unpardonable sins, but I swear on my Kalima power, on the lives of my parents, on every morsel of pride I have left, that I'm on your side." I take a deep breath and force myself to continue. "I'm sorry, Serik. I was awful to everyone, but especially to you. And I'm not asking you to forgive me; I know you never will. I'm simply asking you to give me the chance to make recompense where I can. Let me help you—and the girl we both love."

The apology feels like a knife lancing a festering wound to let the infection drain out. A necessary, if painful, release.

After a prolonged moment Serik says, "My heat will kill you."

"Your power isn't *that* strong," I say with a rueful smile. Even though part of me knows it is. Knows what I'm risking. "You don't need to pump me full of fire—just one strong surge to break the connection."

I grit my teeth and loosen my grip on Serik so he can lift his hands and drag the rope across the blade. He spins around, still caged by my arms, and looks into my eyes. Squinting with suspicion. But beneath this lingering hostility, there's the tiniest hint of surprise. Maybe even respect.

I nod permission as he places his palms against my chest.

Before I can brace myself, Serik's hands flare with light; fire engulfs my body, turning everything red and gold and blazing white. Heat rushes through me and I feel it refining me through the pain. My mind sharpens and quickens as Kartok's icy hold falls. My arms fall too, allowing Serik to burst free.

He darts after Kartok and I stumble to keep up—my legs slow and my vision wavering like the air above a fire. Though, mercifully, it seems to be a dying fire: fading coals and sputtering smoke.

When we're a few steps from where Enebish and Kartok brawl, Serik lifts a hand, forms a flaming whip, and cracks it across Kartok's wrist. The sorcerer yowls as the blade spins across the tiles.

Serik swings at Kartok with a broadsword made of fire, but Kartok dodges the strike and rolls to safety. Before he can spot me and reassert his hold, I launch myself into his stomach like a blazing comet. Kartok screams as my blistered skin meets his. I scream with triumph as the blade he forced me to hold against Serik's throat plunges toward his heart.

At the last second the hilt liquefies and drips through my fingers like hot wax.

I retract my hand, cursing. My burning hands must be too hot to wield a sword. But when the weapon reappears in Kartok's fist, I realize it had nothing to do with Serik's heat. The blade melted because it's Zemyan steel.

I *knew* to be vigilant about their weapons. It's been the one constant threat, the only predictable danger amid the chaos of ascending into a different realm. So of course it's the one thing I overlooked.

Kartok shoves me onto my back and brandishes the traitorous blade. I raise my chin defiantly and continue to struggle, even though the battle's over, desperate to give Enebish and Serik as much time as possible to regroup. To escape. To rescue the First Gods.

I choke on a disbelieving laugh. I should be raging about the injustice of being dragged into this realm. Reeling over how this will affect my legacy. No one will remember my accomplishments and strength. No one will know the true extent of my dedication to Ashkar. I should be begging Kartok to heal me again with his Loridium. Anything to save myself. But as I limp closer to death, none of those things seem to matter. Maybe they never did.

I draw a final breath, waiting for the sorcerer to kill me as callously as I killed Ivandar, but instead of stabbing pain, I feel air whipping past my face. My ears prick with a soft, deadly *whoosh*. And when Kartok's knife hits its mark, it isn't buried in my flesh.

It protrudes from the chest of the Lady of the Sky.

CHAPTER THIRTY-ONE

GHOA

HER BLOOD IS A BAND OF SILVER STARS CASCADING DOWN her breast.

I don't know why my eyes cling to this detail—why the color of the Lady's blood is the one thing my brain refuses to accept when everything about this situation is impossible—but that silver glitter trickling through the velvety-blue is what breaks me.

I lie there, trembling with fury and disbelief, with outrage and devastation. I did everything I could have, made decisions and sacrifices I never would have. I tried to bury my pride and anger. Attempted to forgive and progress, and for what? To watch the goddess welcome death? If She's truly omnipotent and all-powerful, She should have known this was coming, but She didn't even move. Didn't lift a hand to defend Herself!

It feels like a knee to the gut. A thankless dismissal of our efforts—of Ivandar's sacrifice.

The pearly blue sky darkens, as if doused by a bucket of indigo paint. It bleeds down from the clouds as the Lady of the Sky sinks to Her knees. Coughing and gasping. Looking so much like my mother and Shoshanna, I vomit.

Father Guzan's cry booms like thunder. Rivers of tears as wide as the Amereti pour from His earth-brown eyes. As He falls to His knees beside the Lady, the entire mountain shakes. Everything crumbles, from the boulders to the chairs to the tiles. But the most devastating fracture is inside me. It feels like someone has thrust a dagger into my heel, then strung me up like a slaughtered pig to let my blood and life—and *power*—drain out.

The moment we crossed into this realm, I could no longer access my power but I could still feel it there, nestled within me. Now the cold rushes from my body like blood from a battle wound, leaving me so hollow, I wonder if my organs were made of ice. If there's ever been part of me that wasn't hard and cold.

The only good to come from this sudden drainage is that the last of Serik's heat leaves me too. Relief drips across my ash-and-ember skin like rain across a dry riverbed.

Across the parlor, Enebish screams in Serik's arms.

Kartok retrieves the other sword Serik knocked from his hands and darts toward the gods, baying with triumph.

And a small, venomous voice whispers in my ear.

Did you honestly think this would end any other way? You were a fool to let faith and hope infect you. A fool to think of anyone or anything other than yourself.

It's the firm, unflinching voice I've always listened to. The mantras and mentality that kept me strong—made my armor impenetrable.

Only now, that armor is so riddled with holes, it hangs in dented pieces from my chest. Part of me wants to yield. Why continue fighting for a goddess who didn't even fight for herself? But the stubborn warrior within me marches on.

Refuses to accept defeat. This *can't* be the result of everything I've suffered, of all I've given.

Of all *we've* given.

I'm far from the only person who's made a sacrifice. Who's confronted their fears and questioned their beliefs. Who's opened up their ears and allowed themselves to hear the strains of a beautiful song they had all but forgotten.

Now that melody plays loudly, building into a crescendo as I rise up from the ground. Drowning out the voices of fear and reproach. Refusing to be silenced now that I'm finally listening.

I may not know these gods, and I may not be worthy of Their grace, but I am not beneath Their notice. There's a reason I was taken captive into Zemya. A reason Ivandar and I found Enebish and the rebels. A reason I didn't betray them to the imperial warriors or turn my back on them when I had the opportunity. Every step has been too deliberate to be coincidental. Someone who knows far more than we do has been mapping our course. And She didn't lead us here to fail.

I break into a run.

Without a plan.

Without a Kalima power.

With nothing but hope burning in my chest—cleansing and enlivening instead of scorching and ruinous.

Enebish and Serik sprint toward the Lady and Father too, but I'm faster. I always have been.

Kartok is nearly to the veranda where the Lady of the Sky lies.

The Father stands and moves in front of Her.

My lungs beg for air. My legs feel like they're tearing from my body, churning faster than they ever have. But still not fast enough to wedge myself between Kartok and the gods. Not that it would do any good. I don't have a weapon or a Kalima power. The sorcerer would cut me down like chaff and finish the gods anyway.

Like the magic-barren warriors you sent to the front.

Perhaps this is justice coming full circle. Punishment for sentencing so many untrained warriors to certain death. Or perhaps those magic-barren warriors are the answer. An example of dedication and bravery I was too proud to acknowledge. Throwing themselves at the enemy with no prayer of glory or hope for survival but leaping anyway. Giving their lives so that the people they love might live.

That has always been the most powerful weapon. And I have been too selfish to wield it.

Until now.

My eyes fix on a new target. I shift my angle, lower my shoulders, and explode with a final burst of strength as Kartok lifts his blade.

I slam into his ribs before his sword arm slashes down. Not grappling for control of the knife or wrestling him to the ground. My eyes are focused on the railing.

And the expanse of sky beyond.

Air bleats from the sorcerer as I drive him back. He struggles, his long limbs clawing and grasping, but this time *I* caught *him* by surprise.

"You don't know what you're doing!" he howls.

But he's wrong. I'm becoming the commander—the sister and cousin and daughter—that I always should have been.

Splinters of wood spray into the air as we smash through the balcony's decorative rail, and then I'm weightless.

Tumbling.

Falling into a chasm of jagged rocks and shadowy unknowns.

Kartok's screams echo off the peaks, filling the sky with his fury. But I can hardly hear him over that glorious song, still playing in my ears. Only now, with the accompaniment of the wind and the thundering rhythm of my heart, I can finally hear the words.

I'm no longer falling through the sky, but seated in my parents' music room, listening to the harpsichord trill, watching my father close his eyes and wave his glass of vorkhi like a conductor's baton. "Sing, Ghoa!" he insists.

I shake my head. "Why would I sing when you could perform the piece with twice as much skill?"

"I *could* sing," he agrees, "but that would deny you the opportunity. Sometimes the greatest fulfillment lies not in who could do it easiest or best, but in who can improve the most. It's only through that off-key fumbling that we truly appreciate the beauty of the perfected piece. And it's only through that show of vulnerability and courage that the singer reaches their full potential."

From across the gilded music room, my mother looks up from her embroidery and smiles. Her face is the same as I remember, yet changed entirely. She is both woman and goddess. Two beings, but of the same mind. Possessing the same unfailing love.

"Bravo, my girl," she says softly.

I tilt my face skyward and see Ivandar's face in the whiteness of the swirling fog. I feel Serik's heat in the warmth of the eternal sun. And it's Enebish's arms that wait for me in the darkness below. Making me unafraid to fall.

CHAPTER THIRTY-TWO

ENEBISH

EVERYTHING HAPPENS IN A BLUR—KARTOK SCREAMS ZEMYA'S name and bears down on Father Guzan. Sunlight glints off the sorcerer's blade. His face gleams with morbid ecstasy.

A cry tears from my throat and I break into a run. The gods would never allow the Zemyan sorcerer to murder them. They wouldn't! But the Lady of the Sky lies dead in a pool of blood and Father Guzan stands there, letting Kartok come.

I sprint faster than I ever have, but I'm too slow to intervene. Too skies-forsaken slow, thanks to my injuries from Nariin.

I scream again, braced to watch Father Guzan die alongside the Lady of the Sky. But then a streak of chestnut hair flies past me. Ghoa hurls herself at Kartok, slamming into his side with all the rage and speed she carries into battle. Her momentum drives him across the platform, toward an intricate railing that's purely decorative—as curled and wispy as the veil of cirrus clouds.

"What are you doing?" I shout at her, but it's muffled by a thunderous crack.

Ghoa and Kartok break through the fence, and for several inexplicable seconds they seem to skate across the sky: arms whirling, feet skidding. As if Ghoa somehow froze the air itself.

Kartok screams with rage, but Ghoa remains completely silent—her eyes closed, her head tilted back. A shaft of light breaks through the fog and paints a contented smile across her suntanned face.

Then they plummet out of sight.

Tortured wails echo between the mountain peaks, and it isn't until I run out of breath, my throat blistering and raw, that I realize the screaming voice belongs to me. Not to Ghoa. Or to Kartok. My feet have somehow carried me to the edge of the balcony, though I have no memory of taking another step, and my fingertips are bloody from dragging my hand across the splintered shards of what used to be the railing.

It's the same out-of-body sensation that overwhelmed me the first time I was thrust into true combat. I'd been training with the Kalima for nearly a year and had accompanied them on plenty of missions. I'd sat on the sidelines of the most horrific battles. I thought I *knew* what it meant to take a life. I thought I was prepared. But nothing can prepare you for the feeling, the *essence*, that spills from someone's body along with their blood. How it stains you and spatters you, but since you can't see the gore, you don't know how to scrub yourself clean.

To this day I'm still haunted by the eyes of the first Zemyan I killed. The girl couldn't have been much older than I was, and her eyes were a vibrant seafoam green surrounded by the thickest, whitest lashes. Apparently, my sword plunged in and out of her flesh. Apparently, I kicked her body to the ground, as I'd been trained to do. But I remember none of it. Just those eyes, searing through me, until Ghoa gripped my arm and hauled me away from the next wave of Zemyan soldiers.

"Get ahold of yourself," she said as she slapped me across

the cheek. Not in a cruel way. Her face radiated worry. Maybe even a hint of understanding. As if she'd once been the same terrified twelve-year-old who couldn't fathom how her sword had turned so red. Though, the thought of Ghoa being hesitant or afraid, the thought of her being anything other than a seasoned warrior, was laughable. Unfathomable.

Almost as unfathomable as watching her propel herself from a mountaintop to save gods she never believed in.

I glance over my shoulder. The Lady of the Sky hasn't moved, but Father Guzan is slowly climbing to His feet, still clinging to the Lady's lifeless hand.

This isn't real. It *can't* be real.

But the splinters of wood burrowing into my skin, and Father Guzan's mournful cries, insist that it is.

"Burning skies." Serik jogs up beside me, his voice soft and shredded. He peers over the edge, into a chasm so deep, I can't make out the towering trees we passed during our ascent or the sprawling garden that's larger than the entire city of Sagaan. Serik shakes his head. His skin emits billows of steam—like cold water thrown over a bonfire. "Are they . . . ? Did Ghoa really . . . ?"

"She did," I whisper, dropping to my knees.

Kartok is gone. No type of sorcery, in this world or any other, is strong enough to give him wings. Though, I'm certain he tried to conjure them. I imagine him scrambling to craft a pillow of clouds to cradle his fall, only to slam straight through it. His life as fleeting and as hollow as his magic.

The image would be a comfort if Ghoa weren't hurtling toward the same fate.

Sobs grip me and I retch and shudder, dizzily swaying closer to the edge. Imagining how it would feel to fall so far, knowing death waited at the bottom.

Serik wraps his arms around me and tugs me gently back.

"Come away, En. There's nothing to see."

That's part of the problem. If I can't see Ghoa falling, if her broken body isn't splayed across the rocks, there's no evidence that any of this is real. So my brain refuses to accept that she's gone. That she died saving the First Gods.

It doesn't make sense, and I need, more than anything, for something to make sense.

I lash out, clawing and hissing at Serik like a mountain cat. Desperate to stay there, teetering over the void, as my mind flashes back and forth between the past and present. Ghoa had so many layers. She played so many roles.

Savior, assailant.

Caretaker, tormentor.

Teacher, rival.

Which version was real? Who was she truly? How am I supposed to mourn someone who both ruined and saved me? Part of me wants to rage against the injustice and irony of it all. In a way, this is exactly what Ghoa always wanted: for everyone to be indebted to her, in awe of her. She wanted to be legendary, and since she was never going to achieve that after Ashkar's fall, she found another way to ensure she'd be remembered with reverence.

Except no one was here to witness her sacrifice, other than you and Serik. . . .

And no one across the continent will revere her for saving gods they believe to be long dead. . . .

So perhaps her sacrifice was more altruistic. Perhaps the Ghoa I knew and loved from the beginning was still in there, grappling for hold. Fighting for breath as pride and expectations pushed her deeper and deeper beneath the water's surface.

She allowed herself to be captured by Zemyans so the Kalima could escape. She aligned with the Zemyan prince in order to return to the country that forsook her. She helped us free Chotgor, then stood with us against the Kalima. She refused to harm Serik, despite Kartok's hold, and pitched herself off a cliff, defending gods she didn't worship.

I'm certain she wasn't happy about most of these decisions. I'm positive she fought and berated herself every step. But still she stepped, carving a path to her truest self. To the person *she* wanted to be.

We always have that choice, no matter how irredeemable we may think ourselves. No one is wholly good or bad, and nothing is ever as straightforward as it seems.

Ghoa may not have looked frightened as she fell to her death, but I'm certain she was. And she may not have proclaimed with her final breath that she did this for me, but I know it with just as much certainty. She didn't care about my gods, but she always, *always* cared about me. Serik, too, despite herself. I think she was even beginning to care for the Zemyan prince and the shepherds. And this was her way of showing it: by throwing herself at the enemy. Defending her battalion as only a commander could.

This in no way excuses the terrible, unforgivable things she did. But if I only remember her crimes, then Kartok wins, because he will have stripped me of the ability to trust and love. To believe that we are, all of us, capable of change.

"Enebish." Serik tugs my elbow. "I think we're supposed to follow Him." He juts his chin across the ruined balcony, where Father Guzan stands amid the scattered stones of the sacred cairn. Alive, because of Ghoa's sacrifice. The Lady of the Sky, however, droops in the Father's arms like a lifeless swan, drenched in shimmering blood. Her corpse has already begun withering beneath the rich blue velvet of Her gown, and She still wears Ghoa's face.

When the Lady first turned to look at us, I saw my mother and grandmother and my mentor, Tuva, in the face of the

Goddess as well as Ghoa. But now Her visage is frozen on Ghoa's freckled cheeks and furrowed brow. Those brown eyes, which sparked with such ambition and vivacity in life, are glassy and still.

Proof they're both gone.

The ground has stopped shaking, thanks to Father Guzan's control, but the sky continues to mourn the loss of its master. Rain batters us. Wind assaults us. Lightning strikes the ground directly to our right and left as we follow the Father down the treacherous mountain trail. Above us, darkness continues to drip like paint through the eternal blue sky—slowly changing it to night. I flutter my fingers to see if I can summon the threads, but the blackness is as solid as stone. Because it isn't darkness at all, I realize. It is nothingness. The absence of a creator.

The Father says nothing as we walk—not a word of thanks or condemnation—but He does sing. All the songs I know by heart. I find myself humming along, taking comfort in the familiarity of His words and the richness of His voice—like the steady gurgle of a stream.

He holds the Lady of the Sky tight against His chest to shield Her from the worst of the storm. Tears drip from Father Guzan's cheeks and speckle the Lady's dress, causing swathes of green moss to sprout from the fabric. When His tears happen to find the ground, little clovers and flowers spring up from the mountainside. I don't know if He's letting them fall on purpose, but I whisper my thanks regardless because the foliage provides the smallest bit of traction, helping us down the rocky switchbacks.

A crowd waits at the base of the mountain, gathered around a lifeless form at the garden's edge. I immediately take inventory to see who's missing. Ziva and both kings are present, as well as the Kalima and most of the shepherds and Chotgori who stayed to fight. The Shoniin and Zemyans stand still, weapons forgotten on the ground. Their prince is glaringly absent, but the body sprawled across the rocks couldn't be Ivandar's. Ghoa killed him at the other end of the garden. Which leaves only two options.

The two who fell from the summit.

I reach for Serik's hand, needing his warmth, which he readily offers, even though he has none left to give. His fingers are cold and trembling. He keeps shutting his eyes and shaking his head. I tighten my grip, lending him some of my strength to repay all the times he's carried me.

Still singing, Father Guzan steps boldly through the crowd. The shepherds part and bow their heads. Most of the Shoniin fall to their knees. Even the Kalima warriors and the Zemyans stumble back, slack-jawed. Pale as they are, none are as ashen as the Lady of the Sky.

She was the only constant from the beginning of time. The creator of the heavens and earth and everything in between. I don't know what happens now that She's gone. Will the Father cast us from the Eternal Blue? Or force us to stay and be flattened as it crumbles? Does it matter? There's a good chance the entire continent is collapsing in the absence of its maker.

Father Guzan halts in the center of the crowd and looks down. I force myself to look too, expecting to see a mangled heap of blood and limbs. That's all that could remain of anyone after falling from such a height. But Ghoa rests peacefully on her back, completely whole, her hands folded across her chest and not a hair out of place. Her face is smoothed of every scowl line, making it look as if she's sleeping—far more peacefully than she ever did in life.

"Did you cast her from your presence for her crimes?" Ziva pops up from her bow to address Father Guzan.

King Minoak reaches over and presses Ziva's head to the ground, all without lifting his own. Groveling as only the lowliest servants do in Verdenet. "The commander streaked through the sky like a falling star," he explains. "When she hit the ground, the land shook and the sky darkened and a fierce wind drove us to this spot. We assumed you were angry with her, punishing her."

Father Guzan kneels beside Ghoa, still silent.

"Was there another body?" Serik asks Minoak.

"Another body?" the Marsh King asks. The lines in his craggy face deepen even further. "Who else fell? *Where* did they fall from?"

Serik darts a meaningful gaze at the Zemyans and Shoniin, many of whom are trying to retreat as far and as fast as possible without drawing the attention of the Father. A wasted effort. His attention is solely on Ghoa.

Father Guzan lifts Ghoa into His arms alongside the Lady of the Sky before answering. "The assailant will never reach the earth. He'll spend eternity falling."

The Zemyans call out questions, but the Father resumes His solemn march, deeper into the garden. It could be my eyes playing tricks on me. Or I could very well be losing all sense of reality in my confusion and grief. Because, with every step, the Lady's and Ghoa's limp bodies slide closer together. Merging and melding. Until the Lady wears more than just Ghoa's face.

At the entrance of the hedge maze, Father Guzan glances back and beckons us to follow with an almost imperceptible nod.

There's no hesitation. No discussion—not even among the Zemyans. We obey as if compelled by Kartok's Loridium—except this is an invitation, rather than a command.

We wind deeper and deeper into the garden, and the perfectly manicured hedges grow taller and taller until they form a tunnel over our heads.

"We'll never find our way out," Serik whispers.

I feel the same uncertainty emanating from so many of the others behind us. But I also feel the heartbeat of this realm, pulsing through the ground, whispering through the trees. An unwavering rhythm that keeps me walking ahead with faith. If the Father were going to cast us out or punish us, He would have done so already . . . right?

A breath later, the labyrinth ends in a sprawling lawn lined with even more of the jewel-leafed trees. Another gold-dust pathway leads up a rise to a palace unlike anything I've ever seen. It's made of opal or abalone shell that glistens blue and green and pink. The walls ripple, almost like waves, and tall turrets and towers rise into the clouds, connected by bridges that look to be made of nothing but light. Rendered all the more impressive in the ever-darkening sky. The most striking feature of the palace, however, is how it hovers several lengths above the ground—tethered by glittering ropes, as if to keep it from floating away.

"Maybe we won't want to leave," I finally whisper back to Serik. "Have you ever seen anything so spectacular?"

"I've seen *too* many spectacular things. I'm more than ready for the ordinary. And I'd wager so are they." He motions back to the Zemyans, who have fallen onto their faces, crying for pity. Even though Father Guzan hasn't so much as glanced at them.

Or at any of us.

The gold-dust trail is as soft as carpet underfoot, reminding me of the fine grains of sand in Verdenet. It's even warm against my feet, as if heated by the sun. The trees lining the pathway are reminiscent of those in Namaag, with their towering trunks and branches, thick enough to support platforms. King Ihsan touches the face of each tree, his expression full of wonder. And as we approach the palace, there's no denying how the walls glimmer like ice, taking me back to the decimated Castle of the Clans, which we destroyed during the Ashkarian siege of Chotgor.

This place is entirely new yet achingly familiar. Exactly as I thought the Eternal Blue would be. Teeming with a force far stronger than the overwhelming power and frantic energy that was present in Kartok's *xanav*. His world was fueled by hate and ambition. But the true realm of the Eternal Blue is fueled by love.

Father Guzan steps effortlessly through a towering entry hall that hovers just a step off the ground. When the rest of us move to follow, the entire palace rises with a sudden jerk. It's only then that I notice the stalwart figures positioned at intervals along the wall, half hidden by the deepening shadows. There are three of them, and each holds a rope that tethers the palace to the ground.

I know who they are at once. I would recognize them anywhere. The only three people who have qualified to ascend to this realm.

Jamukha the Invincible, with his shock of scorched black hair—the only evidence that he was struck by seven bolts of lightning.

Zen the Devoted, with his hunched shoulders and gnarled hands clasped around his rope as if in prayer.

And Ciamar the Daring, with her confident smile and long gray braid, which waves behind her like a banner—so all the world could see when she leapt from her tower and into the arms of the Goddess.

I've dreamed of meeting these Goddess-touched warriors ever since I can remember. Eager to learn from them. To be strengthened by simply being in their presence. It's the closest I ever hoped to come to the First Gods, and finally I'm here, standing before them. And they're scowling at me.

Unlike them, I was unable to prove my devotion.

We failed the Lady of the Sky.

"We tried," I cry. "So very, very hard. All I've ever wanted is to—"

"Don't bother pleading your case to me, girl," Ciamar interjects. "Judgment is reserved for the First Gods."

"How do you expect us to follow Them?" I gesture to the palace they purposely raised off the ground.

"We don't," Jamukha says matter-of-factly.

I'm too upset to respond, so Serik asks, "Then what are we supposed to do?"

Zen points to the line of trees, which are quickly vanishing in the fading light. "Wait."

And so we do.

We hunker beneath the trees with their gemstone leaves, and the longer we wait, the more they jangle and crash like shattering dishes. The darkness closes in too—an ominous, impenetrable shroud. It crushes me like a chest press, making it difficult to breathe.

"Now you finally know how the rest of us have always felt in your presence," Serik teases as he slips an arm around my waist. He uses his other hand to light the tip of his finger like a candle, but the flame immediately sputters. With a grunt, he tries again. Weroneka and the other Sun Stokers attempt to summon light as well, but none succeed because they're all missing the base element.

The Lady *was* the light; nothing remains without Her.

We huddle in the gloom for what must be hours. So long I begin to think that *this* must be our punishment for failing the Goddess, for entering forcibly into this realm.

Ziva whimpers, unused to feeling so out of control in the dark. I reach out to comfort her, even though I feel just as wild. I'm aware of every rigid hair on my body. My mind feels like it's tumbling end over end—as Ghoa must have when she fell.

Just when I'm certain I'm going to explode, light flares from the palace and slashes through the garden. A beam of brightness more luminous than the sun itself. Or maybe it just feels that way compared to the dark.

I shield my eyes and stumble to my feet as the palace lowers gently to the ground. A silhouetted figure appears in the entryway. At once, I recognize the gauzy splendor of the Lady's velvet gown, the dewy softness of Her skin. But I also recognize the hardness of Her expression and the swagger of her gait.

On the mountaintop balcony, the Lady wore Ghoa's face like a mask while the rest of Her remained flowing and fluid. Omnipotent.

But now She is both hard and soft.

Both Goddess and Commander.

My two lost mothers, forged into one.

CHAPTER THIRTY-THREE

ENEBISH

"ENEBISH." SHE EXTENDS AN ARM IN MY DIRECTION. HER voice is a bewildering blend of a soft, cascading lilt and Ghoa's authoritative clip, and it leaves me so perplexed, I forget to respond.

"It's generally a good idea to answer when your Goddess calls," She says, and it's so unmistakably *Ghoa*, I accidentally let out a baffled guffaw as I take a small step toward Her.

Serik moves to follow, but the Lady holds up a stern hand. "Is your name Enebish?"

Serik sputters and drags his hands through his hair but, mercifully, bites back whatever he planned to say, which makes the Goddess smile warmly and nod with prim approval.

The back-and-forth between Ghoa and the Lady is so sudden and swift, it's giving me whiplash.

"Ghoa?" I whisper as I approach. "Is that you?"

"Come," is all She says, leading me through the arched palace entrance.

As we move down the colonnade, the structure groans

beneath us and rises once again. When I reach out to steady my balance, the wall is closer than I expected. Instead of stone, it's papered with an ornate cream-colored damask. A white-and-burgundy rug covers the entire length of the hall, and I can't stop staring at it. I tell myself it's because I expected a more traditional castle with several curtain walls and outdoor courtyards. I shouldn't give this rug a second's thought. It's undoubtedly the least interesting aspect of the palace of the First Gods. But for some mystifying reason, I'm certain I've seen it before. A small but fierce longing compels me to run my fingers through the shag, to press my face into the creamy softness.

When the hallway opens into a room, I understand why.

Directly across from us, an impressive stone fireplace roars with heat, the mantelpiece heavily laden with trophies and medals and certificates. More than any one person should be capable of earning. To the right of the fireplace, in front of the floor-to-ceiling bookcases, is the little round table where we were supposed to take tea and practice laying place settings, but instead played nik and gambled away the small weekly allowances we earned for completing our chores around the estate.

Serik's filthy boots are abandoned in the middle of the room, as they always were. Purposely trying to provoke the matron. And Ghoa's first saber—the dented hunk of metal she was given when she first enlisted, which she insisted on carrying everywhere, even when she was home on leave—rests in one of the armchairs as if it were the king's personal saber. The air smells of leather books and lemon polish and the buttery aroma of winterberry pies baking in the kitchen below.

This is our home. Our childhood. Somehow preserved inside the palace of the First Gods.

"I don't understand," I whisper, every inch of me prickling.

The Goddess or Ghoa, or whoever She is, takes my hand and leads me to the twin settees with the black and gold stripes. The ones the matron swore she'd throttle us within an inch of our lives if we ever dared to sit in.

"I don't have much time." Again, the delivery sounds like Ghoa, but the graceful way She moves and Her placid expression are all wrong.

"What's going on? How is all of this possible?" I ask urgently.

"I am whoever *you* need me to be. This palace is wherever *you* long to be. My children are as varied as the blues of the sky, so I, too, must adapt in order to properly serve them. Strong for some, merciful for others. Wise and serene, compassionate and long-suffering."

"Where did Ghoa go? I don't understand," I say again, staring into my sister's brown eyes, but seeing the reflection of the Goddess.

Two answers come in unison, rising from the same pair of lips:

"I'm here."

"She's here."

It sends me into an even deeper spiral of confusion. I clutch my head so tight, my bad arm twinges. But I keep squeezing. Praying the pain will bring clarity. I've dreamed of speaking with the Lady of the Sky all my life, but I watched Her die on that balcony. And I'm desperate to know why Ghoa leapt to save Father Guzan, desperate to have some sort of closure after everything we've been through, but that's just as impossible.

Gentle fingers slide beneath my chin and tilt my face upward. "Much to Kartok's dismay, I cannot be killed," the Lady explains. "Not in the sense that you interpret death. My form may pass away, but my essence is infinite and simply finds a new host."

"And *Ghoa* is that host?" I blurt. I know it's impertinent to question Her, but this proves that I am dreaming. Ghoa would *never* let the Lady of the Sky take her form. And the Lady would never want to reside in someone like Ghoa—proud and disbelieving, cruel and selfish.

The Goddess flinches and draws back, even though I'm certain I didn't speak those thoughts aloud. "Not holding back even a little, are you, En?" All of the Lady's softness vanishes, and the challenging glint in Her eyes is so irrefutably my sister, a sob works its way up my tightening throat.

Ghoa's really in there, somehow.

They both are.

"Is that honestly what you think of me?" Ghoa asks, and it could be the ringing in my ears, but it almost sounds as if her voice catches.

"You know it's not," I whisper.

For all her flaws, Ghoa is also bold and courageous and self-sacrificing.

All ideal qualities in a goddess.

As if summoned by the thought, the Lady's aura rises once more, looking bewildered for a moment before settling into this new skin. "The transition is usually immediate," She pants, "but Ghoa refused to cooperate at first. Then she made several demands . . . one of which was speaking to you, which I'm trying to honor." Her face pinches with strain and Her breath grows heavy.

I stare at the Lady of the Sky. Unable to comprehend what She's saying, what I'm seeing. "What do you mean the transition is *usually* immediate? That makes it sound as if this has happened before."

"It has. Three times. I believe you know them well: Jamukha, Zen, and Ciamar."

"The Goddess-touched?"

She nods. "There's a reason so few people have achieved

that designation. It isn't enough to simply be devout or to make a grand demonstration of faith, worthy of legend. It requires sacrificing oneself for my sake. For the benefit of the whole."

"Are you saying Ghoa is *Goddess-touched*?"

"Why do you sound so skeptical?" Once again Ghoa's indignation propels her to the forefront, though her lips are cocked in a grin. "Is it so hard to believe?"

"Yes! You didn't even believe in the First Gods until we were thrust into Their realm. You wouldn't sacrifice yourself for either of Them."

"You're right. It wasn't for Them."

My hands catapult into the air and I leap from the settee. "Doesn't the Lady have a problem with that?"

Ghoa looks down at her lap, and her voice grows as soft as a whisper of darkness. "Why would She ever have a problem with love? What could be more powerful as the source of Her new life?"

It's the closest Ghoa has ever come to admitting that she loves me, and it does something to my insides. My chest feels like it's collapsing and expanding all at once. My eyes flood with tears of rage and gratitude.

You don't get to do this! I want to scream. *You don't get to ruin my life and then expect to undo the damage by jumping off a cliff and claiming to love me.*

I don't want to forgive her. No one has ever hurt me more. Yet I'm desperate to throw myself into her arms one final time because no one has ever sacrificed so much for me either. And no one has taught me so much—both the good and the bad. Aspirations and warnings. Like it or not, Ghoa shaped me like a sculptor, carving away the excess material to reveal the person I would become.

Ghoa places a hand over mine—her skin far too soft and clean, without a single callus from her saber. "You know

I've never been good with words, and I know it will never be enough, but I'm sorry, En. I hope you felt it on the mountaintop. But I wanted to say it. Needed to say it."

A tear slides down Ghoa's face—one of the few I've ever seen her shed. The only one that doesn't harden into ice before it drips from her chin. It makes her feel so much more human, so much more fallible and *real*. It's only when she reaches out and touches a gentle finger to my cheek that I realize I'm crying too.

"I'm out of time," she murmurs.

She starts to pull away, but I grab her hand, suddenly not ready to let go. "What does that even mean? Where will you go?"

"I'll slowly fade as the Lady strengthens. Whatever remains of me will eventually join the other Goddess-touched warriors outside the palace. I believe there's a lovely length of golden rope waiting for me. Though, I have a sneaking suspicion the others won't be eager to welcome me," she says with a wry smile. "Eternity will be interesting."

I'd assumed the dimness of the Goddess-touched warriors was due to the advancing dark of nothingness, but it's all that remains of them after giving their life for the Lady of the Sky.

I try to picture Ghoa among their ranks, standing serenely beside Jamukha and Zen and Ciamar—the tether between the First Gods and the world. And it's all wrong. Ghoa is action and speed and skill. She is decisiveness and control and ruthlessness.

I tighten my grip, crushing her fingers. "But the other Goddess-touched warriors returned to Ashkar to live out the remainder of their lives before returning here. That's the entire point! Sacrificing your life for the Goddess so She can continue to give life to us all. It's one eternal round."

"Just because the Lady isn't giving *me* new life doesn't mean She isn't honoring Her debt." Ghoa gently peels my fingers from hers.

"What does that mean?"

"It means I chose to give my reward to someone else. Zemya needs a wise, compassionate leader far more than Ashkar needs another washed-up warrior."

"You're not washed-up. And the *prince*?"

Her smile is sly, but her gaze is heavy. Maybe even sentimental. "Tell Ivandar that if I were capable of respecting or caring for a Zemyan, it would be him. I expect him to name his first daughter for me. To ensure I'll always have the final word. And tell Serik he was right—he's a far better warrior than I ever gave him credit for. But I'd still whip him in the sparring ring. And you, En—"

Her voice chokes off and her eyes go vacant. I swear I can see the scars on her arms fading one by one. She shrinks steadily lower, ceding ground to the Goddess. Almost gone. But with a gasp, as if emerging from underwater, Ghoa musters the strength for one last charge. "I know you wield the darkness, but for me, you have always been the light."

She lifts her trembling hands, I expect to give me a final Kalima salute, but she drapes them around my neck and pulls me close. Hugging me.

She still smells of horses and leather and iron. Of snow and grass and wide-open air.

My Ghoa.

Sister, mother, and friend, all in one.

"Thank you." I hug her back fiercely. But I don't know if she felt it. Or if she heard. Her body is too soft, her hair too long, and her skin smells of honey and globeflowers. I don't have to pull away to know I'm embracing only the Lady of the Sky. Which is glorious and inspiring and fills me with so much peace—yet somehow leaves me the slightest bit cold.

A fact I find oddly comforting.

I emerge from the palace hand in hand with the Lady of the Sky and Father Guzan. Serik and the others clamber to their feet, looking at us agog as we glide down the gold-dust path. Shouts of praise and hundreds of questions fly at me from every angle, but Ghoa's voice, and all of the impossible things she said, continue to clash like sabers in my ears. Too loud to focus on anything else. My gaze keeps drifting back to the three ethereal forms standing sentinel before the palace, even though I know she won't be among the Goddess-touched. Not yet.

The Lady and Father halt between my group of rebels and Kartok's battalion of Zemyans and Shoniin, standing in a shaft of radiant sunlight that has broken through the black shroud of nothingness.

"We thank you for the bravery and diligence you exhibited by coming here to defend us." The Lady nods at our small but formidable group, fronted by Serik and the kings of the Protected Territories. "As for you . . ." She turns to the group of Zemyans and Shoniin, who throw themselves facedown into the grass, insisting they knew nothing about Kartok's plans. That they never wanted to wage war against gods. The Goddess waits for them to quiet before continuing. "We thank you, as well, for forcing us to reassess a feud that's lasted centuries too long," She finishes with a warm smile.

They glance up tentatively, their faces slack with disbelief—a very different sort of disbelief.

"You're *thanking* us?" Chanar murmurs. "But you nearly died. We forced our way into your realm. . . ."

Oyunna swats Chanar over the head. "No need to remind Her."

"As a token of our thanks, we shall return you to your

home. Come." The Lady sets off across the lawn at a jarringly quick clip that instantly makes me smile. There's a bit of Ghoa in Her yet.

The rest of us scramble to keep up.

Serik appears beside me, questions rushing from his lips like a waterfall. "What happened in there? What did the Lady say? What became of Ghoa?"

I don't have the energy to explain. Or the words. Or the willingness—if I'm honest. I want to keep it all to myself a few minutes more. To imprint the conversations I had with both the Lady of the Sky and Ghoa deeply in my mind before I open them up to the scrutiny of others.

"I promise I'll tell you everything, but is it okay if we're quiet now?" I lace my fingers through Serik's and look up at him. His hazel eyes are no longer guarded or exhausted but as wide and as open as the grasslands in springtime.

"Take as long as you need," he says, kissing the back of my hand. "If I can wait nineteen years for my Kalima power, I can certainly wait a few hours for this. Just tell me one thing. . . . Is she *gone*?"

After a moment's contemplation, I shake my head. Because Ghoa will never truly be gone.

"Good," Serik says with a quiet smile. "I still need someone to blame for all of my problems."

"Really, Serik?" I ram my shoulder against his side and he chuckles.

"You know Ghoa wouldn't have it any other way."

We fall into companionable silence with the rest of our group, taking in the splendor of the garden as the Lady and Father lead us back the way we came. I peer through the thick covering of emerald and garnet leaves. I part the flowering shrubberies with carnelian blooms, looking for a gateway or a tunnel, or even a snag in the air itself. Completely forgetting that we have a final stop to make before we can return to Ashkar.

The corpses of several shepherds and Namagaan warriors, and even a Kalima warrior, lie tangled in the grass where we initially crossed into the Eternal Blue, their blood as bright as the ruby berries dotting the trees. But my gaze goes immediately to the Zemyan prince and his pale, unseeing eyes.

Whispers explode from both groups, and a good number of Zemyans lurch after the First Gods as They kneel at Ivandar's side. Suddenly desperate to protect the prince they were so eager to depose.

Father Guzan raises both hands, and the earth surges up in front of the advancing Zemyans, throwing them onto their backs. Behind this wall of protection, the Lady of the Sky extends Her palms over Ivandar and chants a song that's an amalgamation of every sacred hymn I've ever known. Curls of blue smoke drift down from Her fingers and envelope the prince in a thick haze. The ritual is jarringly similar to Kartok's Loridium, but then, why wouldn't it be? Zemya is a child of the Lady and Father. She may have forged Her own magic, but the foundations of Her power, Her training and tutelage, came from Her parents. Proving yet again that They aren't so different.

As soon as the smoke dissipates, Ivandar surges up from his back with a gasp, as if escaping the throes of a nightmare. He pants and blinks against the harsh sunlight, which continues to punch through the crumbling darkness. His hands rove over his chest and torso, feeling for wounds that are no longer there—though the evidence remains. Blood coats his fingers and plasters his tunic to his chest.

"What happened?" he asks, finally glancing up. He squints and gasps even louder when he registers the faces of the beings on either side of him. "Am I dead? Where's Zemya? I thought She would greet me. . . ." Ivandar tries to scuttle back, but the

Lady places a reassuring hand on his shoulder.

"You *were* dead, but thanks to a friend, you won't remain so. We're going to find Zemya now." The Lady rises with the grace of an eagle taking flight. The Father extends a hand to Ivandar and helps him to his feet.

"What friend? I still don't understand. . . ." Ivandar's round, frightened eyes scan the crowd. Looking for Ghoa. When they fail to find her, his gaze settles on me. I give him a single, somber nod.

His entire frame sags. He clutches his bloodied shirt even harder. "How? Why would she do this?"

Before I can answer, the Lady of the Sky and Father Guzan join hands. Shocks of brilliant green grass and swaying ferns spring up beneath the Father, and another plaque of darkness crumbles from the Eternal Blue sky directly over the Lady's head, enfolding Them in the largest swathe of sunlight yet. They whisper words too low for any of us to hear, and when They raise their joined hands overhead, the garden falls away, bringing us to stand before a high stone wall with a gate large enough for only one person to pass at a time.

Ashkar stands beside the gate, clad in gleaming lamellar armor—the most glorious Kalima warrior I've ever beheld. Yet I'm neither awed nor impressed. The sight of Him floods me with too many conflicting emotions. He gave me my power, for which I will always be grateful. But He also led me to use that power to attack and enslave. To conquer and claim the people and places He feared.

Maybe He truly thought Zemya was a threat. And perhaps She was. Or maybe He was even more afraid of sharing the smallest part of His glory with His sister, of not being the best in the eyes of Their parents. I know better than anyone how the need for praise and approval can drive you to do things you never would have considered. But for some reason, I had assumed the gods were above this. That They had transcended such lowly human emotions. But maybe it's that humanity, that fallibility, that keeps Them tied to us. Bringing out the best and the worst in all of us.

When He spots our group, Ashkar brandishes His saber and moves in front of the gate. "What are *they* doing in our realm?" He levels His blade at the Zemyans.

"Lower your weapon," the Lady commands.

When Ashkar doesn't immediately comply, She flicks Her wrist and His blade flies away on a gust more violent than anything a Wind Whisperer could conjure. "We've had more than enough bloodshed. It's time to lay down our weapons and grudges." She holds out Her hand. "We're bringing your sister home."

Ashkar stares in horror at the Lady's hand. "But She—

"Never had a chance," Father Guzan interrupts. The timbre of His voice shakes the walls of Ashkar's watchtower. The rocks and mortar groan, threatening to collapse. At last, Ashkar sighs and opens the gate.

A current that feels like both wind and water sweeps us up and washes us through a tunnel of shadows. I brace for the glaring brightness of the snow and the unforgiving sting of the cold, assuming we'll return to the ice caves, where we entered the realm of the Eternal Blue. But when my feet touch down, I'm standing on white marble steps, cluttered with singed debris. The blackened husk of the Sky Palace looms over us, and a sore battle rages across the Grand Courtyard. A melee of Ashkarians and Zemyans fight with blind rage, defending their homes and families to the death. Battling for the rights and respect they believe they're owed from feuds that began centuries before.

The carnage is horrific; I've never seen such a bloody battle, not in all my years at the war front. Both sides are so consumed by the chaos, they fail to notice the gods, standing there. Watching them slaughter one another.

I glance at the Lady of the Sky, waiting for Her to unleash a storm of lightning. Or for Father Guzan to rend the earth and command their attention. Or for Ashkar to leap to the aid of His people, to ensure they defeat His sister's followers. But none of them move.

I, on the other hand, am going to burst out of my skin if I *don't* move. The tendrils of darkness shiver in my periphery and whisper in my ears. Ready now that we're no longer in the Eternal Blue.

You can end this now. So easily. If the Zemyans cannot see, they cannot fight.

My fingers twitch. From the other side of Minoak, I feel Ziva's fists tighten in response. Ready to charge with me. But I let out a long, steadying breath and uncurl my fingers. If battering the Zemyans with the sky was the will of the First Gods, They would have called the darkness Themselves.

The Lady of the Sky places a hand on my shoulder, gives me an approving smile, and whisper's Zemya's name. Her voice is so soft, I can barely hear it and I'm standing right beside Her. Zemya will never hear from the barren wastes by the sea. But then the Father joins the Lady, chanting Their daughter's name. After a beat of reluctance, Ashkar adds His voice to His parents' and the fighting instantly ceases.

Every Zemyan in the courtyard stands still enough to be frozen—arms raised, daggers slicing, mouths screaming. Tears stream from their eyes and sweat pours down their cheeks. Within seconds they are drenched and dripping, as if caught in a rainstorm, though the sky is perfectly clear. The water gathers into a puddle in the center of the cobblestones, growing wider and deeper.

"Hot-spring water," Ivandar wheezes as the droplets seep

from his skin as well.

Once the water is knee-deep, it shoots skyward like a fountain and forms the shape of a woman as it falls. Her hair is silver and white seafoam. Her eyes shimmer with the luster of pearls. And the sound of crashing waves follows Zemya as She weaves through the immovable Zemyan warriors and the equally stunned Ashkarians. When She reaches Her parents and brother, She raises Her chin defiantly. A pointed chin, which She clearly inherited from the Lady of the Sky. And Her mane of hair is undeniably from Father Guzan. And Ashkar's eyes are sloped slightly upward at the corners, just like Hers.

Despite the stark outward changes Zemya wrought upon Her body to separate Herself from the First Gods, the family resemblance is irrefutable. It's impossible for a tree to grow without its roots; Zemya wouldn't exist without the Lady and Father.

"I should have known you'd intervene as soon as it became clear I'd defeat you." Zemya flings Her arms and hot-spring water sprays the Sky Palace steps, burning like embers where it wets my skin. "How do you plan to punish me this time? How else can you weaken and debase me? Whatever it is, it won't work. I will always recover. I will always return stronger."

"We were wrong," the Lady says, holding out Her hands in capitulation.

Zemya bristles, crosses Her arms, and says in a spiteful voice, "You are the Lady and Father. Creators of the heavens and earth. You are *never* wrong."

"In this instance, We were."

"About what, exactly?" Zemya challenges.

"Many things: suppressing your drive and innovation, for presuming your magic was evil just because we couldn't understand or control it, and mostly for pitting you and your brother against each other in the first place, by comparing your abilities."

A shiver works through me, dotting my skin with goose bumps. The feud between the First Gods isn't so different from the feud in my own family: some with power and some without, a constant battle for acknowledgment and supremacy. All of it unnecessary.

Zemya stares for a long moment, nostrils flared and jaw working as She struggles to maintain a tight hold on Her rage. "Unfortunately, this realization and apology are several centuries too late."

"Is it ever, truly, too late?" the Lady presses. "Come home."

Zemya laughs and takes a deliberate step back. "My home is with my people."

"You are a wise and caring Goddess," the Lady says with a proud smile. "Your people are lucky to have you. I would never take you from them."

"Then why ask me to return to the realm of the Eternal Blue?"

"Because it doesn't have to be a choice between your people and your family. It never *should* have been a choice. You can mend the rift between us and still serve your people. If an Ashkarian commander can give her life for a Zemyan prince, I think we, their gods, should be capable of reaching a similar truce."

The swirling and crashing of Zemya's watery form gradually slows until She resembles a trickling stream rather than a raging river, but Her voice remains fierce and strong. "And what of my magic?"

"That's entirely up to you," the Lady assures Her. "Continue to innovate if you wish, but I, for one, have grown weary of watching mortals abuse the power of the sky."

"As have I," the Father agrees.

They stare at Ashkar, who grudgingly adds, "And I."

"And if there's no quarrel between us, there's no reason they need the sky to defend themselves," the Lady explains.

Zemya looks skeptically at each of them. "What exactly are you saying?"

"As a show of our commitment, and as retribution for our mistakes, we will withdraw our powers from Ashkar."

My throat constricts around a gasp of utter shock. The other Kalima warriors cry out with even more outrage—Serik loudest of all. In the Eternal Blue, they all briefly experienced how it feels to be powerless. Ordinary. Weak.

A state I was forced to endure for two years at Ikh Zuree. A state I learned to survive. Thrive in, even, once I silenced my oppressors and started trusting myself.

Serik too. He was brave and fierce and battle-ready long before he could wield the sun's fiery rays. And maybe that's the point. Maybe none of us have ever truly needed power beyond our own faith and fortitude and determination.

"Without the sky, your people will be nothing," Zemya exclaims, making the Kalima shout even louder.

The Lady of the Sky gives a little shrug. "Or perhaps they'll be forced to find themselves—to innovate and discover their own strengths—as you once did. . . ."

The Lady of the Sky extends Her hand to Zemya.

She stares at the Lady's offering, then turns to gaze at Her people, suspended in battle. Winning, but for how long? And at what cost? Laying down weapons and grudges doesn't necessarily mean you've lost the war. Sometimes it achieves the boldest victory.

Ghoa taught me that.

After another scowl and an exasperated shake of Her head—as if She'll instantly regret it—Zemya takes Her mother's hand.

The sky explodes with darkness and light, with wind and

rain and stars. We drop onto our stomachs and cover our heads as hail gouges the obliterated palace and sleet washes the blood from the Grand Courtyard. It reminds me of the howling surge of darkness that whipped around me every time I called the night inside the Temple of Serenity in Kartok's false Eternal Blue. An explosion of wild, unbridled power. But unlike that deception, this is both cleansing and punishing. A show of power and restraint. A final reminder of who rules the skies.

The storm lashes us for what feels like hours, growing steadily stronger, until it clears just as fast as it came. As if swept away by a wave of the Lady's hand, to reveal a lustrous, clear blue sky. Everyone in the courtyard peels themselves off the ground and looks to the palace steps.

But the First Gods have vanished.

And so have our reasons to fight.

CHAPTER THIRTY-FOUR

ENEBISH

THE GATHERING OF THE FIVE NATIONS IS SCHEDULED TO TAKE place in Sagaan exactly two weeks after the ceasefire. The warriors conscripted from the territories and the Zemyans wanted to rush home immediately, but everyone agreed we must lay careful groundwork. So the foundation of our new alliance is as immovable as the peaks of the Eternal Blue. We owe it to the thousands of people who perished fighting this endless war. And we owe it to ourselves, too.

The Chotgori clans, Namagaan soldiers, and shepherds who fled the ice caves arrive first, a mere four days after our summons. Readily flocking to join us, now that the danger has passed.

Almost all of Ashkar takes to the streets to welcome the clan leaders as they trudge in from the snowy grasslands, but I remain in the treasury. Inside Ghoa's father's office, where I find myself more and more often—when I'm not tasked with keeping the fragile peace between so many opinionated kings, that is. Or helping to rebuild the homes and shops that were destroyed by the Zemyans.

The rest of Sagaan is slowly beginning to unbury from the rubble, but this room remains untouched—utterly wrecked from the siege. Books and ledgers lie ripped and strewn across the floor, the furniture is hacked to pieces, and the broken window is covered with a tacked-up blanket. It's cold and filthy and Serik and Ziva keep dropping less than subtle hints that my coming here is odd. Eerie. It's where the Kalima betrayed Ghoa and where the Sky King perished.

But it's also where Ghoa was reborn. If I kneel in the broken glass, still stained with blood, I can imagine how her ice bridge must have looked—white crystals spanning the blackness of the siege.

Sometimes I still don't believe she sacrificed herself to save the First Gods. And sometimes I wish she hadn't. It muddled everything. Colored the entire world in maddening shades of gray instead of stark black and white. I miss her and resent her. Love her and loathe her. The balance shifts by the day, sometimes by the hour—depending on how difficult the kings and Zemyans are being.

Serik stomps up the stairs and pokes his head through the door. "You've got to stop hiding out in here. Morbid obsession aside, it's freezing. And it smells."

I shrug. "I don't mind the smell. And it's easier than all of *that*." I wave in the direction of the main thoroughfare, teeming with Ashkarians and Chotgori, with Namagaans and Zemyans. They all came together—exactly as I wanted—but not in the way I planned or expected. *They* were supposed to stand with me against Kartok and the Zemyans.

Not Ghoa.

"Since when do you make your decisions based on what's easiest?" Serik asks. "And do you truly blame them for fleeing the ice caves?"

"No," I groan as I gain my feet, knowing my resentment

is unfair. My expectations were too high. It was naïve to think the Chotgori would charge into battle against Zemyan sorcerers when they were weak and traumatized from the ore mines. When they hardly knew us and had no reason to believe we would succeed. It's a moot point besides; we still managed to save the gods without them. And if the Lady of the Sky can forgive them, I should do the same. I'm trying to do the same. I don't want to reconstruct the fortress around my heart. I don't want to let Kartok wound me anymore than he already has. Which is why I stitch a smile on my lips and plod across the room to join Serik, hoping I look contented. And hoping, even more, that I truly feel that way in time.

"Would it help if I told you the Chotgori brought you a gift?" Ziva appears behind Serik. I don't know if she's been there the entire time, hidden in the wisps of darkness that still respond to our call—though, they grow fewer by the day—or if she just bounded up the steps to join us.

I chuff out a laugh. "What could they possibly bring me?"

"If I tell you, it will ruin the surprise. Come on." Ziva takes my hand and practically drags me down the stairs. Bouncing and giddy, even as her bandaged wounds continue to seep and dark exhausted circles hang beneath her eyes. She's no longer a girl but not yet a queen. Caught between worlds, like so many of us. Hopefully, now that the war is over, she has time to find herself in both.

When we burst out into the courtyard, I squint skeptically at the long line of travelers until my gaze lands on a cart in the middle of the procession, on top of which sits a crude cage that holds the world's most beautiful golden eagle.

"Orbai." I choke on her name. I hadn't let myself hope. I presumed the Chotgori would kill her after we disappeared into the realm of the Eternal Blue, the way Kartok was forcing her to behave. But she's here, rumbling into the city, and I don't know what's flying faster, my legs or my heart.

I wrap my arms around Ziva and hug her tight. Then I elbow through the crowd, gaze fixed on my eagle's flashing yellow eyes. Ears attuned to nothing but her high-pitched shriek as the cart clatters over ruts in the road.

Keep your head. Temper your expectations. Prepare for the worst, the logical part of me insists. But love cares little for logic. And faith cannot exist without hope. It's probably wrong to beg for more after all of the miracles the First Gods have already performed, but I send a silent plea up to the Lady of the Sky anyway. Because this is the only thing I've ever asked for that's wholly for myself. And because I know She cares about these seemingly small requests. She's my mother and sister in every sense of the word.

I throw myself against the crude bars of Orbai's cage, crying her name, wishing I could squeeze myself through the slats and bury my face in her feathers. Orbai lets out a deafening shriek, and the man pulling the cart trips and curses me. I ignore him. No one exists beyond me and my eagle.

"Skies, I've missed you," I gush. I slip my fingers through the cracks and burst into jubilant tears when she doesn't attempt to bite them off. But my joyous cries morph gradually into heartbreak because she also doesn't hop closer or click her beak. She doesn't gnaw on the bars of the cage, trying to reach me. She stands there, as aloof and guarded as the day the trappers brought her in off the grasslands and committed her to my care at Ikh Zuree.

Tears slide down my face. I don't know if they're happy or sad. I never seem to know what I'm feeling anymore. Orbai is alive. And no longer under Kartok's influence. But she's no longer *mine*, either.

I walk alongside the cart until the caravan comes to a halt

in the center of the square. The travelers scatter to procure food and baths, but I remain there, beside my eagle. I can't bring myself to part from her. As I sit there, speaking in soft tones and letting her smell my fingers, watching her eye me curiously, I decide to focus on gratitude, rather than bitterness. This isn't the reunion I wanted, but it's better than the worst I feared. It's a starting point. A new beginning. And like the city of Sagaan and the Protected Territories, and even Zemya, all will be rebuilt with time.

Serik and I aren't invited to take part in the official peace negotiations—something he can't stop grumbling about, but I've never been so relieved. Let the kings argue and angst over how to manage their unruly people. I'd much rather hide away in the treasury or fly off to the stables, where I've converted an empty stall into a makeshift mews for Orbai.

"You'll prefer this," I tell Serik as I slide the barn door open. "It's so quiet and peaceful."

Except the barn is neither quiet nor peaceful at the moment.

Ivandar paces the center aisle, muttering and pulling at the crown of seagrass resting atop his white-blond curls. He jolts when he spots us, as if we caught him pilfering the royal coffers. "What are you doing here?"

"What are *you* doing here?" Serik asks with a mischievous smirk. "Aren't you supposed to be counseling with the other leaders?"

Ivandar groans and leans against the nearest stall door, soiling his seafoam green suit.

"I thought you wanted these responsibilities . . ." I say, venturing closer.

"I do." The prince sighs. "But I didn't want them immediately. And not at my mother's expense. She isn't coming—she isn't strong enough to journey from Zemya. According to our healers, she collapsed at the time of Kartok's demise and didn't rise for five days. And she has no memory of the past eight years. Her attendants say she mumbles and talks to walls. They say she sings strange songs and strokes her neck and laughs at nothing."

"Honestly, you're lucky if that's the worst of it," Serik says with an exaggerated shake of his head. "Can you imagine Kartok sifting around in your mind for *eight* years?"

I shoot Serik a glare, tempted to pinch his ear and drag him away like the abba used to at Ikh Zuree. "I'm sure your mother will return to herself soon," I tell Ivandar, even though I'm sure of no such thing. But I refuse to accept anything else.

Danashti *will* come back to Ivandar because I need Orbai to come back to me.

"But what if she doesn't?" Ivandar presses as he squints through the barn door, trying to hide the wetness pooling in his eyes.

"Then you'll lead your people," I say simply. "You're more than capable."

"But am I ready?"

"Stop dithering and focus on what you can control." Serik presses his palms against the prince's back and shoves him out the door. "If you want to honor your mother and those who suffered and sacrificed, do it by becoming the best damn emperor Zemya has ever known."

Ivandar peers over at Serik, a bemused expression crinkling his usually harsh features.

"Why are you looking at me like that?" Serik demands.

"Because you sounded just like Ghoa."

Serik wheezes and starts to argue. But then he bites his lip and looks down at his feet. A small grin tugs his lips. "For the first time in my life, I'm going to take that as a compliment."

After Ivandar plods across the debris-littered courtyard to the tavern where the negotiations are taking place, I collect my eagle from her perch and take her into the abandoned gardens behind the scorched Sky Palace. Serik follows, settling beneath the larch trees to watch.

I've spent as much time as possible with Orbai, reforging our bond. In a way, it's like time has unraveled and I'm reliving our early days together—except even better. Without the Sky King's other birds, I can focus solely on Orbai and appreciate every little milestone.

Last week, I burst into happy tears when she flew to my glove for the first time. And every time she inches up my shoulder and clicks her beak in my ear, I can't help but coo and praise her in a ridiculous, high-pitched voice.

I wait for Serik to tease me, but he doesn't say a word. He just watches, a small grin on his lips. So much quieter than before. More introspective.

"What are you thinking about?" I often find myself asking him.

"What do you *think* I'm thinking about, in the face of such beauty?" He winks and points deliberately at Orbai instead of me. Though, I catch him staring at his palms when he thinks I'm not looking. Two nights ago, I spied him trying to start a fire by rubbing sticks—like the rest of us. Praying for divine help, for power that continues to lessen every day.

It's during one of these quiet training sessions, on the fifth day of negotiations, that Ziva hikes up the hill to where Serik and I sit, watching Orbai loop overhead. Ziva and Ivandar have kept us informed of plans moving forward: all nations will have open borders and trade contracts and arrangements to send Ashkarians to Namaag and Chotgor and Verdenet for apprenticeships.

So they can learn to hunt and fish and cast gold—actual trades by which to make a living, rather than sucking the resources from other nations. It's a complete reversal; the very people Ashkar set out to "stabilize" are best equipped for success and self-sufficiency. They always have been.

"The council wants to see you," Ziva says to me.

"Why?" I furrow my brow. "I have no place in these negotiations."

I don't want a place, I add silently.

"You're obviously going to be punished . . ." Serik wags his eyebrows. "You led a rogue rebellion and committed dozens of crimes against each country and ruler."

Ziva laughs and rolls her eyes at Serik. "They want to see you, too."

He hooks his elbow through mine and gives me a surprising peck on the cheek. "Just as well. If they plan to take one of us down, they'll have to take us down together."

The entire council stands when Serik and I enter the small room at the back of a tavern. The space is unremarkable in every way—small and cramped with too many tables and benches, everything soaked in the smell of ale and oiled wood. Which would be pleasant enough if it didn't make me think of another group that met in the back of a tavern and their tiger-eyed leader who helped me find the strength and confidence to fight, only to become my opponent on the opposite side of the battlefield.

King Minoak steps forward. Behind him, Ivandar sits between King Ihsan and his orange-clad guards and the Chotgori clan leaders. Varren and the other Kalima warriors round out the group—the closest thing Ashkar has to a ruler at present.

Minoak waits for Ziva to rejoin him before addressing me and Serik. "We owe you both an incredible debt. Through your bravery and determination, the entire continent is free and united for the first time in centuries. In order to maintain this peace, we have unanimously decided to retain a group of Kalima warriors—"

"But how—" I interject.

"You may not be able to wield the sky," King Minoak speaks over me, "but the need for an elite group of warriors, comprised of members from each country, is undeniable. And we would like you, Enebish, to lead this new battalion with Serik as your second, if you're willing."

Serik's hands tighten around my arm and he wheezes, "We are willing!"

But I can't bring myself to immediately agree. My eyes feel as if they're bulging out of my skull as I look from face to face. From Ihsan's craggy complexion, to the golden skin of my rulers from Verdenet, to the blizzard-white Zemyans to the flame-haired Chotgori. All so different, yet not different at all. Not in the ways that truly matter.

My fingers drift to the traitor's mark on my face, then down the old, purple scars on my arm. "You want *me* to serve as commander?"

The title carries so much weight and responsibility. So much longing and resentment.

"You've proven yourself more than capable," Minoak says, smiling proudly at me. They're all smiling proudly. Restoring my honor and position, exactly as I've always wanted. More than I could have dreamed.

But the words of an old Verdenese proverb fill my mind. One my mother used to sing when we were plagued by summer droughts or when Zemyans raided Nashab Marketplace, or when I complained about my chores and the sweltering heat:

The desert is the cruelest cradle. Sun and sand strip flesh from bone.

But bone can break and then rebuild, making man as

strong as stone.

There's no denying that the past few months have broken me. Shattered me into a thousand tiny pieces. And only one place is harsh enough and unforgiving enough to cleanse and harden and reshape me. To knit me back together, joining the dreams and aspirations I've always had with this new person I'm becoming.

"I'm most grateful for the honor," I say, bowing to each respective ruler. "But I don't wish to return to the army."

"*What?*" The smallest flicker of heat surges from Serik's body as he turns to gape at me. I can't bring myself to look at him. I'll be tempted to change my mind if I do. Anything to avoid the disappointment and betrayal undoubtedly haunting his eyes. But I can't disappoint or betray myself either.

"We can't give up this chance!" Serik insists. "This is what you've always wanted—what *we've* always wanted. Riding into battle side by side."

I give a little shrug. "Hopefully there isn't a battle to ride into—not for a long while. And circumstances change. What I thought I wanted isn't what I actually need. I hope you can understand that. I'm not asking you to give up anything."

Serik sputters and pulls at his hair, long enough to hang in his eyes now. "Don't be ridiculous! I can't just run off and join the Kalima without you!"

"You can and you should. A bird has wings for a reason, Serik. Let them carry you where you need to go, then fly back to me. We can have what we need and each other. It doesn't have to be a choice. Just as it never had to be a choice for the First Gods."

His hazel eyes find mine—hurt but understanding. "What do you want, En?" he asks softly.

What do I want?

I don't know how to vocalize the breadth of it, but when I

413

close my eyes, I picture it so clearly: the sand between my toes and the sun on my cheeks. Sandals cutting into my heels and the sweet scent of a grass roof lulling me to sleep. The sound of my mother's voice on the wind and the taste of my father's lentil stew on my tongue.

I want to return to Verdenet.

Not to recreate a time that was before. But to charge forward—into the future by way of the past. To continue reviving and fortifying my home and my people.

And, hopefully, myself.

EPILOGUE

ENEBISH
SIX MONTHS LATER

Zɪᴠᴀ ᴅʀᴏᴘs ʜᴇʀ ᴡᴏᴏᴅᴇɴ sᴡᴏʀᴅ ꜰᴏʀ ᴛʜᴇ ᴛᴇɴᴛʜ ᴛɪᴍᴇ ɪɴ less than twenty minutes.

"Focus, Zivana!" I shout across the sandy sparring ring, using her full name to vex her even more. "A queen must always keep her head. Especially under pressure."

"I *am* focusing!" She snatches her sword—much too forcefully. It jabs her leg and her sparring partner, a Zemyan boy named Josaf, chuckles as she yelps. As do the hundred other trainees spaced across the practice field recently erected outside of Nashab Marketplace.

Any youth across the continent who wishes to hone their skills in self-defense is welcome to attend my training, and I have a good mix of students from each of the five nations. Hopefully the peace between our countries lasts centuries longer than the war and they won't ever need these skills, but it's better to be prepared. To ensure that future generations know how to defend themselves and, more important, how to communicate.

It's a small way I can give back. Something I surprisingly enjoy—Inkar taught me that. And a way to pay homage to my own mentors—Ghoa and Tuva. And the Lady herself, in a way.

"Wielding the night was so much easier," Ziva mutters as she retakes her position.

"Maybe you should cut her a little slack," Ivandar suggests from where he leans against the fence beside me. He visits every couple of months to observe the Zemyan students' progress.

He spoke quietly enough, but Ziva cuts her eyes at him and points her wooden blade in his direction. "I do not want slack. Do you think *your* people will cut me slack when I am queen?"

The group falls silent, tense, awaiting the Zemyan ruler's reply. At times these newly forged relationships feel like treading across a field of sabers. Bloody wounds seem almost inevitable. But every day that we keep on trudging, our feet grow a little bit tougher.

Instead of taking offense, Ivandar tilts his head back, pale skin pink and sweaty beneath the desert sun, and laughs. "By the time you're queen of Verdenet, my people will have heard so many tales of you making a complete and utter fool of me, they would never dream of mocking you."

The group joins in with Ivandar's laughter, and eventually even Ziva cracks a smile.

"You're making impressive progress, En," Ivandar says an hour later, when the trainees put up their wooden swords and disperse back into the marketplace.

"Thanks. They have a long way to go, but they're eager to learn."

"I'm not talking about them. I never doubted for a second that you'd be an excellent teacher. I'm talking about *her*." The Zemyan prince nods up at the sky where Orbai circles and swoops. As constant and predictable as the sun.

After a few slow weeks of reacquaintance, it was like someone pulled a lever in my eagle's mind and Orbai was suddenly Orbai again. Clicking in my ear and chewing holes in my tunic, looking for treats.

I cried so hard and hugged her so tightly, she refused to come near me the entire day after. And I spent so long thanking the Lady of the Sky, She probably never wants to hear from me again. But I had to let Her know how grateful I am. How seen I feel. She has thousands of children across the continent, but She takes the time to hear me. To know and bless me.

Ivandar watches wistfully as Orbai lands on my out-stretched glove.

"I take it there's been no improvement with your mother?" I ask sympathetically.

He shakes his head once. "Not yet. But I haven't lost hope."

"You shouldn't. She was under Kartok's influence so much longer."

"I can't decide if that's comforting or terrifying." His laugh is miserable—and heartbreaking.

"Have you petitioned Zemya?"

"Of course I've tried to call on Her, but the sacred hot spring is nearly drained. . . ."

Part of me is surprised to hear Zemya complied with Her parents' wishes and the other part isn't at all. "She'll find other ways to reach you," I assure the prince.

He nods again, thoughtfully. "Can I walk you home before I return to my caravan?"

"I don't think your entourage will wait that long."

Ivandar's brows lower with confusion. The little shack I rent is just outside the market. But tonight Serik returns from his first tour of duty with the Kalima.

Which means, tonight, I am finally going *home*.

The journey between Lutaar City and the tiny village of Sangatha takes four hours on foot. With my limp, it takes six. Half of the sun has already disappeared beneath the horizon when the first straw huts appear in the distance, but that somehow feels right. My power was born here. It's only fitting it should die here too.

I glance up at the fading threads of darkness, churning and looping above me. Every day they merge a little more into one, becoming an inanimate expanse of black, as the Lady and Father recall Their powers. The night, as everyone else sees it.

Serik waits for me at the outskirts. He's been stationed with his battalion in Zemya for the past four months, studying their tactics and formations in order to incorporate them into the Kalima's repertoire, and since my village is so near to the border, it made more sense for him to meet me here. What doesn't make sense is how he came.

I have to squint and shake my head to make sure it's really him. Not because of the polished lamellar armor he wears and how it hugs his broadened shoulders and trim waist—though I definitely notice both. But because he's sitting astride Ghoa's massive black warhorse.

"Is that *Tabana*?" I call as I limp closer.

"You haven't seen me in months and the first thing you ask about is my *horse*?"

"Well, is it?" I say with a laugh.

"I thought I'd do the beast a kindness and use her after everyone else in the Kalima refused," he explains as he dismounts. "But do you think she's grateful? No. She punishes my generosity on a daily basis—rearing and biting and dumping me in the dirt. Ghoa's probably putting her up to it. Laughing at me from the Eternal Blue." Serik scowls at the horse, but he also reaches out and strokes her neck affectionately. Proudly, even.

"I think you're a good match," I say as I throw myself into Serik's arms.

"Not half as good as *this* match." He pulls me into him, murmuring into my hair, and I marvel for the hundredth time at how my head fits beneath his chin, as if the space had been chiseled just for me. At how his arms curl around my body, knowing just how to cradle my injuries.

"I've missed you," I say, fisting his sunburst cloak—the only part of him that still smells faintly of pine ink and prayer scrolls. He was given a new one, of course, as part of his Kalima uniform, but he "lost" it almost immediately.

"You wouldn't have to miss me if you changed your mind and decided to rejoin the Kalima. . . ." Serik whispers.

With a snap of my fingers, Orbai dives through the swiftly encroaching darkness and screeches as she skims over Serik's head. Close enough that he curses and ducks.

"Well, hello to you, too," he calls as she banks around an outcropping of rock to have a second go at him. "I was going to tell you how much I've missed you, but it's clear the feeling isn't mutual." He shakes his head ruefully and turns back to me. "Are you ready?"

I lace my fingers through Serik's and nod.

Sangatha has been rebuilt in the ten years since Ghoa took me in—and nearly everyone I knew perished in the fire—but the winding streets are still well-worn paths in my memory. My feet carry me to my first home as if I never left it.

As we pass, people poke their heads from their huts to stare at us—at Serik, more specifically—and I'm more than happy for the shield. For the blissful anonymity. Between him and the thickening night, I'm hardly more than a shadow.

A new house has been erected where mine once stood. Thick and sturdy, with a freshly thatched roof. Smoke rises from a vent in the top and candlelight wavers in the windows, but I circle the hut anyway until I find a knob protruding from one of the wooden slats.

419

"What are you *doing*?" Serik demands as I pull myself up.

"What does it look like I'm doing? Climbing to the roof."

"You can't just climb other people's houses!"

"Don't tell me the army's making you into a rule follower," I tease as I heft my leg over the edge.

Serik mutters curses and fumbles around, looking for somewhere to tie Tabana, before finally joining me. "Is this really necessary?" he demands. "Couldn't we have just looked at it from the ground?"

"No," I say without further explanation.

Up here, with the darkness and the stars, is where I've always felt my parents strongest.

Serik gives my fingers a squeeze and we slip into silence. In that silence, I hear the screams and snapping flames from the day my village burned. But I also hear an entire childhood's worth of laughter and heartfelt prayers. So many memories I had all but forgotten.

"Tell me about them," Serik urges, even though I've told him about my parents a hundred times. But I tell him again.

Once more.

And he listens attentively to every word.

By the end of it, I'm sobbing and shivering and I don't protest when Serik pulls me against his chest and covers me with his cloak. "Do you want me to scrounge up some heat? Sometimes I can still summon a spark."

I shake my head and take a deep, burning breath into my lungs, holding it as long as possible. "I actually prefer a bit of cold these days," I whisper.

"Funny, me too," Serik says, and we look upward, into the infinite expanse of sky.

It may be my bleary eyes, desperate to find a glimmer of movement in the blackness, but I swear I see the Lady of the Sky and Ghoa looking down on us. Smiling.

ACKNOWLEDGMENTS

EVEN THOUGH THIS IS MY THIRD BOOK, IT'S THE FIRST SEQUEL I've had the opportunity to write (fingers crossed the future holds more!) and it was a very different beast from my stand-alone novels. The characters and world were already created—which you'd think would make the process easier—but I found myself needing to delve in even deeper and immerse myself more fully in this world, which meant I was much less present and available in the real world.

With that in mind, it only seems fair to thank my family first.

A million hugs and kisses to Sam, the world's most supportive and understanding husband. It nearly broke my heart when you said you feel like you haven't seen me in a year. I know I have a tendency to be a bit obsessive and hyper-focused, but you never complain. Thank you for encouraging me to defend my writing time and for happily playing with Kaia all weekend so I can squeeze in more words. Thank you for cheering the loudest and insisting I'm the greatest whenever I start to panic and doubt. None of this would be possible without you. I love you so much.

Kaia, you may not know how to read yet, but you definitely know how to uplift and inspire me. Thank you for sprinting straight to the YA section in every bookstore to find "Mama's books." Thank you for telling your friends that your favorite characters are Enebish and Orbai instead of Anna and Elsa. And thank you for insisting that I stop writing so we can read more *Fancy Nancy*. You keep me focused on what's most important!

I'm so thankful to the Hair and Thorley clans for their excitement and support. I seriously have the best family in the world. A special shout-out to my nieces and nephews. There's nothing better than getting texts from you guys as you read. Thank you for telling me you'd like my books even if we weren't related—I consider it the highest compliment!

I know every author claims their agent is the best, but Katelyn Detweiler is truly a cut above the rest. Thank you for being so enthusiastic and supportive and for knowing *exactly* when I need a push or a pep talk. It's actually kind of eerie how many times you've popped into my inbox at the precise moment I'm having a meltdown. Thank you for easing my worries and bringing me cake pops. You are magic, and I'm so grateful we're in this together. And a big thank-you to the sub rights agents at JGLM who work so hard on my behalf: Sam, Sophia, and Denise.

I'm overflowing with gratitude for my brilliant editor, Ashley Hearn, who makes my stories so much tighter and stronger than I could ever manage on my own. I know I usually have *way* too many words—without your guidance, my books would be 200K of rambling with the saggiest middles *ever*—but I can never seem to find enough words to express how thankful I am to be working with you.

I'm so lucky to be a Page Street author! Thanks to publisher Will Keister for your continued support. To my publicists, Lizzy Mason and Lauren Cepero, who are not only brilliant and hard-working, but so much fun. Thanks to Kylie Alexander for designing the most beautiful covers I've ever seen. I'm so grateful for my copy editor, Kaitlin Severini, who makes me sound way smarter and more polished than I actually am. Thanks to Lauren Knowles for stepping in and helping me finish out this series. And a big heartfelt thank-you to production manager Meg Palmer, managing editor Hayley Gundlach, editorial director Marissa Giambelluca, associate editor Tamara Grasty, assistant managing editor Mary Beth Garhart, and last, but certainly not least, the wonderful Macmillan sales team.

Massive hugs and chocolate to all of my CPs and author BFFs: JC Davis, Hannah Karena Jones, Erin Cashman, Samantha Hastings, Joanna Ruth Meyer, Nicole Lesperance, Maria Hebert-Leiter, and Breeana Shields. Thanks for cheering me on, listening to me whine, and for enduring long email silences while I figured out how to write a sequel.

Thank you, thank you to all of the readers, reviewers, librarians, and bloggers who've helped spread the word about my books. I appreciate your enthusiasm and dedication more than you'll ever know! It's hard to get noticed in this industry, so I'm incredibly grateful that you see me!

And finally, all my love to Enebish, Ghoa, Serik, and Orbai. It's been an amazing ride. Thanks for letting me hang out with you guys for the past seven years. I'm so glad I got to be part of your journey.

ABOUT THE AUTHOR

ADDIE THORLEY is the author of *An Affair of Poisons* and *Night Spinner*. She spent her childhood playing soccer, riding horses, and scribbling stories. After graduating from the University of Utah with a degree in journalism, she decided "hard news" didn't contain enough magic and kissing, so she flung herself into the land of fiction and never looked back. When she's not writing, she can be found gallivanting in the woods and eating cookies. She currently lives in Princeton, New Jersey, with her husband, daughter, and wolf dog. You can find her online at www.addiethorley.com or on Twitter and Instagram @addiethorley.